HELLOS AND HAPPILY EVER AFTERS

UNTOUCHABLE
BOOK THIRTEEN

HEATHER LONG

Hellos and Happily Ever Afters/Heather Long – 1st ed.

ISBN: 978-1-956264-83-8

For everyone who wanted to know...
what was his or her name?

SERIES SO FAR

Rules and Roses
Changes and Chocolate
Keys and Kisses
Whispers and Wishes
Hangovers and Holidays
Brazen and Breathless
Trials and Tiaras
Graduation and Gifts
Defiance and Dedication
Songs and Sweethearts
Legacy and Lovers
Farewells and Forevers

FOREWORD

Dear Reader,

You know the saying, never say never? Well, here I am returning to the world of Frankie and the guys. While I'd considered something like this all those months ago when I finished the series, I wasn't sure if it would just be a bonus scene or an actual visit to see how they are doing.

Ultimately, I decided it was too long to be just a bonus scene. Of course, the challenge was, could I get back into their heads? To be honest, I wasn't sure. Then I sat down to write and I was just there with them again.

The adult versions of them and their relationship with their burgeoning family was enough to make me fall in love with them all over again. I am so damn happy to be able to share with you Hellos and Happily Ever Afters.

I have also included every bonus scene for the rest of the books in the series. Some have introductions, some are self-explanatory, but so many of you reached out and wanted to be able to pick these up and have them on your kindle with the rest of the series.

As I said in the foreword of Farewells and Forever,

Frankie and the guys have more than earned their happily ever after. Theirs will always be a work in progress

Happily ever after is never the end of the story, and this Hellos and Happily Ever Afters is exactly that. It's the continuation of the big moments and the small.

Thank you for returning to this world with me. I love these characters so much and it was such a delight to come back to them.

Just thank you. Don't forget to check out the afterword, join my group, leave a review, and in general, just keep being awesome.

Normally, this is where I'd do the housekeeping notes, but this is the last book (really, I think—but never say never!). If you haven't read the first twelve, you should probably start there.

xoxo

Heather

P.S. Human voices only. All the work involved in this and all my novels from the stories themselves to the covers, to editing, to the audio are human-produced materials and voices only.

HELLOS & HAPPILY EVER AFTERS

HELLOS & HAPPILY EVER AFTERS

For my beautiful children, you love to hear the stories of how Mommy met your Daddy, Dad, Pop, and Papa. You love the funny stories about fighting that Daddy should never have told you or the stories about dancing that Papa teases me with or how Dad coaxed me into singing with him. Pop says your favorite stories are the ones that tell you we are human, that we love, and have loved, and will always love you.

I get that. Family means security and safety. It means having people in your corner always. It means companions on the journey to chase your dreams and helping them achieve theirs.

Hello seems like such a simple word, my darlings. But every hello that led me to your fathers is also the beginning of the happily ever after we're building every day. You're a part of it, Izzy, Josh, Charlie and our new arrival. You are the continuation of the story, our work in progress—our happily ever after.

Are you ready to hear what happens next?

PROLOGUE

PAPA DON'T PREACH

ARCHIE

A FEW YEARS EARLIER

I eased into the nursery. Josh was awake, but Frankie was still asleep. I wanted her to stay that way. Josh had been a bit of a demanding baby, not settling unless his mother held him. Jake had actually walked with him for two hours the night before, but it hadn't worked until the little one just made himself too tired.

"I know," I told him as I unbuttoned his baby snood to check his diaper. At six weeks old, Josh was not sleeping through the night yet, and we rotated one of us getting up with him. With five of us in the house and Jeremy to spell us when we needed a break, it meant that Frankie could get regular sleep. "I'm not your mother. Totally respect the desire and the hustle to only get her cuddles, but you're going to have to go with Papa for now."

Though she'd been nursing with Josh just like she had with Izzy, she was also pumping so that we could all take turns feeding too. As terrified as I'd been when Izzy was this little, she taught me a lot about being quick, efficient, and to keep a running dialogue.

"Besides, we like it when Papa changes us. I never forget to cover you up cause cold air on a penis…" I shook my head. "Fair warning, that doesn't get better when you're older and if it's icy hands—yours or anyone else—just hard no."

Josh let out a half-grunt then a little toot of a fart. Excellent. Izzy used to struggle with that part, Josh did not. Jake liked to flex that he got the farting from his side of the family.

Frankie did not disagree. Pretty sure it wasn't the compliment Jake took it as, but it was still entertaining. Once I'd secured the fresh diaper and zipped him back up, I scooped him up carefully from the crib.

Josh had been almost eight pounds when he was born. He hadn't lost any weight, which was good. He was already longer than when he'd arrived.

"You're going to grow like a weed," I said as I got the prepped bottle out of his fridge and set it in the warmer. "Probably all the sports talk. Then again, Daddy and Dad are very competitive. Pop and me, not so much."

I almost snorted at myself.

"Okay, rephrase, Papa is competitive too just in different areas."

Josh scrunched up his little face like he was gonna yell, but instead a yawn escaped. I chuckled.

"Yeah, it's not even two in the morning. You managed a whole four hours, I'm very impressed. I'd like to see us work that up to six, but we have time."

When his bottle was ready, I settled in the rocking chair. It was Frankie's favorite. The first time she'd sat in it when she'd been pregnant with Izzy, her whole face lit up. I didn't care if I had to buy the company to keep them making these. It was doable. Anything was doable to keep that happiness on her face.

"So this is a current blend of the finest mother's milk you're ever going to get. Very fresh. She pumped this after you went to sleep and we set it up here for you."

A pair of blue eyes stared up at me steadily. Izzy's had changed to a shade much closer to green by this age. So far, it didn't look like Josh's had any intention of changing.

"The trick is," I said. "To make her laugh while she's pumping so you get an endorphin boost. Sometimes, she's really sleepy and I kind of wish that also worked as an enticement for you, but you seem to be the fussier connoisseur in the house."

Another difference between Josh and Izzy. Izzy didn't mind who took care of her, she settled equally between all of us. Josh was greedy for mama.

I was greedy for her too. I got it.

"Now, here's how we're going to do this. I'm going to set you up, you're gonna eat and doze, then go back to sleep. Then in about four hours, you can wake up again and I bet Mama will be right here."

Teasing the nipple of the bottle against his lower lip, I gave him a moment. At first, we'd worried the bottle nipples were too different from Frankie's and that was why he wouldn't latch. Then she fed him from a bottle so that wasn't it.

His little face puckered but he closed his lips on the nipple and gave it a half-hearted tug.

"That's not working for me there, little man. Put some effort into that suction. You want the milk, I know you're hungry or you'd already be asleep again."

He pushed one of his little hands up toward me and then

bounced it against the bottle. The frown puckering his forehead deepened and his little face flushed.

"Nope," I told him, keeping my voice even. "We're not doing that. No crying for mama. Mama needs to sleep and you've been keeping her awake a lot. She's all curled up with Daddy and Dad right now and we're going to let her stay there. You have Papa and Papa has you."

I gave the bottle a little wiggle, teasing his lips with the nipple again. The milk dribbled a little from the corner of his mouth, then vanished as he latched onto the bottle and began to nurse.

Oh, I wanted to do a victory dance. Instead, I just kept rocking as Josh ate.

"That's a good boy," I said. "What shall we talk about? Since apparently, all you needed was a little man-to-baby talk here. Hey, I know, let's talk about Jeremy and how great he is. You've got all of us, but you also have Jeremy. Grandpa Jere—he's going to be your best friend. Before I met your mother, he was always mine."

Still was.

"Anyway..." I continued, rocking Josh slowly as he nursed. His frantic sucking had slowed and now he was half-asleep. At this rate, he'd be sacked out again as soon as the bottle was done. "Rule number one, never lie to Jeremy. Even if you think we won't like it or he'll be disappointed, never lie. He will always have your back, even if having it means smacking you upside the head verbally. He's really good at it."

CHAPTER 1

MY LIFE

FRANKIE

"Mama. Mama. Mama. Mama." Charlie's chanting from his playpen was enough to make me laugh, but I bit the inside of my lip to keep the chuckles contained. Josh and Izzy were on their way to school with Jeremy. Jake and Archie had to be at the flight lab early today, they had a new engine to test.

Coop stuck around long enough to help me and Ian get the kids ready before he had to head to the community center. It was his week to be there as onsite counselor for anyone who needed it. In addition to his own practice, he maintained a regular volunteer schedule. Once we'd cleaned up in the kitchen, Ian headed to his studio. He had some work before we recorded.

"Mama." Charlie banged his hands on the little wall enclosing his play area. It wasn't just a little four by five spot. Archie and the guys had converted part of the family room into a play area, as well as a secondary one up in the nursery.

It had been perfect when Izzy was getting her feet under her, and then for Josh.

Charlie invading their space had taken some adjustment, but they were all handling it so beautifully. Well, except when Izzy and Josh butted heads. They could go from besties to at each other's throats in no time at all. The tempers they got from their fathers, despite the boys saying that was all me. Nope, not it.

"Yes, Charlie my love, I'm coming." All of the kids had been dependent on me in different ways. They loved their fathers—adored them—but their demands where I was concerned shifted and changed as they got older. It meant, especially with a few months to go until we added another infant, we had to teach them to *share* me.

Izzy had been the most difficult. She'd been an only child until Josh and we'd all spoiled her. Still, once convinced that she would still be my best girl and that I wouldn't love her any less, she made accommodations. Her reaction the day we brought Josh home still made me laugh.

Squatting, I met Charlie's green eyes and winked. They were losing some of the gray, which made me a little sad. I loved Coop's gray-green eyes. He didn't mind so much, said Charlie was getting my eyes. Still…

"Do you know what Izzy said about Josh?"

Charlie canted his head to the side looking every bit like his father. "Mama?"

I chuckled. "Not quite. She said," I continued, rising and reaching for him. As soon as I had a hold, he pushed up from the floor like he could jump. Once I had him on my hip, I booped his nose. "He's all wrinkly, Mama. Did you leave him in too long?"

Between the general soreness from the delivery, the exhaustion of staying at the hospital—I never slept well when I was there—and the delirium of welcoming our new little one, that comment had made me laugh so hard. For a week after, I kept bursting into spontaneous giggles.

Izzy had been very proud of herself.

"So when you came, she was really concerned you would also be all wrinkly. I had to remind her that Josh worked out okay." Lips twitching, I headed out of the family room and made my way down the hall. Ian and I had some recording to do later today. First, however, Charlie needed to be cleaned up, have some quality mom time, and then playtime outside before his nap.

Jeremy usually watched him for me when I had to be in the studio. The soundproofing meant we couldn't hear as well in there and I couldn't have the monitor on while we were working.

"Needless to say," I said. "You were wrinkly and now you have the cutest little cheeks." I blew a raspberry against one of the aforementioned cheeks. Charlie's laughter rippled through the air. I was almost to the stairs to head up when the doorbell rang.

Maxie and Murray both started barking from the back-yard. The pair of herding dogs were just at their first birth-day, while they'd been learning—their enthusiasm often outweighed their obedience when one of the guys wasn't right there.

Miss Abigail was probably asleep in Jeremy's suite. She was thirteen going on fourteen? Somedays I lost track, but despite the grey everywhere, she still enjoyed playing and walks. She also enjoyed good naps. They were quite cross that they weren't in here, but I pivoted and headed back across the house toward the front door.

"Maybe we have a package," I told Charlie as I bounced him a little.

"Box!" He clapped his hands together. He loved opening boxes with me. We always had a delivery of some kind arriving. The doorbell sounded a second time just as I got to the entry hall. I pressed the intercom and camera that let me see who was on the porch.

"Oh, Charlie, it's a grandpa." I was still smiling when I unlocked the door and pulled it open. "Grandpa Eddie is here."

Eddie Standish, Archie's father, and one of the many wonderful grandparents our kids had, stood there in his expensive, three piece suit and silk tie. The touch of silver in his hair gave him a distinguished look. There was also an easier smile in his eyes and on his lips. The resemblance to Archie had never been stronger.

"Gandpa! Gandpa!" Charlie pitched himself forward, grabbing hands demanding attention.

Chuckling, Eddie swooped him up and gave him a little bounce. "There's my little man, and how are you today, good sir?"

"Hungwy."

"Hungry?" Eddie made a comical face. "Hasn't mama fed you?"

Charlie slid me the slyest of looks and I raised my brows. The little sneak was so good at convincing everyone he needed food. The playful streak was just a little too mischievous sometimes.

"Want candy. Gandpa candy."

I swallowed another smile and had to bite the inside of my lip.

"Ah…" Eddie hummed and slid his hand into a pocket before he pulled out the butterscotch treats he'd started to carry with him. Something that Grandpa Ted had used to do with Archie when he was little. The first time Archie saw his dad sneak one to Izzy, he'd been a little rocked by it.

"I forgot…" The whisper and the missing in those two words had me wrapping him up in a hug. Grandpa Ted

always came with candy, so now, Grandpa Eddie did too. I rather loved it for all of them.

Charlie lit up and held out his hand, then looked Eddie right in the eye. "Thank you, much."

I had to turn away to keep from laughing. He was so incorrigible. The little snotweed absolutely could charm his way to what he wanted. As soon as Eddie unwrapped the softer butterscotch, he put it in Charlie's palm.

"Remember," Eddie told him. "We suck on it. No chewing and swallowing."

"Unda my two-ng."

"Yes," Eddie watched him carefully then resettled him before he finally looked at me again. "Good morning, Frankie."

"Good morning, come on in." We were still standing in the doorway. "Did you forget your keys?"

"No, but I don't like using them unless we've already planned for it."

I could respect that. "There's still coffee in the kitchen, I was going to take this one up and give him a good clean up and change his clothes." He was still in diapers, but potty training had been going well, even if he preferred his diaper at night. Sometimes, I wasn't as in a hurry as I should be to graduate them up. He would be fully potty trained before the new baby came.

Oh—had Archie told Eddie yet?

"If you don't mind making me a cup," Eddie said. "I'll take this little buster up and get him ready. I've got a couple of hours and wanted to visit. We can go over some of the new figures if you're up for it."

"Absolutely," I told him. "Play clothes for him? They're in the third drawer. He is in a blue phase and will absolutely not wear anything red or purple."

"Got it." Then he was striding up the stairs, totally

comfortable with the drool escaping Charlie and the way he tightened his fists on the suit. Eddie had been spit up on, actually Josh had an accident on him mid-diaper change, and Izzy threw up after a rather rambunctious ride at the park. It never fazed him, he just stripped off his jackets and rolled up his sleeves.

Dad told me more than once that Eddie *loved* being a grandfather. He was making up for all the missed time with Archie, but our kids weren't a replacement. He was also building a strong relationship with Archie. They were in such a better place now. In the kitchen, I poured my decaf into a cup before I made Eddie a latte. The fact he enjoyed the indulgence hadn't been lost on me. Still, I was glad that he indulged himself.

After his coffee was ready, I pulled out my phone and messaged Archie.

Me: *Have you told your dad yet?*

The decaf was still hot. Jeremy had found a really nice blend since the last pregnancy. It almost tasted like the real thing. Granted, cutting it back was smart and I did all the things the doctors told me to do. But giving up coffee wasn't an option I really wanted to explore. The fake out my brain method worked for me.

My phone buzzed.

Archie: *No, I keep forgetting and you usually like to wait to the end of the first trimester.*

He wasn't wrong.

Me: *That's next week. We have the ultrasound then too.*

Three little dots blinked up at me before his new message showed up.

Archie: *Wanna take him out to dinner and tell him?*

Me: *Yes. He's here to visit Charlie and to talk business, so I wanted to check.*

Archie: *Babe, do you want to go ahead and tell him?*

I smiled.

Me: *Together.*

Archie: *Pick a night for dinner, we'll make it work.*

Me: *Love you.*

Archie: *Love you more.*

I chuckled.

"Before you say anything," Eddie called as though announcing his presence. "I let Charlie pick it out."

When he walked into the kitchen, I laughed. Charlie was all dressed up in his panda onesie that Izzy had gotten him for his birthday. She liked dressing the babies up even more than she did the dogs.

"I see," I told him. "Were you picking on Grandpa?"

Charlie just gave me the sunniest smile. "Pway?"

"We can go outside and play." That onesie was going to be absolutely filthy. Oh well, it would wash.

The dogs were barking as soon as we stepped out onto the patio. There was a play area that was separate from the dogs. The stone patio was one step up from the grass. I carried our coffees and Eddie carried Charlie.

Once he set him down, Charlie toddled over to the little cabin the guys had built out here. It was practically a village, with reinforced everything and pads on edges. Not plastic. It was adorable and they kept adding to it.

"Thank you," Eddie said when I handed him the coffee. He took a drink before he set the cup down and pulled out a handkerchief. There was a sticky spot on his lapel.

"You are so good with him," I murmured.

"Dad used to say that having a stain on your suit was the sign of a family well loved—or an attitude that needed correcting. Strut the first and fix the second."

Another wave of laughter escaped me. That sounded so much like Grandpa Ted. I missed him. He would have loved all these kids and would probably spoil them worse than any of their other grandfathers.

"Mama!" Charlie called and I found him climbing the small slide. He wasn't allowed on the bigger one without one of his siblings.

"I can see you!"

He waved and then slid down with a whoop. Maxie and Murray had come over to watch us through the fence. They wagged their tails and waited patiently. Another lesson that we'd been teaching them. They had to be calmer around the littlest ones. Murray was much better at it than Maxie. She was constantly circling Josh and making him come back to one of us.

But one step at a time.

The dogs loved the kids and the kids loved them.

"What did you want to go over?" I asked as I took a seat. It was a gorgeous day. The sun was warm without being hot and the air was cool. Charlie was racing around chasing a butterfly now, but he kept checking on where we were.

"Oh, I thought we could discuss the quarterly distributions. They're next month, but we've had some new requests."

"The children's foundation from Braxton Harbor. They're opening three outreach centers in various parts of the city. Then in a year, they want to expand to a neighboring city." I'd read the applications. They'd submitted detailed breakdowns on their plans for the facilities, for improvements, and what they wanted to do in the first, second, and third years with longer term goals outlined as well.

"That's one of them. The other is from Blue Ivy Prep, they're seeking donations for a couple of new buildings they want to add. Including a better musical facility. They always start by reaching out to alumni first, but in this case, I think they want you to link it to your work with Bound Hearts and Torched."

"Did that just come in? There are a lot of wealthy donors on their alumni rolls." I'd also never gone to Blue Ivy. KC might be willing to do her own donation, but that was totally up to her. She'd had a unique experience there. Then again, Archie had been one of their students. There'd been a brief discussion about sending the kids.

I did not want to send any of them to boarding school. We had plenty of private schools right here on Long Island. The guys agreed with me, and that was that. Eddie had only proposed it because several generations of his family had attended there, including Archie.

I had to resist the urge to lay my hand over my belly. No, our kids were going to be raised in a home with us. They would have family around them, not a bunch of strangers and distance from us. Just—no. My stomach sank and my eyes burned. It was hard enough to send them to school some days, much less send them to another state to live away.

"Hey," Eddie said, concern in his voice grounding me in the present. "I didn't mean to upset you."

"You didn't," I told him with a sniffle, before swiping away the tears.

"Mama!" Charlie raced over and then clambered up onto the step before toddling to me. "No cwy Mama."

Oh boy, the tears were sliding down my cheeks too swiftly to be just wiped away. "Mama's not crying—well she is, but Mama isn't sad."

Emotions ping-ponging, I scooped Charlie up for a hug. He clung to me like a barnacle and I tucked my cheek to the top of his head. One common thread through all of my pregnancies had been wild emotional swings. They hadn't been so bad with this one.

Until now.

Worry filled Eddie's eyes as I met his gaze. "We can skip giving Blue Ivy anything ever again. I know Archie wasn't always a fan."

"No, it's not that and Archie didn't like being dumped there. His words, not mine. But he did like being close to Grandpa Ted and his Nana."

Eddie nodded slowly. "We could have handled a lot of that better."

"Maybe," I said, then sniffled again as Charlie patted at me. He was trying to rub my back but could only pat my shoulder. It was adorable. "I can't imagine how it was for you and Muriel." Not that I liked the woman. I didn't hate her, but I didn't really like her. Mostly, I just felt sorry for her. "You guys missed out on a lot. I was just thinking, I couldn't imagine sending any of them to boarding school. Just the idea made me miss them so damn much."

"I remember when we discussed it for Izzy," Eddie said before taking a long drink of his coffee. "I know we could have done things so differently. I wish I could turn it all back and fix it…"

"But we can't," I said and held his gaze. There was a lone-liness in his eyes. A sadness that shifted, and sometimes decreased, but never went away. He still missed my mother. Despite everything that happened and all the hell she put him through—the hell she put all of us through—he missed her.

I hated that for him so much. I didn't even miss her these days. I had for a while but after Izzy? After holding my own daughter and the love that filled my chest then seemed to consume me whole? No, I didn't miss Maddy one bit after that.

"We can only move forward, and you're an amazing grandfather. My kids are so lucky." Because Eddie, like

Archie, didn't treat any of them as anything different. They might have different biological fathers, but we were all family. Eddie was every bit Izzy's grandfather too. "I think sometimes you're the favorite grandfather, but don't tell Dad I said that."

That earned a real laugh from Eddie. "No, the real favorite is Jeremy, but I'm definitely a close second."

"Gonna go play again?" I asked Charlie and when he flashed those worried eyes up at me, I smiled. "Mama's not crying anymore. All better, see?"

Charlie studied me like he wasn't quite sure then he pressed a wet kiss to my cheek. "Mama betta."

"Definitely better now." I raspberried his cheek and he let out a shout of laughter. Then he was all squirms to get down. The sadness that had struck so profoundly retreated like a passing cloud on a beautiful day. "As for the children's foundation, I really like what they have in mind. I don't know if the grants they applied for will be enough. Maybe we write into the grant acceptance that we review in one year and increase the amounts as needed to hit their major goals?"

They had some good ones.

"I like that," Eddie said slowly. "I'll put a pin in Blue Ivy until we talk to Archie. What did you think of the language programs for the local schools? It's a smaller charter, but it will provide second language support and tutoring for elementary age kids to help them develop sooner rather than later. There's a lot of studies that suggest longer term language study can lead to greater comfort and more open minds. It also works the other way for immigrants and others who may not have English as a first language at home…"

"Eddie?"

The animation in his eyes was real. "Guilty," he admitted. "This is the program I wanted to talk to you about most."

"Doesn't Helena Endicott currently run that whole program?" I'd met her briefly at a lunch back in the spring. Eddie had been...quite interested in everything she had to say.

"Don't start," he told me, lips compressing. "Helena and I are friends."

"I didn't say anything." I also kept my smile buried.

"Uh huh. Helena is an old friend, her husband was also a friend before he passed away."

"Of course."

Eyes narrowed, Eddie half-glared at me. "Don't bring it up to Archie."

"Why would I?" I went for total innocence.

"Because I can see the wheels turning in your head."

"I like Helena," I told him. "She's really nice. Sharp. Savvy. Absolutely a shark when it comes to closing a deal for raising money. I think the language program is fantastic. It's up there with the arts one. What if we ask them to expand to community centers as well?" Coop's devotion to the series of community centers he worked at was a constant reminder that not everyone had access to what we did.

I liked making sure they had everything they could want or need.

"I can take the meetings with her if you need a break." His offer was delivered in a tone so blasé that I almost laughed.

"I appreciate that. Ian and I are looking at doing a small tour in October and November. Possibly January." We would have to wait and see. "We have to finish the album he's working on first."

"Then let's make arrangements to do a meeting next week...we'll go over the budgets for the foundation, then pick our favorites. We can then handle any negotiations on a case by case basis."

"If this runs up against time, you can take care of Helena

for me." I barely smothered my smile before I drained the last of my coffee.

"You're not funny," Eddie groused and this time I did grin.

"I'm hilarious and you adore me."

"I do adore you," he admitted with a smile of his own before he sobered. "I'm not ready, Frankie."

My own smile faded.

"Don't know if I ever will be. Helena's—a nice woman. A bit prickly and definitely keeps me on my toes. But—I'm not ready for anything more."

"You don't have to be." I reached a hand out to him and he took mine. "You really don't. But don't just shut the door on the possibility, even if you're not ready to walk through it yet."

Eddie squeezed my hand. "Archie and the boys are very lucky."

"Maybe," I said with a grin. "I know I'm the lucky one."

"Mama!" Charlie shouted and we both looked over to see him at the top of the big slide. Took my eyes off him for two minutes and look at him.

"Hey now," Eddie said as he rose and crossed the yard easily but swiftly. "Wait for me."

Like a good boy, Charlie sat down at the top and waited until Eddie was at the bottom. Then he pushed off. He laughed all the way down and cheered when Eddie picked him up and swung him around.

"See Mama! Big boy!"

Yes he was a big boy and those tears flooded my eyes again. Our babies were growing up and our family was growing again. I didn't think I could be happier.

I sniffled.

I was definitely the lucky one.

CHAPTER 2

ISN'T SHE LOVELY?

IAN

I'd been listening to the same track for the last couple of hours. Frankie and I recorded it a couple of days earlier. It was for the new album, but something... Something was off in it.

Using the dials, I minimized my part of the song and just listened to Frankie's lyrics. Her voice was as strong and capable as ever. The softness in her alto didn't rob it of an ounce of its power. The velvety lyrical nature was exactly what the song needed.

Switching over to my own lyric track, I dialed her down and listened to me. Even with the headset on, I always sounded different to myself. I got it, but it also afforded me a good chance to step outside of myself.

It wasn't the song. The song was good. The lyrics were strong. They were emotional...

My phone vibrated in my pocket and I hit pause before I popped off the headphones. Jake's name popped up on the screen so I swiped to answer it on speaker. It was just me in the studio.

"Hey, I thought you and Archie were going to be stress testing the new engine…"

It was something Archie wanted done before we got back from the tour. Booking a smaller tour had annoyed our manager. He had this huge plan to do a slow ramp up to a full tour over the summer and into the following autumn.

While I didn't tell him Frankie was pregnant, we weren't announcing it until after she was through the first trimester, I didn't really care what they wanted.

The tour was going to be smaller, and more intimate. We'd do more social media splashes and keep it lowkey. Traveling would be stressful enough cause she'd have to leave the kids for a couple of weeks at a time.

It worked when we did the tour while she was pregnant with Charlie, two weeks on, one week off. No more than two weeks away from the kids or the guys. They either met us somewhere or we came home.

Period.

"…are you even listening to me?" The dry note in Jake's voice snapped me out of the reverie.

"No, sorry. Got distracted. What's up?" I scrubbed a hand over my face. The bristle on my cheeks reminded me I hadn't shaved that morning. I was debating letting it grow out.

"You've been doing that a lot lately, new album giving you that much trouble?" The change in subject had me shaking my head.

It must have been bad if Jake was worrying about me. "No, it's not giving me that much trouble. It's just…I dunno, I'm probably overthinking it. But it feels like something is missing. I just can't tell if it's the music itself or how we're performing it. But I'll figure it out. "

"Good, cause you guys are leaving for that first set of

dates to soft launch, right?" Jake coughed once, like he was clearing his throat.

"Not until October. As long as everything goes to plan, we're doing the soft launch the weekend after Coop's birthday and we'll be back before Archie's and Halloween."

"Good. Then November, two weeks out and a week back?"

"That's the plan. No holidays missed. If this is anything like last time, she's going to be miserable by the end of week two, so it's about as long as we can go before she has to see the kids." It was adorable in its own way. Her emotions were all over the place when she was pregnant. The poised woman we'd married could turn into an absolute fountain and cry over the fact that her danish tasted like cardboard.

The constant crying would sometimes frustrate my angel. I would just have to keep reminding her that it was just another demonstration of her huge heart. It was why we took great care to protect that heart by making sure she could see her kids.

"Sounds good. She sees the OB next week, right?"

I frowned and flipped through my phone for the family calendar. We color coded it so it was easy to skim. Two kids in school and a toddler meant there were a lot of activities to track.

"Yeah, which you can check. What's up?" Cause this was a weird call.

"Archie's losing his mind," Jake said, sounding utterly reasonable.

"Define losing his mind?" I stripped the headset fully off and stretched as I stood.

"I keep catching him sketching new equipment for the play yard, and new designs for safety features for a car." Amusement filled his voice. So this was something funny and not something to worry about. "Then I mentioned the tour and he pretty much just left to go see her."

Leaning back in the chair, I stared up at the ceiling. "Frankie's in Manhattan handling meetings today." Charlie was with Jeremy and I would take over when he went to get the kids.

"I know," Jake said. "Tried to tell him, but he's heading to the house. Left about fifteen minutes ago."

I didn't laugh. Fuck, it was hard not to laugh. Scrubbing a hand over my face, I shook my head. "I'll take care of it."

"I figured. You had to sit me down and then later Coop."

I snorted. "Why didn't you sit him down?"

"I would have tried but I didn't even realize what was happening until he was in the car and pulling out at speed." Jake huffed a laugh. "I mean, he was a little bit of a space cadet, but he has been since she told us. He's waited a long time and he never said it bothered him..."

"No," I said. "Didn't bother you or Coop that I was first either. Fucked with my head a little but..."

"You handled it. I don't remember anyone sitting you down." Jake blew out a breath. "Lucky bastard."

Yeah, he didn't remember it 'cause it hadn't been them who had to do it. Jeremy did it. My dad did it. Hank had done it. In all their own ways, the *dads* had stepped up and they each offered some useful bit of advice.

It had *helped*.

"Work on the engine, you know when he catches his breath, he's gonna be all over that." I saved where I was at and then shut down the sound board. I'd have to listen later.

Right now, I needed to grab some lunch and get ready for Hurricane Archie to arrive. I left the studio, locking it up behind me and then circled the swimming pool and crossed to the patio leading into the house.

"Da!" Charlie said as I came inside. He hustled away from

Jeremy and Miss Abigail at speed. I caught him racing forward, head first. He was as bad as Josh at charging at things.

"Hey, little man," I said, setting him on my hip as I gave him an inspection. "You're a mess."

"Paint with Gandpa." He showed me his fingers. It looked like he'd dipped each one into a different color. There were flakes drying on his cheeks and more than a little in his hair.

"So, who was doing the painting, you or Grandpa Jere?"

Jeremy snorted softly. "I'm afraid young Mr. Charlie took to finger painting so well, he thought it would be better to be foot painting." The amusement in his droll voice softened any kind of reprimand. "I was going to put him in the bath and see if we could scrub him up before his nap."

Charlie hugged my neck. "No bah!"

"Yes, bath," I told him. "Grandpa is right and you should listen." I tickled his foot after I caught it to check the layers of paint on them. "Where is this masterpiece?"

"Thankfully, in the garage. I'd thought we'd experiment away from anything that could be permanently stained." Jeremy crossed to me. "Come along, Mr. Charlie. Bath time."

"No bah." Charlie pouted and gave me the most soulful look. While he had his mother's eyes, he absolutely had his father's playfulness and he could not hold that expression for long. "Pwease?"

"Bath first. We'll play more later, but you have to be good for Grandpa."

With a huff of a complaint, Charlie went to Jeremy, who carried him up the stairs with Miss Abigail following. Speaking of dogs, I went over to check the yard. Maxie and Murray were snoozing in the sun.

Might take them out for a run with Archie when he got here. It would do all of us some good. For now, I got lunch put together. Jeremy always fixed something if Frankie was home. Since I didn't necessarily eat on a schedule when I had studio time, I just grabbed a sandwich or reheated leftovers.

The first time I'd done that, Jeremy had seemed pretty cross. The second, he'd given me the longest stare before excusing himself. On the third occasion, we had a chat about it. It had nothing to do with liking or disliking his food, I loved it.

But when I was in the space to write or work, I pretty much focused on that to the exclusion of all else. It was just easier for me to breeze in, grab food and breeze out again. When it came to Frankie or the kids, I made time, otherwise...

With all of that in mind, I pulled out the sandwich makings and built two subs. Even if Archie didn't eat his, Frankie might like it for a midnight snack. I chuckled, those hadn't started *yet*. But they were coming.

The fact Jeremy had already begun to restock the frozen yogurt pops she loved told me he was getting ready for it too. I'd just put the food on the table and gotten out a couple of sodas when the door from the garage opened and then shut.

"Frankie..." Archie called as he strode through the living room. I tracked the sound of his path before he stuck his head in the dining room where I was sitting just off the kitchen. "Hey Bubba, I need to talk to Frankie. Be right back."

I opened my mouth then closed it again as he took off. Jake wasn't wrong. I'd seen that panic before. I'd seen it in Jake's and Coop's eyes and I'd seen it in my own. Our love for the kids did not rest on whose genetics they carried. At the same time, there seemed to be a special kind of hell for those of us who were the biological father.

Granted, my panic came closer to the end of the second trimester. So had Coop's and Jake's... Made sense, we hadn't gotten the test results until then. We did the genetic testing just to be on the safe side for everyone. If there was a chance of something being wrong with the babies, we wanted to know.

This was the first time we were certain without a test. Archie had been the only one *not* using a condom and we had been actively trying to go for one more. We were going to vote after this pregnancy whether we wanted to do more or not.

I felt for the guy. No wonder he was panicking now. I'd just finished a bite of my sandwich and popped open the can when he reappeared in the doorway. Still dressed in his overalls for working on the engine and in work boots, Archie looked about as blue collar as he ever could.

"She's not here…"

"Nope." I saluted him with the soda. "Made you lunch."

"Where the hell is she? Is something wrong?" He was patting his pockets. "I'll call her…"

"Arch," I said his name a little more firmly. "Come sit down. She's at Standish in meetings all day with your dad and the accountants and the board of the foundation. They are getting ready to do this year's awards."

One hand on his breast pocket and the other on his back, Archie stared at me. His mouth opened then closed, before it popped open again.

"It's all good, man. Come sit down. Eat, have a drink, and we'll talk." I kept everything as calm and soothing as possible. It was kind of like dealing with a wild animal, there was still a lot of white on display around his eyes.

"You're talking to me like I'm freaking out." He managed to sound worried and a little insulted at the same time. "Why?"

"Because you're freaking out." I leaned back in the chair and let him chew on that.

"I'm not freaking out." Now he was all insult. "I *don't* freak out. I'm very good at *not* freaking out." His tone grew a little more strained.

"True," I said. "Normally. But, ask yourself, why are you still in your work overalls with greasy hands and you drove all the way here from Brooklyn without double-checking where she is. She told us her plans at breakfast."

I took another sip of the soda as Archie turned those words over in his head. I could practically hear the gears and wheels kicking in his brain.

He sat down abruptly, like someone had cut his strings and stared at his hands, then the food, then stood up again. "Oh shit. I am freaking out, aren't I?"

"Yeah, but it's all good man. Happens to the best of us."

"Clearly," Archie said, a hint of arrogance in his smirk. "It's happening to me."

I chuckled. "Go wash your hands and lose the work boots before Jeremy sees you."

He moved like a scalded cat. The water kicked on in the kitchen and he scrubbed up. He disappeared back to the garage before returning in socked feet without his overalls. The jeans and t-shirt were much better and far less greasy.

"Why does it look like someone exploded paint all over the inside of the garage?"

Was it that bad? "Charlie and Jeremy were working on a project."

"Right." Archie shook his head and dragged out the chair. Instead of eating, he just stared at the food. I gave him a minute. The panic might be subsiding, but he still needed to get all the wheels back on the track. "Isn't Charlie a little young for working with paint like that?"

"Probably why it looks like an explosion."

"Point," he said with a slow nod before he reached over to crack open his soda. "She's with Dad today. They're handling the funding…"

"Yep." I raised my sandwich.

"I knew that."

"Yep." I took a bite and chewed it as Archie downed some of the soda.

"I'm losing my mind."

I grinned at him. "Yep."

His expression soured and he gave me a dirty look. "You could have warned a guy."

"You saw it happen to Coop and to Jake. I know you were worried when it happened to me."

"But were you really panicking or just overthinking stuff?" The challenge was a fair one.

"Both. The point is, it hits all of us. It's not fun, when you get hit with the sudden feeling of hope and terror and they spin around inside of you like a top."

Leaning back in the chair, Archie stared up at the ceiling. "It's like—all I can do is think about everything that could go wrong. With me. With her. With you guys. With the kids. Jake and I were talking about the tour and how we needed to balance out our work schedules for those few weeks so one of us is around. Charlie is not going to like the separation, even if it's good for him."

We shared a grimace. Yes, the time apart would be good. He needed to learn to share his mother more and to not panic when she wasn't there. Newborns were one hundred percent dependent and Frankie had nursed them all. She'd been so thrilled that she could and I would never get tired of the look on her face when she cradled one of the babies to her breast.

Never.

"Then it hit you that she was going to be miles away and you wouldn't be seeing her regularly either. Different cities. Traveling. Stress..."

"Yeah," Archie said slowly, then scrubbed a hand over his

face again. "Crap. I can't just lock her up in a padded room, right?"

"Nope. If you try, you're going to be missing your balls or end up in a padded room of your own." To be fair, we were all overprotective. "Here's the thing, take a breath and remember, this isn't our first."

With Izzy, *everything* had been new. While Josh and Charlie had both been different pregnancies, we at least had an *idea* of what to expect.

"We've done this before. She's toured before. We'll be home before the third trimester. She hasn't been as sick with this one, thankfully."

"All good things," Archie agreed and then he looked at his sandwich again as if finally registering it was there. "She has her big visit to the OB next week."

"Ultrasound." Yep.

"Taking the day off." Archie made a face. "I probably shouldn't, she gets annoyed when we hover."

"She also gets annoyed when we don't let her help." Something I was just as guilty of as the rest of them. "You're scared and you're going through all the possibilities. Talk to her. Let her help you."

"But you're right, she has done this before. Technically, we all have. This isn't different and yet..."

"No, it's different. I love Josh and Charlie. No one will ever tell me they aren't mine. But Izzy was different after I found out. It was like—every choice I've ever made cycled through my head. What if the drinking we did in sophomore year has some kind of lasting effect? What if... What if... What if..."

"Frankie worried about her mother," Archie said abruptly and I nodded. "With Izzy, she worried she'd turn into Maddy."

"Yeah, but Coop was the one who figured out she was

worried that Maddy's narcissism and psychosis might be genetic. There's nothing we can do about that if it is, except support the kid in all the ways we can."

Something we'd all accepted. So far, all of our fears proved unfounded.

"I can't believe I just—ditched out on Jake." Archie shook his head.

"He gets it. You're just getting all of this early cause we didn't have to do paternity tests this time."

"True," Archie admitted, then picked up the sandwich. "This is all me, so I get to torture myself longer than you guys did."

"Sounds about right," I told him. "You are always over-achieving."

That earned me a dirty look and then a laugh. "Well, you aren't lying."

No, I wasn't. "Now eat the sandwich and take a breather. I need to get back out to the studio, but we can also take the dogs for a run so you can burn off that manic energy before Frankie gets home."

"Sounds like a plan," Archie said. "But—can you promise me something?"

"Anything," I told him.

"If you think Frankie needs me—for anything—when you're on the road…"

"You're my first call."

Archie nodded. "Thanks."

"Just remember," I said. "Midnight cravings are your job this time around."

He paused with the sandwich on its way to his mouth then eyed me. "It occurs to me, her sex drive surges in the second trimester. You're gonna need one of us on the road."

Not an unfair thought. "Pretty much another solid reason to come home as often as we can."

A real laugh escaped him and some of the tension eased from his expression. "We're having another baby. Think it'll be a girl or a boy?"

"I think they'll be perfect," I said. "Perfect for us."

He finally took a bite and then nodded. "I like that," he said after swallowing. "I like that a lot."

"Just remember the next time you start to freak out... talk to one of us. We've all been there."

"Check. Next time I freak out, talk to someone and don't drive home like a zombie speed demon and risk freaking *her* out."

"And?" I prompted.

"And talk to Frankie. Let her help."

I saluted him with the soda. "Good man."

"Bubba?"

"Hmm."

"Thanks."

I grinned, "Like I said, anytime."

CHAPTER 3

SMALL BUMP

FRANKIE

*I*nstead of Archie's car, we took one of the SUVs to my OB appointment. Reaching over I put my hand on his where it rested on the gear shift. "You still doing okay?"

He'd admitted to having a moment the previous week, but between the kids and the guys, and the hustle for school and getting ready for the tour, we hadn't had a lot of Archie and Frankie time.

That needed correcting. Maybe we should take an earlier babymoon before the tour. If we waited until after, it would be January or February. I'd be a lot further along. It might limit our options.

"I'm fine, babe," he said, turning his hand over underneath mine. "I kind of lost it there for a few. But, I'm really fine. We're kind of old pros at this. Not sure why it just got me all of a sudden. I handled the rest of them okay."

"We've all freaked out in our own ways. Remember when

Coop didn't sleep for a week?" It seemed funny in retrospect. It hadn't been at the time though.

He'd grown crabbier and crabbier. The day he snapped at me had actually given him pause. The very real regret in his eyes earned my forgiveness before he even apologized. After he confessed his exhaustion, I called the guys. Something needed to give and Coop needed us.

Then we all put our heads together. Three days later, Coop and I left for the babymoon. He spent the first three days sleeping, but he felt better and then we had the time that was just us.

"I'm not that bad, am I?" He frowned, then shot me a look when we had to stop at a light. "If I've snapped babe…"

"You haven't," I promised him, then squeezed his hand. This—hesitance and worry—it wasn't Archie. He was always so confident about everything. "And if I didn't tell you before, I'm very glad you told me what was going on. I like being able to help you."

He blew out a breath. "I feel like I'm going to screw all of this up."

"Why?"

He blinked over at me a minute. The honk of a horn behind us jerked his attention forward. The light had turned green. So I waited for him. Sometimes, the best thing any of us could do was be patient while the other person sorted out what was going on with them. All that time in therapy paid off.

We were maybe three blocks from the OB's office when he said, "I don't know. It's weird. This—this isn't me. Or do I just have a higher estimation of myself?"

I couldn't help it, the disbelief in his voice made me laugh. "No, it's not."

The rush of his exhale seemed to make him sag. Lifting my hand, he pressed a kiss to my palm. "Fuck me. Good. Also no listening down there..." He glanced down at the *very* small bump that wasn't even visible in my clothes. I'd reclaimed my figure after Izzy.

Post Josh, I'd had more curves and just a little bit of a belly from how big I'd gotten with him. My tiger stripes fully formed with him too. Charlie just added to the emphasis and I never quite got back into those jeans.

It was all fine. No one was complaining. That said, the illusion of the bump already being there wasn't hard to imagine. Especially with all the guys pausing to kiss my tummy at every turn. Jake liked to pull my shirt tight and Ian would just nudge it up. Coop was somewhere in between and Archie had been putting his hand there every night he slept next to me.

Some of the habits developed with Izzy. Others formed with Josh and then with Charlie. We were going to get new habits with... It was my turn to put my hand over the small bump. The bump needed a name. We would get one, eventually, as soon as we knew.

"You're not going to want to wait until they get here, are you?"

"Absolutely not." He shot me a grin. "I love you more than life, but if I have to suffer for months to find out if we're having another girl or another boy, I might grow crazy."

"Well, currently, that's not a long trip." The dry remark earned me a laugh.

"You're not wrong. But—after the scan today, we'll take Dad out to dinner tomorrow or invite him over?"

"Whatever you want." Truthfully, telling the grandparents was both fun *and* stressful. I loved that they were all always happy.

"Hmm, I want a lot of things, Frankie babe. You may not want to give me that much latitude." At the last light, waiting to turn, he leaned over and gave me a kiss.

"I can handle you," I reminded him and his smile transformed into a genuine grin.

"Hell yes, you can." He tapped his hands against the steering wheel. "Do you want to wait? Because if it's that important to you..."

I shook my head. "We waited with Izzy and I loved the added mystery of it to everything else. We fell in love with the bump, all of us. When she arrived, it was amazing. Jake wanted to know with Josh and finding out we were having a boy a few months ahead of his arrival—it was still magical. Then Coop wanted to know, but Charlie never cooperated."

He'd constantly been turned away during every ultrasound. Even when they tried to get him to turn, he was a hard no. Silly baby.

"Then yes, I really want to know. I want every minute of the anticipation and I want to talk names and plans and..." He pulled into a parking spot and then twisted to face me. "I want every single moment. I never got it when the guys said it was a little different when they knew. It doesn't make me love the other kids any less. I will punch the first person that tries to tell me Izzy isn't mine too, but..."

"But this one is the one we made," I murmured, and the desire that flared in his eyes at the acknowledgement had me reaching over to cup his cheek. "I remember. I love all of you so much. And every baby is just another reflection of how much we love each other. Do you have any preferences?"

"Happy. Healthy. With us." Archie ticked off each one. "I want you happy, and healthy too. So far, the morning sickness hasn't been a problem?"

"Not even a little bit. I know my age might play a little factor, but women have babies later on all the time."

"This isn't our first, but *you* have to be fine. You have to be fine, then *they* have to be fine." The intensity in his brown eyes held me captive there just like it had the first time he told me he loved me. I'd loved them for so long, I really couldn't imagine my life without them in it.

"We're all going to be fine. The benefit of being old pros, you know?" I wanted to make this as easy for him as I could.

"You calling me a pro?" He pursed his lips. "I can live with that." Then with a wink, he was out of the car and hurrying around to my side. The late September weather was almost perfect. Warm sunshine. Cooler breezes. The grass had been cut recently and they'd begun to swap out the flowers for the fall colors.

"Nothing like Texas, huh?" Archie said as he wrapped an arm around me.

"Nope. I like the seasons here and the not sweating all the time." Tilting my head back, I grinned up at him. "You?"

"The best part of Texas came with me up here. Never have to go back again. Dad and I are talking about selling the house there eventually. I mean—I have really fond memories of it, but again, the best part of Texas came with me."

"I love you," I whispered and he grinned.

"Best part of my day, every day."

With a long sigh, I nodded toward the building. "Shall we?"

"Yes, we shall."

Thirty minutes later, we were all set up in the exam room. I didn't have to get naked for this one, so that was always a plus. Instead, I sat on the foot of the little exam table, kicking my legs lightly. Archie parked it in a chair after pacing around the room. The time between the nurse checking my vitals and going over everything, and now, seemed forever.

"Why have an appointment, if they are going to be late?" Archie asked.

"Patience," I counseled him.

"If we were late, you'd lose the appointment."

"True," I said, with a little shrug. "But I need to see the

doctor and they don't *need* to see me. Ergo, we need to be patient. Besides, Dr. Patterson is fantastic and she never rushes us. She spends as much time with her patients as they need."

Disgruntled, Archie folded his arms. "Not a fan of the waiting."

"Tell me about the engine you and Jake are testing, I know you wanted to be ab—" Before I could finish asking there was a brisk knock on the door.

"Hello," Dr. Patterson said as she hustled into the room. The woman always filled the air around her with so much positive energy.

"Hey, Dr. Patterson."

"Frankie and—we have Archie today. Welcome."

Archie rose and shook her hand, polite smile in place. "Hey, Doc," he said. "Hope everything is fine."

"It's great," she said before moving over to the sink and washing her hands. "How are you two doing? I know Frankie said we wouldn't need to do any paternity testing this time."

"No," I told her. "Archie was the only contender this time." I grinned at him.

"Got it. That's good. It means we're already starting ahead. You updated the medical chart with his family medical history?"

I nodded. "Took care of it this weekend when I did my online check-in." I loved not filling out paperwork anymore. While paper was tactile and I liked it for some things, trying to fill out microscopic lines with a long list of anything sucked.

"Excellent." Turning, she swept her gaze from me to Archie and then back. "Any concerns?"

"No," I said with a quick shake of my head. "I haven't really had any issues with morning sickness. Nausea has been pretty minimal across the board. My appetite is definitely fine. Maybe a little more tired than normal, but the kids just went back to school and Charlie was sick the first week of classes and keeping us up."

"That's all relative. The kids will settle down into their schedules and you have a lot of help at home."

"I do. More than enough. Getting ready to do another tour, so that's something to discuss. It's not going to be extensive. We're going to do what we did when I was pregnant with Charlie. A few shows followed by a break, then another few shows. I want to be home by the third trimester unless Archie and I are having a babymoon, but that won't be stressful."

Surprise flickered over his face, followed by a hint of delight. "I forgot about the babymoon. That—is going to be fun." The sudden mischief in his eyes and the way he rubbed his hands together promised that he was already planning. Good, I liked giving him something else to focus on.

"Right then, we'll just dive into the ultrasound. I'd normally have my tech do this, but I know how you are with the first one." The lightness in her tone robbed it of any sting. The guys could be a lot with the techs and with the doctor there, she could answer everything right away. "I will want new bloodwork soon, but all of your labs look great and you're exercising regularly without overdoing it. Go ahead and lay back for me, Frankie."

She was pulling the machine over. Archie moved to the other side of the bed and when I held my hand up to him, he gripped it.

"As a reminder, we're at fourteen weeks. This is our first scan. We may not be able to see any genitalia. Not all babies are cooperative."

Archie chuckled, more of the tension leaching out of him. "We were just talking about Charlie on the way here."

Dr. Patterson paused and made a face before she broke into a sunny smile. "He really didn't want anyone to know."

"That or he just wanted to keep mooning us." That had been Coop's theory. The comment made both her and Archie laugh.

"Maybe so," she said as I rolled up my shirt and then she spread the warm gel out on my stomach. Even warmed up, it seemed a little chilly. Maybe I was just being too sensitive. "Ready?"

She had the screen up and was typing one handed while she held the wand with the other. One deep breath, then another. I had no reason to be all anxious, yet here I was, getting nervous. Archie squeezed my hand and that helped too.

"Ready," I said.

"And if I can tell, you both want to know?" She confirmed as she began to rub the wand against the gel.

"Yes," I said firmly and Archie echoed me.

"Let's see what we can see…" She hummed a little as she began searching. From this angle, I could kind of see the screen but squiggly lines made it harder to read. She paused a couple of times, hit a couple of buttons and then continued. It was really quiet, though.

"Why can't we hear the heartbeat?" We'd heard it during an earlier appt, but…

"Oh, don't start panicking on me, Mom. Here you go." She turned up the sound and there was a distinctive beat. I tried to relax my hand where I'd been digging my nails into Archie's skin. For all that I'd been calm, the lack of sound had actually been the worst thing.

"Thank you."

"Of course, sorry, I didn't mean to worry you. I just wanted to see if our little one was going to give us a good look." The last few words came out far slower than the first few. She frowned as she stared at the screen, then fiddled with something.

"Not being cooperative?" Archie asked.

"Yes and no, give me a second here. They're moving."

I bit my lower lip. Calm thoughts. Focus on calm thoughts. Everything was fine. It took forever with Charlie too, cause he was being so difficult. This was really just our first chance, hardly the last.

"Okay," she said with an exhale of determination. "Here we go…"

Excitement threaded through me as she turned the monitor toward us more firmly.

"Now, we've estimated fourteen weeks and I'd say that we're on the money there, but the fetus was looking a bit small…" She highlighted the screen as she pressed down slightly with the wand. The baby was moving but I couldn't really feel it yet. I wouldn't, not for a while.

"Doesn't look all that small to me," Archie said. "But what is that…"

"That," Dr. Patterson said as she shifted the wand, "is why I was having trouble getting a good image. I thought it was an echo."

"Not an echo?" Was that another head?

"Nope," she said, then marked the images with an AA next to the first and a BB next to the second. "Twins."

Twins.

My mouth opened then snapped closed again.

"Twins?" Archie didn't seem to be similarly afflicted. "Really?"

"Yes, one of them is definitely a girl," she said. "BB right here, she's not at all shy, but AA keeps moving over and is curled. So, not getting a good look."

One was a girl.

"A girl," Archie blew out a long breath then gradually pulled his gaze from the screen to look down at me. "One is a girl."

"The other might be too," I said. Twins. "Can you tell if we're looking at identical or fraternal?"

"Not yet," she said, doing another pass and snapping a couple more photos. "They are curling up together so it's making it hard to see them without seeing it as an echo, but we've definitely got two. That means, Miss Frankie, we will be shifting your appointments around."

A shiver went through me, apprehension and delight. Twins. I couldn't quite wrap my mind around it, but Archie's grin hadn't diminished in the slightest. "How much different?"

"Well, for now, as you go into the second trimester, you might be a little more tired than previously. I need you to keep track of everything. Trust your instincts, Mom. When we get to the third trimester, we'll be seeing you much more regularly. Twins are normal, but they sometimes bring complications. That's not anything for you to worry about, but we will just take precautions." She passed me some tissues so I could clean up. "I'm printing these out for you to take home to the others. Let me be the first to congratulate you both."

"Thank you," Archie said, the shock evident in his voice. "We appreciate it."

"Of course, now, take it easy. Call me if you need anything and I'll see you next month, okay?"

I nodded as Archie helped me sit up. The doctor left us alone and I found Archie staring at me, dazed.

"Twins."

"Apparently, you were an overachiever," I said.

"Me?" He blinked. "What about you?"

"Well… We've always known I've got issues."

He chuckled then cupped my face in his hands before he kissed me. It started out solemn, sober, and serious. Then he chuckled before sweeping his tongue in to tease mine. I swore my toes were curling before he was finished. Hot and cold flashed through me and I really wished we were *anywhere* but the doctor's office so I could climb him like a pole for that kiss.

"What did you think about?" I had to know. Cause that laugh had been downright devilish.

"Just… thinking we know who shoots the big shots." His grin grew. "The guys are gonna have words."

"Maybe, then you waited a long time," I reminded him.

"Didn't feel like waiting," he traced his thumb along my cheekbone. "Felt like living our best life. Still does."

Another kiss and then he helped me off the table. "Do twins run in your family?"

"Not that I know of," he said. "You?"

I gave him a bland look then lifted my shoulders again. "I don't think so. I'm pretty sure Dad would have mentioned it and what I know about the Graysons, none there either."

"Frankie… one's a girl."

I grinned. "Still going just for healthy and happy?"

"Hell yes, but now I'm like, do I want two girls who are identical? Two that aren't? Or a girl and a boy? The possibilities are endless."

"Well, not endless, endless. I need to pee before we go. Meet me out front?"

"You got it." He dropped another kiss on my lips and then headed toward the exit while I slipped into the bathroom. My heart hammered at a furious pace. Twins. We were already talking four kids with one more, this would be five.

We would officially no longer outnumber the kids.

A giggle escaped me at the thought. I couldn't wait to tell the guys and Eddie. The kids. Had to tell the kids. They definitely needed to know. After I peed and washed my hands, I headed out to the car.

Archie leaned against the front of it, his phone in hand but his expression a little distant except for the smile on his lips. When I started forward, he glanced up and I could feel the heat of his gaze.

"What?"

"Well, you know how frisky you get?" His grin widened.

Since I was feeling pretty frisky at the moment, I just nodded. "Yes. I'm aware. Pretty sure I wore all of you out the last couple of times."

Archie's chuckle was downright wicked. "How much more will it be with twins?"

"We might need to buy some toys." I couldn't resist tweaking him, just a little.

His eyes narrowed and he looped an arm around my waist. "Trust me, I'll make sure we keep up. Husbandly duties and all that."

I snorted. "Husbandly."

"Sure, it sounds good," he said kissing me lightly. "Almost as good as you sound when you come. That is one of my favorite sounds."

"Archie…"

"Hmm?"

"Can we go home now?"

He nibbled a kiss along my jaw. "We have to call Dad about dinner."

"We can call him later," I said and spread my hand against his chest. "I'm definitely feeling some of that frisky right now."

"Yes," he whispered. "Then your wish is my command."

"Three orgasms," I said and his eyes lit up.

"Just three?" He raised his eyebrows.

"Let's start with three."

Two of us could play this game.

"Challenge accepted, Mrs. Standish."

CHAPTER 4

BABY MAKES FIVE

JAKE

I was still wrapping my mind around the concept of twins as I set Josh into the bathtub to clean him up. From the other side of the bathroom, Izzy let out a miserable sound as she threw up.

Coop had pulled her hair up and out of her way. Archie and Frankie had picked them both up from school on their way back from their appointment. They weren't the only ones being hit by a stomach flu.

"Daddy," Josh said in a quavery voice. "I don't feel good."

"I know you don't," I said, the bath was lukewarm water only because Josh definitely wasn't. He had a fever and from the way Izzy was throwing up, I'd imagine she had one too. "We're going to fix it."

"I want Mama," Izzy said after Coop wiped her face and flushed the toilet.

Yeah, they always did. "Let's clean you up first," Coop

suggested. "Dad went to the store to get some stuff for your tummies. Mama has Charlie at the moment."

"Is Charlie sick?" The demand in Izzy's tone chased away some of her unhappiness. I stole a glance over to find her staring at Coop with the fiercest expression.

God, she was so Frankie at that age. Our little girl was almost a carbon copy of her mother. Tough. She'd happily throw down if it came to that. Fearless.

Loyal to a fault.

"We don't know yet, little miss," Coop told her in a tone that brooked no arguments even if he didn't have to raise his voice one iota. It was impressive. "Let's finish cleaning you up and then you can try some crackers."

"I didn't get it all over me, Pop. I was careful."

"I know you were," he said, nudging her toward the door. "Let's change anyway. Probably be more comfortable out of the uniform."

Her sigh was everything and I caught Coop's eye roll followed by a swift grin.

"Daddy," Josh said, laying his head against my arm. "I'm gonna be sick again."

I twisted and got the bowl under his face before he puked. Some days, I looked at my life and thought, who planned for this? Two kids throwing up, the likelihood that we'd have a third one doing it anytime now, and the simple fact we'd probably have a round of it go through all of us.

We really needed to avoid Frankie getting this. Granted, we might not have a choice, but fingers crossed.

When Josh finished, I dumped out the bowl into the toilet and flushed it away before going back to him. The hard flush to his cheeks was diminishing and I used a washcloth to spread the cooler water over his neck and back.

"You're doing good, bud," I promised him. "You're doing real good."

"I don't like this."

"Yeah, me neither. We'll fix it though." I gave him another five minutes in the bath. I wanted the heavy flush out of his cheeks and that fever reduced. I checked with the forehead reader before I took him out. Down a couple of degrees.

Better.

When I wrapped him up in a towel and lifted him out, he rested his head against my shoulder. Coop had Izzy squared away, so I took Josh for clean clothes. Jeremy was in his room when we came in and he gave Josh an assessing look.

"I brought up some Sprite and Crackers if we're feeling up for it."

"I'm hungry," Josh said and Jeremy grinned at him. "Thank you, Grandpa Jere."

"You're quite welcome, Mr. Joshua. Do we want pajamas or play clothes?"

Josh looked up at me and I winked at him. "Whatever you feel like, bud. You're not going back to school today." The next day wasn't looking likely either. Not when he had to be fever free for twenty-four hours.

"PJs please," Josh answered.

Jeremy went over to the dresser and pulled out some Transformer ones that Josh had gotten from my parents on their last visit. They'd gotten Izzy the superhero ones she really wanted and Transformers for Josh.

After I dried him off, Jeremy helped him get dressed and then I headed back to the bathroom to hang up the towel. We stored buckets under the sink for these occasions.

The soiled school clothes were already gone, so I just carried the bucket back in to Josh. Jeremy already had him set up in bed with a tray over his lap. I shook my head at the television. The kids didn't have them in their rooms, but we did have one we could roll in when they were sick.

Their "shared" television was in the larger rec room.

There they could watch movies, shows, or play video games. But we could also restrict it when necessary. Unsurprisingly, the Transformers movie was already on. I set the bucket down next to the bed.

"Will you stay and watch with me, Daddy?"

That was an impossible invitation to turn down. "Sure thing, bud. Jeremy can you let them…"

"Absolutely, Mr. Jake. Would you like anything to eat?"

"Probably not right now." Especially since Josh was still pale. "But thank you."

"Of course."

Then he left us alone. Josh nibbled on a cracker and sipped his Sprite, but he didn't rush through anything. I sprawled next to him and when he wanted to cuddle up, I wrapped him up and held him. We didn't even make it to the halfway point and his eyes were heavy.

I eased him down and moved the food tray so he could lay comfortably. The door pushed inward and Frankie peeked in, worry plain on her face.

"He's alright," I said softly, I'd gotten him settled and I eased off the side of the bed as she crossed the room. She'd changed clothes and looked more comfortable. With gentle fingers, she brushed the dark hair off of Josh's forehead.

"He's still warm."

"Yeah, low-grade fever now. Let's get a little more food in him and keep it down and we can go for the kid aspirin if we need too."

I slid my arms around her and settled my hands on the steadily firming bump. The arrival of a new bump was something we all enjoyed. Rubbing my cheek against the top of her head gently, I gave her a squeeze.

"I hate it when they're sick," she admitted. Not that she needed to remind me. Every single time one of them suffered, Frankie's empathy poured out of her.

"I know, Baby Girl," I whispered. "I hate it when you get sick too. So let's ease out of here. If you haven't already gotten it, I'd like to avoid you getting sick if we can."

She rubbed her hand against the back of mine where I cradled her bump. "Izzy wants me to come cuddle, but Coop almost had her asleep too."

"Good." I pressed a kiss to the side of her head. "Come on, they will be fine and we can turn on the intercom so we can hear him."

Her soft sigh tugged at me as I drew her out of the room, just before I closed the door, I pressed the intercom to open it to downstairs. It meant we would be able to monitor. Before Izzy was born, we'd reworked the whole system so we could switch to broadcast and listen in different areas.

Down the hall, we peeked in on Izzy. Coop glanced at us from where he was tucking a sound asleep Izzy in. Like Josh, Izzy had a pail next to the bed. A television had been rolled into her room too. The movie was Fellowship of the Ring. She'd seen it so many times in the last year. It was her favorite.

Coop turned on her intercom before he closed the door. "Josh?"

"Fever still, low-grade. But he's sleeping," I told him.

We both looked at Frankie. "Charlie?"

"He seems fine so far, he's outside playing with Archie. Jeremy was going to fix something light for lunch for all of us. Ian called, he's coming back early."

"He was meeting with the new producers, right?" I asked as we headed downstairs.

"Yep, we need a new tour manager and the producers were bringing in a few for Ian to meet." Frankie smothered a yawn as she followed Coop down. He just took the step ahead of her like we'd practiced it. Then again, we kind of had. "But he doesn't want to get stuck in Manhattan late, and he'd rather be here helping."

"Sounds good." The upcoming tour had been decided on *before* Frankie got pregnant, but it wasn't like we were unaware of the attempts. We'd even tracked ovulation for a while.

"I'll be serving lunch outside," Jeremy told us pointedly.

"Do you want some help bringing it out?" I offered before Frankie did, but Coop was already herding her out the door to where Charlie's laughter floated on the breeze.

"I'll take care of it, Mr. Jake. Half of it is already waiting. I can also hear Miss Izzy and Mr. Josh if they need anything."

"Thanks, Jeremy, seriously." Having a lot of adult backup was amazing, but more kids meant more likelihood they all got something and shared it around.

Murray and Maxie were bounding around the yard herding Charlie. Archie was on his feet, keeping an eye on all of it. Charlie was great with the dogs, but they were still a little too enthusiastic sometimes. Right now, though, they seemed to be behaving well. Murray would lay down and patiently lick Charlie each time Charlie toddled over to him to pet him.

Charlie thought it was all hilarious.

"Come and eat," Frankie was saying and Charlie pivoted at the sound of her voice.

"Mama!" He was already racing as fast as his little legs could carry him. I had to smother a chuckle. Maxie and Murray were hurrying over to her too. Everything revolved around Frankie and it was the best orbit I'd ever been in.

She scooped Charlie up, then gave him a raspberry of a kiss to his cheek. His laughter was so open and happy.

"Pop!" Charlie was already flinging himself at Coop.

"I wish I had half of his enthusiasm," Archie said as he joined me.

"We used to," I said, smirking. "For Frankie, we still do."

"You have a point," he said, clapping me on the shoulder once. "Good man. Big sandwiches to eat."

"Roast beef?"

It was one of Frankie's favorites. Jeremy made sure all cold cuts had been heated before he prepared anything for her. The possibility of bacteria was bad for pregnant women, so he took no chances once we figured out she was pregnant.

"Yep." He led the way over to the table where Frankie was cleaning Charlie's hands. I used one of the hot, wet towels that Jeremy had brought out to clean mine. Good habits.

Then Coop buckled Charlie into his seat between him and Frankie. Archie beat me to the other side of Frankie. His smirk amused me, but I just pulled out the chair opposite her. At least I got the best view.

Conversation was on hiatus while we sorted out food and drinks. We had iced tea courtesy of Jeremy. It had a flowery taste so probably one of the herbals. Frankie had developed a taste for them when she was pregnant with Charlie and Rachel sent her a crate of every herbal tea on the planet.

Or at least that was what it felt like.

Still, it made Frankie smile. While I wasn't banned from real coffee, I'd enjoy the flowery tea with her.

"So," Coop said as I took a bite of my sandwich. "Twins?"

Their message had included a photo of the ultrasound.

"Twins," Archie said and his eyes alternated from wild to determined to delighted and back to wild again. That seesaw was going to get a hell of a workout. "Doc Patterson said we needed to take notice of any significant changes and that starting with the third trimester, Frankie will have to see her more often."

Frankie washed down her bite of sandwich with a long drink. "So far, I feel fine. I've been tired, but it's grant season,

Ian and I are working on tour stuff, and the kids just went back to school. Tired would seem fairly normal."

"Well, maybe we revisit the schedule a little?" I suggested. "You work from here a lot which is convenient, but that also means Charlie and he doesn't nap as often as he should."

Charlie paused mid bite with a handful of fruit gripped in his fingers. "No naps. Not tiwed."

"Of course not," Frankie told him, her voice automatically soothing. "Naps are for after lunch."

"No nap," Charlie said firmly then threw the fruit at her. Frankie actually caught the apple slice.

"Mine now." Then she ate it. Charlie's outrage damn near killed me because I couldn't laugh at the way his mouth opened in an "O." "Next time," she told him. "Don't throw your food."

"How about you don't throw anything," Coop said, his tone firming into what had to be, the ultimate Dad voice. Of all of us to get it, Coop had nailed it from day one. Archie was mashing his lips together to keep from laughing. "We don't throw things at Mama. Ever."

Lower lip jutting out and trembling, Charlie looked from Coop to Frankie. "Sowwy, Mama."

"Apology accepted," she told him, then kissed his fingers. "But it's still my fruit."

Not laughing was incredibly tough. "Anyway," I said in something of a strained voice while fighting to keep my humor contained. "We can look for different ways to give you an extra hour or two each day whether you n-a-p..." Yes, we spelled out conversations. Sometimes you just had to. "Or sit and read. You know, some quality Frankie time. Might ease some of the stress and the tired for you."

She tilted her head from side to side as if weighing her options. "Maybe, but let's see how it goes. She said the third trimester would likely be the toughest. But I will pay attention to any and all symptoms that I might have. That includes the tired and maybe an extra hour a day is not a bad thing when we're home."

"You'll get more on the road," Archie said, though his frown seemed at odds with the sentiment. "Should you and Bubba maybe rethink two weeks on to one week off a different way?"

"We can absolutely talk about it," she offered, her patience fully on display. We got overprotective. Most of the time, she just rolled with it and indulged us. Other times, she countered and proved her point. "Twins is different, but—in my experience, all the pregnancies have been different. I don't know if it's because with Izzy everything was new and with Josh, we were focused on other stuff and then again with Charlie."

When his name was said, the toddler beamed and held out an apple slice to Frankie. She tapped his nose gently.

"You eat it, sweetheart. Mama has to finish her sandwich."

"Otay."

Then she looked back at us, sweeping all three of us with one look. "I'm willing to discuss, debate, and brainstorm anything you guys want in order to make sure that we don't leave a stone unturned. I would like to do the tour... Ian never complains but this is important to him."

"You are far more important to him," I reminded her. "You and our kids. Our family. I'm not saying the tour isn't important. I love hearing you guys perform. Do we get a little jealous when you're gone for a couple of weeks here or there and Bubba gets you all to himself?"

"Yes," Coop answered for us. "We do, but we also know you love us and wish we were there too."

"I do," she admitted and then reached a hand over to Archie. He clasped it quickly, blowing out a breath. Yeah. We'd all been there. "I adore you and I love being here with you guys and I love being out there with Ian. So, we find the best way to make it work for all of us. The two weeks on and one week off for a tour works well because then we get to see all of you. This will also be the first time I leave Charlie."

Her expression tightened and then she laughed, the sound eased one of my concerns.

"And it will all be fine, I know it will. We have plenty of support. The grandparents will all descend soon enough."

"Yeah," Archie said. "We're telling Dad tomorrow night. Then Hank. Then we tell everyone else."

"The best part of when they all come to town is they always want to kidnap the kids and that means we can steal away with Frankie." That was a plan.

"I like the way you think," Coop commented and we all chuckled.

"No matter what happens, I will take every precaution and follow the doctor's advice."

Archie kissed her hand before he nudged her back to eating.

"When are you guys gonna do the babymoon? Especially if the third trimester has more concerns?"

"Already working on a plan," Archie said. "Let's get the tour settled and keep one eye on the doctor reports and worst case scenario, we take the babymoon after they come."

I wasn't the only one squinting at Archie. "You are not leaving them right after they're born."

"No, we absolutely aren't," he said, grinning. "But we have the rest of our lives and I'll just pocket that babymoon for later."

Frankie laughed and Coop shook his head. No, we'd work out something else. The babymoons were important. It was good bonding time for us with Frankie and time to focus on that new parent feeling.

I'd fucking loved the one Frankie and I took when she

was still pregnant with Josh. It had definitely brought us closer. Besides, there were a lot more distractions here now with all the kids.

What if we got them a *pied-à-terre* in the city, then they could escape there for the babymoon but not have to worry about any other travel complications? Maybe. When lunch was done, Coop picked up Charlie.

"Gonna get him ready for a nap and check on the kids. Then I need to do some calls." He gave Frankie a firm look. "Now would be a great time for you to nap too."

I could practically read her desire to stick her tongue out at him, but with Charlie present she resisted the impulse. "Archie and I were already planning a little more strenuous activity when we got home. Might nap after that."

My dick twitched at the low husky note at the end of the sentence. We were rapidly approaching the time her sex drive doubled. Damn those were some good times.

"If you're tired," Archie said and she didn't respond, just covered his mouth with her hand as she looked at Coop.

"If you need to work, we can keep an ear out for them too." Then she removed her hand from Archie's mouth and he captured it to hold with a smile.

"I know," Coop said, bending to give her a kiss and then Charlie wanted one too.

"No nap," he told Coop confidently and I hid a smile.

"Sure thing," Coop said, winking. "It's only a couple of hours, but I canceled some appointments and I want to make sure they got rescheduled, then check in on them."

"We got this," I told him and waved him off. Archie and I pretty much worked for ourselves and Standish, which was also ourselves. So we could and had taken all the time we needed when we needed.

It was a perk, a luxury we could provide when the kids were sick or one of us was or if we simply missed Frankie after a tour and wanted a few days at home with her. Coop bumped my shoulder with his fist as he headed back into the house and I leaned forward to study the two of them.

"Are you really okay?"

"Honestly?" Frankie lifted her shoulders. "I'm not bad in the slightest. Stunned. A little apprehensive maybe, and trying to figure out all the ways that twins are going to be harder than one new one. Charlie will be potty trained in the not too far distant future, that will help, but..."

"I'm freaking out a little," Archie admitted and after the freak out last week, I was glad he had no trouble owning it. "At the same time, I can't fucking wait. This is... we're gonna have twins. Our family is growing. I missed out on having siblings."

"Me too," Frankie admitted. "And I love the ones I have now but..."

"It's not the same as growing up with them." I knew that well. Those two and Bubba hadn't had to share their parents or their attention or put up with little sisters who got into everything. I wouldn't trade mine for anything and at the same time... "I get it."

"I love this family we're making." Frankie said and a tear escaped to roll down her cheek. She swiped it away. "And I know we were going to talk about whether we wanted to go for more after this baby was born..."

"But now it's babies. A girl and unknown. Izzy will be happy about the girl part." She'd wrinkled her nose when Charlie turned out to be a boy. So I had a feeling she'd love a baby sister. "We'll figure it out," I reminded her. "Five kids is nothing to sneeze at and we're enjoying them. If you want more babies after—well, I'm always up for practice one way or another."

"Same," Archie said. "And we will figure it out, but I believe you made a request earlier..."

"Oh yes," she brightened. "Three orgasms."

"Lucky bastard," I said and Archie just grinned.

"You can give me three later," Frankie offered, then circled the table to give me a kiss. I wrapped my arms around her and tugged her into my lap for a moment.

"Anything you want," I promised, then nuzzled the corner of her mouth with another kiss. "Now, let Archie take care of you and let us worry about the kids for a bit."

"If you need us…"

"I know where you'll be." One last kiss and then I set her on her feet. "Go on."

She drifted inside, hand in hand with Archie, and I leaned back. Maxie and Murray looked up from where they were napping in the shade. Once Coop was done, I'd take these two out for a run. Bubba might be back by then.

Tilting my head back to let the sun hit my face, I sighed.

Twins.

CHAPTER 5

PILLOW TALK

FRANKIE

It was almost suspiciously quiet as we made ourselves down to the wing we shared. The kids had their own set of rooms and while it wasn't in a totally separate wing, we were able to give ourselves some privacy when we needed it.

Izzy and Josh being home and sick had me glancing toward their rooms on the way. Without me saying a word, however, Archie navigated down the second hall to the kids rooms. We'd done the remodeling to incorporate the best parts of Archie's wing where he grew up and yet, not isolating the kids far away.

They were *our* kids. If they wanted to come find us at night or climb in bed to snuggle in the morning, they could. As much as I loved that, it made finding quality time for just us a challenge. Not that the guys weren't always up for a challenge.

Quietly, Archie opened Josh's door and we peeked inside.

He was sound asleep. A movie played quietly on the television. With the curtains drawn it was dark and cool in the room. His face was a little flushed and I checked my watch.

After Archie nudged the door a little wider, I went in to check. Josh was a little warm, the forehead thermometer was there, so I did a quick check. Definitely still a fever, but low-grade. I pressed a kiss to his forehead then shifted his blankets before slipping back out.

Next stop, Izzy's room. We did the same, only Archie moved over to close the curtains cause the sun's angle had changed. Her fever was low-grade too, but still there. She opened her eyes when I got close.

"Shh," I whispered. "Just checking on you."

"Love you, Mama," she whispered and I kissed her forehead.

"Love you too."

"Love you, Izzy Belle," Archie said, leaning over to give her a kiss.

"Love you, Papa." She smiled before her lashes drifted down and she went right back to sleep. He brushed some of the damp blonde hair away from her forehead.

Once back in the hall, he pulled out his phone and pressed a button before catching my hand in his. "Hey, Jere," he said. "Yeah, we just checked on them. Still low-grade fevers for both of them, but Izzy's is a bit higher."

He listened as we made it to our room and I closed the doors behind us, then turned the lock. The guys could get in. There was a key above the doorframe that we could all reach.

I leaned against the doors as Archie turned to face me. The concern on his face wrapped me up in knots. They were all the best fathers. They loved the kids so damn much and it made me weepy sometimes—usually when I was pregnant—but I loved that our kids had them.

"Thanks. Frankie and I are going to take some time, but

call if we're needed." He chuckled and some of the worry in his eyes eased. "I will absolutely make taking care of her my priority. No worries there." Another pause, then he rolled his eyes but his grin widened. "Yes, sir."

Call over, he lowered the phone and stared at me. There was so much *love* in his eyes that it soaked through me. Every single day with them had filled me to the brim…

"I love you," I whispered and he tossed his phone in the vicinity of the love seat. Our room boasted a couple of extra bedrooms as needed, a sitting room, then our bedroom, the one all of us shared.

"You going to cry all over me, Babe?" The softness in his voice summoned the tears like they were just waiting for him and he chuckled. Cupping my face, he swiped away the tears with his thumbs. "Twenty years ago, you crying like this would have terrified me."

A laugh escaped me. Twenty years. That seemed—forever and at the same time, just a drop in the bucket. "Not anymore?"

"Nope," he said, then nuzzled a whisper soft kiss to my lips. "No, these tears—they remind me how much you trust me. How much you trust all of us. They're tears of joy, and longing, and hope…"

Another laugh escaped me as I clasped his arms where he cradled my face. "I do love you."

"I'm the luckiest man on the planet. The most beautiful woman in the world is in love with me and she's having our babies again—*babies*." He paused and shook his head. "Wow…"

"Still getting used to it?" I teased as I slid my hands along his arms and when I threaded them up to wrap around his neck, he dropped his hands to my ass and then lifted me like I was still a svelte teenager.

He gave me a look, the corners of his mouth quirking. "Like you're any more used to it yet than I am."

Hitching my legs to his hips, I nuzzled a kiss to the corner of his lips until he sealed his mouth to mine. The first brush of his tongue had me opening to him. I loved kissing Archie. We could kiss for hours and I'd never get tired of it.

Another laugh escaped me and he pulled his head back, amusement filtering through his expression. "It's going to be one of *those* times."

Delight curved through me. "I have no idea what you're talking about."

"Uh huh." He turned, moving easily through our sitting room and into the bedroom. He pushed the door closed with his foot and then stalked toward our bed. It was even larger than the one we'd had in the Brownstone. If we had to all crawl in here with the kids, we could and still have room.

I loved it.

It made my birthday and the games they played so much more fun.

A shiver of anticipation went through me as Archie set me on the bed. When I would have reached for him, he caught my hands and kissed them.

"I want to undress you and play first, Mrs. Standish. There was a request on the table and I think you need the first of three sooner rather than later."

All at once my laughter and tears went up in flames at the liquid heat in his voice. He kissed my hands again before releasing them. Then he took his time undressing me. He started with my shoes, then my socks. When he unbuttoned my shirt, I swore my nipples went on point and the ache in my breasts increased.

They'd been especially tender this time around and now I knew why. Twins... excitement fountained through me as he paused to trace the line of my bra before he unhooked it.

They were already swollen. They'd gotten bigger with each pregnancy and as self-conscious as it had made me at first...

"Fuck," Archie whispered. "I always forget how much more beautiful you get every single day." It was ridiculous and yet love washed through me at the declaration.

"I always feel fatter," I admitted.

"I know you do," he said, then cupped my breasts with such exquisite gentleness it pulled tears to my eyes again.

The tease of his thumbs against my nipples had my pussy contracting as the competing sensations of too much and not enough vied for supremacy.

"You know, you're the most beautiful woman in the world, right? I love every inch of you... from these amazing breasts. God, Frankie... they are so fucking perfect." He pressed kisses to where the stretch marks showed along the sides now. Before he went to his knees and sucked one nipple against his teeth before I could even say a word.

Thought became an abstract as he laved his tongue over the tip. The gentlest of pressure could be right on the edge of pain and I tilted my head back, trying to get my breathing under control. I almost didn't want to inhale or exhale, then increased the suction and the sharpness sent wetness to soak my panties.

I threaded my hand through his hair as he pressed more biting kisses across my nipples. He kept taking it right up to the edge of what I could take then he'd soothe them again. The lap of his tongue was heavenly.

The stroke of his fingers down my sides eased through the haze of passion. When he lifted his head, the cool air against my damp nipples was a whole new form of teasing. Then he gripped the waistband of my stretch pants and tugged them along with my panties down and off.

I was so glad I'd kept up on the laser appointments. Waxing wasn't my favorite anymore and laser was uncomfortable but lasted way longer. In the not too far distant future, being able to see my legs would be a challenge.

"Babe..." The coax of his voice had me opening my eyes. I hadn't even realized I'd closed them. "Focus on me, not all the flaws you're listing in your head, okay?"

"I'm not—" But I couldn't even make the denial sound honest. Not when I had been.

"I know, and you have the right to feel how you feel. It's your body and I know the kids take it over. The cravings come. The desire and the need. Then the emotions slip their leash. You worry about everything and nothing." The description was so damn accurate. "You've been an over-achiever from day one, it's one of the things I always admired about you."

He pressed a kiss to my left knee, then my right. With light hands, he glided them apart, stroking the skin. His touch was so familiar and welcome. It made me hotter now than it had when I was seventeen. Just remembering that first night together...

A shiver raced up my spine.

I touched my fingers to his cheek and his smile softened.

"I see you Frankie Standish. I always have. I fucking love you more than anything else on this planet. You are the best goddamn thing that ever happened to me. With you, I've experienced so many things that I can't put into words but I wouldn't trade for anything in the world."

When he reached the suggestion of stretch marks on my thighs, he teased his fingers along them, following them up to my stomach. The pouch of stretched skin there never went away. The suggestion of a bump was definitely present, a reality more than just the camouflage of previous stretching.

"These babies..." He spread his fingers over the worst of the marks, cupping the suggestion of a bump. "They are already the loves of my life just like their sister and their brothers. Because we made them…you, me, and the guys. Our family is growing and I couldn't love you more if I tried."

Hot tears splashed against my cheeks as he stared up at me.

"Every single one of these marks, the spread to your hips, the thickness of your thighs and your breasts—fuck me, those breasts. I love fucking them, you know that and I can really fuck them now." The husky growl at the end had my pussy clenching and more dampness escaping.

Archie and that devilish tongue of his. He paused and took a deep breath, then leaned closer to my pussy. The whisper of touch and breath sent a wave of goosebumps over my skin.

"Fuck, you even smell better. How is that possible?" Then he pushed my thighs wide. He had no shame, but considering I pushed my hips upward as he pressed his face closer—I couldn't really fault him.

I had no shame either.

Then he licked me from entrance to clit and my thighs started quivering.

"Oh, someone is swollen and eager," he murmured. The vibration next to my clit had me squirming. Then he teased his tongue around it in circles. "Swollen, red, and hot as hell —just like you." He hummed as he sucked against my clit, it was the most sensual torture. Like he knew exactly how much pressure to apply before I would lose my mind and not quite going that far.

It was heaven and hell.

"Archie…" It came out more a moan than a whine.

"I have you, Babe," he said in between swirling his tongue and tormenting me. I was so focused on his mouth and his tongue, that the pressure of his fingers pressing into me was damn near startling. His chuckle was so delighted when I gasped.

Not that he gave me too much time to savor the stretch before he curled those fingers. He was a master at finding the spot inside me just as he applied so much pressure to my clit, I swore I split apart.

A scream left my throat as I fisted both the bed covering and his hair. He devoured me as he used his hand to fuck me and that orgasm rocked me. I came in a rush of dampness, soaking his hand and his face.

The tempo of his licking shifted as I shuddered my way back to earth. It was like he needed to take in every drop before it escaped.

"Perfection," he said in husky tone. "Absolute perfection. I could eat you all day… and maybe I will."

Oh shit. I couldn't grasp a thought as he made good on his promise. He fucked me with his fingers, then his tongue, then his fingers again never quite letting me come. Instead, he edged me over and over again, until I was sobbing from it.

When he lifted his head and let me get a breath, sweat soaked my face and my chest. His face was soaking wet too and he licked his lips.

"Frankie, I fucking love eating you out. But I really want to sink my dick into you and savor the way your pussy wraps around me."

He was massaging said dick with one hand. A little laugh of disbelief escaped me as he moved his grip over his straining cock, from balls to tip and back. Pre-cum beaded over his slit and I licked my lips.

"Then what are you waiting for?" I pushed up on my elbows. My legs were spread, everything was on display. "Come and take me…I want to feel you inside of me when I come this time and I have a feeling as soon as that magnificent dick sinks into me, I'm going to come so hard I won't be able to see."

"That is the plan." He told me. But instead of just thrusting deep, he teased his cock along my slit. Up and down, soaking his length even as he watched me. If not for the vein throbbing in his forehead, I might *almost* buy he wasn't affected.

But this was Archie.

My Archie.

My husband.

He lived to torment me with pleasure almost as much as he did to seduce me with his filthy mouth.

"Does my pussy still got your tongue?" I teased and the absolute light that filled his eyes burst into my heart.

"Your pussy will always have my tongue." Then he angled himself before he pushed in. The gentleness he and they could and did show when I was pregnant was always a test of the waters. How much could I take before I shattered? How much was too much? No pain—ever. Even when a little pain was something I enjoyed, it had to be the pain intended only.

He caught himself on one arm, his cock filled me. The stretch was familiar, and so welcome. A little laugh escaped me on the air that he pushed out of my lungs.

"What are you thinking about?" He challenged.

I could tweak him. My breath was coming in pants, because I hadn't been kidding about how close I was to coming again.

"That people used to think that you had to fuck a virgin so her pussy would shape to that one cock. Too much cock and the pussy gets all stretched out of shape—" I laughed, pleasure and joy twining through me. "Tell me you've never had a baby or seen a baby being born without telling me."

He chuckled.

"Then I feel you…and fuck you were made me for Archie.

71

All of you were. You feel so fucking good inside of me." I would never get tired of it.

"You're the one who feels good, Babe. I can never get enough of this sweet pussy. I fucking love how hot and wet you are. How tight you clamp down on me. How it feels like you can never get enough..." He rolled his hips, then gave a little twist as he drew back then thrust into me again.

I don't know who reached for who first, but his mouth was on mine and I had my arms around his neck as we writhed. I didn't want to be apart. His skin seemed as damp as mine as we slid and glided with each other, then he rolled onto his back and I was leaning over him. I took him deeper this way.

My mouth opened in a silent cry. I dug my fingers into his shoulders and began to ride. Another favorite part of the whole progress of pregnancy. I got to be on top more.

I fucking loved being on top. Almost as much as being on all fours—or being filled with all of them. We'd only managed that a few times.

"Fuck me, Frankie," Archie said, stroking his hands up and down my sides before settling them on my hips. "I want to fill you to the brim. My babies are in your belly...and now I want my cum in there too..."

Real laughter burst out of me as I gripped his hands and pulled them to my breasts. I needed that pain right now. I needed that edging because I was so close and I wanted to make this last.

He tweaked a nipple and it flash-fired through me. I clamped down and he hissed out a breath.

"Fuck. Yes. Right there, Babe. Take everything I have..."

Words were hard as I rode him and Archie met me by thrusting upward. As much as he tried to let me take it all, it wasn't long before he was gripping me, a fist in my hair and another on my hip as he fucked me hard from below.

Every stroke edged me higher, tightening the coils of pleasure until I was shaking my head violently and then he sucked a nipple against his teeth. The combination of tongue, teeth, and pressure fractured everything.

I came with a scream, soaking his lap even as he kept thrusting and he pushed me from one orgasm right into another. Tears escaped me. It was too much. I couldn't do this.

"Yes, you can," he told me, rolling us until I was on my side and then he was still pumping into me from a new angle and I thrashed. "Give it to me, Babe. Give me those screams. You're going to take all of it. You wanted this and now you're going to take it. That's my dick… my hands… my kisses…"

The world went white even as another raw sound burst out of me. He fucked me right out of my body and the rush of his release plunged me back into the quivering shaking mess that was me on the bed, utterly entwined with him.

"Fuck me," I whispered, the cascading shudders had me fluttering around his still half-hard cock. It would soften, but the heat of his release was right there. Frankly, I loved having their cum in me. I loved how it felt when they came. I swore it made me come harder.

Placebo effect or whatever—it was something I craved every time.

Them. It was just them. They were perfect for me.

Light kisses showered my face and I finally opened my eyes to find Archie gazing down at me. "You said three, right?"

"I did." I clenched around him and his lips compressed but he didn't pull away. His cock was always so sensitive after he came. But he loved to feel me around him and I loved having him there. "You really delivered…maybe next time I'll say four."

It was an old joke, but his grin was worth it.

"Give me five minutes, Babe, then I'll eat you out until you scream again."

"Archie... you know it takes a while..."

"I know," he said, his grin growing. "I'm hoping it takes all afternoon. I want to play with every inch of this body. Maybe even fuck your ass later if you're up for it."

I shivered, biting my lip.

"That looked very much like a yes please." He nuzzled kisses to my jaw, then teased the whorls of my ear with his tongue before he whispered. "You want my cock everywhere, don't you?"

"I could swallow your cock right now and suck on you like candy," I promised. It was his turn to give a full body shudder, and it kind of felt like he went from half-hard to a little more firm. Oh that could be interesting... "You up for a bet?"

He raised his head. "Talk to me, Mrs. Standish, because you speak my dirty language..."

"You eat me, I suck you. Whoever comes first, we both win."

Head tilted back and eyes closed, he looked like a man in prayer. "Best. Wife. Ever."

I laughed and we both shuddered when he gave a gentle thrust with his hips.

"Does that mean you're in, Mr. Standish?"

Eyes open, he stared at me with scorching heat. "Get ready to give those lips a workout, Mrs. Standish... because I plan to take a while..."

"Promises promises." It was the tiniest of taunts, but he flipped us around and put a pillow under my hips and head for comfort before he teased his cock against my lips.

Yes, we were both going to win.

CHAPTER 6

BIRTHDAY BOYS

COOP

"Katie," I said, getting my assistant's attention. She was very focused on transcribing notes I'd dictated over the weekend. I tended to write up my own patient notes, but then I dictated the ones that we needed to share with other providers so she could update all the files at once.

She held up one finger then went back to typing at the speed of light. The woman was ridiculously fast. I used to think I had decent typing speed. Then I hired her and it seriously disabused me of the notion. I waited patiently until she hit enter with some finality.

Then she glanced up and took off her earbuds. "What's up, Doc?"

I didn't roll my eyes, but I did shake my head. She gave me the cheeky, unrepentant grin.

"Not a doctor," I reminded her.

"But you have a *doctorate*," she stated before leaning back in her chair. "While you're not an MD, you are a PhD and you help people. Therefore—Doc."

"I'm never winning this argument, am I?" Considering how many times we'd had it? I'd lost it a long time ago. Didn't mean I wouldn't keep fighting the good fight.

"Nope," she said with a sunny smile. "But you keep on trying, *Doc*."

"It's a good thing I like you, impertinence and all."

"Pfft," she scoffed. "You couldn't handle a kissass. You'd walk all over them in five minutes. I talked to Frankie, I know how to keep you in line."

That made me laugh. "Fair enough." I raised my hands. The fact Frankie and Katie got along so well was another reason I'd hired her. In her fifties, she sported blue hair, an attitude and had raised four kids—on her own. All of whom were now in college or had just graduated.

Honestly, she could pretty much say whatever she wanted. She kept the office running even when I had to go.

"So," she said. "What's up?" Then she flicked a glance to her calendar on the left. "Josh's birthday presents were ordered. As was Archie's, but there was a bit of a delay. It should still make it in time. I arranged for flowers at the next two stops for Frankie and I spoke to Ian this morning per your request since you had patients all day, and he said that they would be home for Halloween."

"That's what I thought." Frankie's message the night before had elements of sadness in it. She hadn't called. Instead, she texted. She only did that when she wanted to cover her distress. "Can we move—"

"A few of your appointments around for Tuesday and Wednesday next week? Yes, we can. I already started the process. I had a light day for you on Wednesday already. I can also move Thursday around a bit. I spoke to Ms. H at the center, she can take over the group meetings all week, that way you can go see Frankie on the road."

Well, there was being on the ball and then there was a creepy level of competency. Not that I was complaining. "Right, anything else I need to know?"

Her grin was so amused. "Only that Jake sent over the updates for the latest costumes the kids want. Charlie had a pediatrician appointment today and Jake said he's doing great..." She checked her blotter. "The pediatrician does want to check his hearing again in six months. Said it might be nothing, but there was a blip."

"What kind of blip?" All my good humor fled. This was why I liked going to all of their appointments, but sometimes we just couldn't make it work.

"Hey, easy there, Pop. You're gonna find a lot of repetitive tests come up, it doesn't mean anything until it does. Don't overthink it or panic. Charlie's what? Eighteen months old? He was probably playing and didn't want to cooperate."

I blew out a breath. That sounded utterly reasonable. Totally. And at the same time...

"Breathe, Pop. Call Jake if you need to, but I bet he tells you the same thing."

I scrubbed a hand over my face. "Does it ever get easier?"

"Worrying about them?" She shook her head. "Nope. You just learn to manage your own expectations and fears. There's always something. But that's what love is...managing expectations and fears because you want the best for them."

"Maybe you should have gotten that doctorate," I teased, but at the same time... "Thanks, Katie."

"Anytime, Doc. Anytime. Now—you have thirty minutes before your next appointment. It's also the last appointment of the day. So why don't you get some coffee and some food. Call Jake and check on Charlie."

"I'll get right on that." At the door to my office, I paused and said, "Katie…"

"I'll take care of Friday too. I'd offer Monday, but you have those state assessments due and you wanted to go over them yourself before you made your recommendations."

"You know, I think I'll just let you run the office and the schedule from now on."

Her laughter followed me back to my office. I had to admit though, as assistants slash office managers went, she was the best. I would probably be lost without her.

The coffee I brewed helped perk me up as did the sandwich I ate. When I pulled out my phone, there was another update from Jake.

Jake: *Pretty sure Charlie's pulling one over on the doc and so did the doc. He just didn't like the headphones. So don't freak out when Katie gives you the update.*

"Too late," I murmured aloud. Still, he didn't *know* I freaked out.

Me: *Anything else we need to worry about? Katie said it sounded like all was good.*

Jake: *Nope. Doctor said he's still in the 99th percentile and all that jazz. Just like Izzy and Josh. We make good babies.*

I snorted, but he wasn't wrong.

Me: *I'm gonna check with Arch, but I want to fly out and meet Frankie and Bubba for my birthday. Do you mind if I'm gone? Won't be more than three days.*

Jake: *Pretty sure Archie already got you a ticket, but go ahead and ask him.*

I snorted.

Me: *You guys saw it too?*

Frankie loved to tour with Bubba. She loved performing with him and being out there. She *hated* being away from the kids. Away from us.

Jake: *Yep. I think Archie caught it first, but then she started* *only texting. Classic unhappy Baby Girl. I'd spank her, but I know why she still tries to hide.*

Yeah. So did I. She wanted us all to be happy and she would tie herself in knots to do it. Bubba would have shit-canned the tour in a heartbeat, but she never wanted him to give up those dreams. Neither did the rest of us.

Me: *I'll message him. One more patient, then I'm wrapping up here and I'll head home.*

Jake: *See you then.*

Done, I switched to my message thread with Archie but there was already a show of him typing. So I waited. Not even thirty seconds later a flight booking popped up on the screen along with the seat assignment. First class.

I shook my head.

Archie: *Happy early birthday. Go make our wife feel better.*

I grinned. Sometimes, the fact they could anticipate was such a pain in the ass. Other times?

It rocked.

Me: *Challenge accepted.*

Then my next patient was there and I had to put all of my own concerns away so I could talk to a teenager about the darkness of his life, along with what he could and couldn't handle.

I liked working with kids, even if it broke my heart as much as it repaired it.

THE WEEKEND PASSED BY IN A BLUR. IZZY HAD A PLAYDATE AND she'd taken up dance. Jeremy normally handled the dance lessons, but Josh had asked to join a junior soccer league with some friends. Jake and Archie wanted to finish running some tests on their engine before I headed out of town, so I volunteered to take Izzy to her lessons and checked with the moms of her friends that they were okay with picking her up along with their daughter.

Once I had that squared away, Charlie and I headed to the Farmer's Market with the shopping list from Jeremy. I was the only one outside of Frankie he trusted with this list. My phone buzzed periodically with updates from Jeremy and photos from Josh's first soccer practice.

He would be sending them to the family group chat, so Frankie would get them too. That gave me a pause. She was going to be in tears. Right, we could fix some of this. It probably wouldn't be *that* bad. But she'd had some moments when she was pregnant with Charlie and on tour.

"What do you say we find Mama a present today, little dude?"

"Mama!" Charlie chanted from his carseat. "Want Mama."

"Me too," I said. "But Mama is working, so we gotta find her something."

"Stuff." He said it with such utter confidence, I had to grin.

"Stuff it is," I assured him.

"Want stuff."

"For Mama," I reminded him and he jutted out his lip.

"Me tew."

I chuckled. Charlie shot me a toothy grin. He'd been cutting them off and on, but those two in the front were on full display.

It was a chilly day, the leaves were turning and the breeze was definitely blowing them around. The pumpkins were also fat and gorgeous in one of the display stalls. It was a little early to be carving one, but we'd get one for the kids the following weekend. Then get Mama on video call while we carved if necessary.

I'd brought the stroller with me cause as much as Charlie

liked to run around on his own, there were way too many people here and he'd be tired in no time.

"Okay, little dude, time to shop."

"Stuff!" Charlie announced and pointed at the stalls ahead.

"Yep, stuff it is."

It took us about two hours to get everything Jeremy asked for. Not that they didn't have it, but I also spent some time hunting for something special for Frankie. It was my birthday, I could get her a present if I wanted. What the birthday boy wants, he gets.

That rule had not changed in all the years we'd known each other. So, what I wanted was to give her something that would make her smile.

One of the things I loved about this particular market was the quality of the homemade goods. There were soaps here that Frankie loved. Candles. Bath bombs. Decorative pieces. But nothing that was just...

"Pop!" Charlie waved his arms, demanding my attention and I glanced down at him, then over to where he was pointing.

"Oh, look what you found," I murmured as I pushed us in that direction. I was pretty sure it was the wind chimes with all their crystals and metallic pieces that caught his attention.

What I wanted was just on the other side of them. The lady working the booth was very helpful, especially when I explained what I wanted. She said she could have it ready in an hour.

So I took Charlie to find lunch and when we came back, it was ready to go. I also got him one of the wind chimes so we could hang it on the patio where Frankie liked to take her coffee when the weather was agreeable.

"For Mama," Charlie said. "And me."

I laughed. Yes, for Mama and him.

Josh and Jeremy were home by the time I got there, and Charlie was asleep. I let them unload the car while I put him down for a nap. Then Josh gave me a minute by minute breakdown of soccer and how fun it was and everything he learned.

Jeremy clarified the points he missed out on. Then I left Jeremy to wrangle dinner and keep an ear out for Charlie while Josh and I took Maxie and Murray for a walk. By the time Izzy was ready for pickup, Archie and Jake were back so Archie headed out to grab her.

I'd showed them what I got for Frankie and Jake had laughed at the narrow-eyed look Archie wore as he examined it. After he left, he clapped me on the shoulder. "You know, you just fired shots in a new competition."

I snorted. "If it means a competition for spoiling her, I don't mind that in the slightest. I just need her to feel better."

"Yeah, I get it."

Then Josh was back and Charlie was up and we decided to build a blanket fort. Once Izzy and Archie were home, we had dinner, then baths for all the kids, then time for a movie. Saturday nights we let them stay up late, cause *most* of the time it meant they slept in the next morning and that was nice.

Most of the time.

Tuesday morning I was at JFK early. I put my car in parking for the week and boarded my flight with just a carry-on. I didn't need much. They were in Seattle this week. In fact, based on their schedule, I was going to get in *before* them.

Bubba had given me the heads up on the hotel they were staying as well as the fact he'd booked a suite ahead of time.

They traveled with the band. The tour bus was coming up from Northern California.

My flight landed close to ten local time. They weren't due in until one. Plenty of time to get there, check-in, and be waiting in the hotel suite. Bubba had approved the plan, and he was going to send Frankie up on her own while he took care of some things, then he'd join us later.

My birthday was technically the *next* day. But I liked early presents and my brother-husbands were the best.

Even with the flight arriving a few minutes late and taking *forever* to get to a gate, I was still at the hotel a good ninety minutes ahead of time. Once in the suite, I studied the layout and debated how I wanted to do this. It needed to be perfect.

One glance at my watch and I sent a message to the guys to let them know I was at the hotel. Then I sent a second one to Bubba to check on her. How was she feeling?

His response was swift. The fatigue was better, but she was definitely missing them. The original plan of two weeks on, one week off, hit a snag when they had to leave earlier then spend ten days in the recording studio, which turned into two weeks. That meant they were there for a couple of local events before they got on the road. It was going to be closer to four weeks gone before they got back.

Thus, my plan to surprise her and give myself a present at the same time.

No nausea still. Excellent...

I ordered up lunch, a few of her favorites, a few of mine. Plenty of water and it turned out the hotel offered an herbal iced tea. It was orange blossoms, but she might like that. Once the meal and the flowers I'd ordered ahead of time were delivered, I checked the time.

Fifteen minutes.

Bubba said they were in the city, just making their way through traffic.

I headed for the shower and washed up. I put on a pair of boxer shorts that Frankie had gotten me. They were Aladdin's lamp and featured the genie. It was a joke about blue balls that I appreciated.

That said, I liked to tease her that if she stroked the lamp, I would come out to play. Hopefully she enjoyed the symbolism. Bubba's message pinged my phone. She was in the elevator. I sent him a thanks, then put the phone in DND.

Picking out a particularly lovely rose, I found a nice seat that gave me a view of the door and meant I would definitely be the first thing she saw—I hoped. As soon as the locks tumbled, I tucked the rose between my teeth and waited.

"Ugh," she said as she shoved the door open with her hip and rolled her smaller bag inside. "Stupid thing." She didn't see me, in fact, she had her back to me as she shoved the suitcase over. When the door closed, she put her head down and my heart wrenched at the half-sob she released.

Yeah. No. "Hey…"

Her shriek would have done Fay Wray proud. She spun to stare at me. I soaked in everything about her. The tears in her eyes. The flushed cheeks. The strain around her mouth and the way her teeth sank into her lower lip.

"Coop?"

"Hey, Beautiful," I said as I stood up, rose in hand. "I hope you don't mind the surprise, but the girl I fell in love with when I was five, always told me what the birthday boy wants—"

She didn't even let me finish, half-flying across the room and I braced to catch her. Lifting her up, I hugged her tight and I didn't even mind when she burst into tears. Wild swings of emotion were normal during pregnancy. At least during hers.

It was as much hormonal as it was stress right now and I picked her up, cradling her to me before sitting back down. With her in my lap, I stroked her hair as she got it all out. This was why I'd come, as much to celebrate my birthday with her as it was to take care of her.

Bubba hadn't rejected the idea at all. In fact, he'd been all in. That told me he was very aware of the issue and wanted the backup. Or maybe, it was just what Frankie knew. She always came first with us.

Always had.

Always would.

It took her a while, but she finally slowed the crying and little hiccups replaced the sobs. When she lifted her head to look at me. The red-rimmed green eyes were my absolute destruction.

"I've missed you," she confessed.

"I know, your aim never has been the best..." The dry comment did what very little else would right now.

It made her laugh.

And got me smacked across the shoulder.

I couldn't love her more if I tried.

"I can't believe you just said that..."

"Yes you can. I've said much worse." I gave her a dry look. "You remember when you tried to learn basketball?"

She sniffled. "Mean."

"Maybe, but you're the one who missed me. So I came close enough that you couldn't."

All at once her expression softened into one of those all encompassing smiles that shone out of her. "Tomorrow is your birthday."

"Oh, well, look at that. I'm here for you to spoil."

She stroked my cheek with her hand then let out the longest sigh. "I know you have work and there's so much going on. You probably shouldn't have taken the time, but I don't care—I'm greedy and I am so glad you're here."

"That's my girl," I said, tracing the rose against her face and she blinked. She stared at the rose, then down at me. Since my dick had no objections to her ass on us, we were definitely hard as a rock just for her. I didn't doubt she was aware of it as she flexed her butt cheeks against my lap.

"You're almost naked…"

"Almost," I said. "But I wore your favorite boxers. If the birthday boy gets what the birthday boy wants…"

"What does the birthday boy want?"

"To make you smile."

She grinned. "Mission accomplished."

"I guess I can go then…"

That got me another smack. "Don't you dare."

"Never." Not when I was exactly where I wanted to be.

"The kids?"

"Archie and Jake are working from home this week so I can come out to join you and everyone is looked after. Don't worry, Mama. Your babies are doing fine."

"Even Charlie?"

"Even Charlie. Yes, he misses you. He loves the video calls and he wants you there, but he's doing okay. A little separation is good for both of you."

Her nose wrinkled. "Are you handling me?"

"Yes," I said. "You're going to let me. You've been really unhappy. Bubba is worried. I'm worried. The guys are worried. So, since we promised to love, care, and keep you for all of our lives, I'm here to love and care and keep you."

Tears pooled in her eyes again. "I really hate this part of pregnancy."

"No you don't," I said, cupping her cheek and swiping away a tear when it leaked out. "You really don't."

"How do you know?" There was a challenge.

"Because that huge heart of yours has *always* felt things this deeply. Pregnancy just means you can't hide it. You don't mind it so much when we're all there…"

"But I miss you so much when we're not."

"I know. But you're having fun, right? You and Bubba are performing? He's looking after you? At least two orgasms to start the day and more to finish?"

The blush that turned her red was an absolute delight.

"Oh, so more. Well, tell me what I'm working with—the going number at home was three."

She bit her lip, then held up her right hand.

"Five?"

Then two more fingers on her left.

Ass. Talk about setting the bar high. "Lucky seven." I nodded slowly. "A day, right?"

She was almost shy. "I think the libido demands hit earlier than normal."

"Ha," I said with a grin. "It's my lucky day then. How many have you already had today, Beautiful?"

Suddenly she pouted. "None. We had to be on the bus early and he let me sleep in."

I could have kissed Bubba myself. "Well, good thing for you, I'm here."

"Coop?"

"I love you."

I grinned. "Love me enough to let me take care of you?"

She wrapped her arms around my neck. "I love you enough to do whatever you want."

Well, that was a heady offer. "Let's start with food, and getting you out of these clothes. How does that sound?"

"Like if the birthday boy wants it…"

I grinned.

CHAPTER 7

LOVE ME LIKE YOU DO

FRANKIE

I was going to throttle them all, right after I gave every single one of them a huge kiss. Ian had to have known Coop was up here waiting. His offer to go and find me a decaffeinated mocha made all kinds of more sense now.

While decaf was not my first, second, or even last choice —it allowed me the vaguest illusion of coffee when I wasn't allowed to have any. On really bad days, the decaf mochas worked.

Coop tasted like the real thing, with a bit of spearmint from his toothpaste. He also tasted like home. When he picked me clean up to head into the bedroom, I bit down on his lower lip.

He had one hand under my ass, the other wrapped around my nape. A groan rumbled from his chest, then he was sinking onto his knees before we both "tumbled" onto the bed itself. It was the most graceful I'd felt in a while. I shoved the thought away even as it tried to take purchase.

Ian had spent the past two and a half weeks reminding me over and over that I wasn't allowed to disparage myself. He asked me to write down a tick mark for each time I'd been mentally berating myself.

Then I got a swat for each one. It had left my ass and cunt aching that first week, but by the second, I'd almost begun to miss the "punishment" as the number dwindled. While we didn't practice full-time, I still wore his collar. He was my Dom every bit as much as he was my husband and he took both positions very seriously.

The glide of Coop's hands under my shirt had him pushing it up and I let him tug it off me. Thankfully, I hadn't bothered with a jacket or sweater. One thing these babies were making me was a furnace.

"Hello, gorgeous," Coop murmured as my shirt landed somewhere off the bed. "Twice the babies, twice the boobs."

The droll remark punctured the haze of desire that simmered over the chaos of my conflicting emotions. The crying and missing them had been overwhelming and now...

I cracked up.

Laughter bubbled up through me. It was like cracking through a wall that had gone up around me brick by brick. The mortar shivered before it crumbled. Coop just being here in the first place was enough to disrupt its foundation, but the warmth in his gray-green eyes, the ease in his smile, and the absolute love in his every touch?

That was a wrecking ball for all my loneliness, doubt, and self-recriminations. I had this life because we loved and supported each other. All of us. Yes, I missed them. They missed me too. But I wanted to be here as much as I wanted to be there.

It was okay to want it all, we just had to keep the hands steady on the wheel on our way.

Course, now that I'd equated Coop with a wrecking ball, that song wouldn't get out of my head. My laughter turned into giggles that escaped even as I tried to smother the humor with a hand over my mouth.

Glee shimmered in his eyes as Coop stared down at me. "That wasn't even my best material—not that your boobs aren't the best, Beautiful. Cause, they are. These magnificent mounds of love…"

Mounds.

I died. Laughter shrieked out of me and it just shattered the last of it. Without even an illusion of contrition, Coop's grin grew.

"Tits. Boobies." He ran his nose lightly along the curve of my throat to my ear where he whispered, "Jugs."

The tears slipping down my cheeks now had nothing to do with sadness and *everything* to do with hilarity. Putting my hand on his chest, I skated my fingers down to the tattoo of the footprints he'd begun adding across his heart.

There were three, each one based on the footprints taken from the babies when they were born. Izzy was there first, then Josh, and finally Charlie. Their names were written in lower case letters along the side of the foot. He was going to have to add two more.

"I love you," I said, still chuckling as he nuzzled his nose to mine again. "I am so glad you're here."

"I am a gift to all who appreciate me," he murmured, then bent his head to press a kiss to each of my breasts before tracing a finger along the side of my face. "Better?"

"Oh, so much better. I'm going to have to apologize to Ian too…"

"You can, but he won't need it. I promise, he knows. We

all do. That's the fun of all of us on this journey together. We do know each other."

We did.

"We know when you need one of us or all of us. Just like you always seem to know when we need you."

"Sometimes you guys need everyone too," I reminded him.

"Best brother-husbands in the world," he said, the dry tone perfect. They could all deadpan it. That title had not gone away since the day Sara dubbed them Ian's brother-boyfriends. "Now, would you like to get some sleep or would you..."

I didn't even let him finish before I shoved him over on his back and straddled him. One hand behind me, I unhooked my bra and then shrugged it off. His grin grew as he stroked his gaze over me. It was practically visceral.

When he reached for my pants, it was my turn to make a face. "Stay there."

Then I scootched backwards. Did I purposefully grind on that very stiff erection he sported beneath his boxers? Yes, yes I did. The way his nostrils flared and his eyes narrowed told me he noticed.

Pushing up on his elbows, he watched me ease my feet off the bed. Then I stood and hooked my hands into my waist-band. The clothes peeled down easily enough. I could still squat though, I had to admit, I was gaining more size faster this time.

Head tilted, Coop studied me. I pivoted to give him the silhouette and placed a hand over the bump that had definitely increased. Normally, I put most of my weight on in the third trimester, the bump would grow to prominence closer thirty weeks than twenty-two.

"You're so damn beautiful," he whispered and there was no disbelieving that tone. "I keep thinking it's impossible for you to be more beautiful and then you prove me wrong."

The way he looked at me *made* me feel beautiful. It didn't hurt that they told me over and over. The words were amazing, but it was the way they looked at me. How Coop stared at me now.

When he held out a hand, I glided my palm across his and let him draw me back to the bed. We were in a hotel suite across the country from the rest of our family, except for one other husband that I suspected would be a few hours yet to give us time.

I was going to kiss the hell out of him when he joined us later. My pussy clenched in anticipation. As I straddled Coop again, I let everything that wasn't—

"Wait, the kids are good?"

He raised his eyebrows.

Then before he could say a word, I pressed two fingers to his lips. "I know, but I worry about them and I just need you to tell me they are fine."

Kissing my fingers, he tugged me closer before rolling me over on my back. "They are absolutely fine. Izzy's enjoying her dance class. Josh is in love with soccer, found his new calling. Charlie is cutting a new tooth, but shh, he wants to show you himself."

Warmth unfurled inside of me as he pressed kisses to each of my fingers, then paused when he got to my ring finger. With care, he spread my hand wide and studied it.

"Yes," I told him. "They are on a chain right now around Ian's neck because I was terrified of losing them." My hands had started to swell four days before. I didn't want to risk any issues so I'd taken them off.

It was Coop's turn to give me a firm look. "Did you call the doctor?"

I grinned. "Yes and no. I emailed her through their app.

Her assistant got back to me right away. They wanted to see a picture and for measurements. But retaining water is normal and we've got the blood pressure cuff from last time, so we checked it."

"All good?" Like me, he wanted confirmation for comfort. Ian would never have let the tour proceed if my blood pressure was an issue.

"All good." I used my free hand to cross my heart over my breast. My nipples were taut from the faint chill in the room and his nearness. That said, Coop radiated plenty of heat for both of us. He hadn't lost his lean physique in all the years I'd known him, even when exercise was his least favorite form of recreation.

When he sucked one of my fingers between his lips, my stomach bottomed out and my pussy clenched again. He swirled his tongue around my index finger, then he dragged my middle finger in and teased it.

My awareness of him increased with every slow drag of his teeth and tongue over my finger. Goosebumps were rippling over my skin and my hair seemed to even tighten with every caress. Coop's knowing gaze took all of that in. My lips parted when he bit down on the palm of my hand and I swore my hips lifted all on their own.

The weight of his erection rested on my thigh. His boxers limited the contact, but I was torn between savoring his every touch and going on an exploration of my own.

Every absence seemed to only heighten my need for each of them. Pregnancy just magnified the effect until I practically burned with it.

"I should be doing that for you," I said, even as another shiver raced through me. My nipples ached, but frankly, my breasts did. Ian had a wonderful way of massaging them that helped, but they were still sore. Soon they'd get leaky too. But that was later.

"It's my birthday," he said. "Technically, somewhere in the world."

"Technically," I gasped as he dragged two of my fingers back into his mouth. I worked my free hand down his side until I could massage him through his shorts. "That means I should be doing it…"

"Shh," he whispered, pressing his finger to my lips then past it. I sucked at his finger almost greedily. I wanted to drench myself in the contact. "My birthday. Birthday boy gets what he wants—right?"

I would have said something, but he added a second finger to the first so I contented myself with a nod while swirling my tongue around them like they were his cock.

"Do you know what I want?" He nibbled a path of kisses along my jaw to my ear, alternately biting, then licking, then sucking gently, before moving on. When he reached my ear, I was melting. "I want *you*. I want to make you come. We have all evening and all night and all day tomorrow. Bubba promised that you didn't need to rehearse until tomorrow evening."

Fresh surprise rippled through me, along with a wave of heat that flushed me from my face to my breasts. Coop's lazy smile was all satisfaction.

"Exactly, so first, we're going to get a couple of easy Os out of the way…mostly because if I don't sink my dick into you, I might come in my pants. I'm not seventeen anymore and that's not cute."

I would argue that, the day he'd come while getting me off as we writhed together was one of my favorite memories. Our first real time together though—had been his birthday so this was our…

"Yes," he said, his smile deepening in his eyes. He moved and then nudged me upward a little then over. "Careful of the belly," he murmured, dragging another pillow down to help cushion my hips. It was pushing my ass up higher. The thrust of his fingers was an effective gag and it tickled me.

Coop didn't always play with Ian and I, but he had enough to know that I did like this and I loved it even more when he indulged.

"This ass… damn Frankie. Have I mentioned how hot this ass is? You've gotten so damn curvy the last few years. It makes me think about fucking you everywhere. On a desk. The sofa. The counter in the kitchen…" Amusement speared through me. "We won't tell Jeremy."

Then I was laughing and he thrust into me in one surprising push. He was so hard, so thick, and Coop always stretched me on the most generous of days. As wet as I was, the flush of his balls slapping against me threatened to make me come.

It didn't hurt that his piercing struck in all the right ways.

"No," Coop said, his voice as ragged as I felt. He eased his fingers from my mouth, then gathered up my hair in his hand. Lips next to my ear, he whispered, "You're so fuckable. You've always been amazing, hot, sexy, and hands down the only woman I want and will ever want. But pregnancy suits you, Beautiful. So. God. Damn. Fuck. Able."

He thrust with every syllable and I shook. It should be impossible to come so quickly, but then he'd been winding me up for over an hour. When he tugged my head, I twisted to meet his kiss.

Arms wrapping around me, he pulled me up to a more kneeling position. This was one of my favorites the bigger I got. It took pressure off my belly, but it also allowed him to go deep.

"Still feeling good, Beautiful?"

It felt like I was being stretched perfectly. The pleasure and the pain twined together. I nodded and he gave another shallow thrust.

"Words, Frankie," he whispered. "I need you to say it. I need to hear you're okay."

"I'm amazing," I confessed. "Fuck me, please."

"My pleasure." He ground his hips into me as he began to piston. His hands glided over my breasts, cupping and teasing the nipples before he roamed to my hips then one hand teased against my clit.

That was almost too much and I bucked at the electric contact. His laughter wasn't quite muffled against my throat as he began to caress me from both sides. The pressure was immense, and it threatened to split me wide.

I thrashed as he kept pumping, the push and pull were almost too much. He kept up a steady litany of encouraging words or sounds. My brain wasn't translating beyond the tone of his voice coupled with the strokes of his cock and his hands.

He was absolutely unraveling every part of me. Too much. Not enough. More. I couldn't take it.

"Yes," he whispered, his voice raw and his breath hot against my throat. "You can take it, Beautiful. You take me so beautifully. You always have. Do you have any idea how much I fucking love you? How much I love our life together? All our beautiful kids?" Then he cradled the bump as he pushed in deep and I was shaking. "That you're full of our new babies right here?"

Between the words, the stroke of his dick hitting deeply within me and the tease of his piercing, and the pressure from his fingers, I came in a rush. The cries leaving me escalated, then climbed with every deep thrust he made.

Shaking and crying, I gripped his arm where he'd wrapped it around me, then covered his hand on my belly. He slowed, still deep and I swore *throbbing* inside of me. There was the faintest tremble to his lips where he kissed at my throat.

Maybe it was me who was shaking. His cock was still so damn hard. I loved how it impaled me and then he was easing back. A protest escaped me and he gave my ass a pinch.

"We're not done," he said, panting as he settled me down into the pillows. I was boneless as hell and he was rearranging me so that the pillows cradled me and my hips were up. Then eased another beneath my back before he paused to kiss my breasts, then my belly. "Oh, we're far from done. How are you feeling?"

I stared at him. Was he serious right now? Sweat soaked my face and my hair stuck to me. I probably needed a shower, but I wasn't sure I would ever be able to move.

Like ever.

Another pinch had me refocusing. I was floating at the moment. "What?"

"I asked how you were feeling...I was a little rough." If not for the genuine concern in his voice, I'd give him so much shit. As it was, I reached a hand out to him so he could help me cause I really didn't want to flail around to sit up.

"I feel *amazing*," I told him as he clasped my hand. When I tried to sit up, he tugged me upright. Then I was touching his face and he was showering me in kisses. "You didn't..."

"Oh, not yet," he said, grinning. "I have a few more orgasms to deliver to my beautiful wife before I'm going to come."

I stared at him. A few more?

"Blame Bubba, he raised the bar." Then Coop winked. "Besides, my recovery time is not what it used to be, so I want to get at least three more out of you before I bury myself inside you and come, if you're up for it."

Another shiver went through me. "Coop..."

"Only if you're up for it. That's why I want to know

you're okay. Last I checked, that sex drive of yours is a hot and dangerous thing if not sated."

Fresh heat scalded my face. The first time with Izzy had been insane. We were ready for it with Josh. I kept thinking it would calm down some, but I was already eyeing his very hard, very red, and damp cock with interest and my pussy was clenching around emptiness.

"I'm up for anything with you," I promised him and he let out a long sigh.

"I love my birthday," he said, then nudged me toward the pillows again. "Lay down and spread out, my love. We have a little game to play in honor of our anniversary."

Game? I frowned, then understanding flared through me. "Really?"

He grinned. "Why not?"

"We're not teenagers anymore."

"So?" He pressed a kiss to the bump. "Don't listen to your mom right now, kids. She forgot that we're adults, we get to do whatever we want to do—especially if it makes us happy."

My smile came so much easier and when I poked him gently with my foot, he caught it and pressed a kiss to my ankle. "I love you," I told him.

"Good." His eyes were pure mischief now. "Truth or dare?"

CHAPTER 8

LEAN ON ME

IAN

I gave them a few hours alone while I checked out the venue with the rest of the band backing us up. Then we grabbed dinner. After, I headed back to the hotel and up to our suite. It was almost nine. I'd sent Frankie up almost seven hours earlier.

I needed a shower, a change of clothes, and just some downtime myself. Inside the suite, I found Coop on his phone, still in boxers. He held up a finger to me before motioning to the phone.

It had to be an emergency with one of his patients if he was on the phone, so I left him to it and headed toward the open doors to one of the bedrooms in the two bedroom suite. I dropped my bag on the bed and walked straight into the shower.

Twenty minutes later, and a hell of a lot more relaxed, I walked back out to find Coop staring at his phone. His expression was tight and his mouth compressed. I doubted he even realized I was there.

"Hey," I said quietly. The other bedroom door was closed and the whole place smelled like sex. Frankie was likely asleep and that was a good thing. "You good?"

"One of my kids died," he said, almost bewildered.

I dropped to sit on the chair to his left. "Shit." No wonder he looked wrecked. "What do you need?"

"I have no idea." He still stared down at his phone like he could get all the answers from it. "I—the call came in and Frankie was asleep. There's a code that Katie has the answering service send if it's an emergency."

"Makes sense." I kind of knew that. He'd gotten calls before on vacation or over the holidays. Emergencies were always answered even if he wasn't the psychologist on call. "So they called," I prompted after he went silent for several long minutes.

Surprise flickered over his expression and he frowned as he glanced up. It really seemed to take effort to focus on me. "Sorry…"

"No need to be sorry, man. I get it. You've had a shock. Let me help if I can." We'd all taken our knocks over the years. Coop was the first one to stand up and offer a hand, or a shoulder—fuck even just grabbed a beer and sat next to you.

"I just—I saw him last week. He was in group. He's been doing great. He started coming in to the community center about five years ago. Chip on his shoulder. Shitty attitude. Issues at home. Issues at school. Issues with his sexuality. He just—he was lost, you know?"

Yeah, I did.

"He didn't have a lot of friends, and his parents were always fighting. He didn't know how to ask for the help he needed. So he would pick fights in group. Anger he got.

Abuse he got. A helping hand? Fuck." Coop shot to his feet, phone still in hand. For a moment, it looked like he was going to throw it but he just put it down and paced away.

There was still food on the table and the suite had a single cup coffee maker, so I headed for that while Coop moved. Agitation marked every step. Normally, I wouldn't make coffee in the room. Frankie always said she didn't mind. However, since my angel missed her real coffee, it didn't kill me to wait.

When the first hiss of the coffee echoed through the quiet room, he pivoted to face me. "He was really pissed off one day and he threw a chair. It broke one of the blackboards. Didn't break the chair."

"Good chair."

Coop stared at me for a moment, then let out a sharp half-laugh before he nodded. "Yeah, good chair. Anyway, I didn't say a word, just picked up his chair, put it back where it was and stood there until he sat back down again. After group, I asked him to stay."

Asked him to stay and got his problems out of him, I'd bet. That was what Coop did. He talked and got you to talk until you told him everything. I wanted to be that for him right now.

"Let me tell you, this kid didn't want to stay and he sure as shit didn't want to hear from me. I'm the rich white dude, with the big fancy car and the big fancy house and what could I know?" There were tears in his words. He rubbed a hand over his face carrying them away. "I told him—I didn't know squat. That was why I needed him to tell me."

"That sounds like you," I said, fixing the coffee the way he liked it before sliding the cup over to him. Then I started another for me. "I mean, if he was gonna have an attitude…"

"Reminded me of Jake. Jake does anger real well."

Yeah, he did. "But he's much more laid back these days."

103

In high school? Jake never met a fight he wasn't willing to have. Fuck anyone who looked sideways at Frankie or tried to hurt her.

"Yeah." Coop gave me a half-smile. It had elements of sadness in it. "Sometimes I miss those stupid kids we were. Fucking around all summer, not realizing we were about to lose the best thing that ever happened to us."

"I don't." It came out harsher than intended. "Being a teenager *sucked*. Losing Frankie cause we were stupid? That would have been a thousand times worse."

"But we didn't—that's the part I kind of miss. It was easier sometimes. We knew who was bad and who our friends were."

"Frankie's mom tried to kill Archie and damn near killed Frankie when she screwed with his car. She lied to Eddie and told him that Frankie was his kid and it almost killed Archie thinking they were blood-related. Are you sure we knew all of that?"

Coop stared at me for a long moment. "I had you guys. We had Frankie. She had us. Y'all had me. I knew who was on my side. Even when we were disagreeing—I knew you'd be there if I needed you. Michael didn't have that."

Michael. We'd circled back to the kid. I nodded. "I'm sorry to hear that. You're right, you guys were as much my lifeline as she was. Hell, still are."

He saluted me with his coffee. "Michael didn't have that. He was—alone and a loner. He didn't *want* friends. He didn't want ties or connections. He was counting down the years to graduation and then he wanted to leave and go—you know out in the world."

Coop downed a third of his coffee with a grimace.

"This is shit."

"Well, we're in Seattle. There are like a billion coffee shops out there."

He gave me a faint smile. "That means leaving Frankie."

"Yeah, I didn't think you wanted to do that. So—keep talking, I know the story doesn't end with him not wanting to be friends with anyone or cutting people off."

"No, it was a lot of attitude. Mostly what I got out of that conversation was he wasn't comfortable anywhere. Not even at the community center. Then he took off. Didn't see him for two weeks. One of the things we try to do is just make it a safe space for the kids."

He blew out a breath, another faint smile creased his mouth.

"Then he walks in, two weeks later, like it was the next day. He takes a seat in the group and he says nothing. He's there every day for the next week. I shifted my schedule around cause I worried if I wasn't there..."

"He might leave again." It wasn't a question.

"That was my thought. At the same time, we can't cater to every single kid all the time. We need them to trust the process, but—"

"But the process can fail." Which had happened in the past.

"Yeah." Coop downed the rest of the coffee, then flopped back on the sofa. "I started posting my schedule where the kids could see it and not just in the office. Then I gradually resumed only coming a couple of times a week. Michael was coming to group, he still wasn't talking—but he came. That was a big step.

"Eventually, he talked. It started when one of the girls confessed to being jumped in the bathroom at school. She was scared to go back to one. She'd rather hold it all day or go across the street to the convenience store, or whatever. She couldn't go back in the bathroom. She went to Michael's school. He told her if she needed to go to the bathroom, text him. He'd make sure she could."

There was an element of pride in Coop's words.

"She was scared to take him up on the offer. But he was scared to make it. They both looked at me and I asked them what they wanted to do... It was a first step of him reaching out. She could have blown him off or dismissed it, maybe undoing all that work. But—she didn't. She hesitated, but she asked him how could she know she could trust him?"

That made me curious but I waited him out as Coop smiled for real, for the first time since I came in.

"He said, 'I don't know. I just—think you should be able to go to the bathroom when you want. I don't like bullies and bitches. So...you want to piss, I'm your guy.' Then he pauses and they both look at each other and then laugh. She said she'd think about it. Couple of weeks went by, and she mentions she can go to the bathroom at school again. It helped build her confidence and his."

He scrubbed both hands over his face and then sat forward again. The grief was raw and visceral.

"It was such a small but huge step for both of them. They tried to reach out and someone was listening. Friendship followed. No romance or anything just—good friends. He was still trying to figure himself out. It wasn't that he liked guys or girls, he just—he didn't like either. Thought it was weird or made him freaky. The day he finally told me that, I said, 'you're probably asexual. Or you haven't met the person you want. There's nothing wrong with it.'"

Real emotion ripped through his expression and he was fighting to hold onto it. I moved to put a hand on his shoulder. He didn't need me to press him or force him to do or say more. He just needed to know he wasn't alone.

"He cried. This big, buff fifteen year old kid who looked like a linebacker, sat down and fucking cried. Cause he didn't know it was a thing. Why do we always have to put labels on everything? High school is so damn tough to begin with then you throw all that social shit into it."

"You're the expert," I reminded him and he snorted, giving me a misty-eyed glare before he stood and I let my hand fall away. I got the need to move, so I reclaimed my coffee cup and watched as he picked up one of the water glasses on the table, then filled it up with water from one of the silver pitchers.

"She ate, by the way," he told me. "Not a lot at first, but the appetite hit around the second or third round. Then she was starving."

I nodded. Sex and food, two ways guaranteed to take care of our wife. "Good."

"Anyway... Michael's spent the last three years busting his ass to graduate. He was gonna go into the military. He weighed all his options and he was thinking about the Army. Get the training and the experience, get out of his home where he wasn't happy and build a future. Then maybe college after..."

"He didn't graduate until the end of this year, did he?"

"Yep, he was gonna graduate before Christmas... he didn't care about walking, just wanted the diploma." He was a million miles away.

"What happened?"

"Car accident." Coop didn't look away from the water. "He was waiting for the bus. Car jumped the curb. Plowed right into him and three other people. He and an older man died at the scene. The other two were taken to local hospitals. Driver was arrested, probably already out on bail and Michael's just gone."

"I'm really fucking sorry, Coop."

"Yeah... Me too."

He didn't say much after that. Instead, we sat out there

drinking piss poor coffee. If he was going to be up, I'd stick it out with him. He didn't tell me to fuck off.

We were still sitting there at three in the morning when Frankie opened the bedroom door. Naked, hair mussed and tangled from sleep and the imprint of a pillow on her cheek, she looked at us with confusion.

Then the sleep vanished from her eyes as she laser focused on Coop. I didn't have to say a word. She just walked across the room to crawl onto his lap. I rescued the coffee cup as she wrapped her arms around him.

At the first choked sound of his sob, I moved to wrap them both up into a hug. He clung to Frankie and I held onto both of them. It took time, but eventually, she coaxed him back into the bedroom.

I'd have left them to it, but she caught my hand and Coop gave me a faint smile. "Stay, Bubba. I think we'll all feel better."

I could do that. "Come on then, both of you. In bed." Frankie vanished into the bathroom to pee, when she came back out, she had a washcloth. She used it to clean Coop's face and I gave them a beat while I made sure the hotel room door had the safety bar on, then I shut down the lights.

Back in the bedroom, I climbed in on one side of Frankie as Coop curled up on her other side.

"I'm here," she whispered to him.

"I know you are," he said. "I'll tell you tomorrow...or maybe the next day. Right now I just—I just want to hold you and the babies. Is that okay?"

"It's always okay."

She stroked her hand through his hair as he lay there, one hand on her stomach. I kept a hand on her hip, just being there for both of them. Eventually, Coop's breathing evened out. It was a little nasally from his tears, but Frankie didn't go back to sleep.

"He'll be okay, Angel," I said, rubbing my hand up and down her side. "Go back to sleep."

"I—"

"I know," I said, then nuzzled a kiss to her cheek. "We only have rehearsals tonight so I can afford to be awake. You sleep. I'll keep watch."

If he had bad dreams, I'd wake his ass up. But I'd be here.

"I love you, Ian," she said and I gave her hip a squeeze.

"I know you do, now be a good girl for me, and sleep." I dropped another kiss to her lips and she sighed.

It didn't take her long to drop off and while I could probably sleep, I stayed awake and read on my phone while I kept an eye on both of them. One luxury I had on the road, I could catch sleep when I needed it. Right now, they needed me to be on watch.

I could do that too.

CHAPTER 9

CHICKEN DANCE

FRANKIE

"Mom!" Izzy streaked into the kitchen where Jeremy and I were already working on getting the turkey hustled into the oven. It was the second turkey. The first had already gone in. There were easily a dozen other dishes prepared. The moms would be down shortly, as it was still early for almost everyone except me, Jeremy, and apparently now Izzy.

She slid to a stop next to me, blonde hair escaping her braid in wisps, her eyes huge and her expression panicked. The last is what had me wiping my hands to meet her intense gaze. Our eldest daughter was something of a perfectionist, didn't always know when to take a break, and could often work herself up into a fit of anxiety trying to do everything.

"Hey," I told her as I crouched. Then she threw her arms around me and I cradled her close. "Shh, what's wrong?" She was actually shaking. "Bad dream?"

I caught Jeremy's eye as I stood, still holding her. I was

five months pregnant now, the bump was there with our fourth—and fifth children. We'd announced it to the whole family. But I had the balance down for carrying even my big girl.

He'd wiped his own hands before running a hand over her head. "I'll make you some hot cocoa."

"Thank you," Izzy said in a muffled voice that came out small and a little worried. Leaving Jeremy to the prep, I carried Izzy out of the kitchen and down the hall. The house was huge and we'd made some changes over the years. Other parts, we'd kept the same. Grandpa Ted's study was exactly as it had been, right down to the pool table and the big chairs in front of the fireplace.

Archie had so many memories in this room. So did Eddie. More than once I'd found them here after a meal or a day, just sharing a drink and chuckling. We'd put up Christmas decorations everywhere else, but we kept it light in here. This year, we'd achieved twelve trees. I rather suspected next year, one would end up in here whether we planned for it or not.

Still, I nudged the door closed and carried Izzy over to one of the big armchairs. It was the one Archie favored and it always made me think of him as I sat. There was no fire at the moment, though the wood was set up. The room was more than warm enough, so I settled Izzy on my lap just holding her until she lifted her head.

"I had a bad dream," she admitted, tear tracks on her cheeks a testament to that.

"Bad dreams are no fun," I said and she gave me the most solemn of nods.

"I don't like them."

"Most people don't like them, babycakes. Do you need to talk about it?" I didn't ask if she wanted to because, well, I never wanted to talk about mine. Sometimes, I needed to talk about them. Sometimes she needed it and sometimes she just wanted cuddles.

"I don't know," she said, lower lip jutting out for a moment. "I—"

Jeremy opened the door quietly, carrying in two nice mugs of hot cocoa. While I was stuck on decaf coffee, I could have hot chocolate and he'd loaded it with whip cream, and candy canes. Oh, he'd broken out the peppermint hot cocoa.

He set the mugs down next to us and I had a feeling my eyes were as large as Izzy's at the moment. "For my two favorite ladies."

"But we're not supposed to ask for the special hot cocoa," Izzy said, the wonder in her voice dazzling.

"You didn't ask," Jeremy told her with so much kindness it squeezed my heart. "Besides, what good is a rule if I can't break it now and again?"

Izzy giggled.

"It'll be our secret," I said and Izzy bobbed her head.

"This is why you two are my favorites." With that, Jeremy slipped out as quietly as he'd come in, leaving Izzy and I to sip our hot cocoa. While there was a lot of prep to do, I didn't want to rush her. Especially because her lower lip was still a bit wobbly and the tears on her face were still damp.

After helping her balance her hot cocoa cup, I took a sip of my own. It was like a chocolate orgasm and I sighed at the breathless bit of peppermint adding its soothing kiss to the bomb of chocolate. The whip cream crowned it all with sweetness.

"You have whip cream on your lip, Mommy," Izzy warned in a too solemn voice.

"Hmm." I licked it off. "I was saving it for later."

That made her laugh all over again. So we sat there in the quiet room, just savoring the hot cocoa and the cuddles.

When she finished her whole cup, she curled up with her head on my shoulder. "What if the babies are a girl?"

"Then you're going to have little sisters," I told her. We hadn't told them that we knew one was a girl. Our second little nugget was quite shy apparently. The doctor offered to do a blood test and if our next scan continued to keep the mystery for us, well... then we'd discuss it.

"But if they're boys, then I will have *four* baby brothers." She didn't sound terribly certain of that fate.

"This is also true." I waited her out. When she set her hand against the bump, she bit her lip. "Was the bad dream about the babies?"

I'd been known to have them myself. Especially with Izzy, the dreams hadn't been as bad with Josh or Charlie. Maybe because I'd relaxed? I didn't know. I hadn't had any this time around, but the fact Izzy was worried kept me focused on her.

"Kind of," she admitted. "Are the babies asleep right now?" Her favorite thing to do when I'd been pregnant with Charlie was "talk" to him when he was awake, but she always whispered if she thought he was asleep.

"Maybe." I was twenty-six weeks and I'd been feeling them for a bit now. But not at the moment. Twins meant the bump grew faster than my earlier pregnancies, still, we were doing all right.

"Okay," she said, pitching her voice a little lower. "Do you want boys or girls, Mommy?"

"I want healthy babies," I told her honestly. "Boys or girls or both, I'll love them for being them. Just like I love you and the boys."

"Will you be mad if I kind of want them to be boys?"

"Why would I be mad about that?" I wasn't going to laugh at her or tease her, not yet. Izzy was being so serious. Sometimes, she took after Ian in how hard she would look at something before she decided. If she wanted to ask me this question, then it was important.

"Because maybe you want girls."

"Do you mind if I ask you a question?"

She shook her head.

"Do you *not* want a baby sister or two?"

Guilt filled her eyes and I wrapped her up in a hug. "I—in my dream it was a girl and I wasn't special anymore. No one paid any attention to me. Not Daddy or Papa or Dad or Pop." She swallowed hard. "You just played with her and kept calling her your favorite little girl…"

Setting my hot cocoa aside, I curled Izzy to me closer and pressed my lips to the top of her head. "Izzy, baby, there are three things I need you to remember for Mommy."

"Okay," she snuffled the word. My baby was trying to be so brave.

"One," I said, leaning back so she and I could look each other in the eye. "No one can replace my Izzy-belle. No one. You are *my* baby, you will *always* be my baby. You are my favorite Izzy ever. Girls or not, I am not going to love you any less. I didn't with Charlie or Josh, did I?"

"But they're boys, Mommy," she told me in all seriousness.

"This is true, we have a lot of boys in this house, so maybe another girl or two will help us keep them on their toes."

That gave her a beat and she looked surprised.

"Two," I continued before she could latch onto that. "Daddy, Papa, Dad, *and* Pop have so much love in them they could never not find time for you or love for you. They *adore* you. If I have more girls or even just one, they are going to need you even more."

Confusion filled her eyes. "Because I'm already a girl."

"And the oldest. You helped so much with Charlie. You still do and you help with Josh."

"Oh."

"And three," I pressed onwards and gave her another kiss, "Do you remember how big our family is?"

"It's huge."

"Yeah, you have lots of grandparents, aunts, and even a few uncles…"

"I do," she said slowly.

"That's a *lot* of love. Don't you think?"

She bit her lip then looked at me sideways before she nodded slowly.

"Besides," I said. "Another girl might save you from all the pink."

Izzy's eyes grew huger if possible. "Wait—you mean that I wouldn't have to wear the pink dresses just because one of the grandmas got them?"

"Nope," I told her. "I mean these little ones might love pink and then we'll have to hose everything down in it."

Her little nose wrinkled.

"He or she, they could both like pink."

At that, Izzy snorted.

"Either way, they are going to be their own little selves and you're going to be the very bestest of big sisters ever." I tickled her a little, cajoling her smile to grow. "Do you know how I know?"

"Josh told you?"

I laughed. "Nope, Charlie. Josh thinks you're a big ol' meanie cause you took the last cookie."

That got me a real laugh out of her and then Izzy hugged me again.

"I love you, Mommy."

"I love you, too, Izzy-belle. Do you feel better?"

She gave it all the appropriate thought before she leaned back and stared up at me. "I think so. It's okay if one of the babies is a girl."

"Yeah?"

"Yeah," she said then leaned down closer to my stomach, "But if you are a girl, you *have* to be on my side in everything."

Laughter floated out of me again because the babies gave a flutter of movement. One of them was waking up. "You may have to keep reminding her."

"Don't worry, Mom," Izzy told me in all seriousness. "I will."

"Come on, then," I told her. "We need to go help Jeremy with the food."

We had a lot to do.

~

"You should go sit down," Kelly said as she moved into the kitchen. The grandmothers had descended in force just before breakfast. We had already set up a breakfast bar in the bigger dining room with a waffle maker out there that Jake took charge of.

The grandfathers weren't far behind the grandmothers. Siblings, aunts, uncles, and cousins drifted in. Thanksgiving had *everyone* here this year in particular because I was pregnant and everyone wanted to be a part of it.

Christmas, however, was ours. We floated some of the holidays from Fourth of July to Thanksgiving each year. Sometimes we had part of the family, other times not. Jeremy and Eddie were regular attendees for Christmas. Every other year, Ian's parents came up. With the girls all graduated, they were planning a world cruise with Jake's parents and Klara.

So much to do.

"I'm fine," I told Kelly. "I just wanted to check on the last of the desserts so the pies would be hot from the oven." As it was, I also didn't want to sit still too long. We'd been home from the tour for a little over a week. We had another week then we would spend two more weeks on the road.

I had to see Doctor Patterson next week first though. So far so good, except for the swelling in my legs. That had been happening far more quickly this time and it was making riding on the bus a challenge.

"I know you are," she said, raising her arm with a question. I appreciated the fact she never just hugged on me or invaded my space without asking. We'd grown to be very good friends the past few years. She'd been invaluable when Izzy was first born and I second-guessed everything.

I couldn't ask for a better stepmother.

That said, I still wasn't totally used to it. Maybe I never would be. Then, I would never take her for granted either.

"Let us spoil you some," she said, then lowered her voice as Josh raced through the kitchen with Kyle right behind him. The cousins were close. Charlie was too young to be a partner in crime yet. Kyle was not.

"Boys," Jeremy said without even glancing behind him. I swore you could hear the screeching brakes as the kids halted.

"Sorry, Grandpa Jere," the boys said in unison.

He spared them a look and both ducked their heads. "I'll let the infraction go this time. No running in the house."

"Yes, sir."

Then they were nudging each other and hustling out only to start sprinting as soon as they were clear of the door.

"It's a circus," I murmured and Jeremy chuckled.

"Even circuses have ringmasters, Miss Frankie."

A whistle cut through the din beyond and Jake's voice rose. "And I nominate Jake for today."

Jeremy and I grinned, then I looked at Kelly who was still waiting patiently.

"Jeremy—"

"Go," he said, moving over to take charge of the pie I'd been prepping for the oven. It just needed crimping on the edges. "Enjoy some peace and quiet in the old drawing room before the kids notice. Dinner will be in forty-five minutes."

Needless to say the chaos would begin, followed by game night. The guys were in the other room watching a football game, but they were also rotating with the kids.

"Sounds good, thank you, Jeremy." I pressed a kiss to his cheek before I rinsed my hands off and dried them. There was a cup of hot tea waiting, like he'd known I'd be taking a break.

Then again, maybe he'd planned it. Sounded like him.

"Wonderful," Kelly said, wrapping an arm around me as we went out via the dining room and then down the hall to the drawing room. It was the old drawing room because the piano was still here, but we'd been debating what we wanted to do with it.

For now, we had a couple of sofas, the piano, and some guitars. I had a feeling it would eventually become a music room. Maybe.

The upside of it though, was it was quiet. It was a rare, sunny day and though it was cold, it was dry and the kids were outside and in. We'd put the dogs up for a few hours cause this was just too much chaos.

Overstimulated kids were bad enough.

As we stepped into the room, I had to swallow a laugh. Sara, Alicia, Klara, and Carly were already ensconced. Chloe was here along with Becca, but Blake and Trina were missing.

Blake and Trina also had kids, so they were probably wrestling them. Someone had moved some more seating in here, including one of my favorite arm chairs and I settled into it with a sigh.

My back and feet were both annoyed. While I had tea,

they all had wine. "I'm suspecting a setup," I teased as I shifted a pillow into a more comfortable spot.

"Yes and no," Alicia said. "But you've been in the kitchen all morning, and you were up early. Sometimes, it's nice to just have a breather."

"That's true."

"Speaking of breathers," Sara said as she sat forward. "We wanted to talk to you before we talked to the boys. The babies are due in May, right?"

"Late April, though Doctor Patterson said twins can and do come early."

"They do," Kelly said as she took a seat on the corner of one of the sofas. "So, we plan for the idea they come early and that means if they do, they do and if they don't—you five don't miss out."

"Miss out?" I had a sneaking suspicion we were about to have our older kids stolen. Or at least usurped. It would hardly be the first time.

"I was talking to Eddie," Carly said, recrossing her legs. "He told me that Archie isn't as eager to babymoon because of the possible complications and the tour."

"Then Carly called me." Alicia set her empty wine glass down and waved off Becca when she would have refilled it. "Now, you know we're planning the cruise. It leaves right after the New Year. It's eight weeks, but we'll be home by the first of March."

I took a sip of tea rather than comment beyond my nod.

"Which is when I suggested we call Kelly," Klara joined in. "Then we got Carly back on the line..."

"And basically called us," Becca said, her eyes practically sparkled as she saluted me with her wine glass. "Blake, Trina, and I are little tied up but Mom was planning to visit me in March and then head to Blake's to play Grandma. That said... we came up with a plan."

I was not smiling but it was almost impossible.

"I'll come and stay for January," Carly said. "If you kids don't mind. Trina's doing just fine with her baby and she's not that far away at the moment if she needs me. But I can help out with errands and school stuff along with Jeremy. That will give you and the boys more time when you're home."

"Then I'll come up in February," Kelly said. "With work, Becca and Chloe can't take the extra time…"

"But I have weekends," Chloe said. "Graduate school is way easier than regular lectures. A lot of my work is research. So, I can do that just as easily here. But basically, I'm available for weekend drop-ins whenever you need a break or just want company."

I chewed the inside of my lip as we circled back to Alicia. "Sara, Klara, and I will be back in March as I said earlier. The five of us, granddads too of course, will come and the five of *you* can take a break together. Even if you just find a place in the city. Even if Archie is worried about the babymoon, if all of you are together it will make it easier."

"It also puts them closer for when the twins come." The last came from Becca. "Since all the grandparents have a bet, they want to see who wins."

"Rebecca," Alicia scolded but the girl was absolutely unrepentant.

"Hey, you guys were the ones who said it."

"It's also about helping Eddie too… He was so gracious when Charlie was on the way and kept flying me up to surprise you kids."

He had done that.

"Your dad is worried about you," Kelly added, putting the final bow on top of their proposal. "He says you've been more tired this time around and you're exhausted every single time he talks to you."

"I agreed with all of them, Miss Frankie," Jeremy said as he joined us and brought me a fresh cup of tea. Which was lovely cause I'd finished mine. "You are a fantastic mother, a devoted wife, and a consummate professional, but all of you are going in too many directions. You have the support of family."

"This really was a setup," I said, exchanging teacups with Jeremy.

"The most well meaning of setups. Mr. Archie, Mr. Coop, Mr. Jake, and Mr. Bubba will be hard pressed to tell you no and they need this too." Jeremy sealed the deal and I smiled.

"Well, when you put it like that..."

"Excellent," Kelly said and she wasn't the only one blowing out a relieved breath.

"Am I really that terrifying to talk to?" I had to know 'cause they were all looking much more comfortable.

"Not at all," Alicia told me even as Carly scoffed a little. "But you've spent most of your life being the one who does stuff for others and it's never easy for you to accept help. We want you to know that you have five mothers to lean on whenever you want or need it."

Tears burned in my eyes, but I kept the waterworks dialed back. "I do know I have all of you. I love that. I love that my kids have you in their lives too."

I knew the loneliness. I knew it all too well. I never wanted that for my kids.

From the other room the music suddenly spiked and I wasn't the only one groaning. The chicken dance and then I had to bite my lower lip. "Who do we think lost the bet?"

Klara tilted her head. "The grandfathers."

A laugh from Joseph cut through the music and the kids were cheering. Sara gave my shoulder a squeeze as she drifted out to see the fun.

She wasn't alone, Alicia and Becca followed with Carly

right behind them. Chloe made a face and pulled out her phone. I didn't blame her. Klara was in no hurry either.

Jeremy chuckled as he closed the door on his way out. Every year, there was a bet on the football game and whoever lost had to do a dare.

Apparently, the chicken dance was this year.

Hopefully someone videoed it.

CHAPTER 10

THERE YOU'LL BE

JAKE

"*D*id you see me, Daddy?" Josh asked as he slid to a stop on his skates.

The kid was a natural. Soccer was on break with the weather, so I'd been working on his ice skating cause he liked hockey. My little man.

"I did," I told him, leaning against the wall with the other parents. "You should be out there though, listening to the instructor."

He grinned, and I swore it was Frankie's smile shining right back up at me. The "watch me do what I want smile" she wore when we were in second grade and she was more than willing to throw down.

"Go on," I said, sending him off. I checked my watch as he went, then focused on how he was moving.

"He looks good," a woman said as she drifted up to stand next to me at the rail. "He's young though, yes?"

"Five," I told her. "He'll be six soon. He enjoys it. That's the important part." I'd loved sports when I'd been younger. Loved the competition, the struggle, and the work. I never intended to force Josh into any of that.

At the same time, I'd played hockey in a recreational league for a while. I'd taken a break for now. But I could go back to it in a few years when the kids were older. Or maybe I could just coach the kids. Bubba and I were debating volunteering with the local Little League in a couple of years.

"He's good. That's mine over there…" She pointed to one of the boys hesitating at the edges. "He does fine when he's on his own, but in a group of kids…" Faint frustration rifled over the words.

"He's shy. Give him time, don't push. The kids will do that for you and once he makes a friend or two—it'll help." It was one perk for team sports, they did foster friendships. Of course, there were always exceptions.

The kids were moving again and I tracked Josh's practice. He was practically vibrating with excitement. Not all of which was for the game. Frankie and Bubba were coming home today. They'd be home from now until Christmas. They had a New Year's performance and five more stops, then the tour would end so she could be home as she edged into her third trimester.

She had a doctor's appointment in two days to also make sure she still had the sign off to go. Thankfully, they'd saved all the East Coast stops for this part. It meant we were all going to be closer.

"I hope so," the woman next to me said and I blinked. I'd half-forgotten she was there. "I'm sorry, I'm Jeanine Trox."

"Jake Benton-Standish." Still sounded weird sometimes and a hell of a lot more high brow than I felt, but the family name also fit.

"I know, Melodie told me." She motioned to where the

other moms were standing in a cluster. Yeah, I didn't know which one was Melodie and I didn't ask.

I shook her hand then went back to tracking Josh. He was chatting again. The kid was so damn social. I liked that for him. It made adapting—

"So, I don't know if you'd be interested, but Mack and I like to grab lunch after, maybe you and your son would like to join us?"

I thought I was reading too much into it until she stroked her finger down the back of my hand on the rail. Yeah. No.

"Appreciate the invite, but playdates are usually something we run past Mom before we do them and she likes to meet the other moms."

"Oh. I thought since you have him this weekend..."

Now she had my whole attention. "This weekend? I have him every weekend."

Dammit, this was what happened when I forgot to put the wedding band back on. I'd taken it off to finish some engine work on Coop's car this morning, then forgotten to shove it back on in my hurry to get Josh here on time.

Surprise marked her expression. "Oh."

"Happily married for well over a decade. Three kids. Two on the way." Planned to stay happily married. Period.

She didn't say anything for a long moment and I kind of hoped she'd excuse herself. Then, she said, "Well if that changes..."

"You'll be the last to know." Archie said from behind me. His voice was cold, precise, and ready to draw blood. "He gave you the polite answer. I'll give you the impolite one. Go the fuck away."

Flushing, she shot a wild look around then just left and retreated past the other moms. They were giving us speculative glances but immediately found elsewhere to look. Shaking my head, I caught Archie's smirk.

"You know how they say couples begin to take on each other's traits…"

"Shut up." Asshole. It was an effort to not smile though.

He chuckled. "You missed the flirting."

"I did not miss the flirting, I shut it down."

"No, you missed it at first." Archie folded his arms and leaned on the rail. Josh was racing with the other boys and keeping it clean.

"I was being polite."

His scoff at me earned a glare. "Shut up." Weak defense but it was what I had. No, I hadn't noticed the flirting. I was focusing on the kids. "The moms don't usually hit on me."

"Eh," Archie said with a shrug. "I've had a couple now and then, but my charming personality is such a turn off for them that they back off."

His charming personality.

I snorted. "Thanks, I appreciate the backup."

"It's all good. She wasn't getting subtle. So I took care of it." Like me, he tracked Josh on the ice. "Damn, is it me or is he moving even better than he was three weeks ago?"

"Not you. He's a natural. We should have seen it with how easily he picked up snowboarding. But I'd swear he'd been born on the ice for how he moves."

"As long as he's having fun." Yep, the cardinal rule for all activities. Some needed to be challenging and to push them. But the rest? No one was strong-arming them into anything they didn't want to do.

"What are you doing here? Not that I mind the company." He'd been working with Charlie asleep in his lap when I'd left.

"Bubba and Frankie are getting in early. Flight cancellation shifted them around. Figured I'd see if you two wanted to come with me to get her."

"Hell, yes." Not even a question. I reached for my phone and when I patted my pockets, I frowned. Then Archie held it out to me.

"Other reason I showed up. You left it in the garage. I have a feeling you were using it for a light and then put it down."

I grimaced, even as he laughed. "Thanks."

"Yep. When your phone was vibrating on the work table, I figured I'd come on down and deliver it. Then grab you too. Leave the car here, we can pick it up on our way back."

"Works for me." I scanned the phone for messages. Yep, there was one from Frankie and Bubba saying they were getting on an earlier flight. Excitement amped through me. Having them home at Thanksgiving hadn't been long enough. "I'm ready for this tour to be over."

"Same, but she's doing a lot better. It took her a minute to adjust." Archie keeping his cool settled my nerves too. "They have just two, three weeks tops after Christmas. Then they're home until the babies arrive."

Grinning, I nodded. "Good. The kids will like that."

"So will we," he commented and I couldn't really argue.

"You still not sure about the babymoon?"

"Been thinking about it. She sees Doc Patterson in a few days. Then another visit after Christmas. If she gets the all clear when the tour is done, I'll see about taking her somewhere close. But I don't know that she's gonna want to be really far from the kids."

"Fair." I got that. Selfishly, I also didn't want her far but we would do whatever she and Archie needed. Sometimes, Frankie forgot she needed to look after herself too. "We've got backup coming though." Starting in January, the grandparents had all set up a rotating schedule.

"Dad's actually excited about that," Archie said with a

faint smile. "He likes when the other grandparents visit. Apparently, they now have their own regular group chat so they can keep up on everything."

"And gossip about us." I harbored no doubts about it. My father had mentioned it the year before. The moms *loved* to talk and the dads enjoyed the information. Not all the parents were in the chat. Coop's dad and Archie's mom… "Have you talked to your mother?"

He cocked his head to the side like he needed to consider his answer. "No. But she sent a card for Christmas, one addressed to me only, as usual."

Damn. "She's still salty about the lack of wedding invite?"

Archie just shrugged. "I don't care what she's salty about. Not anymore. Dad and I—we've come a long way. I extended an olive branch to her after Izzy was born. Then she was such a bitch about wanting to know if Izzy was actually my child versus you know…'the pretend game' we're all playing."

The absolute hostility edging his voice was something we all shared. The kids were *ours* period. For medical reasons, we needed the DNA knowledge and Frankie loved picking names that went with our initials. Beyond that, Izzy was every bit as much my daughter as Josh was Archie's son and these twins would belong to us as well.

Our kids.

Our family.

"Well, fuck her." The last time I'd even *seen* Muriel Standish had been senior year when Maddy had Eddie convinced that Frankie was his daughter. We'd flown all the way to Manhattan, Archie and I, to confront her and see what she knew.

"Pretty much."

I bumped his shoulder and he just gave a shrug.

"Don't worry about me. I got a dad for real out of all this

and Muriel is where she chose to be. She wants to be out, she can be out. My family and I will be just fine. Looks like we're done."

We were but I still hated this for him. Granted, I'd had my own issues with *my* father for years. Issues I'd really needed to grow up to understand. I didn't think all the years and the distance would ever help out Muriel.

Her loss.

"Papa!" Josh yelled as he spied Archie as he skated over.

"Little Big Man," Archie held up his hand for a high five, and Josh smacked it.

"Did you see, Daddy?" Josh practically glowed with his accomplishment. "Coach says I'm good."

"I'm with Coach," I told him and then helped him put on the covers to his blades before I just picked him up and moved him clear of the other kids.

Between me and Archie, we got his skates off and his shoes on. "I'm starving," Josh said. "Can we get pizza?"

"We can look at that later," Archie said. "I actually came to get you and Daddy to go get Mama and Dad."

Josh's expression transformed. "Mama's coming home?"

"Yep." Archie checked his watch. "Flight should be here in just under an hour. We have time to get food on the way."

"Yay!!"

Josh half-skipped out to the car, then screeched as we cleared the doors. "It's snowing!"

I caught his shoulder before he could tear off into the parking lot.

"Sorry, Daddy," he apologized then clasped my hand.

"I know, no taking off."

"I won't."

Archie had actually brought the minivan. The first one we'd ever owned, but we actually needed the space when *all* of us wanted to ride together. It amused us both to be the *minivan* dads but here we were. It also had entertainment in the back for the kids—and sometimes us when we wanted to keep playing a video game on the way somewhere.

We picked up a small order of burgers and fries. Including extras for Frankie and Bubba. They might not be piping hot when we got there, but no one wanted Frankie getting in a car that smelled like food if there was nothing to share with her.

Their flight landed before we even got to the exit for JFK. Bubba and Frankie both messaged that they were on the way to luggage claim.

"We want to park, or do you want to drop me off, circle and come back, and then we'll meet you?"

We could do it either way. Archie glanced at the dash-board clock then at the traffic in front of us. "Message Bubba and ask him to tell us when he has luggage. If it's before we get up there, I'll drop you off, if not…"

Well, if not, we'd just pick them up. I fired the message off and got a thumbs up back. Archie drummed his fingers on the steering wheel. Impatience crept through his careful facade.

Behind us, *Transformers* played to keep Josh entertained. We'd seen the movie so many times at this point, I could quote it.

And once upon a time, I'd actually liked the movie.

It was also why we were working on making him a remote control transformer for Christmas. It wasn't quite working yet. Still had a few bugs to work out. Traffic crawled but we made it to the arrivals lane and started to circle up as my phone buzzed.

"They have the luggage."

"Yes," Archie said and made a fist.

"Yes!" Josh yelled enthusiastically from the back seat and

we were both laughing by the time I caught sight of her red coat and gorgeous blonde hair.

"You want me to drive back?" Cause otherwise, I was tossing Bubba up here and climbing in back with her myself.

"I got it." He flashed me a grin.

Then we were there and I was out. The bump was looking fantastic, though nowhere near as fantastic as she did. Her smile was equal parts relieved and elated. I picked her right up when she wrapped her arms around me.

Bubba chuckled as I cradled her, but he went ahead and got their luggage and guitars stowed away. Frankie dug her fingers in so tight I rubbed her back gently.

"What is it?" I murmured.

"Just happy to be home," she admitted.

"That's all?" Worry crested right through me as I set her down carefully. The chaos of passengers arriving and getting into cars and rushing around faded as I studied her. The lack of tears in her eyes was a good sign, but her grip was firm as hell.

"Talk later?"

"Mama!!" Josh was waving wildly and she glanced at him before looking up at me.

"Promise me it's not bad and we can wait. But I need to know you're okay, Baby Girl."

"I promise," she offered it so easily and without hesitation. "Just, it was a very long eighteen days. I'm ready to be home with the trees and the fire and the kids and you guys."

"Well, we're definitely ready to have you home." With that, I opened up the back sliding door and helped her inside. Josh cheered as she slid into the seat next to him and then he was trying to get out of his car seat.

"Nope," Frankie told him when he would have unbuckled himself. Then she started dropping kisses all over him and he squirmed, but laughed.

"Hey, Babe," Archie said over his shoulder. Then Bubba was in the passenger seat and I moved to the other side to get in on Josh's left.

"Hey," she said, smiling at him. "Kiss you when we're home."

"I'm holding you to that," he told her and I wasn't the only one chuckling. Still, I kept a firm eye on her all the way home. Josh populated the car with conversation as he told her all about ice skating and his new coach.

The tired radiating off of her utterly softened for our son. She listened, she played, she commented and once she glanced up at me and made a comical face. I was pretty sure that by the time we got back to the house, Josh had her briefed on every single second from when she left to when we picked her up.

At the house, Coop and Izzy came out to greet her and the volume increased as the kids vied for her attention. We got the luggage inside along with the guitars. Bubba went on child distraction while Coop got her upstairs so she could shower and change.

By the time we reconvened downstairs, Charlie was awake and crawling all over her. Some of the trouble and distraction in her expression had eased and she looked happier.

When I leaned down to brush a kiss to her lips, I stroked my knuckles down her cheek. "You sure you're okay?" Something seemed off and I didn't want to ignore my instincts.

"I'm much better now," she said and I caught Charlie before he could land on her.

"Little man," I scolded. "We do not jump on the furniture or Mama."

"Want Mama." He gave me an imperious look and I tucked him onto my hip.

"Ask nicely and no more jumping," I told him, then

focused on Frankie again. Her lips were twitching like mad as she watched Charlie without quite looking at him. It was a skill we all mastered over the years. Largely because we enjoyed the kids antics even when we couldn't reward them.

"Otay. No jumping." Then Charlie tried to just fall forward and it required restraint to not laugh at him. Not that I let him land on Frankie.

"Be nice, Charlie or Santa won't bring you anything." Izzy sounded like the absolute authority and Josh froze in mid-motion climbing onto the sofa with Frankie.

I wasn't the only one clamping my teeth to keep from laughing.

"Want Mama no Sanna." Charlie's declaration got all of us and Frankie laughed as she held up her arms. I settled him into her arms and then nuzzled a kiss to her forehead.

The fire burned, the pair of trees on either side of the fire place glittered, and the snow fell outside the window, turning the landscape into a postcard. Jeremy carried out cups of cocoa for all of us. We were all home and the family was whole.

Frankie's laughter filled the room and eased one of the last concerns off my heart. Course, I wasn't the only one keeping an eye on her. While she hated when we hovered, I didn't want to take an eye off her until I was one hundred percent certain she was okay.

It could be just as simple as needing to be home and I got that. Didn't mean I couldn't keep watching out for her, until she got her equilibrium back.

"Jake…"

"Yes, Baby Girl?"

"Come sit down and stop glaring at the air." The amusement in her voice looped around me like a siren's call and I almost broke our own rule and hopped over the sofa.

Bad Daddy.

Still chuckling, I slid onto Frankie's other side, lifting her and Charlie both so I could settle her in my lap. Her eyes glittered and there was more happiness glowing there.

Better.

Much. Better.

CHAPTER 11

HOME FOR THE HOLIDAYS

FRANKIE

hristmas remained one of my all time favorite holidays. The new year could be bittersweet, thinking of Grandpa Ted. I expected this year would be even more so with the twins coming. I wished...

Well, I wished he was still here. My grandparents too, though they'd both passed a couple of years after Izzy had been born. My grandmother first followed by my grandfather.

I'd made a point of spending more time with him in those intervening months. The guys even supported me moving him down here with us, but he preferred his house in Connecticut.

The maudlin thoughts invaded the dark hours of Christmas morning. Easing out of the bed, I made my way into the bathroom. The twins were growing healthily, but it also meant they were compacting my bladder.

Archie and Coop were both sound asleep. Ian and Jake

were absent but they might have been on Charlie duty. Charlie was so much better about sleeping through the night, but not totally.

Standing in the doorway to the bathroom, I studied the guys. They were sprawled, Archie was more toward the center with Coop on the far side. Usually I was the one in the middle but it was hard enough to get up and down sometimes, I didn't want to feel like a beached whale in the middle.

The tightness around Coop's eyes had begun to ease. I'd been worried about him. He'd taken Michael's loss so hard. He cared about those kids—all of them. It didn't make me any less concerned, but at least he seemed better. I tangled my fingers around the miniature pocket watch turned pendant he'd brought to me in Seattle.

A reminder that we made the time for each other. We always had. We always would. The words resonated with me and had every single day. I still missed them while touring, but I would hold the necklace like I had my rings or my charm bracelet. Their love made tangible.

Another reason I was glad to be home. I would absolutely be making time for him. For all of them. My gaze tracked to where Archie slept. His expression was downright peaceful. It almost seemed like he was smiling in his sleep.

Good dreams, I hoped.

As tempting as it was to wake them, I slipped out quietly and closed the door behind me. The sitting room was also dark, save for a single small lamp by the main door. The doors to the other bedrooms were open. They weren't sleeping elsewhere.

We all did it. Just sometimes we were tired or restless. Sometimes we needed a little privacy. I loved that everyone was comfortable enough to not be insulted when one of us needed it.

I'd snagged my robe from the bathroom and I pulled it on. I also had on the slippers for the colder floors out in the main house. Pregnancy always made me seem to run hotter, but—

A flutter of movement had me pausing. Then another. Oh good, time for morning calisthenics. "Thank you for almost sleeping in for Mommy," I murmured to my belly. It was just before four in the morning, so it wasn't sleeping in by *that* much.

I let myself out of our room and then down the hall. I checked on Izzy, she was sound asleep with one arm thrown up and her blankets kicked off. I tugged the sheet back over her and a lighter blanket so she wouldn't get cold. Her Christmas stocking lay on the foot of her bed just waiting for her to discover it.

Josh was next. He had two of his toys in the bed with him. Toys he hadn't had when we put him to bed. I moved one to the nightstand and left the other tucked in next to him. His stocking was still on the foot of his bed as well. He might have been trying to stay up to catch Santa. No luck though.

Charlie, predictably, wasn't in his room. Off I went in search of them. I found him downstairs in the movie room sound asleep against Jake's chest with a blanket over them. The fire was low, but it burned merrily, so I pulled the pocket doors closed to let them sleep.

I padded through the darkened rooms. Jeremy wasn't up yet, or if he was, he hadn't left his suite. Izzy and Josh would be awake within the next couple of hours.

Their stockings would keep them busy for a short bit, but then it would be time to rush downstairs for breakfast then presents. Speaking of presents... I nudged open the door to the big living room.

Ian glanced up from where he was setting another present under the tree. His smile was as warm as a hug.

"Merry Christmas, Angel. Don't tell me the kids are already up."

"They aren't," I said, letting myself in and closing the door. There was a fire going in here too, along with some Christmas music playing softly. "I thought Santa and his helpers were already done."

They'd sent me to bed and promised to take care of all of it, though I had done a fair bit of wrapping myself. *My* personal elf took care to place those presents and since I'd already seen them, I had no questions about Jeremy taking care of the requests.

"They were done." He set the box down toward the back before coming toward me. "I wanted to add a couple more presents that I'd forgotten to wrap."

I wrapped my arms around his neck and he dropped a light, sweet kiss on my lips. He couldn't pull me quite flush to him. The bump was in the way, but before I could say anything, they tumbled around in there. The fluttering increased.

Dropping his chin, he glanced down. "Ahh, it was these kids who woke you up then."

I chuckled. "Maybe, I definitely had to pee and then..."

"You wanted to come down and savor Christmas before the chaos?" He knew me well. One of my favorite things to do was make love to one or all of them under the tree or in front of the fire.

"Getting harder each year," I admitted. He shifted us so I was leaning back against him. It gave me a wonderful view of the fire crackling, and the beautiful trees framing the fireplace. They were comically loaded with presents. Some wrapped, and others not.

The not wrapped ones were from Santa—a decision I had never regretted when I realized just how much all of us would spoil the kids. Not to mention the grandparents. Our babies wanted for nothing, materially or emotionally.

A long sigh escaped me and Ian rubbed his cheek against mine. Now that we were home again, he wasn't shaving. Like Jake, he almost had a full beard. The softness had me closing my eyes as I let him soothe me.

He didn't ask. Maybe he didn't have to or maybe he just let me decide if I wanted or needed to tell him more. Ian could just be there for me and let me lean on him. They all shared that strength with me, without question or hesitation.

"I keep thinking about Ted," I admitted softly. "And my grandparents. It's weird..."

"Why is it weird?" While he waited for my answer, he tugged me back to the sofa and I eased down to sit next to him.

"It's—I miss them. I mean, I always miss them." That wasn't a tough admission. "This morning, it's like... I wish Ted was here to meet his great-grandchildren. I wish my grandparents had gotten to meet Josh and Charlie." A long sigh escaped me. "I know this is pregnancy hormones and then..."

The words were failing me. Ian didn't say a word, just stroked his fingers through my hair. He took his time detangling. The repetitive motion soothed me.

"Why do I miss Maddy?" I asked finally and Ian wrapped his arms around me. By the time she died, she'd done so much damage. If she'd had her way, I wouldn't have Archie. I wouldn't have anything.

My grandparents never really recovered from her loss. Eddie *still* grieved her. I didn't want to grieve her too.

"Because you are a wonderful, loving mother who wants everything for her kids. You are now on the other side of that equation," Ian said, stroking the hair back from my face. "You remember what it was like to not have your mom there. Or to have a mom whose agenda was always at odds with your success and happiness."

All true.

"That's why when we go on tour, it's so hard for you to be away from the kids. You spend all that time remembering how your mother would just up and disappear, abandoning you to raise yourself."

I met the understanding in his warm blue eyes. When I curled into him, he wrapped me up and tucked his chin against the top of my head.

"We get it, all of us. It's okay to miss her. I know it ties you up in knots cause you hate her choices and hate how she treated people. But you don't ever have to justify that to me."

I swallowed, playing with his shirt. "I think I need to justify it to myself."

"Okay. What do you need to do that?"

"I literally have no idea. A few months ago, I tried to nudge Eddie into seeing a woman he liked. But he said he wasn't ready. He wasn't sure he'd ever be ready."

"He might not be, Angel. Fixing him up or fixing his loneliness or whatever it is you want to fix—that's not on you." The steadiness in Ian helped. "Eddie's a good guy. Once upon a time, I don't think I would have said it. But…he and Archie have mended fences. He and Ted were at least reconciled before Ted died. That gives both of them some peace. Eddie's great as a granddad."

A real smile curved my lips. "He really is. He loves the kids. *All* of them."

"I know. It was hard for some of them, in the beginning, but everyone has adapted."

Everyone except Muriel. Well, Muriel and Coop's dad. The distance between Coop and his father just never recovered, particularly after he found out about him and Maddy.

Maddy destroyed so much.

"Okay," I said, lifting my head. "Enough of the maudlin. It's Christmas. Are we ready for invasion?"

"Pretty sure, we're good, Angel. The kids won't be up for at least another hour. You want to try and sleep some more?"

"No," I said. "I'm awake. I want to—I want to have all of it. I want to hear them yell and shout as they come down the hall. I want Jeremy to scold in that prim and proper tone that gets the kids to obey. I want Coop to be grouchy cause he doesn't like early mornings and Archie to hopped up on sugar and caffeine, ready to put all the big things together."

These were all some of my favorite things.

"Did Jake and I make the list in there somewhere?" The teasing tone erased any possible sting and a giggle escaped.

"Well, you're doing it now. Cuddling, making sure everything is taken care of—I've been running you ragged the last few weeks. Don't think I haven't noticed the overtime you've been putting in to look after me."

"Well, I appreciate that," he said, stroking his fingers through my hair again. "I love taking care of you. I love that you *let* me do it. Especially when your hormones and emotions put you on some huge seesaw."

"I never even see it until it's happening and then you're right there, already making it better."

"Good," he murmured, dropping another kiss on my nose. There was a sound of running feet in the hall and I sat up a little as a very naked Charlie came charging in.

"Oh boy," Ian said, laughing as he caught our little rug monkey. "Where are your clothes?"

Charlie burst into giggles then pointed.

"I have them," Jake said in the dryest of tones. I twisted to see him standing in the doorway with Charlie's pajamas on his head.

Like Charlie, I started laughing.

"Tell you what," Ian said as he stood. "Let me go wrangle

143

the monkey into some clothes and you get some coffee and decaf for the wife."

I laughed when "the wife" had become a popular endearment when I was pregnant. Then again, it started right after the wedding, so it wasn't like I could fault it.

"You got him?" I asked as Ian balanced Charlie against him. The little one had his head pressed to Ian's chest and his cherubic smile promised the only thing holding up his halo were the two little horns sticking out of the top of his head.

"I got him. Go let Jake look after you, Angel. That's an order."

"Yes, sir," I murmured and that earned me an entirely different kind of heated look. Being Ian's sub gave me a lot of privileges and we rarely channeled it into everyday life. But now and then... Well, I needed to just turn off the pressure and let Ian decide.

Right now, that helped.

Everything helped.

Ian caught the sleeper from Jake as he passed him. I rose to move over to Jake, and he tugged me in for a proper kiss good morning after a breath check that actually made me giggle.

"Good morning, Baby Girl. Merry Christmas."

"Merry Christmas," I murmured. We'd just celebrated his birthday earlier in the week. The year had gone by so quickly. "How are you?"

"Not bad," he said around a yawn, then gave me another kiss. "Much better now." He studied me, the alertness in his pale blue eyes at odds with being up so late.

"Charlie?"

"Didn't want to sleep. He kept winding himself up. That's why I brought him down. Easier to settle him and not risk him waking up the kids or you."

I lifted a hand to scratch at his beard. He tilted his head, eyes half-closed at the petting.

"Keep that up and I'll be asleep in nothing flat."

I laughed. "Later," I promised. "You need to get a nap in."

"Don't worry, Baby Girl. I'll be fine." Then he gave me another kiss. "Coffee?"

"Hmm." I was more than willing to be distracted. The smell of coffee was at least something I could still savor. We'd just gotten the decaf started in the pot while Jake actually made a latte. It wouldn't be long before the others drifted in and they'd want their own.

"I feel like I should tell you something," Jake said, folding his arms and studying me. Shirtless and dressed in jeans with his dark hair disheveled from sleep and his beard…he looked practically edible and I swore my whole body went liquid at once.

"Hmm? What's up? Also…if there's time today, I'd very much like to give you a blowjob."

He blinked once, the corners of his mouth twitching. "Noted. We'll make time." Then he winked and I grinned. Honestly, if Jeremy weren't going to be out here any minute or Ian back down with Charlie, I'd drag Jake off somewhere right now.

"Thank you."

"Oh, my pleasure." He shook his head. "That said, I still feel like I should tell you about the other day before you got back."

"Then I return to my earlier question. What's up?"

He made a face then lifted his shoulders. "I took Josh to the skating rink. Mini hockey, but it's all still learning phases."

"I remember." I moved to start preheating the ovens. It would be nice to make blueberry muffins up before Jeremy kicked us all out.

"Well, before I went I had been working on Coop's car. The engine is still doing that faint ticking. I think I fixed it this time." Annoyance filled his expression. Then he shook it off. "Anyway, I had taken my ring off and then forgot it on the counter out in the garage."

"It's okay to forget the ring," I told him. I held up my bare fingers. "I can't wear mine at all right now." I probably wouldn't until *after* the babies came and I lost some of the water weight.

"Well, you're also *very* pregnant."

"True," I said as if just noticing and his eyes flashed with humor before he finished making his coffee then he focused on me again. "One of the moms hit on me and I didn't even notice what she was doing until she mentioned me having Josh on the weekends."

I bit the inside of my lip to keep from laughing. The mournful look on Jake's face told me he felt *really* bad about this.

"I should have seen it and shut it down, but it dragged a little before I realized then I told her. I'm a happily married man with three kids and two more on the way."

"Okay."

"It's not okay, I should have seen it sooner. Then she says something stupid like if that ever changes—"

My eyes narrowed. "You can point this woman out to me at Josh's next lesson."

"I didn't tell you so you'd go beat her up." He actually looked worried for a minute and I lifted my shoulders.

"I'd smack her for making you feel so uncomfortable. But —" I held up a hand before he could dive back in. "I get it. I know I'm not always the sharpest when someone is hitting on me. You guys have had to deal with that for years. I'm better now… but…"

"Yeah," he said and the affection in his eyes tempered the

exasperation. "Still, I hate that for an instant this woman thought I was available. I am very much not."

"No, you're not and I adore you that you were worried about telling me and yet decided to tell me anyway." I closed the distance. "I love you," I said as I put my hands on his chest and he covered my hands with his. "I love every part of you and I love you even more for telling me. But you know what I'll love more?"

"I promise if she does it again, I will absolutely let you kick her ass."

"Hmmm." I considered it. "We are supposed to be setting a good example for the kids."

"We are," he said, then he cradled my face. "We can't start the fights."

I supposed not. "It won't be a fight. It'll be a knockout."

I rose on my toes and he dipped his head to give me the sweetest of kisses. A moment later, shouting came from upstairs and there were deeper voices and high-pitched ones.

All of the earlier loneliness and dark thoughts evaporated. It was Christmas and we were all together.

"Merry Christmas!" Izzy yelled as she raced into the kitchen. Josh was right behind her followed by the other three loves of my life and Charlie.

The shouting. The chaos. The love.

It was perfect.

CHAPTER 12

CATS IN THE CRADLE

ARCHIE

"So we still don't know?" Dad asked as he brought our drinks over. We were at his apartment in the city. Even though it was the week after Christmas, he was still working despite giving most of the staff the week off.

"No," Frankie said with a half-smile tossed in my direction.

"Yeah, yeah," I teased her. "I know I'm impatient. But we still have a very shy one."

"Or..." Frankie prompted me before she accepted the glass of water from Dad. "Thank you, Eddie."

"More than welcome." He passed a soda over to me. Normally, we had cocktails when Frankie and I came to dinner in town, but since she couldn't have them, none of us were.

"Or, it's two girls." Anticipation threaded through me.

"You don't sound thrilled?" Dad frowned as he reclaimed his seat. Frankie rubbed her hand up and down my arm. I let out a huff. She was the one growing rounder by the day. She shouldn't have to comfort me.

"It's not about being thrilled or not, it's about—*not* knowing for sure. I want—I want to plan. I want to get everything ready, and the nursery redesign is just waiting for the final colors."

"You know, we discussed that we could just go with blue. We all like blue and blue is soothing." It would save us some time. The blue sky paint was still on the ceiling. We could do some touchups.

"I know, but in my head blue is for boys."

"How very traditionally sexist of you." Yeah, I deserved the tweak. "But I do understand. The fact we're decorating for two and doubling up on everything."

We'd used the same crib for all three of them, this was the first time we'd actively gone in search of a new crib. Then we weighed our options on matching or not.

"I'm sorry," I told her, putting aside my drink and covering her hand on my arm. "I know I'm obsessing…"

"You're fine," she said, squeezing my arm before leaning toward me. I accepted the invitation and kissed her lightly. "I know how much you want to know and the fact our child is being quite obstinate should not come as any surprise to either of us."

Dad suddenly let out a laugh. "Listen to Frankie, Archie my boy. You were such a stubborn baby. I was half-convinced you learned to talk early so you could tell everyone off."

"What was Archie's first word?" The question had me sliding her a look, the fact she wore a soft, intrigued smile just made me adore her more.

"Pretty sure it was 'no,'" Eddie said, as he rubbed his chin. "Check with Jeremy, but I'm almost positive. I know the first word *I* heard Archie say was a very emphatic *no*."

"Like I said, I like to know things and I like having a firm grasp on everything that is going to happen when."

"Well, we have one more shot at this," Frankie assured me. "We definitely know at least one is a girl. That may be all we get until they get here."

I didn't have to like it so much as just accept it. When she eased forward, I stood and held out a hand to her. Standing and sitting were growing more challenging. There was a little more swelling in her hands this time. The rings had been absent for a while.

She wore her bracelet more and more. The bracelet that had new charms for our life after marriage. She also had little heads with their names and birthdays inscribed on them for the kids. Once our new pair arrived, I'd add two more.

"You okay?" I checked and she nodded.

"Yes, I just have the world's smallest bladder. So, if you two will excuse me."

Dad was also standing. Old habits, ingrained throughout his life. I got it. Frankie stood, so did I. It wasn't quite so firm for other women. Not that I paid any attention to them.

"Food will be ready shortly," Eddie told her. "I thought about holding it a little later for us to make together…"

Her pout was downright adorable.

"Then I remembered what your appetite is like pregnant, so I put it all together earlier and slid it into the oven a little while ago to heat."

"I adore you," she said, pausing to give him a kiss on the cheek and he returned the affection easily enough. "Excuse me, gentlemen."

After she made her way down the hall, I glanced at Dad to find him studying me. I retrieved my glass and took a seat and he followed suit, albeit more slowly.

"Spit it out," I told him.

"I don't know if you really need any advice from me." Not unfair. Once upon a time, I would have agreed with him.

Once upon a time...

"Well, we won't know until you give me the advice," I told him.

He looked at his glass, then set it aside. "Don't be in such a rush all the time."

I raised my brows.

"You want to know and you want to know yesterday. I get it. You like knowing things. You want to be in a position to anticipate everything. It's—you like to fix things. You like control even more. It's a fundamental part of what makes you, you."

I couldn't really argue with the assessment.

"I know we might not find out about the gender and that's fine." It wasn't but I would accept it because what else would I do. "They did offer to do a blood test."

"Feels like cheating, doesn't it?" Dad asked, his brows raised and I spread my arms wide.

"Thank you. It does. There's something about seeing it on the screen or in the scan when they brought them home. I just—I want to know. But... I can wait. The important thing, the only important thing is that Frankie and the babies are healthy. Babies."

I made a face and he grinned.

"I will say that twins surprised me," Dad mused. "Not that it isn't amazing. It absolutely is, but usually, it runs in the mother's side of the family and I don't remember Maddy having that many twins. A lot of only children, but no twins."

He let out a long sigh.

It was my turn to ask. "You okay?" I flicked a look toward the hall Frankie had disappeared down then back to Dad.

"Some days, I can think about her and I'm fine. Other

times…I miss her. Then I wonder why I miss her when so much was wrong. It's a challenge."

"You're allowed," I told him. "I know I never liked her. I hated what she did to Frankie. The more I've learned about her, not a huge fan of what she did to you."

"We've never really discussed her," Dad said, then he spared a glance toward the hall. "We don't have to start now."

"You and Frankie talk though." I knew this. I'd heard them and I left it alone. Her feelings toward her mother would always be complicated. Just like Dad's were. Mine were much more delineated.

"Sometimes. She reminds me of her mother, but—not in a she is just like Maddy way. Not remotely. But, she's all the good pieces of Maddy if she had—if she had let herself be happy with life."

Hard for a sociopath to be happy, I supposed. But then again, I wasn't sure how much of her issues were mental health and how much had been she was just a bitch.

"You kids being together…"

We were hardly kids anymore.

"I don't know," Dad groaned as he pushed to his feet. "I guess I'm feeling my age. Frankie suggested I start dating again."

"I thought you had gone on a couple of dates." I glanced toward the hall and then followed him into the kitchen. I had a feeling she was giving us time.

"More business acquaintances," he said, then opened the oven. The smell of the Beef Bourguignon filled the air as he removed the covered pot. I'd seen Jeremy use those before—it was a brassiere or a braiser maybe…whatever, it cooked food. "More often than not these are business meals."

"You're not ready," I said, folding my arms. "Do you need me to do anything?"

"Absolutely not," he told me as he set the covered pan on

the top of the stove. "We've both learned we have weaknesses in some areas."

I chuckled. "Look, at least you don't mind it when I walk in the kitchen here." The table was already set or I would offer to do that.

"You blew up Jeremy's oven—twice. I can understand why you are still grounded from the kitchen."

We shared a grin, and then his smile faded.

"I'm not ready. I just told her that a few months ago. I know she worries about me. But I think I'm—alright with being on my own. I've still got to win favorite grandfather, and the lack of dating means I have more time to win over the grandkids." The lack of any sarcasm promised he wasn't kidding and at the same time...

"You know, I'm alright with it if you decide you do want to try dating."

He lifted the lid on the Beef Bourguignon and the scent was enough to make my mouth water. He opened a warmer and pulled out fresh dinner rolls that had a bit of honey on them, or at least they smelled like they did.

"Have you been raiding Jeremy's recipe box?"

Dad chuckled. "Actually, yes and no. Jeremy got that recipe from your grandfather. This is the first time I've been able to make it right. It seemed appropriate."

Yeah. It did.

"As for you being alright with me dating, I appreciate it. I really do. Maybe I'll get there, eventually. I'm pretty satisfied with my life right now. I have you kids, I have your kids and soon, we're going to have two more babies to spoil."

Frankie drifted out of the hall and the small smile on her lips suggested I hadn't been wrong about her giving us time. "You okay?" I checked regardless and she held up her cell phone. "Oh, Izzy sent pictures of—what is that?"

I stared at it, frowning.

"Flowers," Frankie said. "From a boy at school."

I scowled. "They aren't back at school yet."

"Nope." Her smile was so cat with the canary, I couldn't fault her but at the same time. Who was giving flowers to our little girl? "Apparently, his mother drove him over and he rang the bell and delivered them. He also added a card."

She swiped the screen to the left and the little greeting card with his careful little handwriting did not make me feel better.

Roses are red,
Violets are blue,
Flowers are pretty,
And so are you.

"That's quite sweet," Dad said as he came to look. "Is this young man well? Or was one of the other fathers right there?"

Frankie's giggles were worth the question, cause I wanted to go and roll security footage back. "She's seven."

"Almost eight," Dad reminded me and I scowled at him. "I'm just saying, it sounds like the young man has the right idea."

"Hmm-hmm." Seven was too young for me to beat up.

"I think Eddie is right," Frankie said. "It's sweet. She wasn't as impressed, however, and wanted to know how long she had to keep them before she could throw them out."

Now I grinned. That was my girl. Excellent.

Frankie swatted me and I didn't mind in the slightest. "Anyway, dinner smells amazing, Eddie."

"Speaking of which, let's get you seated and I'll bring the food out."

"I can help," she offered automatically, but I intercepted and turned her toward the table.

"Absolutely not, since I can actually *serve* food even if I'm not allowed to cook it, I'll help and you sit."

She wrinkled her nose at me but let me usher her to a seat. I didn't miss the faint tightness to her expression when she sat down or how quickly she tried to smooth it over.

I squatted and studied her closer. "What's up?"

"Just a little sore," she admitted.

"Sore?" I raised my brows then glanced at our bump then at her.

"A little sore. More my back than my—" She glanced toward Dad who had joined us, his concern mirroring my own. "It's not like when I was dilated with Charlie before."

"Okay. Do we need to call the doctor? Or head to the hospital?"

Thankfully, she didn't downplay it. "I don't think so. Just my back is achy and it could be because they are both in rapid growth phase. Doctor Patterson did say we would notice more changes in the third trimester."

The doctor had also indicated that was the time when more complications might also be an issue.

"I promise," Frankie said, cradling my cheek. She glanced at Dad once then back to me. "I'm a little sore, nothing terrible. I will report if it changes and maybe I can talk someone into a foot and back rub tonight."

"You want it, it's yours," I said. "But would you like to sit somewhere more comfortable?"

"This is fine but I would not object to the flat pillow for my back."

"You got it," I kissed her knuckles, then her palms before I stood. I went back out to the living room and snagged her pillow. Dad had found it when she was pregnant with Izzy. Now the pillow only came out when she was pregnant. It was shaped perfectly for her back.

"We're good then?" Dad asked, glancing between us and her smile was drenched in warmth and affection.

"Absolutely. I'm starving though and dinner really does smell good."

"Then let's get you fed." He was on the move while I helped her with the pillow.

"I'll get you some more water, or do you want the iced tea with lemon?"

"No no, the cucumber water. I don't know what Eddie did to it, but it's perfect." The eagerness accompanying her desire and the ease in her expression settled some of my last nerves.

I'd keep a closer eye for now. She and Bubba still had a few stops left on the tour. The doctor didn't say she couldn't go, but selfishly, I kind of wished she had.

A few minutes later, dinner served out and Frankie eating with gusto, I had to hide a smile. She wasn't exactly *racing* through the food but she was devouring it at a good clip.

"I'm really rather glad I made extra," Dad said, a bemused look on his face.

Her cheeks flushed with a hint of pink, but then she just shrugged. "What can I say," she told him after dabbing her mouth with her napkin. "It's excellent. Your grandchildren approve. Oh…"

"Moving?" I was out of the chair like a shot and around the table. The kids had been moving more and more, but *we* couldn't always feel them, even when she could. I palmed the bump and Frankie moved my hand.

There…

The feeling was fleeting, but it was there. Then another and this one had a little more force. I reveled in it. In the not too far distant future we were going to meet these little gremlins.

I couldn't wait.

"Eddie?" At her invitation, Dad glanced at me.

"C'mon, you can get that inside line on spoiling these grandkids first."

"Oh, good call," Dad said as he stood then moved to Frankie's other side. The kids were definitely being active.

"Here," I told him and he put his hand where mine had been. His quick grin said the twins weren't hiding at the moment.

"It's not too much for you, right?" His check with Frankie made me appreciate him more. The past few years had been a revelation in our relationship. His fondness and connection with Frankie had also flourished and I loved it for both of them.

Not to mention for the kids.

But I got it. I got why she'd been trying to encourage him to date. Dad deserved so much better than he'd gotten. He wasn't ready yet, but not yet didn't mean forever.

The twins entertained us for the next half hour. I moved so I could keep one hand on her belly while she ate. I wanted them to settle enough to let her relax. Dad kept glancing at her and the bump with fondness.

I totally got that.

"Can I ask if we've discussed names?" Dad waited until we'd finished dinner and moved back to the living room. Frankie smothered a yawn, then gave him a shy smile.

"Sorry, full tummy and I feel like the kids. I want to nap."

I settled my arm on the back of the sofa and stroked my fingers through her hair. "You can sleep in the car on the way back."

"I love you."

"I know." I chuckled and she grinned. Then I glanced at Dad. "Well, we've discussed one name for one of the girls if there are two girls. We've been disagreeing on the other name."

"Then there's if one of them is a boy." Lips pursed,

Frankie studied Eddie. "I know tradition would be to name him Edward Archibald Standish the IV."

"God that's a mouthful," Dad said and I chuckled.

"Right?"

"But the custom has been to name each of the kids using the initial of their biological father. So it works perfectly for our girl name, not so much for a boy."

"The girl?" Dad asked and I shared a glance with Frankie.

Her quiet nod made me smile. "Amelia."

Dad's expression shifted. "For Mom?"

I nodded. "For Nana, if we did go the IV route, we'd probably call him Teddy."

"For Dad." Dad nodded slowly. "They would be so damn proud of you and they would love that. They would also tell you to follow your heart and not custom if that wasn't what you wanted to do."

He wasn't wrong. "I think since we're having twins, then Amelia can by my initial, but bump number two, male or female, needs to have an F name."

"I am not naming a girl Francesca." She absolutely steadfastly hated her name.

"Well there are other F names," I reminded her and she made a face. "Thus, the disagreement on the second name."

A chuckle left him, but he nodded. "I can see the issue. Why don't you write your favorite names down for girls and boys on slips of paper, put them in separate bowls, then each of you draw one? You seal them in an envelope for girl and one for boy. Then you open it when you find out."

Frankie frowned. "Then we decide on a name without deciding."

"Something like that. But if you only put the names in that you both agree on or that you both love, then you are guaranteed the right name when you draw them."

She glanced at me and I lifted my shoulders. "If we ultimately don't like whatever is drawn, we have time to change our minds."

"True," she murmured. "We can think about it. We have time."

We absolutely did. Another twelve to fourteen weeks. I hoped. That was if they went full-term.

"Well, now that we solved that," Eddie said. "What other problems can I solve for you two? I need all the best grandpa credit I can get."

CHAPTER 13

ON THE ROAD AGAIN

FRANKIE

"Ow," I said, with a groan as Ian flattened my foot out. It had cramped while we'd been on stage. Since more and more, I sat while we performed, it hadn't been that hard to ignore the cramps in my legs and feet.

At least until we were getting ready to walk off stage and he'd taken my hand when I stood up. If he hadn't been holding onto me, I would have fallen.

"Easy," he murmured, adding a little more pressure that took me to the point of tears. It hurt so damn good. "You should have said something at the break."

There was the scold. Not that I didn't deserve it. "I would have," I said on a groan. "Oh ow… Ow. Ow. Ow."

He had magical hands, the agony was survivable only because relief was right there as he worked on my calf then back down to my foot. It was almost like he could tell just how much I could take before he needed to ease back and switch to the other set of muscles.

Maybe he could.

"Frankie." Aggravation punched up the syllables of my name. "Angel, we have two shows left. We can cancel them and make it up to the people in a few months…"

"No," I said, shaking my head as I blinked away the tears that kept trying to form. "Really, no, when we're done, I want to wrap and go home for at least a year or two."

His expression gentled, as he worked his way higher to my quads. "Then we need to do something about this. The swelling is getting intense and if you sit too still for long, you're having issues. If you stand you're having issues. Call Doctor Patterson first thing in the morning?"

He was offering a compromise and I appreciated it. When I tried to sit up, it wasn't the easiest, but he moved to grip my hands and tugged me upright. Not a single one ever teased me about the need for help. If anything, they were moving to assist before I even thought to ask.

"You're an amazing husband," I said. "Have I told you that?"

Ian's smile gentled and he squeezed my hands once before moving a pillow behind me and going back to work on my legs.

"You may have mentioned it once or twice." He lifted those stunning blue eyes to meet my gaze, then winked once. "Doesn't mean I won't keep a tally of swats for you letting yourself hurt through a whole set."

It was my turn to cradle his face. The action slowed his massage. As much as I loved him doing that, I needed to comfort him. "I promise, I wasn't hurting *during* the show. I didn't even notice at first. I mean I'm *always* uncomfortable now. It's just the lesser discomfort. When I stood up though…"

He frowned, then pressed his forehead to mine. It was

comfort and affection. Love and passion. Need and desire. "I hate when you hurt. I hate it more that I can't make it better."

"You do make it better. All of you do." This was something he really needed to understand. Every single one of them made it better for me. "We should be experts at this pregnancy thing by now..."

"Yeah," Ian agreed with an almost wry note in his voice. "Save for the fact that you are carrying twins and as stubborn as ever."

"Hey now, being stubborn is one of the things about me you love." The chastisement pulled a real smile out of him.

"God help me, it definitely is, Angel." His smile made my heart flutter.

"I love you," I whispered. "I keep thinking we're going to hit that maximum amount somewhere—like you can only love someone so much. But every year, it just feels like I love you more."

"That's excellent for us," he teased. "Come on, walk some and then shower."

I groaned, but let him help me to my feet. Currently, I was wearing one of his *old* football jerseys. We'd discovered with Izzy that it hit me about the top of my thighs with the belly and I still had room in it.

Made it easier to get comfortable. Though right now, the twins might make us have to use alternatives.

One arm around my waist, he balanced me easily as we started to walk. The soreness was there and I had to fight the urge to be ginger about each step. The best way to handle the cramps was to do full stretches. Use each and every muscle so that they could warm up again.

The shower would be better still. I'd rather soak in a bath, but not allowed at the moment. Though I could put my legs in I supposed. Eh, it would probably be awkward.

"And I love you too, Angel," Ian said as we walked. "I get it when you say it's more every single year."

I grinned.

"You're an excellent mother. A phenomenal wife. An absolutely amazing partner. The best and only lover I ever want." The pride resonating in every word made it impossible not to believe him.

Despite the fact I flushed a deeper pink, I didn't shy away from the praise. It had taken me years really to accept not only how much they loved me, but also how much they demonstrated it.

I leaned into him, slowing our pace. When I turned toward him, he wrapped me into his arms. He cradled me there, rubbing my back slowly. I could have stayed there forever, but he nuzzled a kiss to my forehead.

"Shower time."

I groaned. "I hope there's enough room in there for both of us."

He chuckled. "Don't you worry, Angel. I've got this."

Fifteen minutes later I stood under the rainfall shower spray. I had my back to the water and as much as I wanted it to be super hot, that was another luxury that had to wait until after the babies were born.

The warmth though, penetrated the tight muscles as he worked his magical hands up and down my spine. When I began to sway, he put a hand on my hip.

"Am I losing you?"

"No, but you can keep doing that forever." I was half-floating from the combination of massage and shower.

He chuckled as he moved his hands up to my hair. "We're going to wash this now."

"Okay." My awareness of him grew as he worked the shampoo into my roots. If I'd thought the foot and leg massage had been agony and ecstasy, while his work on my back had left me floating—the scalp massage? It absolutely untethered me.

I moved where he put me, he rinsed out my hair then added conditioner. A few minutes later he was soaping me from head to toe. The gentle rub of his hand over my belly got the kids moving.

"Nope," he murmured, flattening his hand to the side of my belly. "Back to sleep, both of you. Mama is getting a break tonight."

Probably not, but I loved the way he was thinking. The simple fact was, my bladder was the size of a microdot at this point and the quieter it was around us, the more active they became.

Then again, maybe they would learn to listen to Dad too. A grin curved my lips.

"Hmm, I recognize that smile," Ian said as he knelt to finish rinsing my legs. Then he pressed a kiss to the bump. "What are you thinking about?"

"Just—you're a great dad. All of you are so amazing as fathers. Granted, I don't have as much experience—even if I think Hank is the best." My dad. I didn't meet him until I was eighteen and more than done with all the growing.

I wished I'd known him from childhood onward, but he was also a great dad. The guys more than measured up to him and beyond.

Granted, we were lucky to be together from the beginning with all of the kids, but Hank definitely set the bar high. Over the past fifteen years, so had Eddie.

I sighed.

"Thank you," he said, then nudged me over to the shower bench and helped me sit down. "If you don't mind giving me a moment, Angel."

"Hmm. Gonna give me a show?" I teased and his eyes lit up.

"Do you want one?" The dare was right there, omnipresent in his words and I grinned wider.

"I will never say no to you." I could drink in the sight of him all day long. While he wasn't as cut as he'd been in high school, there was no mistaking the comfortable muscle mass he maintained. His abdomen wasn't as ripped, but only in as much as his six pack was a slightly softer four pack.

He tilted his head back to let the water wash over him. The once golden tan had definitely faded. It showed more on his arms and face. Less on his chest and legs. Not that I cared. He was Ian, and he would always be my golden guy—and the first one to really kiss me.

I sighed.

As I let my gaze drift over him, I hummed.

"Feeling better, Angel?" The liquid heat inside of me unfurled, blanketing the aches and the tired in a coat of pure need.

"Feeling like I want to suck your cock," I told him before flicking a glance up at him. I could almost taste him on the back of my tongue and the idea of feeling him glide over my lips had my pussy clenching tight.

He rinsed off the soap, and handled his own rapidly stiffening dick with care before he moved forward. The angle wasn't perfect, but it would work. The shower bench was low. Probably meant more for bracing a foot to shave your leg than to sit on.

But it worked for me.

"Not going to tell you no…but no hurting yourself either." He locked his gaze on mine. "That's an order."

The order looped around me and sank into my bones. "I promise. May I suck your cock please, sir?"

If his desire hadn't been evident before, it seemed to blaze out of him now. He gripped his cock and teased the head against my lips.

"You may, Angel. You can control all of it..."

Oh, that was a gift. I parted my lips the moment I had permission and he eased inside. I didn't get to suck them off that often once past the second trimester. We were right there on the cusp and they were so careful with me.

The heavy weight on my tongue was heavenly. I teased my lips along his length. I slid my hands over his thighs and then up. It let me brace myself against him and I could almost feel his legs locking so I could lean if I wanted.

I worked my way slowly to the base then back again. Everything about playing with him was about craving the feel of him in my mouth. I loved the way the vein pulsed along the underside of his cock. More, I savored how he would blow out a harsh breath, then suck in another.

The tease of salt in his precum wasn't all that bitter. Someone had been having some sweets today. A laugh vibrated in my throat. If he indulged in too much soda, his cum always tasted just a bit sweeter.

We'd indulged in some experiments over the years—for science of course. I was so damn lucky these guys would let me discover what I wanted and didn't. I wasn't a huge fan of the soy, but the teriyaki? Oh yeah.

"You're killing me, Angel." The husky growl of his voice rushed over me and I opened my eyes to look up. He stared at me with so much *love*, my heart fisted. These men *loved* me. Me.

All of that love filled in a hunger I'd never realized I had and I would always crave. They didn't love me like boys in high school or with the desperation brought on by nearly losing each other or even the ferocity of discovering how much we wanted to be together—all of us.

No, they had loved me like that. But now they loved me with a kind of all-encompassing heat that promised safety, security, *and* sex. I bobbed my head faster, swallowing him toward my throat.

As much as I could indulge myself with edging him, I wanted to taste his cum. I wanted to give him the release he gave me so much. The love. The caring.

"Fuck..." He groaned and braced his hands on the wall above me. "Your mouth is heaven, Angel."

I wanted to smile, but it would alleviate the pressure. I was determined to ramp up his pleasure. With care, I kept one hand on his hip for balance and the other I used to caress his balls.

The vein along the underside of his cock seemed to pulse and I could have sworn he swelled a little harder. I added the barest of scrapes from my teeth to the suction. Then I swirled my tongue around his head at the end of each retreat before I swallowed him again.

I locked my gaze on his and when he slid a hand from the wall to my hair, I hollowed out my cheeks. The suction pulled a genuine gasp from him.

"I'm coming, Angel..."

I could hardly wait. The warning came a split second before the first spurt of him hit my tongue and I closed my eyes as I savored him. Another rush hit my throat as I kept swallowing. I wanted every single drop of him. My whole body hummed with the need ignited from his pleasure.

When he shuddered at the rub of my tongue along the side of his length, I eased up. He was so sensitive after he came. Almost too sensitive and I didn't want to disturb the pleasure I'd already given him.

Easing back, I let him go and then he went to his knees and his mouth fused to mine. The kiss had my toes curling. It was almost a battle for those last drops of cum, but I won. His chuckle triggered my own and then he stroked my cheek.

"We're getting out of the shower and then it's my turn..."

Oh, the delicious shiver that climbed my spine had me wanting to stand. It took no time to towel off the extra moisture. He paused long enough to squeeze out my hair, comb in the leave-in conditioner, then tossed the brush before he picked me up.

"Ian," I protested. I was getting too big for this.

"One word about your weight, Angel. And our first session after recovery will involve five swats right off the bat and no orgasm for you."

My mouth dropped open as he met my shock with an even stare.

"Understood?" He continued to eye me. "You don't have to say anything, just nod."

There was just the smallest element of humor to that last bit, but I didn't mistake his announcement for anything less than what it was—a promise he would *keep*.

Snapping my mouth closed, I nodded once.

"Good girl," he murmured, then carried me out of the bathroom and to our bed for this stop of the tour. He wasted no time settling me on the bed before he crawled right between my legs and sucked my clit to his teeth.

The demand of his mouth on me held no patience or ease. He wanted me to come and he wanted me to come now. Thank fuck, because that was exactly what I needed. I writhed under his expert tongue and when he glided his fingers in to fuck me, I came on a shout.

He lapped up my release then hummed as he eased me down before ramping me back up. "More orgasms," he said, his voice coiling around me like the most sensual of kisses. "You relax and then the babies will... so hold on, Angel. I'm going for the magical eleven."

Eleven?

I couldn't even find the words before he was pushing me up and over. By number six, I was sobbing from it. It hurt and felt so good at the same time. He gave me the barest of breaks, kissing me until I lapped the taste of myself from his lips. Then we had water. Then we started all over again.

Sometime around midnight, he eased into me and the first push of his cock detonated my system. To be perfectly fair, I wasn't sure what number we were on when I blacked out.

I surfaced to a cool damp cloth on my overused pussy. It eased the heat down and the soreness. I floated everywhere else. My cramps were barely a memory. He nuzzled kisses to my face and lips, then coaxed me right back to sleep.

I could figure out the number the next morning. A couple of hours later, I surfaced cause I had to pee. Ian's hand cradled the bump and I was lying on my side.

"Already?" he asked in a voice drenched in sleep.

"Yeah," I said. I didn't apologize for it anymore. They didn't need that.

"Okay." He rolled off the bed then came around to help me. The trip to the bathroom was efficient, but oh...I was sore. He gave me a smile that was all lazy satisfaction.

"You're very proud of yourself," I teased and he winked.

"No complaints?" Was he asking or telling?

When I finished peeing—not that there was that much stupid tinkle tinkle tinkle—I stood and washed my hands. Meeting his gaze in the mirror, I let out a little sigh. "None here."

"Good. I think you're sore enough, but if another orgasm will help..." He wiggled his fingers at me. "We can make that happen too."

A real laugh worked its way free. As tempting an offer as that was, tired still swamped me. Once we were back in bed with Ian wrapped around me, I tumbled right back to sleep.

CHAPTER 14

ALL OF ME

FRANKIE

*M*arch came in like a lamb, which meant it would probably leave like a lion. The kids had spring break in April. This far north, it made sense for spring break to be later toward summer. Snow days were not things we had to worry about when we were kids.

I roused slowly, the caress of a hand stroking over my side and then down to where I was already naked under the shirt roused me from the half-drowsing state I'd been in. Such a lovely dream, I shifted my hips so I could rub against the stiff cock pressed against my ass.

We were just past thirty-four weeks. Both babies were easily four pounds according to Doctor Patterson. If they came now, no one was going to stop the labor.

Thank fuck.

I honestly felt larger than I had during any of my other pregnancies. I was either damn tired or I couldn't sleep. Most of it at the same time. Frustrating, but there. My breasts were beyond heavy and the colostrum had started to leak.

Especially when Charlie was crying. Even though I'd weaned him at a year, it was like he wanted to go back to nursing again. That had been fun.

Warm lips trailed along my neck and I let out a low sigh. Oh, I thought it had been a dream. I tilted my head back, eyes opening in the dim light of the room. "Jake?"

"G'morning, Baby Girl," he whispered against my ear. "I thought I was going to have to work a little harder to wake you up."

"Hmm, you feel very hard." I loved the feel of him touching me, stroking me. When he eased a hand between my thighs, I let out another sigh.

"Oh, someone is very wet too." Jake practically hummed under his breath. "How are you feeling this morning, Baby Girl? Fingers or cock? I'll even put lips and tongue on the table."

The most delicious of shivers danced through me. "Hmm, is yes to all of the above on the menu?"

He scraped his teeth against my throat, before he eased one of my legs up and then he was sliding into me. The shallow thrusts didn't take him too deep, if anything he kept teasing me with a little deeper.

A little deeper.

Then he settled inside of me as he teased his fingers over my clit. "Oh, Baby Girl," he sighed. "You feel so damn good."

So did Jake. But I went from lazy, slow arousal, to inferno. When I pushed my hips backward, he chuckled again.

"Demanding," he teased even as he fisted my hair and braced my hip then he fucked into me with a lot more deter-mination. I had no idea how long he'd been trying to wake me up, but I writhed against his cock as he kept his thrusting steady.

"I love how you feel." A keening sound tore from my throat. I adored how he felt. Hot and heavy inside of me. The stroke of his fingers on my clit, edging me higher and higher.

"Come for me," he ordered, his thrusts growing fiercer and his fingers firmer. The orgasm splintered on a wave and I came in a shudder. I swore I wet myself and fuck if I could be bothered to care.

The feel of his release as his hips stuttered suggested he really had been working for a while to wake me up. I savored the feel of him and how he cupped his hand against my slit. His cock was still buried inside of me and his mouth moved on my throat.

"I was really happy that Doctor Patterson hasn't taken sex off the table yet," he teased, drawing lazy circles with his tongue over my pulse point.

"No, she said I'd been active all the way through and my cervix isn't incompetent. It also helps reduce stress and improves sleep, releases oxytocin and helps to mask my aches and pains." Her very clinical assessment way back when had been hilarious. The guys hadn't been terribly sure during that first pregnancy and the last thing they wanted to do was hurt me or the baby.

"Hell yes, it's a wonderful thing to know my cock is good for your health." He bit down on my earlobe this time. "But as soon as you're all healed up from the birth, Baby Girl I want you on top and making me work for it."

What a wonderful idea. "Endorphins are so good for what ails you." I stretched against him. I wanted to be more active in these little assignations of ours. But the guys were definitely doing all the heavy lifting. And I couldn't even really lay here for long to enjoy the feel of him.

With a grunt, I sighed.

"Yep, pee time." Just like everyone else, he didn't seem to mind that my micro-bladder got in the way of everything. Currently, I was the one it bothered most. But still... He eased out of me and I swore there was another rush of fluid.

Okay, here was hoping I really *hadn't* peed myself. The low light in the room let me see where I was going as he helped me get up. I barely made it a step though when the rush was a lot more than it should of been.

"Oh shit," Jake said. "Don't move."

I froze for a second as he got the light on and then we both looked down.

My water had broken.

"You still need to pee?" He checked and I made a face.

Unfortunately, yes. He didn't waste time on working out how to get me out of the middle of the mess, he just picked me up. As soon as I was in the bathroom, he went back for his phone. Then he was back in the bathroom to help me clean up.

Within ten minutes, the rest of my husbands arrived and the plan we'd had in place for months commenced.

Coop helped me get dressed in something warm, but easy to remove. Ian worked on cleaning up the floor while Archie went for the vehicles. Jeremy was up and by the time Coop and I left the bathroom, he was sending all of us out.

"I'll take care of this. Get Miss Frankie to the hospital. I've also called Doctor Patterson."

"Thank you, Jeremy," I said, pausing to kiss his cheek. He put a hand on my shoulder. It was tantamount to a full on hug. "They'll call you as soon as we have any news."

"I know."

Eddie was downstairs with Carly. It was her week to be up helping us. "Go," she was telling him. "I'll stay with the kids. You can help keep the boys calm."

Then she gave me a hug and kiss as they got me in a coat. Ian was behind us with my hospital bag.

"I'll call everyone else," she continued and then Eddie was offering me an arm. Once in the car, I worked on trying to keep my breathing even.

My heart raced, but I hadn't felt any contractions yet. That didn't mean anything. I felt no contractions with Josh until right before he came and then they were fast and so was he.

Eddie was upfront with Coop driving. They'd both sent Archie into the back with me. Hand clasping mine with Jake on my other side and Ian behind me, I said, "I suppose now wouldn't be a good time for road trip songs?"

Coop grinned at me over his shoulder then hit something on his phone before he pulled out of the garage.

Aerosmith.

Good choice.

THE DRIVE TO THE DELIVERY CENTER DIDN'T TAKE LONG. Doctor Patterson wasn't at the hospital, which was a bit further away. That worked out. As soon as we pulled up, the gray skies gave way to rain.

Eddie was out of the vehicle first and striding inside, then he was back with a nurse and a wheelchair. I hated wheelchairs, but I didn't complain. The ache in my lower back was beginning to spread.

Jake lifted me out and Archie was there to help me sit. Then my feet were on the little footboards. The nurse wheeled me inside with the guys following. Coop still had to park.

Doctor Patterson was standing at the desk as we came in. She gave us all a smile. "How are we feeling?"

"Not bad," I told her. "Actually—pretty calm." Which after all the months of anxiety and sleeplessness, I had to admit—this was amazing.

"Good. Let's get you in a gown, and set up on a monitor and I'll come take a look, shall I?"

The rooms at the delivery center were very nice. You could *almost* forget it was a hospital. The spacious design let all the guys be in there without it feeling crowded. Eddie stepped outside of the curtained off area so we could get me in a hospital gown.

Granted, I wasn't shy anymore but there was no room for that at all during delivery. Once I was in the gown and on the bed, Jake pulled a cover over my lap. Then the nurses descended.

I had an IV in and then the monitor on the bump. Doctor Patterson came in to do her exam and I tried not to think about the mess from Jake.

To be fair, it was hardly the first time this happened. Her amused glance said it all.

"I don't think we're going to be waiting on them for long," she said. "You're already dilated to six centimeters. Contractions are steady. How are you feeling?"

"Still not totally feeling the contractions yet. It's more like Josh. My back hurts."

"Okay, that's normal. Could just be the angle of how they are laying. We've got two very steady heartbeats and your blood pressure is holding, but we're going to keep watching it. Any distress for any of you and it'll be a c-section."

I nodded. "Agreed." She'd get no argument out of me. Sure, we could do this the vaginal birth way, I'd done it three times before so at least I knew what to expect.

"Okay, let's keep you comfortable and I'll be back in a little bit."

As she stepped out, Eddie came to join us. Archie had

become a statue at my side and I tilted my head to look up at him. His jaw was clamped, a muscle ticked away in his cheek, and his gaze was a thousand miles away.

"What do we think of Armand?"

Coop mashed his lips together to keep from laughing. Jake grinned and Ian shook his head. Archie didn't quite respond yet.

"Maybe Andrew."

No response.

"Atlas," I said and that snapped Archie's gaze to me.

"What?"

I grinned. "Looking for more boy names that start with A. You didn't seem to mind Armand."

His expression turned comical. "We are not naming him after The Vampire Chronicles."

"Pfft," I said. "Alaric would work then."

"That's Vampire Diaries." He gave me a narrow-eyed look, but I didn't mind in the slightest. He was talking again and we'd broken through the terror and the shock. "Besides, I think I prefer Filbert."

"Okay," Eddie said with all due sobriety. "At this rate, neither of you are getting to name these kids."

I grinned. "You don't like Filbert? What about Fairbanks?"

The laughter felt good. So did the kiss Archie gave me. The next couple of hours passed by swiftly. Nurses came and went. I had to talk to the social worker who asked me the same set of questions they always asked.

While I appreciated it, it always felt kind of silly for me. Yet I loved the idea of the help being there for everyone. The contractions actually began to hit more firmly at the top of the third hour.

Jake offered me some ice chips. I would kill for coffee. But no food or drink. Doctor Patterson was back. "You don't appear to want to take our time today."

"Sorry, Doctor," I told her and then had to hold that thought as another contraction hit.

"Keep breathing, Babe," Archie said. "You gotta breathe with it."

Yeah, breathing with it sucked, but I tried to push out the air and then as the pain eased off I took a deeper breath.

"No waiting today," I said, licking my lips.

Eddie retreated to the top of the bed and Ian lifted his chin to him. The guys were taking turns and they were all keeping an eye on the time, the monitors, and me. Coop stationed himself near Archie. None of them had ever passed out, but Doctor Patterson horrified them with that story of the dad who fainted so now they watched out for each other.

It was adorable.

"We are definitely ready to get you into position." Oh right, the doctor was checking how dilated I was. It said something that I barely noticed anymore.

The next contraction hit and I'd remembered to suck in the deep breath first, then I pushed it out as I rode the pain. When it passed, they were getting me more forward, feet in the stirrups.

"Okay, pushing twins is a lot like pushing a single baby, you just get to do it twice. You've already got one ready to crown and they are in position—you ready to do this, Mama?"

I grinned at the doctor, though it might have been a grimace too because the contractions were coming again and a lot faster.

"Archie…"

"Right here," he said clasping my hand with his. Jake had baby duty, when they came out they moved them to test them and do all the things. Jake would go with them. Sticking close. Ian would back him up.

Coop moved around to take Ian's spot and he clasped my

free hand. "Let's do this, Beautiful. We're about to grow this family."

"We've been growing it," I said with a laugh and then sucked in that breath a second before the contraction rippled through me. I swore the bump moved.

"Next one, we're going to push," the doctor said as the rest of her team poured in. I suppose I could have asked for the epidural.

Probably should have, but then the pain was there and the contraction.

"Push, Babe," Archie said. "Five. Four..."

He counted it down and then I could breathe again. Not for long. The babies were determined. Three more rounds of pushing and I felt the baby moving and then they were out and the relief was so profound.

For a split second the room was almost too quiet, even with all the beeping then a healthy cry filled the air. There was a baby lying on my skin and Doctor Patterson was helping Archie cut the cord. I wanted to hold them but the contractions were already back.

"Okay, sounds like baby sister doesn't want her big brother getting all the attention."

Brother.

Sister and brother.

Tears sparked in my eyes and I glanced up to find Archie grinning wildly. Jake nodded to me as he followed the baby boy and then I was in the middle of the contractions again.

She took a little more effort, but Amelia arrived five minutes exactly after her brother. I was sobbing in both relief and joy.

Healthy.

Almost five and a half pounds each. Nineteen inches long for Amelia and nineteen and a half for...

"Aidan," I said, and Archie glanced from the baby boy he was cradling to me. He nodded slowly. "Aidan Edward."

I liked it. Amelia for his grandmother. Edward for his grandfather. Aidan for us and the new lives we were celebrating.

It was the fastest labor I'd ever had and the babies were perfect. They needed some time and monitoring, but they were a healthy enough weight. Much longer and Doctor Patterson indicated we'd definitely have needed a c-section.

I was already in love with them. The guys were too. Eddie —he cradled Amelia like she was the most precious thing on the planet and he kept glancing over at Aidan. Archie wore an expression that was equal parts awe and adoration.

Our happily ever after kept growing and changing. It was the best kind of ending.

Another beginning…

RULES AND ROSES BONUS SCENES

FISTS & FRIENDS

FRANKIE - KINDERGARTEN

"Cooper Brennen," the teacher called.

"Here."

"Francesca—" I grimaced. "—Curtis."

"Here."

The kid sitting next to me crossed his gray-green eyes and I wrinkled my nose and then focused on the teacher again. He lived in my apartments and I'd seen him outside a couple of times, but I hadn't met him before class today.

I was nervous enough about being here. My tummy kept doing these weird flippy flop things. Mom had told me I wasn't allowed to cry so I hadn't. I also had to be good, so I was doing my best. I'd been to pre-school before, but I had friends there. It was in the same building where Mom worked.

This was not.

And it was so much bigger.

I didn't know anyone.

Tears pricked my eyes but I blinked them back because a girl at another table just started crying. When all the attention swung to her I let out a breath. The kid next to me crossed his eyes again when I glanced at him and I frowned.

"Fran-Chest-Ca?" he sounded out my name and I scowled. "Frankie."

I liked Frankie *way* better. Francesca was a terrible name. Mom only called me that when she was mad.

The kid grinned. "That's a boy's name."

Ugh. I made a face. Then stared at the board when the teacher started talking again. She had the crying girl all cuddled up when she called us to sit in a circle. We got to tell each other something about ourselves. I didn't have much to say, but I did get to tell them I was Frankie and the teacher promised to remember my name.

By lunchtime I was exhausted, we got to go out on the playground right after food. We didn't get our first break because we got to go to the library instead.

I *loved* the library.

The lady in charge of it was Mrs. Fredkins. She was the nicest lady ever and promised that by Christmas, we would be able to take books from the library home to read then bring them back.

Best.

Place.

Ever.

I could already read. That was something not every kid in the class did yet. I could even write most of the alphabet neatly. I ate as fast as I could because as soon as I finished I could go outside. The kid who sat next to me in the class also sat next to me at lunch. But like me, he was hungry, so he ate as fast as he could, too.

I won and shot my hand up in the air. My teacher laughed and told me I was excused. I remembered to throw away my trash along with the brown paper bag and then raced outside. It was hot and sunny and there was playground equipment. I knew I had to be careful of the dress, even if I hated it, but I *never* got to go to the park.

Mom never had time. She had to do a lot of work and it was important that I entertain myself. This was the best part of preschool and I needed to know if it would be the best part of school school too.

The playground was *huge.*

I wanted to do everything.

I was up the slide in a heartbeat and flying down.

Stupid skirt got in the way, but I bunched it and made it work. I had on shorts underneath.

The boy from class was at the top of the slide when I got to the bottom and he wooted as he raced down. Then I was back up again.

Next was the jungle gym and I watched him scamper across the monkey bars and I was right behind him.

He laughed when I jumped off and landed next to him. "Swings?"

"Yes!"

We turned and he ran into another kid. "Hey," the kid groused and shoved Cooper. Cooper stumbled into me and then shoved the kid back.

He was a bit bigger than Cooper. But I was taller than Cooper too. Then the kid hit Cooper. I scowled. "You want a knuckle sandwich?" I demanded.

The other kid smirked at me. "Give it to me," he demanded and pushed right at me. I balled up my fist and socked him. The big bully landed on his butt in the dirt. My hand hurt and the kid on the ground stared at me for a beat and then burst into wailing tears.

What a baby.

I was so disgusted.

Cooper stared at me, wide-eyed with his mouth open as one of the teachers charged over to us.

An hour later, I had to explain for the third time why I punched the boy John in the face. "I asked permission," I argued tartly. I didn't understand the problem. We weren't supposed to touch other kids without their permission. I learned that *last* year. So I asked.

My teacher seemed to be struggling, mightily. The principal who had come in to talk to me was a big guy and I was a little scared when he'd first come in, but he listened to me tell the whole story and then he and the teacher both seemed like they were going to cry.

"Am I in trouble?"

"Francesca," my teacher began.

"Frankie," I said. "Please."

"Frankie," she continued, this time with a smile. "I am going to have to call your mother."

My stomach dropped. I was in trouble. Mom was gonna be so mad. "But I asked first."

"Yes, you did," the principal said with a sigh. "We have to talk to your mom because those are the rules, and I need you to not ask other kids if they want a 'knuckle sandwich' again."

I frowned. "He said yes."

"John claims he didn't know what it was," my teacher said gently and I scowled. "That said, you shouldn't hit."

"He was being mean to Cooper and shoved him."

"Then you get a teacher," the principal told me. "I know this is new for you, but you have to follow the rules, too."

I folded my arms and leaned back in my seat. "I did follow the rules. I didn't touch him without asking."

The principal cleared his throat. "I'll leave Frankie with you, Ms. Diaz." Then he left the room. It sounded like he was choking or coughing as he left.

Then it was just me and Ms. Diaz. The other kids weren't

here, they were in another classroom. I'd had to come sit with Ms. Diaz and talk after the fight. Not that it was a fight. John was just a big ol' baby.

"Frankie," she said, pulling my attention. "Do you understand why it was wrong?"

"No, because I asked first. I didn't touch him without asking."

"That was good. But even if you ask for someone's permission to hit them, you shouldn't hit."

That didn't make any sense. "Do you have to call my mom?"

"I'm afraid so, sweetheart. That's the rules. You're also going to need to sit out from the playground for the next couple of days."

"Fine."

That wasn't so bad. Mom was going to be so angry.

"But Mom is at work and if you interrupt her at work, she'll get mad."

"I'll take care of it. You don't worry. Okay?"

Yeah. I worried.

By the time the other kids came back and Cooper and I were sitting at our table, my stomach was in knots. Not because I was scared of school, but because I was scared of going home.

Cooper leaned over when the teacher told us to color our sheets and whispered, "Hey Frankie...will you be my friend?"

Really? I blinked and stared at him. "Okay."

"Yeah?" he said, grinning.

"Yeah."

He bumped my shoulder and then shared his crayons.

I didn't get to play for the next couple of days and Cooper sat out with me. He wanted to be called Coop. I called him Coop.

Mom picked me up that first day and she wasn't mad at

all. She did ask me about it, but she wasn't angry. If anything she laughed then asked me if I really hit the kid hard and I told her I had. She nodded and that was that.

Whew.

Mom picked me up every day after school that week and she met Coop's mom and then...the next week, Mom took us both to school and Coop's mom picked us up after.

It was awesome.

Three weeks later, I was in the principal's office again. I'd torn my last dress and I had a bloody nose. Felicia MacNamara had a black eye. I made sure she hit me first. But she'd been really mean to Coop and called him names.

So I made her mad.

They called my mom.

I got in trouble for this one.

Totally worth it.

Coop wanted to be my best friend after that.

BOYS & BOOKS

FRANKIE - 2ND GRADE

"Let it go," I ordered Alan Graves. He had his grubby fingers locked around my book and I wasn't giving it up. I'd worked for two weeks straight to earn enough quarters from Mom to buy this book myself. Alan did not get to take it. We were supposed to be having free time on the playground right now and I'd brought my book out to read.

Alan made a face and yanked the book free. "Mine now. Whatcha gonna do?"

Balled up my fist and punched him in the nose was what I did.

He whacked me right back. Even though I had tears from the smack of my book hitting my face, I didn't get to retaliate. A blur of dark hair slammed into him and they both went flying. So did my book. I barely scrambled to grab it and turned when I found Alan on the ground while a boy a little bit bigger than him wailed on him.

We were just out of sight of the monitors but one of the other kids yelled "fight!" and I whistled between my teeth. It sounded pathetic since I was actually missing a tooth but it was enough to get the second kid's attention. Oh, it was the new kid. "C'mon," I told him and curled my fingers. "You're gonna get in trouble."

He scowled. At first I thought he was glaring at me, but he jumped to his feet and then kicked Alan. I winced cause Alan made the mistake of rolling and the new kid got him right in the no-no square. The little squeal Alan made told me, hurt as much as it looked. Then the new kid stomped over to me and looked down at my book.

"You're bleeding," he said.

I swiped a hand at my face and winced at my nose. Yep. There was some blood. "He hits like a little girl."

The new kid snorted.

"What?"

"You hit him pretty hard," he said. Alan had dragged himself up and limped away. One of the playground monitors glanced over at us and I grabbed the new kid's arm and hauled him over behind the jungle gym and the slide. We weren't totally out of sight, but didn't want them to see the new kid with the dust all over him.

He looked like he'd been fighting.

"I said *little* girl," I told him sternly and dusted him off before I straightened and stuck out my hand to him. "I'm Frankie."

"Jacob," he said with a grimace. "I like Jake better."

"Okay, Jake." I said as he shook my hand. "Thanks for helping."

"No problem." He squinted at me. "You sure you're a girl?"

I yanked my hand out of his and glared at him. "Why do you think I'm not a girl?"

"Cause you don't hit like one."

"You've never had me hit you, you don't know." Course, I kind of liked the compliment. Just glad I didn't get caught. I belted Sue Marie last week cause she called Coop stupid.

Mrs. Diaz was pretty disappointed in me and Mrs. Hoffman told me I'd lose playground privileges for a week if I got caught fighting again.

Worth it.

"Heh," Jake said, then scratched his ear. "Well, if you wanna hit me so I can find out for sure, you can. I won't hit you back or nothing."

I stared at him. "Why would I hit you?"

"So I can see if you hit like a girl."

I rolled my eyes. Boys were so dumb.

"What?" Jake said. "I could take it."

Yeah. Really dumb. "I don't want to hit you. I wanna read my book."

He shrugged. "Okay."

"Anyway...thanks." I carried my book away from the playground equipment and the other kids and found a place to sit. My nose was tender and there was only a little bit of blood. I rubbed it clean and then wiped my hand on my jeans. So far Alan hadn't told on us. But he was also sitting at one of the picnic tables near the door crying.

I kind of felt bad until I looked at my book and the part where he ripped the cover and I scowled.

He better be crying.

A shadow fell over me where I sat and I glanced up to find the new kid Jake standing there. He dropped to sit next to me and I frowned. "What are you doing?"

"Sitting here," he told me. "What are you doing?"

"Reading my book." I mean, obviously, right?

Still, I hated that Alan tore a piece of the cover. I smoothed it down and opened it to the first page.

"What's it about?"

"It's about a girl detective."

"Is it any good?"

I looked at him. "I like all her books. But I haven't read this one before."

"But you read the others?"

"I just said I like the other ones."

"Oh," he said slowly. "Right."

Going back to my book, I turned to the first chapter and Jake scooted closer. Glancing up, I stared at him. "What now?"

"Just wanted to see if it's good or not." He stared at me for a minute. "Is it okay if I read it too?"

I squinted at him and pushed my tongue at the gap in my teeth. I was losing valuable reading time to this conversation. "I read fast."

"I can keep up." He lifted his chin and gave me a grin.

"I won't slow down." Fair warning. Cause Coop always complained about how fast I could read.

"Okay." He nudged my shoulder and nodded to the book.

Fine.

I leaned a little so he could see and then started reading. Like I promised, I didn't slow down. We were on chapter three when a shadow blocked out the sunlight and I glared up to find Coop staring at us. Well, staring at Jake. "Hey," I said with a grin. "I thought you were gonna miss recess."

"Nah," he said, flopping down in the dirt on my other side. "Just had to get my teeth cleaned." Then he looked at Jake. "Who are you?"

"Jake." He scowled right back at Coop.

See, I told you boys were dumb.

I elbowed Coop then said, "Jake's the new kid. He beat up Alan for me."

Coop glanced from me to where Alan was playing now and then back to me and Jake. "Yeah?"

"Yeah."

"Cool," Coop said and stuck his hand out. "I'm Coop."

"You her boyfriend?" Jake asked and I rolled my eyes.

"No," I said.

"Yes," Coop answered.

"I don't have a boyfriend, Cooper Brennen." I pinched him.

"Yes you do! I'm a boy and your friend. So you have a boyfriend."

We glared at each other. "Fine. I'm reading."

Then I stuck my nose back in my book.

"Can I be your boyfriend too?" Jake asked and I stared at the sky. "I mean I'm a boy..."

"If I say yes, can I go back to reading my book?"

He grinned. "Sure."

"Great, then fine. I have two boyfriends. Now lemme read before the--" Too late the bell rang and I sighed. I closed my book as they scrambled to their feet. Both of them offered me a hand and I snorted, I could stand up on my own.

We were almost to the door when Jake said, "When you're done with the book can I borrow it?"

I glanced at him. So did Coop. Cause I didn't lend books. I didn't have that many.

"I have some books you can borrow," he offered. Coop and I looked at each other and then back at Jake. "I can ask my mom if you guys can come over after school and see."

"How many books?"

He grinned again. "I got a lot of books. Mom likes that I read."

Lots of books?

"Yes," I told him. "Coop and I would love to come."

"We would?" Coop grumbled but I stomped on his foot.

"We would."

"Cool," Jake said, grinning wider. "I got video games too."

"Now you're talking," Coop suddenly didn't seem to mind. Games were fine.

I wanted the books.

I finished before school was over and I offered the book to Jake to see if he still wanted it. He grinned. We didn't get to go over after school that day, but Coop's mom promised to talk to Jake's mom and it took us almost a week--Jake brought me my book back the next day and brought one of his with it. Then he asked if I had another of the Trixie books.

We traded books all week.

Coop made fun of us.

But it was still fun and finally, a week later, I got to see all the books he had.

He wasn't wrong.

He had a *lot*.

Boys were dumb but boys with books were cool.

A few months later, I punched Jake. He deserved it.

And you know what, he said I didn't hit like a girl.

MATH & MEETINGS

ARCHIE - 9TH GRADE

*T*he car rolled up to the high school, and I leaned back in the passenger seat. Jeremy cast a sideways look at me. "There's still time to change your mind, Mr. Archie." It was the first day of ninth grade, and not only had we moved over the summer to a new house in Texas of all places, but I'd decided to go to school locally rather than remain at boarding school.

"Nope," I said with a lot more confidence than I possessed. The last couple of years at Andover had been less than stellar. With Nana gone now, there was no reason to stay. She'd been the driving force behind my attendance. Particularly since she and Grandpa lived a few miles away. I could spend weekends with them. Grandpa didn't want the house anymore, and I couldn't blame him.

The last weekend I spent there, it had just been the two of us rattling around in that big empty place. Now that Grandpa and Edward were no longer on speaking terms, I didn't even have that escape available. Grandpa's last missive —passed through Jeremy since Edward, the asshole, had forbidden me direct contact with him—included the fact that he was selling the house, but would put the money into my trust for me.

I didn't give a damn about the money. Honestly, I didn't even care about the house. It was just a building without Nana.

This school though was a far cry from the boarding schools and preparatory academies I'd spent the last few years at. No uniforms in sight. The temperatures outside were sizzling. A hell of a lot more kids trailed up the walk-ways, got off of buses, and made their way in from the parking lot than had been at my boarding school.

A lot more.

Public school. Time to make my own way.

"I'm good," I continued, glancing at Jeremy. The guy who was pretty much the family manager—from butler to chauffer to cook to confidant—regarded me steadily. "Seriously, I'm good. I want to do this. I need air to breathe that isn't loaded down with expectations and plans made three generations ago."

Also, I didn't want anymore damn arguments about what my next steps would be. Edward and Muriel both wanted different things for me. From prep school to Ivy League to diving into the family business.

Yeah, none of those were on my list.

There had to be a life outside of the moneyed halls with their polite stabs in the back and poisonous arguments.

"You have your phone, I'll be along directly at four to retrieve you. If that changes for any reason, just let me know."

"Thanks, Jeremy."

"Of course, Mr. Archie."

At least riding up front meant it wasn't as conspicuous that I had a driver for school. We'd finished all my enroll-ment the week before. Jeremy had come with me to do the paperwork and signed everything. He'd pretty much done that since I was five. I doubt Edward or Muriel had ever set foot inside one of my schools.

Ever.

Somehow, I didn't think it would change here

"See you later," I told Jeremy as I stepped out into the muggy heat and slung my backpack over my shoulder. One look at what the other kids were wearing, and I was glad I had swapped out the polo shirt Jeremy put out for a band t-shirt I'd picked up at a concert over the summer.

As it was, the khaki shorts were gonna stand out, but fuck it. I tapped the top of the Lexus before walking away. I had my schedule in my back pocket, and I may or may not have memorized the layout of the school because it was three times the size of the academy. They like everything bigger in Texas apparently.

The first three classes of the day were boring as fuck. I might need to revisit my academic schedule. I was ahead of a lot of these classes, but Jeremy had been right in his advice to test the waters first. Fourth period had potential. I liked math. My engineering classes were in the afternoon, so those were something to look forward to, as well as foreign language. Two years of French to meet the requirements.

Another perk for public schools—so far, there was no assigned seating. I could skate in and grab a desk in the back row. It put me in the perfect position to watch kids as they hustled in. The other freshmen seemed to be a mixed bag of totally not giving a damn and seriously anxious. The anxious ones earned my sympathy, 'cause if I hadn't practiced hiding my feelings for years, I'd probably look just like them.

The last four to skate in the door laughed their way into the classroom. Two jocks, though the third guy could be one, too, I supposed, but they weren't what snagged my interest. No, the blonde in their midst with a faint smirk on her lips as

HEATHER LONG

she punched one of the jocks in the arm captured all of my attention.

"Shut up," she muttered, then hip-checked the second jock. "Asses."

"Awww," the third guy complained. "It was my idea."

She flipped him off so fast, I had to snort a laugh, then she slid into the chair in front of me, which worked for me. I didn't mind the view at all.

Her friends, however, scowled, and the dark-haired guy gave me such a narrow-eyed look, I planted my gaze anywhere but her.

For. The. Moment.

As soon as the teacher walked in though, I kept studying her. She barely looked up from her books, except to answer questions. That kind of laser focus was scary. Still, math just got a hell of a lot more interesting, even if the subject material was easy

"Psst," the blond jock leaned over and tapped her arm. I'd ended up sitting right in the middle of all of them, but I didn't mind.

"Yes, Bubba," she said over her shoulder with a grin. "I'll help with homework after school."

"Awesome," he said, grinning.

With him distracted, I could see his answer sheet. Why did he need help? He had all the problems answered already, but he tucked the page into the back of his book and then put a blank sheet on the problem set.

Huh.

Still, the glimpse of her profile had been like a donkey kick. She really was gorgeous. All too soon, the bell rang, and she and her escorts were gone before I could introduce myself.

That had to change the next day. Hell, I hadn't even caught her name. I'd do better. I had first lunch, so I headed for the cafeteria along with the rest of the herd. A couple of girls smiled at me, and a guy from my first period class lifted his chin. I nodded back, but I couldn't remember their names, if they'd been said at all. Probably better to just play it cool.

I stood in line with everyone else and grabbed a tray of the most frighteningly greasy pizza I'd ever seen, some French fries—who served fries with pizza?—and grabbed bottled water. I'd kill for a soda, but apparently, they didn't sell those in the lunchrooms here.

Healthier options, or so it had said in the orientation packet. Looking at the greasy pizza, I had to seriously question that particular description. Whatever. Food paid for, I scanned the cafeteria seating. The tables were packed. I didn't know enough of these people to just swing over and ask for a spot, so I navigated the room looking for an open table, when the blonde from math intercepted me.

Damn if I didn't nearly swallow my tongue.

"Hey," she said, and my brain went on hiatus for a solid five seconds. "I'm Frankie. You can sit with me if you want." She indicated the nearly empty table behind her. Well, nearly empty except for her tray and backpack. "My friends will be here in a minute."

The communication lines between my brain cells zapped to life, and I grinned. What was I going to say when a beautiful girl—seriously freaking hot—asks me to sit with her? I was not stupid.

"That'd be great, Frankie. I'm Archie."

"Awesome! Those of us with 'e' at the end of our name need to stick together."

I snorted a laugh as I slid my tray onto the spot next to hers and pulled out the chair. She said her friends were coming. I assumed that meant the guys from math, but maybe she meant girlfriends.

"You're in my math class," I managed as I unscrewed the top from my water bottle. Pithy one there, Arch. Really pithy.

"I know," she said with a grin. Unlike me, she was in jeans, but they were ripped around the knees, and her t-shirt was tie-dyed. She kind of reminded me of a cool hippie. The green of her eyes held all of my attention. "Saw you when we came in. Did you go to Freeman?"

I had no idea what that was. "No, just moved here this summer."

"Oh, cool..."

"We can't leave you alone for five minutes," said the guy she'd flipped off during class. "Don't you remember you're not supposed to talk to strangers?"

"Bite me," she said, pointing a plastic spoon at him. Like me, she had a slice of pizza and some fries, but she also had a chocolate pudding cup and was eating it first. "Coop. Archie. Archie, Coop."

"Hey, man," Coop said with a grin as he set his stuff down on the other side of Frankie.

"Hey."

"Why are you all the way over here?" Ah, here came the other two guys. The darkhaired one pinned me with a look that was far from friendly. "Who are you?"

"Jake, don't be an ass."

"Hard for him to do that when it's his default mode," Coop said with a laugh. The other blond with Jake snorted.

"He's sitting in Jake's spot, and Jake never takes that well."

Shit, she was already taken. That figured.

"Jake can sit there," Frankie said, pointing opposite her. "It won't kill him. Also, Archie, that's Jake. He growls a lot, but he's much nicer than he sounds, and that's Bubba."

"Hey," Bubba said, sliding his tray onto the table. "I don't growl, and I'm apparently not very nice." But his laughter decried that as Frankie rolled her eyes.

I found myself grinning as Jake scowled but took the chair she pointed out. I could have offered to move, but I didn't want to. Besides being pretty, she was adorable.

"Guys, this is Archie. He's new, just moved in this summer, and he's gonna hang out with us for lunch, so don't be dicks."

"When was the last time we were dicks?" Coop asked with a laugh, then bumped his shoulder to hers.

"This morning," Frankie and Bubba said almost in concert, but Jake just snorted. He didn't say much while we ate, but he did slide his pudding cup over to Frankie when she finished hers. The weight of his glare wasn't lost on me, but I played it cool. Frankie chatted with all of us, and her enthusiasm for school just seemed to bubble over.

"Wait," I said when something she just mentioned penetrated past my just soaking in her voice. "You have French this afternoon?"

"Yep," Coop said, popping the p. "Both of us do. Sixth period."

Excellent. "Me too."

"Hey, that's two classes together. What else do you have?"

"Engineering next, then history for seventh."

"You're with Jake next period then," Frankie said, grinning. "Who do you have for history?"

I had another class with Jake. He met my gaze with the same amount of enthusiasm I experienced. That was going to be fun.

"Um...Rogers, I think." I had to pull out my phone and look at the schedule

"Sweet, you're with me and Bubba."

Three classes with Frankie, but one of the other guys was in it? I could live.

"Well, at least now I have a reason to survive my first three classes of the day."

She laughed, and Bubba snorted. He and Coop shared a look. Yeah, I was definitely treading on unwelcome territory, but she invited me so I wasn't going anywhere. The next couple of minutes, she quizzed me about my last school, and I didn't mind answering the questions, but I kept it vague.

She'd finished her pizza and was down to half her fries when she said, "I see Tiff and Sharon. I gotta go talk to them about spirit squad." As she wiggled out of the chair, her hip bumped my arm before I could move out of her way. "Sorry." Then she pointed a fry at Jake and Bubba. "You two owe me for this."

Jake grinned at her, and it was his first real smile since sitting down. "You're the best."

"You really are," Bubba told her. "Also, if I could put in a cookie order for my spirit box…"

"Yeah yeah," she said with a flick of her fingers before walking away. "Don't touch my fries, Coop," she called back without looking behind her as she hustled across the cafeteria. Coop yanked his hand back with a laugh, but I tracked her progress until Jake leaned into my line of sight.

Snapping my gaze to him, I raised my eyebrows. "Problem?"

"Keep looking at her that way, and there might be."

"Dating?" I asked because sure, if she was taken taken, I could bide my time.

"Nope," Coop answered before Jake could say anything. "Frankie isn't dating anyone."

The other guy glared daggers at him, but I grinned. "No one, huh?"

Jake scowled, then drained his water bottle. Bubba shrugged. "Frankie doesn't date."

Maybe she just hadn't met the right guy. "So, I'm not stepping on anyone's toes if I ask her out?"

Across the room, she was talking to a table full of girls.

Girls who alternated between chatting with her and glancing over here at us. But I wasn't interested in them. Frankie's grin was so damn open.

Finally, Jake sighed as I realized the dead silence meeting my question also involved the three guys exchanging looks. "No," he said after a beat. "But let's be clear, if she says no, you take her no, and if you hurt her, I'll beat your ass."

"And I'll help," Coop said. "You know, like bring the first aid and stuff."

Bubba just shrugged. "What he said, but Jake usually does the hitting first and warning later. So take the warning for what it is."

"Duly noted," I said with a nod. She was on her way back, and when she grinned at me, I didn't bother to hide my own smile. "Definitely need to do lunch again."

"We do lunch everyday, genius," Coop said.

"Great, you're just going to open the door?" Jake grumbled.

"I didn't have to," Coop retorted.

"Y'all behaving?" Frankie asked as she dropped back into the chair, a little flushed and breathless. "Also, apparently, I have to do this spirit thing every day after school for the next couple of weeks. I officially hate you both."

"Aww," Bubba said. "We'll meet you after football practice."

"Pfft," she said, but Jake offered her the pudding cup from Coop's tray, and she laughed.

"Hey," Coop complained. "I was going to give it to her."

"You snooze, you lose," Jake said with a grin, and I shook my head.

They were nuts.

But they were my kind of nuts.

Frankie popped open the pudding cup and looked at me.

"We're probably going to walk down to the diner after practice and spirit meeting stuff. You're welcome to come with."

Oh yeah. "Sure, just let me know when. I'll have to text my ride."

Yeah. School was definitely looking up. Tomorrow, I was definitely grabbing a pudding cup to give her, too.

MISTLETOE AND MISCHIEF

FRANKIE - 9TH GRADE

First Christmases are fun. The first Christmas Frankie and all four boys were together, they were in ninth grade and they thought they were smooth. Really, they were just adorable.

"Rules are rules, Curtis," Jake informed me as he stood on the other side of the pool house door.

I rolled my eyes. Coop's mom had dropped us off on her way to work. This Christmas was a weird one for Coop and he stood right behind me, waiting for me to go inside. The fact Jake had thrown open the door as soon as Jeremy showed us outside and pointed to the pool house hadn't been lost on me.

Nor the fact he wore a smirk.

In the last three months, he and Coop had both shot up taller than me and then some. For a while there, we'd been neck and neck. But even Bubba had already begun to leave me behind. Fine, I could handle being the short one, but...

"What are you up to?" I peered at Jake and his grin widened.

"Nothing."

Right. I didn't believe that for a second. His birthday had been the day before. Today, the five of us were celebrating Christmas before everyone else had to go hang out with their families. I would probably end up at Coop's for Christmas dinner. That or Mom and I would be eating fried chicken and watching terrible Christmas movies together. That could be fun.

Still...

Coop gave me a gentle nudge, but I locked my legs. It was warm this year. In fact, outside of like three days where the temps hit the forties for five minutes, we'd been warm all December. I was in shorts and so were the guys. They were up to something.

"Come on, Frankie," Bubba called from deeper in the pool house. "We've been waiting for you two to get here."

Uh huh.

"We're not getting any younger," Archie threw in when I still hesitated. Behind me, Coop bounced from one foot to the other. Right. They were *all* up to something. I didn't know Archie as well as these guys but we'd spent a lot of time together the last few months.

This was all suspicious.

Arms folded, I shook my head. "You know what, I'm gonna stay out here." Cause if it was a water gun war or a water balloon waiting to hit me, they were gonna have to catch me first.

"Come on," Jake said, arms dropping. "It's us."

"Exactly."

"Hard way it is," Coop announced. Not like his agitation wouldn't give him away and I squealed as he tried to pick me up. That just had "throw me in the pool" written all over it. Jake tried to help and I eeled out from between them and the two collided in the door frame.

And then I saw it.

The mistletoe hung right inside the door.

Laughter exploded out of me.

"Oh hell no," Jake said as he gave Coop a shove. But bless Coop, he made kissy noises and smacked his lips against Jake's cheek in a noisy raspberry that set off my giggles. "Get off."

Despite his complaints, Jake was grinning and Coop snickering as they broke apart.

"Sneaky," I informed them. "And rude."

"Rude?" That got me twin looks of wtf. "Why rude?" Coop asked.

Archie popped his head around the door as if he hadn't been hiding back there the whole time. "Well, if we asked you nicely, will you stand under the mistletoe?"

I considered it and him.

"Tell you what... You guys stand under the mistletoe."

They all looked at each other, I could almost *hear* the mental debate. I was also dying to know who bet who what.

"You know what," Archie announced. "You only live once." He stepped right into the doorway and then got shoved out by Coop who took his place. Only Jake wasn't going for it, so he moved Coop. I saw it coming and lost it laughing when Bubba gave Jake a solid shove out of the way himself and then he was in the door.

The next ten minutes involved a lot of scuffling and wrestling. It was worse than the last time we played Twister, but it was funny as hell. When Jake had Bubba in a headlock and Coop parked himself in the door and Archie almost managed to make it in there, I walked over. They were too busy shoving each other to grab me.

One by one, I gave them each a kiss on the cheek.

That stopped all arguments.

"I win," I said, then scooted right between their legs to

crawl inside. One perk of everyone getting suddenly taller than me.

Their laughter chased after me, but none of the guys complained as we all piled into the living room of the pool house. The big television was already on and a game paused. The guys might have been waiting for us, but they were already entertaining themselves. There was a tree in the corner and it had a few presents under it.

Jeremy came out with sweet treats, hot cocoa, and more. We cranked the air conditioning down until we needed the fireplace on and we played games. More than a few, cause they'd stashed mistletoe just about everywhere.

Archie snuck a kiss when I came out of the bathroom. Jake got me when I switched chairs. Coop pounced when I grabbed something from the tree. Bubba bided his time, but he snagged me when we decided to go jump in the pool.

They were bad.

But I had to admit, my sides ached from laughing and if I had to kiss anyone under the mistletoe, at least it was them.

Though I did spot the sprig right before it was time to go home and I gave Jeremy a kiss on his cheek. Course, I learned my lesson. From that year forward, watch out for the mistletoe traps.

LOST & LONGING

IAN - SUMMER PRIOR TO SENIOR YEAR

*T*he music cranked up a notch and I had to remember to thank Archie for letting me have the party here. My parents volunteered to host it. One, we didn't have this much space in our yard or pool. Two, our neighbors would care if the volume was even half of what it was now. Three, I loved my mom and dad, but considering how many people were making out and half-naked already or the couple of girls who'd flat out ditched their suits entirely?

Yeah. Not a good idea.

I lifted the cold bottle of beer and took a long drink. Besides, alcohol wouldn't have flown there either. I met Jake's bland stare across the pool where Maria was currently glaring at him. He rolled his eyes and I shook my head. Jake had broken up with her twice, but she kept coming back.

Sharon slid onto my lap and looped damp arms around my neck blocking my view. "You're just sitting over here, birthday boy, why don't we go somewhere and make it fun?"

"Not having fun at my party?" I took another long drink of the beer even as I glanced around the throng of kids dancing, swimming, laughing, and playing. The blonde in my lap wasn't the one I was looking for. She did a little grind against me and my dick twitched, but he had about as much interest as I did at the moment.

When she leaned in to nuzzle my ear, she whispered, "Just think about how much more fun we could have if we were naked?"

I might be able to work up to that. When she pressed in tighter to me and tried to suck on my ear, I scanned the crowd again and then paused.

Right there on the other side of the pool, near the side gate that let people in without having to go through the house. A blonde turned around, a small birthday sack in her fingers. It wasn't fully dark out here yet, but the movement of others kept blocking my view, then she faced the pool and seemed to be searching.

Fuck me.

It was the first time in nearly three months she'd shown up anywhere. I started to stand and Sharon jolted.

"Off," I ordered her.

She frowned. "You don't have to be rude..."

I didn't have time for this. I scooped her up and stood, then dropped her back in my seat.

"Bubba!"

Ignoring her complaint, I shotgunned the last of my beer then left the bottle on the table and walked away. People moved between us, but I threaded my way through the crowd. When I didn't spot her right away, I frowned

No fucking way I imagined—

"Hey." The soft huskiness of her voice was a hug I hadn't even realized I'd been missing. Turning around, I found Frankie standing there with a hesitant expression in her perfect green eyes and a tremulous smile on her lips. "Happy birthday."

Fuck my birthday. I wrapped an arm around her and

dragged her in for a hug. Beyond going to Mason's to grab a burger and hopefully a snatch three or four words of conversation, I hadn't been close to her in months. She didn't answer text messages or phone calls. Fuck, if Coop hadn't made a regular point of checking on her when she did her damn laundry I might have camped out at her back door.

A part of me still wanted to, but she'd said something about traveling for colleges and... fuck it. She was here. She *came*. I would make the most of it.

Her shoulders were a little stiff at first but then she softened. Finally, she hugged me back. "Sorry, I'm late," she told me as she gripped me tight and I closed my eyes as I held on probably a few seconds longer than I should. But it was my damn birthday.

"I haven't seen you since I was seventeen," I tried to tease her and keep it light, but I didn't want to let her go even as I made myself take a step back. Accepting we'd only ever be friends was one thing. Accepting I didn't get to see her anymore?

Impossible.

Her rolling her eyes at me was the second best thing I'd seen in months. Lifting the gift bag, she glanced past me to the party and shifted on her feet. I swore, it looked like she was ready to bolt so I moved to block her view of the insanity. Fuck, there were actual naked girls out there. I was pretty sure at least a couple of people were screwing. We'd never have let the party get this out of hand if she'd been here...

"Bubba?"

"Let's go somewhere quiet?" I suggested more to get her out of here than anything else. A hand on my back almost made me want to punch something, I didn't even have to look to know Sharon had come to lean against me.

Fuck. My. Life.

"Don't be greedy, Frankie. The birthday boy can't disappear from his own party." The possessive arm she tried to wrap around me irritated the fuck out of me.

"Sure he can," I told her and stepped out of her grasp even as I caught Frankie's hand in mine. The tautness in her fingers and the fact she immediately tried to pull away was a sharp little stab. "It's my birthday and on my birthday..."

"Birthday boy gets what he wants," Frankie finished.

"Exactly." I grinned at her and a faint smile turned up the corners of her mouth but then she flashed a look beyond me to the party again. Definitely time to get her out of here. Fuck, I wish I hadn't let Jake talk me into picking me up. If I had my bike here, I could take her for the first ride on it. I'd been dying to show her the bike since I finished that class. "What I want right now is time with my friend," I told Sharon and jerked my chin back toward the pools. "Go hang out somewhere else, okay?"

I didn't wait for her to answer as I walked Frankie away from the party and toward the gate. It only took walking around the corner of the house to get away from some of the noise and I blew out a breath.

"You didn't have to leave the party."

"Hush," I said, letting go of her hand and slinging an arm around her shoulders to tug her close. She smelled like Frankie. Hints of her shampoo, but none of the burger smell. She'd gone home to shower after work probably. "Indulge me. It's my birthday."

Okay, low blow, but if the guys caught sight of her, they'd be here in a heartbeat. And I kind of wanted to be a little selfish. A lot selfish.

She huffed out a laugh and I did a little internal fist pump. We walked slowly together and she didn't try to pull away. Archie's parents' place was huge and there was one of those side patios up around the way not far from the kitchen. We could probably sit there.

"I should have grabbed you a drink." Shit. Idiot.

"I'm fine," she told me. "Besides. That was a lot of booze flowing back there and I'm driving. So no drinking for me."

"There's Cokes and stuff, too," I admitted, then ran a hand over my face.

"That's why you smell like a keg."

I grimaced.

"Ignore me," she added quickly with a wave of her hand.

"Never."

We reached the patio and there were no lights on and with the sun's descent the fading light left us in shadows. The air was hot and sticky, but that was all of August and I let her go, albeit reluctantly, then pulled out a chair for her.

Once we were seated, she set the bag in front of me. "Happy birthday, Bubba."

"You showing up is the best present I could have." No lie. The last few months had been so fucking weird without her. But I hadn't even realized just how *much* I missed having her around until she showed up. Or how much I'd been looking for her. The one girl I wanted to ask out more than anyone else, but she just didn't date. She was flat out oblivious to the fact that guys and girls alike looked at her.

So, we kept the hordes away and kept her safe. It was the least we could do.

"Uh huh…are you opening presents now or do you want me to put it somewhere?" There was an element of weariness in her voice that had me leaning forward.

"Let me open it now," I said reaching for the bag. "I don't know if there are other presents. It's really not that kind of party."

"What kind is it?"

I opened my mouth and then winced. "A little out of control," I admitted.

"Uh huh. Drinking. Screwing. Just—cutting loose?"

Another wince and I squinted at her. Getting her away from the party had been a stellar idea. But tucking her here where I couldn't really see her was a terrible one.

The lights cut on overhead and we both squinted. Then one of the glass doors to the kitchen opened and Jeremy paused to glance out at us. "Mr. Bubba and Miss Frankie...it's good to see you. We've missed you around here."

"Hey Jeremy," she greeted him with a far warmer smile than she'd given me. Then again, Frankie always had liked his cooking. "Sorry, we can shuffle back to the party..."

"Certainly not," he intoned then gave me a mildly reproving look. Message received buddy. Not that I wanted her back there anyway. "You two make yourself comfortable and I'll change the light settings so we don't attract the insects. Can I get you anything to drink?"

"I'm good," Frankie told him.

"Maybe some water?" I tried. Hopefully I didn't look as desperate as I felt.

"Sure," she agreed.

After Jeremy delivered a pair of ice cold water bottles, he locked back up and as promised dimmed the lights. So far the bugs hadn't bothered us, but it was Texas and August, it was more a matter of if than when.

She nudged the bag toward me and I pulled the ribbon she'd tied it closed with loose then eyed her. "Should I guess first?"

A real laugh escaped her this time, half-hearted at best, but still real. "Go for it." There was a genuine smile and I grinned. I rattled the bag, and made a big show of examining it without opening it.

"Nothing breakable." I checked with her, but all she did was take a drink of water. Yes, her eyes were still on me and the dim light didn't hide their amusement. "Hmm...not heavy enough for a book." I squeezed it. "But not hard either."

Okay I was a little puzzled. I shot her a look and all she did was raise her brows. "Any guesses?"

"It's something I'm going to love."

"You sound certain of that."

"You gave it to me," I admitted and tugged the top of the bag apart. "And you came to my party." Opening the bag, I stared inside at the sheet music books. I'd been wrong. It was a book, but it was soft covered and...

Before I could say anything though, Jake's voice cut through the dark. "Bubba, if you're gonna sneak off to fuck some chick could you possibly get rid of the other girl first. Sharon is a pain in the—oh, fuck. Hey, Frankie..."

"Frankie?" Archie was a half-step behind him and then they were both there and she scooted the chair back to stand. I closed the bag as they both shoved their way into the alcove. "What the hell are you guys hiding over here for?"

Archie snagged her hand and for the first time in a long time, I wanted to punch him. I hadn't wanted to hit him this hard since ninth grade when he spent months trying to date Frankie. Probably would have if I hadn't ended up feeling bad for him.

"Let's go. It's been too damn long since you came to party."

Jake grabbed her for a hug and she squirmed a little at the contact and then sighed as she gave him a hug back.

"Let go," I muttered and shouldered Archie gently. "Birthday boy here and you know the rules."

"Lucky bastard," Jake murmured, then surrendered her. I really didn't want to take her back to the party, but they were herding us there.

"Come on," Archie said. "I'll get you a drink and we can catch up. It's been months, babe. Way too long."

The minute we got back to the rowdy party, it was hard to miss Coop and Laura making out on one of the lounge chairs. Patty made a beeline for Archie, while Sharon was right there glaring at me because I'd told her to get lost.

Great. Mitch cut in and thumped me on the shoulder. The whole football team was here and Mitch was half-trashed. "Hey, Frankie girl. Where you been? I thought you dumped these losers."

"Fuck off," Jake told him even as Maria wrapped herself around him. He wasn't paying an ounce of attention to her. Hell, I didn't blame him, I was watching Frankie, too. Mitch just shrugged off the verbal threat, but he also didn't stick around. We ran a pretty tight ship and Jake had made it clear, more than once, what the rules regarding Frankie were.

Archie didn't take long to grab beers for all of us and he handed her one, but she didn't take a sip. Then the music changed and Sharon dragged at my arm. "Come on," she told me, taking the present out of my fingers and tossing it on the table. "I love this song."

One dance and I'd get rid of her. "I'll be back," I told Frankie and squeezed her hand before I let Sharon lead us to the makeshift dance floor. More kids had arrived while I'd been talking to Frankie. They were everywhere. Some of the girls were topless and there was more than one blowjob going on. Fuck, the guys better watch out for her.

I ended up dancing twice with Sharon because Maria dragged Jake out there and then I was done. I wanted to get caught up with Frankie.

But she was gone.

Archie handed me a beer. "I sent her in to grab a suit so she could join us, but she slipped out." He didn't even have to ask who I was looking for. He sounded like I felt. "And before you ask, I already checked to see if her car was gone."

"Thanks." I should never have danced with Sharon. It took me a minute to find the present Frankie had given me. Some asshole had tossed it near the bin with the used and empty bottles. Sharon slid right up on me again and this time, I really did shrug her off.

"Come on, Bubba. Let me make you feel good…" She had her hand in my swim trunks and I tugged free.

"Enough," I snapped and this time when she reached for me, I caught her wrist. "I meant it, Sharon. Fuck off."

She blinked. "What?"

"You're not getting the picture. You and me, we're not a thing. We had some fun, but you're getting on my nerves now. So fuck off."

And I'd had enough of that, I downed the beer and dropped it with the other empties and stalked away, sheet music in hand.

Jake caught me heading inside. "Done?"

"More than done," I told him. "I need a real drink and to get the fuck away from…" I waved to the party.

He nodded. "Head up to the deck. I'll tell Arch and we'll clear it out. Might take a while."

"That's fine."

I needed a while.

Upstairs, even with the dull throb of the music from the party still playing, I checked my phone.

No messages from her, but I sent her one anyway.

Thanks for the music. I love it. Maybe we can get lunch this week?

I thought about adding more, but then just shut off the message. There were a few above that she'd never read. I didn't even know if she'd read this one.

But she'd gotten me sheet music. She remembered.

She was the only one who ever did.

Fuck, I missed her.

SHOWCASE & SHUTTERBUGS

RACHEL - BONUS POV

*F*ive minutes after I got the last restriction removed from my driver's license, I had to resist the urge to scream. Despite all her protests about me spending money on driver's ed, wasting some of my college money on a car, and even all the hours I plagued my poor uncle to play the role of guinea pig and licensed driver while I practiced, my mother crowed like it was her achievement and not mine.

She hadn't gotten off the phone, not once. First it was the grandparents. Then my other aunts and uncles. My cousins. Her cousins. All the way back to the house, she chatted away to everyone who wasn't me about the achievement. It was eye-roll worthy, but I ignored it. Let her crow.

I had a driver's license, a car, and the insurance paid up for the next six months. I was doing *great!* The funny thing was, Mom didn't even notice I didn't follow her out of the car after I pulled up to the house to let her out.

With so many family living with us, the driveway was already a jigsaw puzzle of parked cars in varying ages from a couple of years to a couple of decades old. My uncle's favorite clunker was parked proudly *in* the garage. Then again, it earned that spot because it was broken down and we'd have to shove it out and down the driveway.

Periodically, he went out and tinkered with it. More than once he'd gotten the engine started, it would bellow black smoke, backfire a couple of times and promptly die all over again.

Then again, it was a forty-five year old car, that was older than he was. But he loved the damn thing. In fact, he was out there smoking a cigarette with a kind of indulgent grin on his face when I saluted him from the car. He gave me a thumbs up and then I pulled away.

The car gave me the kind of freedom I'd craved for the last four years. Well, more like for my whole life, but it was only in the last four years that I'd begun to discover that I was an oddball even in my quirky, non-traditional family. Go figure.

Too tall. My nose was too big. My attitude too sharp. My laughter too loud. My voice too cutting. I didn't participate enough in school. I didn't run with the right crowd. I didn't have *goals.* The last one was laughable. Also, most of those weren't my immediate family's opinions, but my far more conservative grandparents who'd wanted me to move to Ohio for high school.

Kill me.

As Uncle Basil would often say, "Fuck that."

Keeping my eye on the speedometer, I cut across town toward the Rappaport Center. It housed the senior community center, the library, recreation center, the new town hall, and a few city offices. It was also host to some *modern* art installations including a huge metal piece that played a tone as the wind passed through it.

Creepy fucking thing.

It was also located on a huge park area that had walking

trails, creeks, trees, and the best places to get some "nature" photography that didn't involve going all the way out to the lake. Perfect for my latest assignment. I wanted to submit a series to a showcase in autumn. I'd won two years running, both offered up a nice tidy sum toward college.

The more the merrier.

Parked, I pulled out my favorite camera. It was older than I was, but it still took excellent depth images. I had a much newer digital one—Uncle Basil had given it to me for Christmas—but when it came to art, I liked working with my shutterbug.

I was halfway across the parking lot and doing my best to ignore the melting temperatures sending up dizzying waves of heat from the pavement when a squeal of laughter erupted ahead of me. A familiar, gorgeous blonde pursued a much larger, thick-headed jock.

Her shirt was soaked revealing the curve of her bathing suit beneath it. The dark-headed jock cut away as she sent a splash of water from her cup at him, but she missed.

"Asshole," she declared and the asshole in question just laughed.

"Aww, you're gonna hurt my feelings."

She shot him her middle finger as she turned a disgruntled expression on her clothing. In this heat, that thin cotton shirt would dry in no time. She plucked at the fabric and let out the most pitiful of sighs.

I was thirty or forty feet away and in the shade of one of five trees growing up on the little green strips between the parking spaces. On a whim, I raised my camera up and focused on her.

Frankie Curtis was a pain in my ass. Smart as a whip and twice as beautiful, we competed in a lot of areas from grades to—well to not much else. I didn't worry about the social scene. I could play the game well enough to keep the school's more vicious bitches off my back and cultivated my reputation with care.

Curated you might say. Very few fucked with me because I would fuck with them right back. Except Frankie. She never tried to sabotage me and she never minced words either. Surrounded by four of the most besotted, numbskull idiots, she also didn't know what she was missing either.

Most people gave her a wide berth. Guys anyway. Girls who wanted to date said besotted idiots, swarmed her. It was enough to nauseate me. I narrowed the focus, I almost had the perfect shot, her head tilted down, the shadow of her chin just adding depth. Even the wet shirt would make for a solid texture.

If not for the lens focus, I probably would have missed it, but the wickedest most mischievous smile was on her face. I pressed down on the shutter release, not letting up as it snapped photo after photo.

Jake—the jock—had already returned to her, a half-formed apology on his lips. Aww, guilt was a beautiful thing. It didn't let him see the trap. As soon as he got to her, she twisted away and when he sighed, she spun and then dumped all the ice in her cup over his head and down his shirt and right into his shorts.

Damn she was fast. Admiration burned through me. I caught every slice of the action. His yelp was a thing of beauty. Smart girl took off running at speed, with Jake right behind her as she plowed right into another jock.

Bubba. Half-climbing him, Frankie put him squarely between her and Jake.

It was adorable and hilarious.

The last shot I got of her, she looked right at me. Her smile was so damn open it yanked my heart up into my throat. I lowered the camera, ready to give her a smile in response but she wasn't looking at me. A whistle came from my right and I sighed.

Should have known. The other two Musketeers had arrived. Their laughter cascaded through the park. That stunning smile hadn't been for me.

But I'd captured it.

Glancing down at my camera, I crossed my fingers. Even if it wouldn't work for the showcase, I kind of wanted it for me. Another laugh rolled toward me. I tracked the five of them as they headed for the rec center. The ache in my chest burned.

It wasn't until they disappeared from sight that I headed toward the walking trail. Sweat trickled down my neck, but I ignored it. I had five rolls of film in my camera bag.

I'd already burned through one.

Time to see what else the old shutterbug could capture.

What I wouldn't give to have had her smile at me like that for real.

UNADORNED & UNDILUTED

RACHEL - WHEN FRANKIE LEARNED ABOUT BEING UNTOUCHABLE

"*H*e said he's going to wear red, who wears a *red* tie?" Sharon smirked in the mirror as she checked her eyelashes, but Patty gave her a shove that nearly had her poking her own eye with the mascara. "Watch it."

"Then don't be rude about Archie. He looks damn good in red."

"But he drives an orange Ferrari, it's going to clash." In Sharon's world that probably registered somewhere between laughable and apocalyptic.

Maybe both.

I rolled my eyes.

"Who cares if it clashes," Patty said, her voice all breathy. I used to think that was attractive, now I just wanted to offer her an inhaler. "He *drives* a Ferrari and he definitely knows what to do with a stick."

"Oh you didn't," Maria said with a snort as she joined them.

"Of course, I did," Patty told her with a playful pout. "What's a matter, Jake still not giving it up for you?"

"I wouldn't tell you even if he was." Well, at least discretion and Maria appeared to be acquainted.

"That means no," Sharon said as though confirming that in other news, water was wet. "Poor Maria, you just have to distract him. Maybe do something with your hair."

"Like what…"

Was that bitch really going there?

"Dye it blonde," Patty finished. "You'd make a great blonde."

"Then throw in green contacts," Sharon added with the worst kind of laugh.

Bitch was supposed to be her friend.

I flushed the toilet. I'd been done for a while, I just hoped the boob crew would move their tight little asses, slimmed down by starving-themselves diets, the fuck out of the bathroom before I had to deal with them.

"You know, you really suck sometimes." Maria told her as she pulled down some paper towels to dry her hands.

"That's what Bubba says," Patty said with another laugh that actually got Sharon to glare. Which wasn't true. The guys might talk to each other, but they sure as shit didn't spread it around who was giving it up for them.

Hypocrites.

All three of them turned as I let myself out of the stall. A flash of fear in Patty's eyes followed by a guilty flush on Maria's face amused the fuck out of me. For one split-second, they had forgotten someone else was in here. Not Sharon, no, she just looked disappointed.

I'd like to boob punch her right back into training bras not that the B cup she sported was anything to brag about.

"We gotta go," Maria announced as if I cared. Sharon and Patty followed her with Sharon asking, "If he's wearing red, are you going to wear red? With your hair?"

Bile coated the back of my throat. I fucking hated the idea

of those bitches talking about her like that. Worse, I hated that they weren't wrong. The shitheads waved off anyone who even looked in Frankie's direction. If the rumor was right, Jake damn near put a senior in the hospital three weeks earlier because he announced that he was going to nail Frankie at the dance.

I appreciated the effort, but goddamn, they were all asking girls out and getting laid. Why the hell couldn't she? It pissed me off.

It was still pissing me off two hours later as the last bell of the day rang and I watched the girl who'd become something of my own personal obsession gather up her things. She was talking to math whiz Jane about helping her study for her lit test. Frankie had been tutoring her on and off when she wasn't working at Mason's or hanging out with the guys

Jane was cool. Nerdy. Smart. Totally my type and yet it was like trying to appreciate a rare gem while the brightest diamond in the world kept pulling all the light and refracting it back out. Frankie outshone them all and was so damn oblivious to it, she hurt my fucking heart.

Maybe that was why when Jane waved goodbye and shot me a shy smile, I winked at her.

And maybe that was why I packed my shit slowly because Frankie was staring down at her phone and texting furiously. Not with any kind of smile or bounce, but with a look of such profound disappointment it burned. Probably one of the asshats scaring everyone off from asking her out.

"Hey."

She startled with a jerk like she'd forgotten I was even in the room. Yeah, that would probably sting more if I was actively trying to get her to notice me, but bless this girl's beautiful eyes and brains, but she wouldn't see someone interested in her if they walked up to her and hit her over the head like some caveman.

Fuck, it would probably take something like that.

"Hey," she said, shooting me an apologetic grin. "Sorry! Didn't realize anyone else was still in here."

For all of two seconds, I debated ripping the Band-Aid off. Not everyone wanted the blinders removed. Sometimes, we were a lot happier in ignorance. But if it were me and my best friends were cunt-blocking me at every turn, I'd sure as fuck hope someone would tell me.

I'd hope someone would break the little conspiracy of silence they'd wrapped around her. No one crossed those boys.

But I was about to because fuck them and their goddamn double standard.

"No problem, you got a sec?"

"Sure." With a wary look I probably deserved, she tucked her phone into her pocket and then slid her backpack on. "What's up?"

"Look, we're not besties or anything. But you're basically a cool chick."

"Thank you?"

"You're welcome. We don't always get along, but I've never lied to you." Well, lied by omission but this wasn't about me goddammit and I sure as shit wasn't cock blocking her.

"Rachel, is something wrong?"

"As matter of fact, there is. You're not going to believe me, probably not at first and you won't want to hear this but I promise—it's the unadorned and undiluted truth."

"Okay." Arms folded, she met my stare. Goddamn if she wasn't gorgeous doing it, shoulders squared, feet slightly apart and her lips pressed closed but not clamped. Defiant. Defensive. Delightful.

Right. Not a pussy call. I was going to give it to her straight and walk away. Maybe then she could get out from under the shadow they cast. She deserved to shine and not be hidden away like some damn possession.

"You don't have a date for the spring dance."

"So?" Aww, sweetheart, don't look at me like that. I'd take you in a heartbeat if I thought you might go for it but you don't even pick up on the most straightforward clues. "What does that have to do with anything?"

It was the hurt lurking there in her voice that pushed me the last two steps I needed to make.

"It has to do with those so-called friends of yours. You know, your four Musketeers? Or maybe I should call them Stooges—look it doesn't matter. You don't have a date because there isn't a guy in this school they haven't warned off either with verbal threats or beating the shit out of them. No one is going to ask you. Ever."

It was like kicking a puppy. Before she could hide it, the hurt in her voice reflected in her eyes. "What are you talking about?"

"I'm talking about the fact they made you untouchable, girl. It's about damn time someone told you. They are so busy sticking their dicks in anything that moves, but if a guy so much as glances in your direction—they are taking their lives in their hands."

"The guys wouldn't…"

Yeah, I thought she wouldn't believe me, so I opened one of the multitude of chats that I'd managed to get looped into over the years. I lurked in a lot of them. I swore these guys never checked to see who was also in the chat when they started talking.

I just handed her the phone and she read the messages. The thread had been started by the senior Jake beat the crap out of. He wanted to know what the hell was up with the untouchable girl. The explanations ranged from the blunt to the crude, the same thread was present in all of them.

You didn't want Archie, Bubba, Coop, or Jake coming after you. Especially Jake. Though Archie could probably pay someone to destroy his foes. They were merciless and relentless in their protection of Frankie.

You'd have better chances of breathing if you hit on one of their girlfriends than on her.

Cheryl had appeared in the doorway. Fuck, I forgot I was supposed to give her a ride. Frankie glanced from the phone to the door and back again. "They wouldn't. I could walk out there and ask someone right now."

God, the denial hurt me. "Good luck with that. The guys know you're untouchable. No guy is going to risk it and ask you out, so go by yourself or don't go at all."

Looping her arm through Frankie's, Cheryl gave me a look like what was I thinking? I yeah I was thinking I was tired of the damn double standard. "She's not lying. I mean, I know she sounds like a bitch, but Archie and the guys? They made it clear. No one touches you; no one dates you. There was a guy last year who was gonna ask. I'm pretty sure he got a black eye and busted lip from Jake because he'd been looking at your ass when he said he was going to ask you out."

Ahh, Kent. On that one I totally agreed with Jake. Dude was a damn douche. He was all about tapping it and leaving it. Pretty sure at least three girls in our classes had STDs because of him.

"Don't believe us? Try asking out a guy. See what happens."

Always a hugger, Cheryl gave her a quick one. "It's sweet, how they want to look after you." Not in my opinion, but whatever. "Also, Rach, I gotta stay later than I thought so I'll just get Mitch to pick me up after practice."

"Sounds good." Fortunately, Cheryl didn't stick around. Sweet girl. Too sweet sometimes.

Licking her lips slowly, Frankie handed me back my phone. "Why are you telling me this?"

"You need to know."

"Today?" She sniffed and turned but not before she swiped a hand against her eyes. "I needed to know today?"

"Yeah," I said with a sigh. "Today. If I'd told you yesterday it wouldn't be any better and if I waited until tomorrow—it could get worse."

"Right." She shook her head and headed for the door.

"Frankie?"

Without looking back, she paused, "What?"

"I'm sorry."

"No," she said with a snort. "You're not."

"Well, I want to be sorry."

"Yeah well, I want you to be wrong."

I guess we were both doomed to disappointment. She didn't look back as she left and I sighed.

God I hated high school.

DATING & DECISIONS

COOP - SENIOR YEAR

"*C*an I come over tomorrow?" I asked, the sight of Frankie in her underwear had been one thing, but the hurt in her eyes–that had gutted me. It had been a long time since I'd seen her really hurt.

And I don't think I'd ever seen it because of me.

"I have to work," she reminded me. "And I'm busy tomorrow evening."

The words gouged into me like fish hooks dragging at my skin. She always had work. She worked harder than any other person I knew except maybe my mom. At the same time, the rejection in each syllable stung. Especially the last part.

Busy.

Too busy for us.

"We'll see you Monday," Bubba said, clapping a hand on my shoulder and tugging me toward the door. Frankie didn't say a word, just followed us to the back door and once we were out, she locked it.

The snick of the bolt sliding home had never sounded so final.

Dammit.

I blew out a breath as I shook off Bubba. No one said anything. Archie stared at the back door like he had x-ray fucking vision and Jake glared at me the same way.

"What the hell did you do?" he repeated his earlier question in a much lower voice that held a lot of aggravation and, if you knew him, worry.

I shook my head. "Nothing we haven't done a hundred times before." It wasn't even the first time one of us ended up with torn clothes. Granted, it had been a while, but Frankie—what the hell had we fucked up? How had I done it? I was her best friend.

"So now what?" Bubba asked. "You guys planning on setting up camp out here?"

"Gonna grab something to eat and figure out how to fix this," Archie announced. "I'm guessing none of us wants to do the escape room now."

Yeah, that held zero appeal. "Sorry, man, I'll…"

"Don't worry about it, you might have stepped into the crap, but we all waded in after you." Archie slapped me on the back once. "You two coming for food?"

Jake and I locked gazes for a moment and my phone buzzed in my pocket. The only reason I pulled it out was because I hoped it was Frankie. When Laura's name flashed up at me, I scowled. "No. Actually, Jake can I borrow you?"

"Depends," Jake said, almost drily. "You planning on giving me back?"

I rolled my eyes at the quip, but it was hardly the first time either of us uttered that old joke. We parted ways with Archie and Bubba leaving in Archie's Ferrari while I climbed into the passenger seat of Jake's SUV. While he started it up and turned up the air conditioning to dry the sweat from standing around outside, he didn't pull out. We were both staring at Frankie's apartment.

My phone buzzed in my hand.

"Is it her?" Jake asked and I shook my head before showing him the screen.

"What the fuck, man? Is that where you want to go?"

"Actually," I told him. "Yes. I figure I need to break up with her in person."

"I thought you weren't really dating."

I hadn't intended to hook up with her again and I sure as shit hadn't planned to make it anything serious. Laura had been kind of fun in the beginning, but she was a quiet thing. Sad. A little lonely. I liked the idea of supporting and encouraging her. But she'd long since come out of her shell. The last week…no, I let her tears and her neediness tug at me. She was open in a way Frankie had shut down and I wasn't making excuses for myself because fuck that.

But Laura wasn't the girl I wanted.

"We aren't and we shouldn't be." Another text hit my phone. Laura again. What the actual fuck?

"Sounds like desperation, you sure you wanna see her in person?" The hostility bled out of his tone. "Cause the last thing you need is for her to go all nuts on you."

"She won't," I said, then pinched the bridge of my nose. "Just, drive me…" I checked the phone. She was at the mall and wanted to know if I wanted to hook up for a movie or just to hook up.

I grimaced.

"Let's go to the mall."

"Your funeral," Jake commented. Then he fell silent until we pulled into the parking lot at the mall. I'd told Laura to meet me near the northeast exit by the Jenson's. "It's Frankie, right?"

I cut a look at him. "You're not stupid. Don't ask stupid questions."

"Fuck off," Jake retorted, but there was no heat. "Just answer the question."

"It's always been Frankie," I told him. "Same for you." I wasn't kidding myself. It had been the same for all of us. I'd had the unenviable role of watching each of these guys secure themselves a spot in her life. It helped that they were all my friends, too. But I'd have to be blind to not know she was who we all wanted.

We talked about it without talking about it. We danced around the subject like experts navigating a minefield of possibilities. The closest we'd come to a direct conversation had happened in ninth grade when Archie said he planned to date her and wanted to make sure we were all okay with it.

Four months later, he'd admitted defeat. Frankie hung out. Frankie didn't date.

It was a fact we'd all kind of learned to live with because being her friend was totally worth it. More than worth it…

"I'm not doing this past summer again," I told Jake as he pulled up near the doors. Laura exited as soon as she saw us. The smile on her face made me feel like a jackass. "If Frankie wants to date…"

"Then we're dating her," Jake said flatly and I didn't disagree with him. "I get that Archie and Bubba want her, too."

Yeah.

"But she was ours long before they showed up."

I chuckled. "Glad you included me." The humor was fleeting. "I'll be right back."

"Guard your nuts."

Yeah.

Blowing out a breath, I left the SUV and met Laura about halfway. The slant of the sun created these weird shadows and the spot where we stood was in one of the diagonal shadows.

"Hey," she said with a smile and reached up to kiss me. Yeah, I dodged that because no more mixed signals. "I didn't know you were bringing Jake–I know you guys like to…"

"Stop."

We were seriously *not* having that conversation.

She blinked those big ol'doe eyes at me. "What?"

"Look, Laur, you're a great girl…" Was there an easy way to break up with someone? Most of the girls I'd dated had never been long term. They'd always seemed to understand and had been perfectly happy to go back to being friends. Most of them hadn't had Laura's neediness though. And I was the jerk who put her in this position. "I mean that, but…I made a mistake this week."

Her whole expression crumbled and I made myself *not* reach out to comfort her which would be the automatic thing to do. Right now, I needed to communicate clearly that I wasn't interested. And honestly, I wasn't. She'd needed someone to talk to and a shoulder to cry on. The kissing never should have happened.

"I led you on and I get that. But–we're not a thing. We're not going to be a thing." Thank fuck she hadn't brought her friends with her. "We're friends, more acquaintances than anything else. I need you to understand that."

Tears pooled in her eyes and I felt about two inches high.

Then her hand caught the side of my face and that sting burned.

She didn't say a word before she marched back into the mall leaving me rubbing my face.

It could have gone worse, I suppose.

I turned to find Jake watching and the minute our gazes connected, he gave me a questioning thumbs up and I snorted.

Asshole.

Still, I checked my phone before I got back to the SUV and I sent Frankie a text.

If groveling was necessary, I'd do it.

But I was getting my best friend back and if that involved dating, too.

Well, then count me in.

CHANGES AND CHOCOLATES BONUS SCENES

CARING AND CONFLICT

IAN - END OF CHANGES AND CHOCOLATES

As promised, here is your bonus scene for reaching 200 reviews on Changes and Chocolates. Because there was such a pivotal scene at the very end of the book for all of our characters, I decided to rewrite it from Ian's point of view both to take you on the journey of what was going through his head that morning as well as to wish Elisabeth the very happiest of birthdays. She's never given up on Ian. Not once. Please note that if you have not read Rules and Roses or Changes and Chocolates, this bonus scene will contain spoilers.

****

For Elisabeth. Chaos Coordinator. Wonderful friend. Champion cheerleader. Fabulous alpha reader. Sweetest person. Happy birthday. xoxo Heather

Frankie spent most of the first movie curled up next to me. As worried about her as I was, I couldn't help but soak in her presence. The last few days had been hell. The dinner with her mother and Archie's father had only served to shine a light on just how ugly and complicated this whole situation had become.

Even when she shifted to curl up with Coop, her head on

his stomach. Jake started giving her a foot rub and what little oomph she'd had left after her brutal day just melted away. I barely paid attention to the film when so much of my attention lingered on her.

It lingered on the growing sadness in her eyes. The signs of loss as she worried at her lip. The long, deepening sighs as the world around her shifted. Some of those sighs were our fault. Directly. Indirectly. But the blame lay squarely on all of us.

Frankie had never responded to our flirting beyond friendship. Her friendship was worth more than any date I'd ever had. Yet at the same time, we'd *assumed* her lack of interest in directly or indirectly meant she didn't want anyone.

Mistake number one.

Then we set the terms for who could or could not date her. If we couldn't then no one could. As much as I wanted to tell myself it had everything to do with *her* happiness and *her* safety, a part of me couldn't help but feel that it was also very much about our possessiveness. Even if we couldn't be the ones to have her, we wouldn't let her be anyone else's.

She was our girl.

She always had been.

Now?

I cut a look at Archie. He leaned back against the chair, legs stretched out in front of him and his face turned toward the movie but his gaze was a thousand miles away. His father and Frankie's mom. The whole thing was a convoluted and complicated mess. One made more so because Archie had taken the very first opportunity presented to stake his claim.

I *hated* it. Hated the fact I didn't like the idea he'd made that choice for her even if I knew damn good and well, if Frankie had said no, he would have stopped. Yes, jealousy factored into that some and so did envy, but below all of that was an undercurrent of worry.

As excited as I was that she'd suddenly noticed *us*—noticed *me*—I couldn't escape the very real feeling we were going to do her irreparable harm. Look what had happened already? She was getting hell from the girls and that was so fucking on us it wasn't funny. It was also pissing me off that I couldn't do anything about it.

Throw in the complication that Jake had his hat in the ring and her bed and we were going to take far too much advantage of the situation.

Fuck. I rubbed my eyes. The conversation I'd had with my father kept replaying over and over in my head. I needed to not hear him right now. When the movie was over, Coop scooped Frankie up before Jake could and then we were all piling into her room.

They snagged the bed, tucking her in between them, and she was so out she didn't even wake up. Archie and I made good with the floor and one by one their breathing all evened out around me and I was left staring at the ceiling.

Staring at all the possibilities of what could go wrong if we mishandled this situation. Frankie wanted to date. She wanted all the "benefits' of high school we'd been indulging in but she'd somehow missed out on. Dating. Sex. Parties. Fun.

Those words weren't anathema to a girl like her, but they were a cry for help.

A cry I don't think we'd all heard in the same ways. Frankie had drive like no other person I'd ever met. Her focus was unshakeable and her determination unwavering. When you earned her loyalty, she'd have your back to hell and back.

We'd all had her loyalty. We'd had her affection. Hell, we'd had her encouragement, zeal, and passion for what we wanted to do. I had it. She was one of the only people I played for. The only people I let hear my music. More, she was the only person who always encouraged me and seemed far more confident than I was that I could even do it.

Again, a wild benefit to her friendship—an utter and total belief in me that was so intense, it made me believe in myself. What had I given her in return?

Doubt. Loneliness. Exhaustion. And now—terror. Because the girls were going to keep on terrorizing her. They were angry that we'd finally admitted what we felt, but none of them should pretend we hadn't felt this way the whole time.

I'd pretended. I'd tried with Sharon. Really tried, but the fact it took effort at all when being with Frankie was so effortless should have been my first clue.

Fuck.

We were going to fuck this up. We made up those rules, but it wasn't enough. The ride toward loving her was something we'd all been on for years, only the crowded access and the fact she seemed oblivious to our feelings beyond friendship, had kept us in check.

Now?

Now we were all in a race to win her affection and cement our place. It was like some game of immortals. There could be only one. What happened when our jockeying for her attention pulled her apart?

Or worse, what else had we missed all those times we'd shut down other guys looking at her? What would we continue to cost her?

The very idea of hurting her was repulsive. But how were we *not* going to end up hurting her? Sure she could date all of us, but what if she only wanted one? Or worse—what if she ended up wanting none of us?

What if…

What if we all lost her? What if the cost of all of this dating was the destruction of years of friendship. This was the single concern she'd brought up over and over. She didn't want to lose *us*.

Already what made all of us, *us*, was shifting. The very last thing I wanted to see happen was for Frankie to be hurt *ever* again.

More hurt was coming.

Her mother.

The girls.

School.

Now us.

Something had to give.

I didn't sleep all night as I wrestled with what to do. I could talk to the guys but I already knew their responses. Archie wouldn't back off. Not when she'd already welcomed him into her bed and more, they were allying against their parents.

Jake? I loved him like a brother, but he charged ahead nearly as forcefully as Archie and Frankie was his dream come true.

Coop? He'd been here long before the rest of us and I had a feeling long after. That said, he went with the flow and that flow took him to Frankie. Why would he want to challenge that?

By the time I dragged myself out of the room and away from where she slept so soundly between the guys, I'd already admitted to myself that I knew the answer.

I'd known the answer for the last week but I didn't want to admit it. She needed to be protected. She needed to be cherished. She needed to have her *needs* looked after. It would be difficult even for a lover with so much going on, but with a lover in competition with the others? I couldn't afford to let my own possessiveness overwhelm what was good for her.

So if anyone took a step back, it needed to be me. She didn't want to lose our friendships, then I had to fight to preserve them and if that cost me my shot with her but at the same time provided her with a safety net, then that was exactly what I would do.

Even knowing it was the right thing didn't make it the easy one.

I didn't *want* to walk away from her.

I didn't *want* to lose the chance at being the one she picked.

At the same time, she needed us to look after her. Or maybe she just needed me. Fuck if her mother had ever bothered. I kind of understood why Coop hated her now. Still, it didn't make it any easier when Frankie walked out, all rumpled and warm from sleep.

It grew almost impossible when she kissed me and wrapped her arms around me. I wanted so much to just soak her in and keep her there. I could win this race. I had...

No. It didn't matter which of us won, in the end Frankie would be the one to lose and I couldn't do that. Protecting her even if it hurt me was worth it.

Dad—Dad hadn't been wrong when he said Frankie had been damaged by her mother. Probably damaged in ways we couldn't see yet and that we could easily overwhelm her.

Sex didn't always equal love. Sex definitely complicated things.

Didn't mean I didn't want to have it. But right now, I wanted her to have stability more than anything else.

When I left, it wasn't easy and my heart burned with all the things I hadn't said. There'd been confusion in her eyes and I needed to find a way to explain so she would understand. No matter *what* happened between us or didn't, I was *always* going to be here for her.

Period.

The last thing I expected was to say it so badly or miscommunicate in any way. Yet that was exactly what I had done.

The day she officially *broke* up with me because she didn't want the push and pull—it was already too late to repair my mistake.

Didn't make me love her or want to fight for her any less. It just meant now I had a whole new battle to wage.

She was still my angel.

That was a hill I'd die on if necessary.

Maybe she'd forgive me some day.

Maybe then I could forgive myself.

Caring and concern should never hurt the one you loved. That need to protect her just grew even more fierce. More desperate.

We could fix this.

We would.

We had to.

RADIANT & REUNITED

JAKE - SUMMER BEFORE 7TH GRADE

*C*ongratulations on hitting 500 reviews for Changes and *Chocolates* all of you! And in honor of Stephanie Hein-ritz's birthday, I saved this bonus scene just for her. Jake coming back from Germany was a great moment for Coop and Frankie (Jake too) reuniting the three of them once more. It's not a long scene, but it is a fun one.

Summer heat rose in radiant waves from the sidewalk and black-topped roads before it was even ten in the morning. We'd barely gotten our bags unzipped and the new beds set up so Louisa and Becca could get their naps in before I'd asked Mom if I could take my bike over to Frankie's and Coop's apartments.

"You should probably wait another couple of hours," she told me and I stared at her. "They're still at school."

Oh. Right.

Shit.

Thankfully, I didn't spit that last word out. They still had another week of school before summer break here. "I forgot."

"I know, help me unpack the stuff for the kitchen and as soon as school is out, you can ride right over there."

"Yes ma'am."

"Oh, and Jake?" She motioned to the fridge. "Remember I need to go shopping, tomorrow we're going to the junior high. They said you can try out for the football tea—"

I crashed into Mom and hugged her. I half-picked her up. "Thank you!" She'd promised she'd reach out to them to see if there was a chance for me to try out for the junior high team even though it was late into the spring and they'd begin practices over the summer.

Her laughter was a sweet sound, one we didn't get to hear that often anymore. She kissed me on the top of the head and I hustled into the kitchen. A lot of our gear and stuff had been left in storage when we'd gone overseas, so Mom had it delivered the day we came in.

It took me almost the whole two hours to get the full kitchen unpacked. Fortunately, I remembered exactly where Mom liked everything. One thing I could thank the military for, I could pack and unpack in nothing flat. I was already changing my shirt when Mom said school was out. They had to take a bus home so I would have time to make it the mile and a half to their places on my bike.

"You sure you don't want me to drive you?"

"I'm good," I told her. "You don't want to drag the girls out anyway." I kissed her cheek. "Is it cool if I stay there for dinner?"

"As long as you don't invite yourself."

"I won't!"

New keys in my pocket, I was out and on my bike before she could change her mind. It was weird how familiar everything was. We'd been gone almost three years. Almost. But I knew exactly where to go and I picked up speed as I raced along the sidewalks, crossed streets, and then along a back way to where they lived.

I didn't even question that they were still there. They had

to be. Frankie was probably going to punch me in the nose and Coop was going to make fun of me. I caught sight of the yellow bus ahead and kicked up the pace.

Cutting across the grocery store parking lot, I found the little alley that cut right through their back fence into the apartments' parking lot and I skidded to a halt right in front of the back stairs that led up to Frankie's apartment. Ahead of me, at the top of the drive, I caught sight of golden blonde hair as she bounced off the bus.

Coop was right behind her. She pivoted without missing a beat, walking backwards and from the way her hands were moving—she was giving him hell. I dropped the bike and started up the hill. They were about fifteen steps away when Coop's head jerked up, he stared right at me.

"Holy shit—"

Spinning around, Frankie stopped almost as abruptly as Coop did. I grinned at them. How mad was she going to—

I barely had time to finish the thought before she slammed into me at speed. The hug actually knocked me back a step. Man, she'd gotten taller. So had Coop. All arms and legs, Frankie squeezed me. Then she pulled back and wow—the blow caught me right in the cheek and my eyes watered.

"You asshole," she said.

"Yep," I said with a wince. "That's me."

"I missed you."

"Nope, I can pretty much tell you that you didn't." I rubbed my face but she hugged me again and all was forgiven.

"So," Coop said as Frankie checked my face then pulled away again. "We were just arguing about pizza and movies since her mom is working late and my mom is gonna be late cause Trina has scouts tonight."

"Yeah?"

"Yep," Frankie said, then grimaced. "Sorry about the punch."

"Nah, I deserved it."

I really did. I hadn't written them. Not once. I was an asshole.

"You did, but I am still sorry."

I hooked an arm around her shoulders and dragged her to me. "Pizza and movies?"

"Yes!"

She bounced against me and Coop laughed.

"Welcome home," she told me, then gave me a quick kiss to the cheek. "I'm gonna go feed the cats and change. Meet you guys at Coop's!"

Then she was gone, running like we were chasing her. I stared after her for a minute, a stupid grin on my face.

"She's still my girl." Coop informed me.

"I'll get her back," I promised.

He laughed, then punched me in the arm. "Good. She's missed you."

I'd missed them too.

KEYS AND KISSES BONUS SCENES

DRESSES & DEVOTION

COOP - ALTERNATE POV FOR DRESS SHOPPING

ongratulations on reaching 500 reviews with Keys and Kisses. Funnily enough, this is probably the toughest book for me to come up with a bonus scene for, largely because the first five of the series were getting bonus scenes every 100 reviews and because so many seeds were planted in this book that were then paid off later.

So, after some brainstorming, I decided to do something a little fun. Hope you enjoy it. *winks*

****

"You have to try the blue one," Cheryl said. Her too sweet voice was just this side of irritating, but for the most part I tuned her out. My attention was firmly on Frankie. The last place she wanted to be was trying on dresses.

It was almost comical, except she was unhappy. I debated trying to get her out of this. However, as much as she disliked this whole thing, she also craved "normalcy" and what every other high school girl had.

Dates. Dances. Dress-up.

So…if that's what my best friend wanted, then that was what she was damn well going to get. It was also why I was flipping through a rack of dresses trying to picture her in each one and find one that would make her happy.

"Not really my style," Frankie answered, her expression a contrast between dismay and confusion. She really didn't want to be here.

"No, it's perfect. You have a great body and the ruching hides anything you might think you need to hide." A half-snort and laugh later, Cheryl added, "Not that you need to hide anything. Does she, Coop?"

That wasn't even a question. "Nope. She's perfect."

The absolute note of disgust in Frankie's scoff almost made me laugh out loud, but she held the skimpy blue dress up to her chest and faced me. "Really?"

My dick swelled with approval. But this wasn't about making *me* happy. Frankie would look amazing in a paper bag.

And out of one.

Right. Not the time to think with my dick.

I focused on the dress. The blue wasn't bad, except… "Do they have it in green? It would match your eyes better."

The "are you for real?" look in her eyes made me grin.

"But this matches Bubba's eyes, and he may not notice," Cheryl argued, catching Frankie's arm to pull her attention away from me. "Trust me, guys don't notice it consciously when you do it, but their subconscious? It's the perfect prey, it recognizes the colors, and then they're drawn in by the symmetry."

That sounded almost profound coming from Cheryl.

Almost.

"Right color or not, I don't wear skimpy dresses." Frankie glared at her. Well, it wasn't a real glare. I'd seen Frankie's real glares. They'd tear the strip off the concrete if you weren't careful. But she was so disgruntled it was adorable.

"It's not skimpy," Cheryl said in an impatient tone. "Just add it to our rack there."

The rack for their dresses waited, very loaded on one side for Cheryl and with only one for Frankie. A fashion show wasn't what she had in mind. Okay, time to make this a little easier for her, especially since I wasn't sure how much of this was real nerves.

Right, I yanked out the next dress on the rack and with the most straight-faced expression I could manage for the nightmarish dress that looked like a bad recital costume for a dance class, I held it up.

"What do you think of this one?"

"I think you'd look great in that," she deadpanned. It was almost as good as flipping me off.

I grinned as I shoved it back onto the rack.

Cheryl's giggle was nails on a chalkboard though. "Oh, do we get to dress Coop up, too? Why didn't you say so!"

"I'm good," I informed her. The only person I'd let dress me in anything *was* Frankie. This wasn't about me. "Let's focus on Frankie." Ignoring Cheryl, I went to the next outfit I'd uncovered and this one was—sexy as fuck. "But seriously, what about this one?"

It was a two-piece outfit, a lacy high-neck crop top with a satin mini-skirt. It was almost the exact color of her eyes, the perfect green. She'd look *amazing* in this.

"Oh, I like that," Cheryl said. "Find it in blue, too." She immediately dove into the rack next to me. "We may have found your calling, Coop."

I didn't say a word and just got out of her way.

Then she whooped. "Royal blue. This will match Bubba's eyes, right?" She all but thrust the outfit at me.

"How the hell would I know?"

"Hang on, I have a picture, let me check…"

Now I rolled my eyes. When Frankie shot me a look, I made a face until a flicker of her smile returned. Cheryl consulted her phone and tried to match the dress, but I ignored her as Frankie pulled out a lovely gold dress.

Well, I ignored Cheryl until she said, "No, Frankie. You need to work on your tan if you want to go for that. Too cold and pale. It will wash you out."

Ugh, she was cracked. Frankie barely pulled out another dress before Cheryl grabbed it to add to their rack.

"It's like watching a hurricane in action," I commented as I moved to look at the rack she'd been perusing.

"Kind of feels like one. She had a picture of Ian?" The discomfort in her voice was a clarion.

"Yeah." I'd seen the one she'd been looking at. "It's just from one of the parties over the summer." I had no idea when she'd even taken it, to be honest. Pretty sure it was before Ian's birthday but after the fourth.

"Cool."

It was not cool.

"Frankie…" If I lived to be a hundred, I didn't think I could feel more like an ass than I did right now. We'd hurt her and we hadn't even realized we were hurting her.

Now? We were still hurting her.

She was so steadfastly not looking at me, I sighed and looked at the dress she'd pulled out. "That's beautiful. You'd look great in it. 'Course, you'd pretty much look great in anything here." I did a quick scan for Cheryl before leaning in to whisper, "Even the cold and pale colors."

There. The corner of her mouth curved. "Thanks, Coop." She bumped my shoulder, so I hip checked her with equal care.

"Anytime. Want me to go add that to the rack?"

She frowned at the price tag though. Yeah, she didn't have

to buy it to try it on. Right now, I'd sell a kidney to get her what she wanted.

"Come on," I said, bumping her shoulder again. "Try it on. I bet it looks amazing."

"You know what…why not?"

"That's the spirit." I added it to the collection.

By the time Cheryl declared they had enough dresses to begin trying on, poor Frankie looked like she was ready to flee or to collapse.

Maybe both.

"Divide and conquer," Cheryl said. "We walk out in every dress. Coop, you are going to be the tie breaker if we can't agree."

"Oh. Joy. I was about to offer to get you ladies something to drink." Or food. Cause if Frankie was really tired and hungry, Cheryl might actually be in danger.

"Nope." Cheryl pointed me toward the puffy flat square seats. "Park it. You have to give us feedback."

I checked with Frankie, cause really didn't want her starving. "You said this would be fun, remember?"

There was my favorite girl. Reminding me that since I got her into this—at least partially—I was stuck doing it too.

I stuck my tongue out at her and she returned the favor, but then she grinned when we both shot our middle fingers at the same time.

Something akin to relief flooded me. It was the most "grounded" and "normal" she'd managed since everything went sideways the last couple of days. If she needed me here, then right the fuck here was where I'd be.

The next couple of hours were a deceptive exercise in sensual torture and entertainment. Despite her uncertainty, Frankie looked flat out fucking amazing in everything. She looked almost too good in some.

Especially the skimpier ones that made her so uncomfortable and would give way too many people a solid look at her ass and her panties.

Yeah, not a fan of those for public events.

Still, by the time she came out wearing the dress she *loved*, it radiated off of her.

Thank fuck.

Now to get rid of Cheryl and go feed my girl.

RAGE & WRATH

IAN - POST DANCE

The following bonus scene takes place over time both in the hospital and after in the scenes between the end of K&K and the beginning of W&W.

The whole time I sat in the hallway outside of her hospital room, I replayed the scene in my head of walking in on Mitch looming over her. The fact her eyes were so dilated. How limp her hands had been. The fact there was a whimper in her voice. They haunted me through the conversation with the cops, the interview, the questions. It played on a loop when a nurse wanted to look at the bloody wreck of my knuckles.

The scene echoed when I went back to her place to feed the cats and get her a change of clothes. Frankie filled these rooms with her presence, a sweetness and a kind heart that had been so badly treated. It just flooded me with fresh rage at Mitch all over again.

His jaw had broken. I knew that much. Every single time I flexed my bruised knuckles, I could feel the way his jaw cracked when I slammed my fist into it. I wish I'd broken his skull open and then pissed in the hole.

261

The sheer violence threading through my veins each time the *thought* of his name came up was bad enough. Yet, it intensified whenever I caught the flash of the bruises on her face. I couldn't bring myself to go into her room at the hospital. She needed the guys. She needed their steadiness, their devotion, and the fact they had been there for her.

It was my damn fault I hadn't been the official date. I'd tried and failed to communicate what I was trying to do and I had no one else to blame for the situation than myself.

Me.

And Mitch.

As much as I despised her mother for the things she'd done to Frankie, I'd never hated anyone the way I hated Mitch.

If I'd been even five more minutes.

Or worse—I hadn't found them at all.

Homicidal didn't cover it.

Dad spent my whole life stressing how to resolve with my words and not my fists, but right now I didn't have the words to express the depth of my rage that she had gone through this. I told myself that night as the music etched itself into my soul that I had to find the right words. Each note a hard chord that drew blood as it was struck.

It didn't take away the need for vengeance or to hunt him down. Not when Dad counseled me to take a step back. Not when Mom asked me to take a breath and let the law work. It didn't curb the bloody dreams of ripping him apart or from listening to Jake as he detailed how badly he wanted to eviscerate him.

On that subject we were in perfect accord. Yet, the words weren't there. The first night Frankie woke us sobbing, the chords grew heavier and darker. I stared up at the ceiling as Jake held her or Coop comforted her or Archie murmured until she went back to sleep.

Every night, when the dreams came, the notes fell into a bleak riff that ripped my heart open. With every tear, long look into the distance, and dark dream—the notes grew in strength and force. I could hear the song every single waking hour.

The first time I picked up my guitar though, I couldn't play it. I didn't dare let it out. If I did, I might never be able to bottle that rage and the next time I saw Mitch, I'd kill him. Playing the "what if" game was as dangerous as Russian roulette. It didn't stop the notes from coming.

A week.

Seven days.

And it wasn't until she napped in the other room while the guys were at school and I knew she was safe that I played it for the first time.

The full measure of the song. Every single blood-drenched half-note, treble, clef, and sharp. The rage boiled in the music, crackling and popping like kernels of corn in a fire. The eruptions came in a series of violent notes that descended back to something like a baseline of normal.

Rage.

Rage.

Breathe.

Rage again.

She woke the last time I played it, but I put it away when she came out of the room. "Just practicing some-thing," I told her and there was a faint smile on her lips at those words. Later, when she would ask me to play, those notes quieted. They would return when I woke each morning.

Every day, with my pulse as the metronome, I refined the notes. Until I could finally add lyrics to them.

The rage was in the music, the wRath in the lyrics. I never sang it. Not once. Occasionally, I pulled it out and looked at the song sheets, I'd created. It was a rock song filled with pathos. A threat and a promise.

One day, Frankie found the notebook with that song in it. When she asked me what it was, I told her the truth. "Just working out some stuff. Not sure we need to use that one."

"Okay," she said and smiled. Her smile was back. That let me put the notebook away, and keep the song sheets filed. She had her smile again.

But the song sat there, a Pandora's box for my fury. One day, when I was ready, I'd either let it out or I'd burn it.

Today, however, was not that day.

WHISPERS AND WISHES
BONUS SCENES

RIPPED & RACING

JAKE - ALTERNATE POV SCENE

"Shh, we've got you. You're safe." I sat on the edge of the bed, smoothing the hair back from her face as Coop hugged her from behind. The flicker of troubled emotion in her expression never failed to send a fresh surge of anger through my system. If only we were in one of those sci fi or fantasy movies we loved so much. I'd love to slide into her mind and just defeat the bad dreams for her.

But we weren't.

"You got her?" I checked with Coop.

"Yeah." He yawned. We woke him while we were getting ready to go. It had been more impulse than anything else, but the minute Archie brought up running, I was in. I needed to burn off some steam. The last week had left all of us more than a little restless. Frankie didn't need our restlessness on top of her own issues.

So, running it was.

"I got her," Coop continued. "Go do your sickeningly healthy thing."

Whether he had her or not, she'd opened her eyes a couple of times and currently seemed to be staring at me. So

I leaned my head to the side so I could meet her gaze. "Hey, Baby Girl. Go back to sleep. It's still early."

"Where are you going?" The barest hint of a pout decorated her words.

I sighed, more for effect than anything else. "Arch, Bubba, and I are going running."

"Why?" The absolute disgust she filled that single word with made me laugh. Frankie had never been fond of "regular exercise." She just liked to do things that were athletic.

"Because they're getting lazy," Archie answered. Dick. "And I haven't gone running all week. Coop's here, and we'll be back in a couple of hours."

"With donuts," Bubba tacked on.

She made a face and it took everything I had not to laugh at her. "Want to go?"

"No." Zero hesitation or prevarication. Instead she just burrowed back against Coop.

"Go back to sleep, Baby Girl." I couldn't contain all of my chuckle as I kissed her forehead. After, I made way for Archie and even Bubba to give her a kiss as well. Look at that, he was working his way back in, one step at a time.

It didn't take long to feed the cats or give Coop shit for calling us pussy-whipped. I mean, we were and I was fucking proud of it, but he got to stay in bed with our girl so he could have a little more shut the fuck up.

Outside, Archie put in his bluetooth headphones and even Bubba did, but I skipped that. I didn't want music. I wanted to just—*run*. The one thing about the guys, they didn't spend a lot of time "warming" up. We just started out slow, then picked up speed.

Not even five minutes from the apartment and the wild tug to go back and check on her went taut. She was safe, I reminded myself. She was with Coop. We weren't that far away. It took me picking up speed and reciting that to myself mentally a few times to keep from turning back.

More than once, I caught sight of Archie glancing back and so did Bubba. Yeah, I wasn't the only one questioning our choices. But she needed time without all of us hovering and if I didn't get at least some of this edge off—well there was a real chance I'd pick a fight with the guys and none of them deserved it.

Anger management annoyed the fuck out of me. But it had helped Bubba and me come to one conclusion, the last place our anger needed to be was around her. So, running it was. We hit the first mile in almost no time and headed for the second. By the time we hit the third, the inexorable pull to go back had slacked. It wasn't gone, but it wasn't ripping at my insides.

If anything, Bubba pushed to pass me and that drove me to go faster. Archie had zero trouble keeping up with us. It was easy to forget that he ran constantly. He got up earlier than most to run every day and we didn't see him doing it, so we didn't think about it.

I was more winded than normal and Bubba's face was ruddy with sweat. You could definitely feel our lack of working out this week. But even as oxygen burned in my lungs and my muscles protested until they heated up, there was an edge of euphoria creeping in.

The runner's high. We were there by mile five and we rode it all the way through the next forty minutes until we were cooling down on our way back. Slower than our usual pace, but fuck that felt good. Not that seeing the apartment didn't add to that internal sense of glee.

More than ready to be back with her, I was up the steps and unlocking the back door before the others could get up there. Frankie and Coop were both in the kitchen, but more… Frankie was glowing and there was a real smile on her face.

The apartment also smelled like sex. Not overpowering and the stench of our own sweat would probably blot that out in no time. But I didn't even care that it wasn't me. In fact, I was fucking glad it was Coop. Not that I'd tell him that, but I was really fucking happy to see that smile on her face.

Beyond fucking happy.

TEASERS & THREATS

COOP - DELETED SCENE

"Nope, I think Jake is just the right touch. And it's a quick conversation. We'll be right back. Not going to lay a finger on him." The promise cost me nothing to make. Amusingly enough, Frankie didn't buy my crap for an instant. If anything, she smiled at us and rolled her eyes without rolling her eyes. We weren't fooling her.

Then again, I wasn't really trying to fool her.

"Hmm-hmm," Frankie said. "I've heard that before." Then… "Just remember, if Sis likes him, you have to be careful."

"So does he," I reminded her. This wasn't our first rodeo. It was one of the first for me to have to deal with some little punk eyeing my sister. I'd had plenty of practice with the guys who used to check out Frankie.

She gave it a beat, then nodded. "Well, go get 'em."

"Like I said," I spread my hands. "It's just a conversation."

She chuckled and shook her head, but shifted in the chair to watch us, and emotion fisted tight in my chest. Not only did she not try to stop us, she offered her support. I bet if I asked, she'd help me threaten the guy. Not that I'd ask.

Or that I would threaten him.

No, threatening him was why *Jake* was going with me.

He had zero issues delivering threats he could not only back up, but had already paid interest on in the past. His reputation gave us a leg up.

"This is going to be fun," Jake admitted as we headed right for the little shit.

I snorted. "Not as fun as this morning."

This morning had been amazing. Irritation flamed through me at the fact that I had to go and deal with Auburn when I'd rather be back at the table with Frankie.

Check that, I'd rather be back at Frankie's place with her. I hadn't expected to find her right on the cusp of orgasm when I opened my eyes, but I sure as hell wasn't sorry about it. And it had been everything I thought it might be and more as Jake took her apart.

Fuck. I was already half-hard. Mood souring rapidly because the little jerk had decided to hit on my sister, which meant I had to do this rather than be where I wanted to be, I stalked forward.

Jake hummed as he strolled along next to me. The kids at the table spotted us coming. Two of them were freshmen, and they paled. They also abandoned their buddy without even a gesture from me or Jake. I tapped the kid on the shoulder sitting to Noah's right.

The arrogant expression on his face faded as he looked from me to Jake. Then he muttered, "I gotta go be somewhere…"

He left, and the kid on the other side of Noah wasted no time following him. Jake hadn't even had to ask.

Biting back a smirk, I dropped down into the first kid's spot, and Jake bracketed Noah on his other side. With a dismissive look across the table, Jake said, "Go away."

The other kids scrambled, and that left us with Noah. He

started to stand, but we clamped a hand each down on him and kept him in place. All friendly-like, Jake slung an arm over his shoulder as I turned half-sideways so I could study his expression.

Noah wasn't a bad looking kid. A little bit on the scrawny side. He didn't do sports, but that wasn't a crime. I didn't do them either. He did smell like a fucking ashtray though. "So…" Jake said, opening the conversation. "How you doing?"

Sliding a look from me to Jake, Noah cleared his throat. "I'm…fine. I think."

"You think?" I mused aloud. "You having trouble figuring out the answer to that one? It's pretty binary. Yes and no."

The kid swallowed convulsively, and his Adam's apple bobbed. Jake grinned wider and gave Noah a little squeeze. "So, either you are fine or you're not. What's it going to be?"

"I was fine before you sat down," Noah admitted. Then he slanted a look at me. "Am I going to be fine when you get up?"

I didn't smile. Damn good answer though. Look at that, the kid scratched out a point. "Undecided," was how I answered him, and he paled a little.

"My friend tells me you've been giving cigarettes to his little sister." Jake leaned in and took an audible sniff. "Not that I needed the update. Here's a tip—you stink."

"I smoke."

"No shit, Sherlock," I retorted in a dry tone. "Only the nose blind wouldn't notice."

"And…your sister's Trina, right?" Noah squinted at me, uncertainty etched into every facial contortion. The kid really didn't know whether to piss his pants or try to bluff his way out of this one.

Okay, so he wasn't stupid because he took the mid-line. That might scratch him out another point.

"Yep," Jake answered for me. "She's just turned fourteen."

"She's cute," Noah admitted. "Funny, too."

"Fourteen," I repeated. "You're what?"

He swallowed. "I'll be sixteen next month."

So almost two years. Still, a long way between sixteen and fourteen.

"And how many dates have you been on, Auburn?" Jake asked.

"Um...a couple. Maybe three." The uncertainty stampeded its way through his features again.

"Three dates. Same girl? Different girl?" I pinned him with a look, but I tried to keep my features pleasant. No glaring.

The kid was already sweating, and it looked like he had some acne along his potential beard line. I said potential because if this kid had to shave every day, I'd wax my balls.

I wasn't waxing my balls.

"Why is that important?" His lower lip firmed from the trembling, and he lifted his chin.

"Noah," Jake said, all friendly like and gave his shoulders a firm squeeze. "We ask the questions. You answer them. That's how this works."

"Look...Trina's cute, okay? Just—cute. She hangs out. I like her. Asked her to go to the movies."

"Still not an answer to the earlier question." I propped my chin against my fist and studied him. The kid really had lost all the color under his tan and looked like he wanted to puke.

"Fine. Three different girls. Not really good at the dating thing." Then he tried to smirk, but it looked more sick than amused. "Maybe I should get a couple of my buds to go in on the dating with me. Maybe that would make it work."

I didn't say a word. Jake's grip slid to the back of Noah's neck, and the pressure had to be unbearable because tears sparked in his eyes.

"Let me be very clear," Jake said in a low, deadly voice.

"You say shit like that again, and I'll do more than just get friendly with you. I'll introduce you to the table. At speed. Do you understand?"

"Yes," he choked out. "I was just kidding."

"I wasn't," Jake told him. "You want to ask Trina out on a date, there will be rules and you will follow them to the absolute letter, or you will piss me off."

"You really wouldn't like him when he's pissed off," I commented, and reached over to pluck one of the mini-muffins out of the bag the kid had been eating.

"Okay," Noah said.

"Good, rule number one," Jake said. "Stop fucking smoking around her."

"Just stop smoking," I told him. "You really smell like shit, and I'm going to have to wash these clothes just from being next to you." I didn't want to imagine what Jake's shirt would smell like.

Noah swallowed.

"Rule number two," Jake continued. "You keep your hands to your fucking self. Any body part you touch her with is subject to me ripping it off and beating you with it."

I didn't think the kid could pale any further, but damn, was he going to pass out?

"Rule number three," I added. "She's my sister. You treat her with respect and if you're dating her, she's the only one you're dating, and if you can't hack more than one date, you don't ask. She's not there for you to create notches. Clear?"

"Crystal."

Noah slid his gaze from me to Jake, then back.

"Anything else?"

I considered it and met Jake's gaze. "Yeah," I said as though I really needed to think about it. "Don't ever make another crack about Frankie again."

Jake murmured something to him, and Noah gave a full

body shudder. Then he said, "We're good now, right? We understand each other?"

"Yes," Noah pushed out in a shaky voice.

"Great," I told him with a grin and clapped his shoulder before I grabbed the rest of his mini-muffins and stood. "Good chat. Trina asked me to double-date with you. Looking forward to it."

I swore the kid shrank.

Jake snorted, then rose and glanced at the kid's apple. "You mind if I have this? No? Thanks." He winked, then took a bite of it as we walked away. I didn't look back. Not when the kid's chair fell over or when the sound of his shoes slapping against the floors echoed back to us.

Even with distance between us, I could still smell the cigarette smoke. Ugh. I offered Jake a muffin. He chuckled, and across the cafeteria, I met Frankie's amused look as she shook her head. Archie said something, and she laughed.

That was better.

"That felt good," Jake admitted.

I snorted. "Tell me how it feels when it's Becca getting asked out."

His amused look vanished, and he scowled. "She doesn't get to date until she's twenty-one."

I laughed and clapped him on the shoulder. "Keep telling yourself that."

"Asshole."

We were still chuckling when we got back to the table.

"All done?" Frankie asked.

"Yep," Jake said. "Good chat."

I nodded. "Definitely." Then held out the bag to her. "Muffin?"

LOVE & LACE

ARCHIE - ALTERNATE POV SCENE

*a*s birthdays went I'd never particularly looked forward to mine as much as I had this year. Frankie dating all of us—well three of us at the moment, though Bubba looked to be improving his chances—and after the disaster of Homecoming, it was more important to me than ever to share tonight with her.

Yes, we would have lots of other nights. But those rare nights where she was just mine were something I would treasure. I could share, I would share, and I loved that she was happy but I also liked being a little selfish, too.

The fact Rachel had popped around to help her with her make-up and hair amused me. Dinner with Grandpa probably wasn't high on Frankie's list of dinner dates for my birthday, but spending it with her and Grandpa? The only thing that would make it better was Nana being there.

Also, Frankie had a rule—what the birthday boy wanted, he got.

By the time she emerged, she looked like a million dollars. While I loved seeing her all dressed up, she was just as beautiful in a pair of cut off shorts and a tank top as she was in a silk dress. My favorite was nothing at all, but I didn't relish sharing that view with anyone besides the people currently present.

Even Rachel got a pass.

Sort of.

Coop was a dick laying a kiss on her after he pinned her to a wall and removed nearly all of her lipstick. The fact he'd made sure to get a lot of fun pics of Frankie and me together with him only photo bombing one or two helped alleviate the need to punch him.

I added the shots to my locked folder of Frankie images. I'd started the collection not long after we met and it wasn't about creeping. I'd even had a couple printed and framed in my room—it was for way more than spank bank material. Far more. Nana had all these huge photo albums and when I was younger, she would pull them out and go through them.

"Why?" I'd asked. We didn't know hardly any of the people in those pictures. Well, I didn't. Even the ones of Edward as a kid didn't really register as being my father.

"Because, they're memories. They're my memories and every one of these pictures reminds me of a moment and they make me happy."

"Like the one of baby me on the mantle?" She had a picture of me from each year I'd been alive. Several in fact, but the infant picture taken just minutes after I'd been born when I was red-faced and screaming was her favorite. She had it in a frame with a lace doily around the edges. She said it was a handkerchief, but it looked like a doily.

Anyway, she said it was her favorite because it was the moment I came into her life. That would be one she would always treasure. The handkerchief held her tears of joy. I thought it was kind of hokey, but I wouldn't argue with Nana for anything in the world.

Until I saved that first picture of Frankie, I hadn't quite

understood what she'd meant. Now I did. Every single picture I had of her also held a story, a moment in time, a slice of emotion. Even when we'd been *only* friends—she was someone I would always treasure and I never wanted to forget a single instant.

The minute Frankie returned, I led her to the backdoor and called, "Don't wait up for us, I might not bring her back until tomorrow." In fact, I had zero intention of bringing her back before the next day.

We had a suite booked at a hotel and we were going to have it all to ourselves. I was going to get to spoil my girl in style.

Once we were in the car though, Frankie put a hand on my arm. The thrill that went through me at the contact never got old. Seriously. There were times when she stunned me now almost as much as she had that first day I met her.

"Before we go, can I give you your presents here?" The offer sent a pulse straight to cock.

Hell, even before I'd buried my face in her pussy and had her pulse around my dick as she came, it would have. Now? Well, now my dick and I both knew what we'd love our present to be.

"Right here?" I said, trying to ignore my rapidly stiffening cock. She'd also just finished fixing her lipstick. Course, she could leave a ring of that around my dick—I wouldn't argue. "Cause the seats aren't the best for it, but I'm totally game to try."

"Not that and not here, perv." She rolled her eyes and I just grinned. Playful Frankie was amazing. I adored the fact that just because we were dating didn't mean I got a free pass. It was a hell of a lot more fun to have to earn it anyway.

"Damn. Though after the other night, you're really going to need to work it to match that as a present. I still get hard thinking about it."

A hot flush crept up her neck and flooded her face. It just added to her beauty and made me want her more if that was possible. "Archie. Let me give you your present."

"Fine." I sighed and mimed zipping my lips. Birthday boy might get what the birthday boy wanted, but I'd give it over to Frankie every damn time.

"Thank you." She pulled out her phone. "Do you mind if I pair this with your car?"

Like I'd tell her no. It took me no time to get her phone paired with the sound system. Curiosity was like a restless beast in my system, it wanted to unwrap the present and devour her right there.

"Have I mentioned how hot I find it that you're giving this moment a soundtrack?" I grinned at her and she wrinkled her adorable nose. Yeah, yeah, I was supposed to be quiet.

"Hush."

Obedience was not my strong suit. Leaning back in the seat, I eased the pressure on my dick and moved him over a little in my pants leg. Excitement or nervousness or maybe both seemed to shimmer over her skin. The first notes began to play through the speakers and I nudged the sound up a bit. I was way more rock and roll, but I assumed she had a point here.

Then a voice joined the piano music.

Frankie's voice.

"The first step was the hardest one. You walked in and I invited you to sit and talk. I smiled at you and you joined in. You were a stranger then you were a friend."

Holy shit, she recorded a song for my present.

"The second step was harder still. You wanted me and I was blind. Whispers and wishes, so many misses. Dancing. Playing. Laughing. Crying. You were the one who wanted to take my dreams flying."

My heart pounded so hard, it threatened to drown out the music and I didn't want to miss a note. I took her hand. No wonder she'd been nervous. She didn't think she could sing...

"The third step and we fell off. My whispers became shouts and my wishes so many doubts. You were there every step of the way and when I tumbled you had to have your say."

Sitting forward, I locked my gaze on hers. The leap of her pulse under my fingertips before I caressed her cheek told me that it had definitely been nerves. She was terrified and embarrassed and she'd—she'd recorded this for me.

"But here we are, crash and burn, rise and fall, song and singer, friends and lovers..." The last word trailed off. *"If I have my way, this is where we'll stay but I want your whispers and your wishes every day."*

The music rose again and then trailed off.

"Happy birthday, Archie. I always want your wishes to come true. So whisper them or shout them, but this song? It's just for you."

As it ended and she bit her lip, I lunged forward and kissed her. Every ounce of emotion she'd poured into that song flooded me and I was desperate to share it with her. She clung to me as I thrust my tongue against hers. Everything I asked for she gave and gave and gave.

"God, I love you," I admitted between one pause for breath before kissing her again. I didn't need oxygen. I needed Frankie. I'd loved her for so long.

Truly loved her.

The words were right there and the easiest declaration I'd ever made. This was another moment I planned to never forget and I was keeping that song.

And I was keeping her.

Forever.

HANGOVERS AND HOLIDAYS
BONUS SCENES

TURTLENECKS & TEASING

JAKE - SKIING

So, here's a quick look at the Ski Lessons from Jake's PoV and why he and Archie decided to take over with Frankie.

THE SKY WAS VIVID BLUE, THE AIR CRISP, AND THE SNOW fantastic. From the moment Archie mentioned this trip, I'd been dying to get out on the slopes. Okay, I'd been dying to be with Frankie *and* get out on the slopes. First things first, get Coop and Frankie a ski lesson. "You guys don't have to stay," Frankie said, grinning. She looked *fan-fucking-tastic* in the red ski clothes. Honestly, she looked good in them and even better out of them, but I was definitely enjoying the view.

"We're fine, Babe," Archie told her. "Besides, we want to be here."

Coop smirked at us. "Right, you just want to *hang* out." Yeah, he got it. We wanted the time with her. Besides, I also wanted a good look at the instructor to make sure he had some clue of what he or she was doing. No one was risking my baby girl.

I resisted the urge to flip him off. Jerkface should appreciate the fact we were looking out for him too.

"Hey there—I'm looking for Coop and Frankie?" At the sound of the guy's voice, I pivoted to see the college guy staring at my girl with a hint of pleasure in his eyes.

Oh. Fuck. No.

"I'm Frankie," she said, taking his hand as he offered it. "This is Coop."

Coop just lifted his chin in hello. Okay the guy shook her hand super brief and she had her gloves on. We could do this.

"Great. Neither of you have skied before?" He double-checked then glanced down at their booted feet. "Okay, we'll start with the skis and go from there." He gave Frankie a fucking once over.

Bubba gripped my shoulder.

"Right, let's get you both outfitted." He shot us a grin. "You boys joining us?"

"Oh, we'll be following," Archie told him. "Lead the way."

Good plan, get him going first. Instead, he fell into step with Frankie as he took her over to the ski hut. The whole time he got them kitted up, I glared.

"Dude, you've got serial killer eyes," Bubba told me.

"I'm keeping an eye on our girl." And on the guy who was right on her there walking her through putting her skis on and off. Frankie wasn't an idiot. Nor was Coop. But he repeatedly walked them through locking the skis on and getting them off—including using their ski poles to trigger the release.

We headed out together and he walked them through putting their skis on and then went over the basics. I kept my arms folded and my gaze pinned on him as he explained wedging and turns. They walked up the half little bump—at the base of the bunny slope and to the side—put on their skis and then had them ski down.

"It's all about momentum. Downhill skiing means gravity does a lot of the work, but you also have to control your descent. Wedge, wedge… that's better." After a few passes at that, he directed them over to the rope pull to head up to the top of the slope. Frankie shot us a nervous look and I summoned a smile.

That died right about the time the asshole—*Josh*—skied up to her where she struggled with the rope and braced her as he gripped the rope and up they went.

"Did he just…"

"He sure the fuck did."

"Guys," Bubba said. "Take it easy, she was having trouble. He just helped her."

That was fine. I dropped my skis into the snow and stepped into them. Archie was doing the same, Mister Handsy needed to keep them to himself. If she needed help on the rope pull that would be us. Frankie and Coop came flying down the hill. Coop had the wedge but Frankie nearly crashed. I winced for her, but she was laughing.

Before we could get to her, Josh was there giving her hand. "Okay, beautiful, I can tell you what you did wrong. Can you?"

She grinned. "I thought I was wedging, but I couldn't angle them right."

"You just have to engage your ass and there's gonna be a pull down your thighs and you shift your weight to the outside of your feet as you angle the ski tips together. Don't cross them."

He stood right behind her, hands on her hips as he urged her to lean in a little.

"And I'm done," I said bluntly as I headed over.

"Me too." Archie was right behind me. Bubba, it should be noted, didn't object.

"Tell you what, *Josh,*" I began as I reached them. "You focus on Coop and Arch and I will take over with Frankie."

She blinked at me with a frown. "Guys, I didn't do *that* bad."

"You didn't do bad at all, Babe," Archie assured her but Josh took a hot minute to get his hands off her hips. He backed off, hands raised. He better back the fuck off. He should retreat to the other side of the damn mountain.

"Come on, Baby Girl. You get two skill teachers for the cost of one." I grinned at her, but she just rolled her eyes.

"I can get this wedging thing down."

"You absolutely can," I assured her and Archie and I got her moving back to the rope pull. I helped her go up this time and she glanced at me.

"Are you mad?"

"Nope," I promised. I wasn't. Not anymore.

"You look kind of mad."

I grinned. "See? Not mad."

"Uh huh."

Arch and I spent the next few minutes taking turns with her. Wedging took a couple of passes. Experience was the best instructor. Way better than Josh and his wandering eyes and hands. If he looked at her ass one more time...

"Woot! I did it." Pleasure flooded Frankie's voice and I shot a look over to find her holding her arms up. Fuck, I missed it.

"Okay, let's do it again," I said and tried to put *Josh* out of my mind. I wasn't missing another thing with my girl. Mr. Turtleneck was way too preppy. I bet we could strangle him and that turtleneck would hide it all.

"You're growling," Frankie said as I braced and gripped the rope tow to get us up there. She kept struggling.

Arch, Bubba, and I took turns helping her. Josh wasn't putting his hands on her again. Not unless he wanted me to rip them off.

"You're hawt," I retorted. "Makes me hungry." Then I growled against her ear and she burst out laughing.

There we go. Much better.

GUYS & GAMES

FRANKIE - HOLIDAYS AT THE CABIN

The best part of vacation is the games we play.

MAKING UP OUR OWN RULES TO PLAY THE VARIOUS BOARD games had been hilarious. We'd done everything from strip poker to kiss trivia—I was pretty sure my lips were a little bruised from Jake's earlier winning streak at the trivia game.

"Why are we playing this one?" I asked as I looked at the stack of question cards they'd put in front of me. Also, I wasn't gonna comment on the "Frankie Trivia" game that Archie had added to the back of every "card."

"Cause it's fun," Ian said with a slow smile. "And some people can't decide whose turn it is to sleep with you so we're wagering on it."

Laughter bubbled up through me. "Maybe I should get to pick and we don't sleep in my bed, I come sleep in one of yours."

That got me more than one interested look, but Coop just

winked. "Nah, this is more fun. I mean we all know you'd pick me cause I'm your favorite."

Giggling, I enjoyed the pair of pillows that winged right at Coop. He managed to catch Jake's but Archie's smacked him upside the head. Not even missing a beat, Coop settled both pillows next to him.

"Mine now."

"Right," Archie said. "For that, you get skipped in the first round."

"Seconded," Jake said with a smirk and Ian hid a laugh.

Coop flipped them both off. "Like I said, I don't need to 'win' her affections, I've already got them."

I reached for my coffee and took a sip as they mock-glared at each other. "Speaking of which," Ian said, raising his voice just enough to talk over them. "Who is going first?"

"If we go by age, it's Jake for youngest," Archie suggested. "Or you for oldest."

Before this could devolve into wrestling or more, I raised two fingers. "Why don't I just go first with asking the questions and you guys get to write down the answer? Then reveal it at the same time."

"That's ridiculously fair, Babe," Archie said with a slow grin. "You sure I can't bribe you into something more slanted in my favor."

"Nope," I teased and he laughed.

"Fine," he gave a mock sigh and then they were passing out the little whiteboards Archie had found in the game closet. Grandpa Ted had stocked this place well. I glanced around the cabin, I almost hated the idea that we would have to leave it at some point soon.

I loved it here.

The fire crackled in the hearth and the scent of pine from the tree just added to the overall effect. Touching my tongue to my teeth, I flipped over the first question and giggled.

Coop's handwriting. No wonder he was certain he had an edge.

"What is my love language?" My face warmed as I read the question. It had nothing on the scorching heat in their eyes.

One by one, they flipped their answers.

Archie's just said, "Coffee."

I burst out laughing.

Coop's read, "Acts of service."

Ian had written, "Patience and forgiveness."

Jake wrote, "Your huge ass heart."

"Technically," Coop retorted, "We all said the same thing."

"Archie said coffee," Jake argued.

"Which is an act of service for our lovely girl here."

I couldn't help it but laugh. "You all get a point. Next question…"

There was grumbling but they erased their boards in prep. I caught the twinkle in Ian's eyes. I got the feeling he was enjoying the grumbling as much as I was.

"What is the most romantic thing I have ever done for you?" The flush on my face went to my neck on this one, but I was also curious as hell.

They flipped their boards at the same time. Every single one said the same thing.

"Forgave me."

Now I was going to cry.

"Ah," Archie said as he leaned forward. "No tears. It was romantic as fuck—the second most romantic thing you ever did was say yes to a date. I'd say that was first, but it took a while to get you to notice we were asking."

I sniffled, my tears fading some into a weepy laugh. "Fine, everyone gets a point. This is a terrible game."

"I like it," Jake said, nudging my leg. "You need to hear things like this more often."

I stuck my tongue out at them but their expressions remained indulgent. "At this rate, we're all five going to be sleeping in the same bed."

"Told you, I'd win," Coop said, his grin firm and smug.

"Next question." I blinked at this one then re-read it. The handwriting was definitely Archie's and his grin spread. He had to know. Such an ass.

Adorable ass, but still.

"What is my favorite food?"

Groans and laughter greeted the question. They answered with varying forms of coffee, chocolate, coffee and chocolate. Coop added "me" to his and I laughed so hard, he gave himself an extra point.

There were another five or six questions and the guys were neck and neck. Arguably, even when their answers were different, they weren't wrong. I had a feeling this was not going to solve our" who was sleeping in my bed tonight" conundrum and I didn't mind it.

Maybe we could all camp out down here again.

"Last question," I said because we were on the last card. "What is my favorite memory of our relationship so far?"

The briefest of hesitations as the guys glanced at each other. "Individually or as a group?" Archie asked.

As one, Coop and Jake said, "Group."

They nodded then started writing. I took another drink of my coffee as I watched the four of them, the fire warming the room, their faces flushed from laughter and their eyes bright.

I didn't doubt their answers, but right now? This was my favorite moment. My favorite memory.

My favorite guys.

BRAZEN AND BREATHLESS
BONUS SCENES

DRUNK & DISORDERLY

JAKE - ALTERNATE POV

*T*his bonus scene features Jake's alternate PoV from a scene within Brazen and Breathless when he and Frankie arrive home to find Coop drunk.

"Okay," Frankie murmured, the compassion in her voice the kind of warm hug everyone needed when shit went sideways. "Can you drink some water for us? And maybe let me clean up your knuckles?"

He glanced at his hand and then shrugged, but he didn't let go of her face. While Frankie didn't flinch, Coop's grip tightened enough to press into her cheeks. "Hands don't even hurt. Why are parents so bad at parenting? Mom is great. Mom's been a damn saint. So much makes sense now, and I don't know why I didn't see it. But fuck me, I wish I didn't see it now."

"Hey, bud," I said, bumping his arm, and he eased up his tight hold on her cheeks. "Water, man. Before you puke all over Frankie then have to look her in the eye later."

Frankie shot me a look. It wasn't like it hadn't happened before. Granted, not our proudest moment but...

"Dude, you puked on her the first time you got shit-faced," Coop said with a snicker, but he took the glass of water from me, and I braced his shoulder and kept a hand on the glass so he didn't slosh it around. Gradually, he slumped back on the sofa. "You remember that, Frankie? Threw up all over your shirt and your shoes. First time I saw you with tits for real. I mean, we'd seen them before, kind of knew they were there, but you had on that pretty pink bra."

Shoulders shaking, I was hard-pressed *not* to laugh. "Do we tell him?"

Frankie shook her head. "Leave him alone. I want to know what happened."

"His dad, apparently." I raked a hand through my hair. Dads were just not good news around any of us it would seem.

"Course, then I threw up on you," Coop said, his voice almost mournful. "And you said you threw that pretty pink bra away, and I felt bad."

"It's okay," she murmured. "Really, there was no getting burrito and beer stains out of it."

"Fuck, why do you even kiss us when we did shit like that?" Coop groaned.

"And there he goes." I had a hard time containing my laughter. But in the great grand scheme of things, the memories we shared were worth a hell of a lot more than one stained, pink bra. "Dude, don't remind her, or she might not want to kiss us."

Then again, it had been a beautiful pink bra.

Not as pretty as the girl wearing it but…not much was.

Four Years Earlier

Drunk didn't begin to cover it. We'd known Archie what —a week now? This asshole lived in an honest to god mansion. He had a driver bring him to school and he lived in a mansion. Not only that, he had free run of the place and the liquor cabinet.

"Not the hard liquors, Mr. Archie," his butler—who the fuck had a butler?—informed us. "That cabinet shall remain locked. You may however, using restraint, visit the beer and wine fridges."

Beer *and* wine fridge.

Frankie elbowed me so hard in the gut, I oofed and I caught her give me a hard look. I mouthed 'what?' I mean, I'd been minding my manners since we arrived at Castle Standish. The only thing the place was missing was a fucking moat.

"Stop glaring at Archie," she whispered without moving her lips at all. "It's rude."

"I'm not glaring," I whispered back at her, then curved an arm around her shoulders so I could press my lips closer to her ear and hide my mouth with her hair. The last thing I needed was the rich little shit getting any ideas.

"You are," she muttered, but didn't pull away. The fact the rich little shit in question glared at me when I hugged Frankie made me want to hug her more. Dude needed to get a grip. He was late to this party.

"Am not," I countered in mature fashion. "You're not the boss of us."

Her inelegant snort pulled Bubba's and Coop's attention in our direction. Coop crossed his eyes and reached over to snag Frankie's hand. I had to let her go or risk choking her when he tugged.

"We got it, Jere," Archie was saying. "Thanks, seriously. Did you guys want to swim or hit the game room?"

"I didn't bring a suit," Frankie said and Archie laughed.

"We got lots of suits you can borrow…" But her face shut him up. "Tell you what, let's split the difference! Jere, we're gonna use the game system in the pool house. You mind setting us up with snacks out there?"

Not waiting for the response, Archie led the way outside

and around the *giant* fucking swimming pool. They had a hot tub because of course they did and I caught Coop gaping as much as Frankie had accused me of. Only, she wasn't yelling at him. She did make a little face as Archie pushed open the double wide french doors to the pool house.

"Wow," she said slowly and turned around in a circle. We'd all come pretty much straight from school. The plan was to hang out and spend the night. We'd had to do some wrangling and since Frankie's mom didn't know Archie's parents yet, she told her mom they were crashing at my place and my mom was away with the girls this weekend at some dance thing and I was supposed to be at Coop's place.

It coordinated well. Since our moms didn't talk that much these days, we'd probably be safe. Frankie set her bookbag down by the sofa inside the pool house room and my need to stare stuttered completely at the huge screen on the wall and the gaming systems.

Never one to feel uncomfortable for long, Coop leapt over the sofa and landed on it with a bounce. "What are we playing first?"

Just like that, arguments erupted over what we'd play and Archie settled it with a whistle. "Ladies first," he offered with a sly grin at Frankie. Coop groaned and so did I.

There was only one game Frankie chose first.

"What?" Archie asked, but Frankie pinched Coop and he laughed as Bubba made room for Frankie to sit between him and Coop.

"I want to play Mario Kart," she said at the exact same time we said, "She wants to play Mario Kart."

"Done."

Man, he'd learn.

The next two hours were fucking hilarious as we plowed through the races and tried to sabotage each other. It was hard to do five player, someone always had to rotate out, so we made the lowest score drop each time. It seemed fair and we were all so damn competitive it changed often. Not Archie though, he got in nearly every game.

Well, so did I.

Frankie stayed in far more than she fell out though neither Coop or Bubba seemed to mind. Pizza arrived and we fell on that like ravening beasts, cleaning out the two larges in record time and we were still hungry.

"Tacos?" Archie offered.

"Hmm, quesadillas," Frankie said as she reached for a controller.

"Burritos," Coop and I chose and Bubba went for tacos with Archie. Though when this spread arrived, there were literally trays of everything.

It was getting dark when we broke out the beer and gave it a shot. It wasn't too bad. Ice cold it was actually really nice. We'd switched to a first person shooter which was hilariously harder than it should have been. I was damn good at these games. Frankie was kind of scary accurate at them.

Archie kept the beer coming, and twice I finished Frankie's for her because her nose would wrinkle up if it got warm at all. I wasn't sure when Coop caught on to what I was doing cause he snaked her next half-full one when it was room temperature.

Ass.

I had to take a leak bad, but the warm haze enveloping me coupled with the fact I'd finally gotten to sit right next to Frankie made me not want to get up. Move your meat and lose your seat.

The game perspective switched and I had to squint to stay focused because fuck it was like we were drunk waddling through this level. Then Archie took me out. Asshole. But Frankie squealed with laughter. Oh, he got her too—but she threw a grenade and Coop whooped because they died at the same time and Coop won by default.

"Champion!" he shouted and we were all laughing.

Frankie pushed up to stand and glanced at me with flushed cheeks. "Come on stinky boy," she ordered and held out her hands to me.

"What?"

"No more bean burritos for you."

I did a test sniff. "Wasn't me. Had to have been Coop."

"I don't care which of you did it, you're gagging me."

I opened my mouth to protest that and vomited all down her shirt.

Nobody moved.

Oh shit.

"Frankie…"

"S'okay," she said, holding up a hand like this happened all the time. "Just—someone get me a towel and a bucket." She sounded like she'd stopped up her nose and was breathing through her mouth.

Oh fuck. I was a dick. "I'm sorry…"

"I got this." She stripped out of the shirt with care and this time my gaping was real. Because beneath the oversized shirt she'd been wearing was the prettiest pink lace bra covering the prettiest tits I'd ever seen.

I mean. Yeah, Frankie had tits but…fuck me, Frankie had *tits*.

Half my drunk seemed to pass out from the hot wind blowing through me.

"Wow," Coop said, echoing my internal dialogue. "Look at that…you have lace on your nips."

Then he threw up on her as Archie lunged across the room and Bubba covered his face. It was like slow motion destruction.

I clapped a hand over my mouth because I didn't want to join the puke fest but seriously, it was such a pretty bra.

And now it was pretty spectacularly ruined.

Fuck my life.

I was still thinking about that bra the next morning when I was hungover and ready to die. Frankie kept telling us to not worry about it, but holy shit. I'd always known she was a girl. Always known I liked her.

But now...now all I could see was that pretty pink bra and if I hadn't puked on her first, I'd have punched Coop for ruining it.

Even more when I saw the bra in the trash.

We were the worst friends ever.

Could we buy her a new bra? Would that be weird?

Now

"Shut up," Frankie told me and stuck her tongue at me. I winked. Fuck I loved her. She had lots of pretty bras now, but she still had the prettiest fucking tits I'd ever seen. "I kiss you because you brush your teeth. You also held my hair back when I got puking drunk. You guys were doing all kinds of things for me with my broken wrist, including helping me in the bathroom."

And we'd do it all again, no question or hesitation.

"Why do you kiss me when you've had to do that?"

"'Cause you're fucking beautiful," Coop answered promptly. Good boy. "Inside and out."

Yes, she was.

And she was ours.

Just as long as we kept the bean burritos to a minimum.

Pretty sure we got the best end of that deal.

HEARSAY & HICKEYS

RACHEL - ALTERNATE POV SCENE

"Speaking of pig farms, I have a new series for you to read. You are going to *love* it. But you'll probably call me a liar and a fake, because you'll hate it first." Laughter escaped me because of all the series I could recommend, this one was definitely just—wow. Frankie would figure it out. I had money on Jake being jealous of at least one of the characters.

Maybe more than one. I flicked a look to where Coop and the guys had gone. He'd been...yeah. I liked him most of the time. A fact I didn't share often, but he was a pretty decent guy and rolled with everything.

What a shit thing to discover about one of your parents. Then again...what was family for but making your life miserable?

"Sign me up," Frankie said. "I could use a new series with someone else's drama."

"Girl, let me tell you, they have *drama*." Behind her head, I locked gazes with Archie. His dark brown eyes held a lot of anger, and more than a little malice. That expression also said he was planning something. I just raised my eyebrows.

Count me in, I more or less said with just a lift of a chin. He narrowed his eyes for a split second, then nodded with a half-smile. He would and he appreciated the offer.

Look at us being all diplomatic and shit.

Instead of wandering off, I continued into the cafeteria with Archie and Frankie. Sometimes, their dynamic was a little claustrophobic for me. They were all so focused on her and that's where my focus was too. But the push and pull they often showed when I was around seemed absent.

And for once, I didn't want to just nut punch the whole lot of them. I paused to consider that, maybe we were learning to get along better.

When Archie pulled out a chair for me, I almost smirked. But you know, if we were gonna continue this armistice, I would keep any and all scathing comments to myself for now. The coffee and the welcome should be appreciated.

We'd barely taken our seats before Jake focused on me. "So, who's the new girl?"

Shots fired, Benton? "Excuse you?"

"Unless you're dipping your toe in the XY gene pool, there's a new girl." He motioned with his coffee cup toward my neck.

"Jake." Warning lingered in Frankie's tone.

Unrepentant, he winked at her and pressed on. "Hey, she'd be the first one asking us if we showed up with fresh hickeys like that."

"I don't *give* you hickeys like that." That warning climbed a notch. Oh, Benton. Take a good look at the land beneath your feet before you decide to tease me.

"You're making his point for him, babe," Archie said with a slow smile, and even Coop laughed.

"Not really," I informed the smug little shits as I thumbed the screen of my phone to unlock it. "What she's saying is that if you showed up like that, I'd be gutting you because she doesn't leave hickeys like that."

They marked her up. Not the other way around. Sharon and the bitch squad, however, loved to mark their territory. I'd be removing testicles with spoons if I caught sight of hickeys.

There was a particularly sweet and juicy moment where all four of them paused. Finally, Coop lifted his coffee cup and said, "Touché, Your Majesty. Touché."

I just grinned and returned my attention to catching up on who was doing who on social media. The boys kept their gazes and their conversation off my hickeys. I also resisted the urge to check them. I thought I'd used cover up on all of them.

Oh well, I'd swing by the bathroom before class. A message popped up inviting me out again later tonight. I considered it a moment before flicking a look to where Frankie murmured to Coop and he seemed to relax against her.

Sure, I answered the invitation. I could go for another night of experimentation. I caught Archie's speculative look and this time I did smirk. He just shook his head but he could hide the soft laugh.

Suck it up Standish, neither of us are going anywhere. He just raised his coffee cup and I took a sip of mine before Frankie pulled my attention back to her. Man, hanging out with them in the morning could get addictive.

PATERNITY & PREROGATIVES

JEREMY - DELETED SCENE

*T*he door slamming just after the sound of tires squealing to a halt that surely painted black stripes of rubber on the drive alerted me to young master Archie's mood before he burst into the kitchen. The day before had been Valentine's and he had plans with Miss Frankie.

Plans that seemed to have not gone well.

"Mr. Archie," I greeted him calmly before turning on the kettle. I hadn't planned on tea, but the act of making it would give me something to focus on while we sorted out the latest twist in the path of romantic travails Mr. Archie had experienced since he'd finally admitted his feelings for Miss Frankie *to* Miss Frankie.

"Jere…I need your help."

Four words he rarely ever spoke. I pivoted to face him. "Tell me." It allowed me a great inspection of his state from the disheveled hair to the wrinkled shirt he'd probably slept in if he hadn't just dragged it back on after leaving it on the floor all night. The sleeves were rolled up and he was missing a coat. Though somehow I doubted that bothered him.

If we were in some mad farcical comedy, I believed steam might legitimately pour out of his ears.

"Your mother or your father?"

He clenched both fists and his teeth ground together. Definitely one of them. Ms. Muriel was in New York, she'd moved the bulk of her things from the house and what she'd left behind I'd packed and had stored. The cold snap between mother and son showed no signs of warming.

His relationship with Mr. Edward was far worse and had grown increasingly frosty over the last year to the point that they seemed to exist either in the middle of volcanic dispute or a Siberian wasteland of contact.

"Fucking Edward told Frankie that he's her father." The words exploded out of him, each one fired like a bullet from a gun. Of all the issues I could have imagined bringing him to this state…

"I'm sorry," I said slowly. "Could you repeat that?"

"Sounds unfuckingbelievable, right? But no—apparently he and Maddy have been tight for years and he managed to knock her up while Muriel was knocked up. That whole, they had to get married for me thing broke up an epic love story for the ages."

The sarcasm dripping from his tone threatened to stain the tile.

"She looks nothing like him." That was my first thought, but Archie just stared at me.

"Jere—the bastard cornered her last night and told her she was his daughter. She's completely devastated and has no idea what to believe because if it's true…"

"If," I said sternly. "That's a very large if, Mr. Archie and, personally, I do not see it. Mr. Edward may believe he is her father, but without actual proof…"

"There are paternity tests."

"Tests as in multiple?"

"Shocking that her mother wasn't sure, right?"

"Not shocking so much as suspect." I turned the idea over. My job was to look after Mr. Archie, the home and the family generally in that order. It wasn't on me to judge any of them their choices or weigh in on their personal affairs. "If she suspected Mr. Edward was the father, I find it improbable she would have waited this long."

Archie groaned and scrubbed a hand over his face before he slumped down onto one of the stools. "Apparently she told him months ago. They were going to spring this on Frankie last September. I've never been so fucking glad I butted in where I wasn't wanted."

The fact he'd taken a seat was a good sign. He was thinking again. I resumed pouring the hot water into a pot then gathered the loose leaf tea into a ball that I could set inside the water before closing the lid for it to steep.

"How conclusive were the tests?"

"They clearly list one of the four as her father, but instead of names, there are only ID numbers."

Of course. Privacy laws and such.

"Then we'll make arrangements to do our own tests."

"She's not my sister, Jere," Archie said but it held far more of a question and hope than it did of determination and conviction.

"Agreed," I said, then poured the tea into each cup. Despite his preference coffee, the last thing Mr. Archie needed right now was more caffeine. This blend was more soothing than pick me up. After adding a touch of honey and lemon, I stirred it before sliding the cup across to him.

"Tests are going to take time...and I'd really rather not deal with Edward if I don't have to. I'll probably hit him." He picked up the cup then added, "Again."

"We don't need Mr. Edward for the tests. You and Miss Frankie can submit DNA samples and we can send it to a vetted laboratory where discreet tests can be made. Then you'll have your proof."

"Muriel can confirm some of this bullshit."

"She could," I agreed with him. "But do you really feel the need to take on this battle on two fronts?"

Because this was a war he'd been caught between for so long, I rather suspected he didn't know how to not fight it.

"I need answers." He sipped the tea and then wrinkled his nose as he looked at it, but he took another swallow. "I deserve them and so does she."

"Then we will get those answers. Calm down, shower, change your clothes. I'll make some calls…"

"I want to go to New York. She's there right?"

"I'll take care of it."

The front door opened and Mr. Archie glanced over his shoulder. "That would be…"

"Yo," Mr. Jake's voice carried. "You drive like a fucking maniac man, do not break every speed law in the city just to get here."

"I don't drive like an old man," Mr. Archie corrected and then, at my look of reproval, he mouthed "sorry." "Come have tea with Jere, I'm gonna grab a shower. Then we can do some digging here while Jere books a flight for me."

Mr. Jake walked into the kitchen and paused. "Where are we going?"

I smiled and nodded to the young man. I wouldn't torture him with tea, but I could start the coffee. This late in the day I doubted either would sleep and they would want a flight in sooner rather than later.

Once I took care of that, I would reach out to Mr. Wittaker. We would disentangle this messy knot. Mr. Archie needed Miss Frankie. The agony in his eyes left me angry with Mr. Edward. While it was not my place to judge or to interfere in their personal matters, I was quite certain, like

Mr. Archie, I might find myself compelled to punch the man if I were to see him.

Mr. Archie, after all, came first in the list of my duties and it was my prerogative to look after him. If that mean dealing with Mr. Edward, then I would very much handle that matter as well.

TRIALS AND TIARAS BONUS SCENES

ATTACHED & ADORING

ARCHIE - ALTERNATE POV

*F*ucking Frankie gave me life. From the first kiss she let me give her to just now, sucking my tongue and every ounce of breath from me as I fucked her against the wall. I lived to be right here. The feeling of that sweet pussy pulsing around my cock and all of my bones turning to liquid as I filled her up.

Yeah, this was life.

I traced my tongue over her pulse point, lapping at the salty sweetness of her skin. The smell of sex wreathed her. Wreathed us. Cum smeared my thighs, but she was full of it. Full of me.

Need flared to life all over again, even as my dick began to soften, I kept myself firm against her. I wasn't leaving her body until the very last second. In fact, I wanted to move in. This pussy was my pussy.

A laugh escaped her, the convulsing of her inner muscles flexing around me made me groan. Goddamn, it was heaven and hell, but I was slipping free. Fine. Just needed to get a little harder and we'd fuck right back in there.

Frankie needed to come a few more times today. It was

my personal mission in life. Right now, my only mission in life, to put a smile on her face and keep it there. No more tears for our girl.

None.

Then her laughter turned into the giggles and I dragged my head up to see what had her attention. Coop sat there staring at us with a boner and a grin.

"Hey," Coop said. "Good day?"

I glanced back at Frankie then up at the ceiling. Sharing meant sometimes the other guys were around, and while I could share her…didn't always mean I liked it. But there was no denying the gleam in Frankie's eyes and the pleasure in her flushed face.

I searched for resentment, irritation, or even just—impatience. None of it existed. It was Coop. He made Frankie happy. He was a damn good friend.

"You know, I don't even fucking care." She needed to hear that from me. It was the truth. I really didn't fucking care. Let Coop watch. I kissed her again and then added, "It's a damn good day."

Behind me, Coop let out a chortle of glee. "Good to know."

"Hey," Frankie said as I set her down slowly. I swore there was an imprint on my body as much as my soul from how tightly pressed together we had been. Would be again.

Oh, definitely again.

"Hey, beautiful," Coop answered. "Feeling good?"

"I feel amazing…and a little sweaty. I also need to go suck Archie off if he'll let me."

My cock gave a hard pulse and twitch at that declaration. She still had my cum in her and running down her legs and she wanted me to come down her throat?

Sign. Me. The. Fuck. Up.

"And if you want to wait with that," she continued in a voice drenched in sex. "I'll totally take care of you too."

Okay. That was fucking hot. She wanted me first, then him.

"I can wait," Coop offered. Magnanimous of him. I just grinned. Her kiss swollen lips were going to look so fucking good wrapped around my dick.

"Where do you want me, babe?"

"Right here is good," she said as she pushed me against the wall next to the kitchen. We'd barely even made it out of there. When she went to her knees, I swore mine wanted to give out but my cock was already straining. Her eyes held a thousand questions and all the love in the world.

All the love I would never need.

Was this okay with me? Her sucking me off while she let Coop get an eyeful of her bare ass and dripping...

Fuck, yes this was okay with me.

It was heaven and hell. Every touch had me jerking, from the smooth strokes of her tongue to the warm softness of her hands. But I just let go and rode the ecstasy as she took me deeper and deeper.

You'd think I'd last longer, but fuck this was Frankie.

My babe.

My heart.

She wanted me and when she stroked my thighs to let me thrust, I fucked into her mouth and kept my gaze on her the whole time.

Best.

Fucking.

Feeling.

Especially when her lips spread into a dazzling grin and a drop of cum clung to the corner of her mouth.

I needed a picture of that. And her pussy.

Hmm...

Coop cleared his throat and I glanced at him. Really?

"So…is it too soon to ask about how you did that thing with your hips?"

That thing with my…

Laughter swelled up inside of me. "Trade secret," I told him as I dragged Frankie up and then kissed her. I liked that she tasted of me. I like that she was going to go over there and suck him off, soaked in me. "But I could be convinced to tell you…"

The last I directed at Frankie and her eyes lit up.

"Let him convince you to convince me, Babe," I whispered. "Make him work hard at it."

Then I pressed a kiss behind her ear before I added, "I want to hear you scream until your eyes roll back in your head and your pussy spasms in a cascade of orgasms. If he gets you there, I want to slide inside you and feel you as I fuck you."

"That will convince you?" she asked, pure and delicious devilment in her eyes.

"It's a start."

She licked her lips, then trailed her fingers down my chest. "I like this plan."

Me too, Babe. Fuck, me too.

I liked it enough that I let myself enjoy the sway of those hips as she sauntered over to the sofa and the way her swollen pussy lips pushed out when she bent over just before going to her knees.

Yeah.

I was really invested in this plan.

FOOLS & FIXATION

EDDIE - UNSEEN CHAPTER

"*Too little too late, old man. As for Frankie, you don't need to have anything to do with her life. You're not her sperm donor.*"

The moment the door closed behind the kids, I stared at Maddy. The day she walked back into my life, I'd counted it as the happiest. A second chance. A real chance to make up for the fools we'd been when *we* were the kids.

"*Every word that comes out of your mouth is a lie. Every story you've ever told me. Every piece of garbage you try to sell about the life you lead or the life we lead has been a lie. I'm tired of it.*"

Her mutinous expression. The stubborn tilt of her chin. The way her eyes could flash from fire to ice then back to fire. They all captivated me. I loved the fight in her. The refusal to bow to her parents wishes. She'd held strong when I'd caved.

"*She was supposed to be yours.*"

The agony cutting through me might have echoed what she experienced all those years ago. But when I slept with Muriel, I hadn't intended to get her pregnant. I hadn't even thought about it. A careless decision one careless night. I'd wanted to hide from my own pain and maybe inflict some back for what Maddy had done to me. Once again, here we were, slashing and cutting at each other. I'd promised Archie I would handle this.

Handle her.

"Will you now? Like you've been handling everything else so well. She played you. She has been playing you, and she used her daughter to manipulate you."

"Eddie…"

"Don't."

I kept my hands in my pockets as I turned away from her. If I took them out, I worried I might throttle her. The vindication in Archie's eyes—I deserved it. I deserved every ounce of his scorn and disdain. Just like I deserved Frankie's. I'd wanted to be her father so badly. I'd wanted it because it meant…

"Eddie…" She was right behind me sliding her arms around me. "You have to believe me."

"Don't."

Her hands stilled against me. I gave it to the count of three. She didn't disappoint as she shoved away from me. "You believe them. Of course you do. You believe anyone that isn't me whether your father is demanding you marry that slut…"

It never changed. From sweet to sour then back to sweet and Archie was right. She played me. I let her vent, but I wasn't listening anymore. One part of me desperately wanted to fix this for her. To make right the years I'd taken away because I'd let my need for power and control—no, I'd let my *fear* make the decision for me. For us.

That was the day I'd lost her.

"You're not even listening to me." The snap in her tone and the viciousness beneath it all scraped against my skin. When confronted by a snarling dog, I needed to remind myself that it was about self preservation. Maddy *always* attacked when she thought she was on the cusp of losing.

"I should have seen it." Each word cut the inside of my mouth like so many slivers of glass. "I should have known the moment you spoke to her like that at dinner—"

"Like what? Like she's an ungrateful…"

"Shut up, Maddy," I exhaled the words because I'd been a fool. A fool for so damn long. "Don't disparage her that way. She certainly doesn't deserve it."

"Oh, so you're still taking her side," Maddy challenged, folding her arms as she glared at me. Yes, direct that attack at me. Come at me. "Even if she isn't *yours* when she should have been?"

"Of course I'm taking *their* side. You made me complicit in the pain they've both been put through and I might have been a shit father…something my own has been trying to drum into my head for years and now I see it. That it took me so fucking long is on me. But this…what we did to them because you wanted to punish me and own me at the same time?"

I could wrap my hands around her neck and squeeze. I could literally see myself doing it and yet I couldn't. For all her flaws and as twisted as it was, I loved her. I'd always loved her.

There was no way I could let this one go.

Not now. Not when I'd finally seen past my own misery and selfishness. I'd lost so much with my son. Pissed it away.

"I didn't do a damn thing that didn't need to be done." She raised her chin as if daring me to deny it. "Frankie *should* have been your child. That should have been *our* life."

"It was going to be," I told her. "But you weaponized sex to punish me. You wanted what you wanted, when you wanted it. Once upon a time, you were worth it. Even if I took a lover every time you did. I never wanted them the way I wanted you. I would have given them all up—just to have you. But there isn't a loyal bone in your body and I'm not your lapdog. Not anymore. I ruined a marriage, stole years from Muriel and Archie? I'll never be able to give him back what should have been his. Fine—I accept that, that's on me."

"Well, good for you. I'm sure Muriel will be so eager to take you back from my bed…" She sauntered toward me all sex appeal and desire. My cock hardened at her nearness. Still, I caught her wrists before she could touch me and surprise burst through the cloud of seduction she wore like second skin. "Eddie…"

"Don't. The apartment is yours. You can keep it. The car as well. I'll make sure everything is in your name and I'll add a tidy sum to cover your expenses until you find another job." She'd quit hers and I'd agreed at the time. She was a brilliant marketing executive, but leaving her job meant she'd been with me full time and I'd been the stupid, selfish bastard who craved that. "Your credentials here will be revoked. Don't call me. Don't text me. Don't look for me."

"Eddie…"

"You heard me. You and me? We're done." It was like cutting my own heart out with a spoon. I should have scooped it out long before the cancer devoured it.

"But—we're partners. What about us?"

"There is no us. There's never been an us. I was just—too blinded to see it. I wanted to see you—my beautiful Madeleine. The gorgeous girl who took my virginity and introduced me to a world of pleasure. The girl I wanted to marry five minutes after we said hello. That girl has held me in her sway for decades. The problem is…that girl died a long time ago. Frankie is everything I thought you were, the way she looks at Archie? It was how I'd always wanted you to look at me. But seeing what they have? It's a burning light on what we don't."

Releasing her wrists, I took a step back as she gaped me.

"Get out of my office, out of my building, and out of my life. Don't come back."

Her hand flew through the air and I took the full brunt of her open palmed smack. "You can't just abandon me."

The discussion was over, so I just stared at her a beat before I walked over to the phone and lifted the handset. Two buttons gave me security. "I need you to escort Ms. Curtis from the building and revoke her security clearance."

Now tears welled in her eyes as if right on cue. "Eddie... please don't do this. I..."

I tuned her out, arms folded, I waited. She went from sobs to shrieking and back again by the time security walked into the conference room. I watched with as much dispassion as I could muster, but it was all a front. I could still hear her strident tone in the elevator as the doors closed.

Alone, finally, I pulled out the chair and sank down in it. The DNA tests were still on the table. Regret was the bitterest of companions. I'd wanted Frankie to be my daughter so I could make up for all the ways I'd failed Archie.

Dragging my phone out, I stared at the blank screen a moment, then paged through the photos. There were dozens of Archie on there. As a baby, a toddler, even a precocious child when he'd already mastered that disdainful coolness he held for me. A six year old should not ever have had to feel that.

I failed him in so many ways.

Never again.

Then I did the one thing I'd never expected to do again, I called my father. We had been on bad terms for years but after Mother died, it was like the chasm between us turned into a frozen tundra. That was my fault, too.

"Eddie?" Dad answered. The surprise in his voice was so profound it drove home my own selfishness.

"Dad." I hadn't really called him that in years. Father if I was pushed, Ted at most business meetings, then nothing at all if I could help it. "I screwed up. I've been screwing up for a long time." I pinched the bridge of my nose to try and drive back the pain throbbing so deep in my soul it echoed everywhere. My heart broke a long time ago, but today it finally admitted that it would never heal. Not the same way. "I'm sorry."

A long sigh greeted my words. "Eddie, it's going to be alright," my father said in a gentle tone I didn't deserve. "Where are you?"

"The office—in Texas." Because we really did have offices everywhere.

"I can be there in a couple of hours. Or you can come and meet me."

"After everything I've done?" After how badly I'd messed things up and kept messing them up?

"You're my son," he said, as straightforward and simple as breathing. "You'll always be my son. That's what family is. A chance at forgiveness even if we don't think we deserve it. Now—are you coming to me or am I coming to you?"

"I'll come to you. I need to get away and break some ties here…"

I didn't have to explain, but I needed to. I needed to explore the depth of my own stupidity. Dad said nothing throughout the whole thing and at the end, he said, "Then we'll take care of it. Now come home."

SLUGGISH & SCRAPBOOKS

FRANKIE - BEING SICK SUCKS

I hated being sick. Not a little bit hated, but actually loathed. Worse, I hated sleeping all the time and feeling groggy. Though if I wasn't sleeping and hot, my nose was running and tickling and making me crazy. The night before in the bathroom, I stared at my red nose, swollen eyes and made a face. Archie slid up behind me and tucked his chin on my shoulder.

"If yew caw me bewtifuw like this, I'mma sneeze on yew." The stuffy nose left my voice all kinds of thick and spoiled words with mashed consonants.

He kissed my nape. "I'll survive, besides, I was going to say adorable."

I'd made another face and then just leaned back into him. I was so tired. "I thwow something at yew tomowwow."

Bless him, he didn't laugh in my face.

Despite Jeremy's threats, he also didn't leave me to sleep alone and anytime I woke up needing something, Archie got it. Ian was there, first thing in the morning, with Jeremy and breakfast. Then Jeremy shooed them out for school.

I'd had texts from Jake and Coop as well as Rachel. I

managed a shower which pretty much sapped all my energy, so I didn't argue with Jeremy when he gave me medicine, checked my temperature and insisted I drink all of the hot tea he'd made me.

Hot tea with a heavy dose of whiskey and honey, holy crap, but it helped and I was asleep until just after lunch. I woke up to a huge bowl of soup, crusty bread that was still warm from the oven and more water. Jeremy fussed.

No one ever fussed over me.

Jeremy fussed.

The guys had after Homecoming, but this was different.

He even moved me over to Archie's desk to eat while he stripped and changed the bed.

"You don't have to do all this," I said for like the hundredth time and Jeremy gave me a mild look before pointedly staring at my food. So far, I hadn't won a single argument. After he stripped the bed and remade it with fresh sheets, he vanished and then returned, there were fresh pillows, a pitcher with water, a clean glass and even some throat lozenges and... "Jeremy..."

He paused and glanced at me.

"How did you get so awesome?"

"Well, yours is not the first cold I've had to tend to, Miss Frankie."

I smiled at that. "Sorry, I'm being so difficult."

"Oh, you are not remotely as difficult as you might believe." His chuckle was real. "I'm going to make you some more tea. Finish all that up, then leave it and get back in bed."

With a sigh, I debated arguing that point but settled for... "Do you know where my backpack is?"

"Yes," Jeremy said. "You don't need it." Then he was gone and I stared at the closed door, mouth open, more than a little shocked.

He'd meant it, too. I was back in bed by the time he returned with my tea.

"I could work on…"

"Getting better. You're going to work on resting." He set my tea next to the bed, then turned the television on. "The history channels are pre-programmed in, but you can also watch any of the movies we have in the digital library. If there's something you want and it's not there, let me know and I'll get it added. Drink your tea. I'll be back up to check on you in a couple of hours." He didn't slow as he gathered my lunch plates. "Also, if you need me before then, just press one on the phone there next to the bed, it will ring the kitchen."

It will ring the kitchen. Then he was gone.

That night, the guys all teased me when I tried to complain but even then I couldn't complain. Not really, Jeremy was being sweet. On the second day, I was already at the desk when he came up with lunch. I'd managed another shower and I hadn't had the energy to blow dry my hair so I was resting up for that task.

"And how are we feeling?"

"A little antsy," I admitted. The guys had been texting me on and off all morning and I'd nearly made my way through a full rewatch of *Lord of the Rings*. I loved the extended editions. I figured I could knock out the third movie after lunch if I didn't sleep.

"Hmm." He left my lunch and changed the bedsheets out then remade it before disappearing to get my tea. The amount of whiskey he put in it lessened each time and while it was *different*, I wasn't complaining. I had actually felt better after each dose.

When he came back he had a tray with a teapot, cups, a couple of books stacked on it and I grinned. Was I getting to do some homework after all…

With a knowing look, he set the tray down. The books were not textbooks at all. But he didn't pull them out, taking the time to pour the tea and preparing it before he moved a chair over and took a seat next to the bed.

Lifting the first book, he set it on the bed between us and then flipped it open and I swore my heart did a backflip of its own.

Baby Archie stared up from one of the photos on the page. I'd recognize those eyes anywhere. He looked pissed.

"Why is he so mad?"

"Because he had mastered the baby gates and figured out how to free himself from his crib by sliding open the bottom, then letting himself out of the room. He'd cheerfully stripped off his diaper and pee'd a path down the hall along one of the Persian rugs."

I jerked my head to find Jeremy smiling fondly.

"He was always very clever."

"I bet…but why is he mad?"

"Because I reversed everything and it took him another two months to figure out that he could still open the bottom if he went to the other side, but he couldn't reach the locks on the gates."

I giggled. That was hilarious.

"And here…" Jeremy touched the next page, Archie was dressed in a sailor suit. God, the cuteness was killing me. "We had to attend a function at a country club and Miss Muriel insisted on the outfit, this is the only picture we have of it before he figured out how to upend an entire bowl of punch."

That picture was on the next page.

For the next hour, Jeremy entertained me with tales of Archie's escapades as a child. Precocious didn't begin to cover it. The pictures often included anecdotes that he'd written down about Archie and the events that happened.

There was even one of him with a red nose, swollen eyes, and looking like hell. He also had the surliest scowl on his face.

"As I was telling you, you're far from the worst patient I've had to take care of…"

The note next to the picture read: *When young men don't listen and go out even when they have a fever. They not only lose privileges, they get to suffer longer.*

"Sometimes, when he's ill, I trot these out for him so he remembers to listen."

I grinned. "I'm almost afraid to ask…"

"Do I have a photo of you in a similar state? Well, we shall find out if you decide to be difficult again. Now. This book I'll leave you to enjoy on your own. Then you should get some more rest. You're looking better today. I'd say at least another day of rest and good medicine and you'll be bouncing back."

"Thanks Jeremy."

After he left, I flipped open the next book and grinned. This scrapbook was all of us. Jeremy had made notations about us in the margins just as he had about Archie. Including the fact that we were good kids and good for him.

I was still holding the book when Archie got home and woke me as he eased out from my fingers. "Hey," I said with a yawn and he settled onto the side of the bed and chuckled.

"Go back to sleep, I didn't mean to wake you up."

"It's okay, I've had a lot of sleep today."

He glanced at the book before setting it on the nightstand. "And someone busted out the photo albums. Please tell me he didn't get out the baby pictures."

I grinned and Archie groaned but when he laid down next to me I curled up against him. "You were adorable."

"I'm still adorable," he corrected, but chuckled. "Jeremy must really like you. He doesn't get them out for everyone."

That much I figured. Still… "He wanted to show me I wasn't his worst patient."

That got a real laugh. "Sorry, babe. I'm afraid that honor is definitely all mine."

I tilted my head back and smiled up at him. "Well, the next time you're sick, be ready to be spoiled rotten."

"Will you play nurse for me and wear a sexy little number?" He wagged his eyebrows suggestively and it was my turn to groan. "I mean, if you're feeling up to it…the doctor is in and I could totally give you a check up."

A throat clearing at the doorway had me blushing so hard, I was sure my face went neon.

"You're a killjoy, Jere."

"So, I've been told. Dinner will be ready in an hour and Miss Frankie is due for another dose of medication. I can assure the doctor that checking her out is unnecessary."

Yep.

This is where I was going to die.

Right here.

I hid my face against Archie's chest and he rubbed my back. "Fine, I'll behave."

"Well," Jeremy said as he left the room. "There's a first time for everything."

I snickered then coughed. Then laughed a little harder as Archie's shoulders shook and he dragged me up to sit with him and curl against his side. He held over the meds and the water, then turned on the television.

"The doctor will check on you tonight," he murmured against my ear. "Promise."

I was still grinning when Jeremy brought up dinner and gave us both a look before he headed out.

Nope, not going there, just gonna watch the show.

And the doctor definitely came to call later.

GRADUATION AND GIFTS
BONUS SCENES

COCKS & CREATIVITY

COOP - DELETED SCENE

*R*e-reading the instructions, I scratched at my chin. The silicone mold didn't seem so bad. All I had to do was get it hard, shape the softened and warm silicone around it, let it set and then peel it off. Afterward, I could work on getting the customized dildo made.

On the computer screen were a list of different piercing types. The one that had started this whole line of investigation had already been crossed off as no way in hell was I doing that to my dick. Not even for Frankie.

Well, okay maybe for her if she really wanted it but she didn't so fuck that noise.

That left me with a few other options. After double-checking the door was locked, I finished getting everything set up. The warmer was basically a glorified wax heater, but I'd bought all the different pieces and just had it shipped in rather than talk to Jeremy or Archie about it.

One, I didn't need that kind of grief. Two, that was a conversation I would never have with the guys if I could avoid it much less Jeremy.

Just nope.

Fortunately, Rachel had proved to be a fount of knowledge on the subject. And, she could keep a secret. Something else to be applauded. Warmer going, I glanced down at my dick and sighed.

"Okay buddy, you and me got some work to do." We'd gotten as familiar with my hand as we used to be and neither of us were impressed with the return of this blast from the past. Frankie's pussy was a lot warmer, fuck loads softer, and damn, the sound of her gasps when I first pushed in were enough to give a man life.

My dick twitched at the possibility. Missing her was like missing a limb. We talked almost every day or at least texted. Not the fucking same.

Also watching her go down on Jake over video chat was hot, but the pops and blurs when the signal decided to fuck up could leave me with some awkward, and frankly disturbing frozen screen images that I was *never* telling Frankie about.

Yeah, that wasn't doing a damn thing for my dick.

I checked the timer, the silicone would be ready in about five minutes. So five minutes to get my dick on board with the plan. A plan that was going to be epic, my dick just had to get that picture. Standing in my bathroom where I'd plugged the silicone in, I went ahead and stripped the rest of the way down, pulled on the gloves I'd need, added a little oil—not a lot, just enough so the silicone didn't stick to the skin then began a slow massage.

With my free hand, I lifted the phone and let out a sigh. It'd been two weeks since we'd left Frankie and Jake to go to Germany while we returned to the states. Two long weeks. I unlocked the private files and then hit play on the recording of Ian and Frankie that Jake had made when he'd also called us so we could listen.

To be fair, we'd told Frankie and after she got over being

embarrassed, she made us play it where she could hear—that lasted for exactly ten seconds and then she said we could keep it and hidden her face.

It was as sexy as it was adorable. But the first audible cry of hers sent a pulse straight to my dick. Fuck. In no time at all, I was so hard, my balls ached from it and I had to hang onto that erection and soak it in silicone.

The first layer of warm silicone was almost nice but still wasn't Frankie. Just the images her sounds made on that recording were enough to keep me there. Once I my dick was sheathed fully, I let out a breath and then stripped off the gloves and started the timer.

I was so jerking off as soon as this was over.

Then I took a picture of my dick painted up in the blue silicone because at some point, Frankie was going to need the laugh. Grinning, I waited patiently and skimmed through our cloud account of pictures from summer vacation. I was glad Archie added another layer of security to some of these because they were positively illegal and I fucking loved how happy and serene she appeared.

When the timer rang, I blew out breath. Thank fuck. Peel it off, hop in the shower and rub one out before I finished washing the rest of me. As promised the oil helped with the removal except no one mentioned the hairs on the bottom near my balls.

Fuck.

Me.

Tears popped in my eyes and my dick sank like a flagging ship as I pulled out what had to be every fucking hair on my balls.

I didn't cry.

Barely.

It definitely took a while to catch my breath.

The silicone sheath formed just like it was supposed to. Fabulous.

When I tested my balls, I winced.

They weren't quite baby soft smooth, but they were close.

Maybe I owed Frankie for doing that wax job she did for us this summer.

I owed her big.

"Totally worth it," I whispered as I hopped into the shower and tried not to let my balls rub on my legs. "Totally worth it."

Ow.

RHYME & REASON

BUBBA - FLASHBACK/DELETED SCENE

*W*hen Dad retired to private practice and a civilian life, I'd actually been looking forward to getting away from living on bases while also soaking up stability of maintaining the same address as well as school for more than two years at a shot.

With his degree and specialities, Dad had often pulled overseas duty assignments. I'd enjoyed seeing the world, but I missed the normalcy of America. Hamburgers. Coke that tasted like coke. The right ratio of onions to burger and the vital ingredient to all of life's pleasures—ketchup

Right, I was a simple guy and I liked simple things. We'd only finished our move the week before once we'd gotten back to the States, done the house-hunting, then pulled everything out of storage in San Antonio. The new place was located in a much smaller town, but I kind of liked it. The open roads. The huge fields. The lakes.

And tons of places to go hiking or fishing when the air wasn't so hot it could cook you in place. Add to that they'd gotten a pool with the house and I was in heaven. Still, enrolling at the junior high so late meant I'd missed out on the pick of the classes and had to stick with whatever was left. I didn't care, honestly, I was kind of looking forward to that "all-American" experience even if it meant homework.

First period was language arts and I found the classroom right before the bell. There was only one desk open. Second row right behind a gorgeous blonde. I'd only gotten a quick look at her as I passed by. She had a book open on her desk and her whole attention seemed focused on it.

I ignored the glances tossed in my direction. Being an unknown wasn't a new experience for me. I'd learned to shrug those glances off a long time ago. Still, I kind of wished she'd glanced up or at least around at me so I could get a better look at her.

The guy on her left reached over to grip it and she smacked his hand without looking up. It was hard not to laugh. The class flew by. Actual textbooks were assigned along with our first visit to the library to get authorized to check out books from there. Independent reading lists and the syllabus for the first six weeks of assignments were also handed out.

Before I realized it, she'd vanished in the library and there just wasn't time to track her down before the bell rang and I had to hurry. My next class was a PE training class. Weights, since all the tryouts for the various teams had happened over the summer, was clear on the other side of the school. I had gym clothes in my bag, but the teacher waved us in without having us get changed. There was a note on the door for the same thing.

"Let's go, I want to go over all the safety rules and expectations before you guys even touch the weights…"

Right, I knew how to use all the visible equipment and had been training with Dad pretty regularly for the last three years. Still, I focused on what he was saying right up until I caught sight of a familiar face. Locking gazes with Jake Benton had me grinning stupidly.

Of all the people to be in one of my classes was someone I actually knew from going to school with him before. Only then, we'd been in Germany and not the U.S. Our parents had also been friends, our dads at least, which meant Jake and I had hung out quite a bit before he'd returned stateside with his mom.

We didn't get much of a chance to talk before the end of class when the teacher—coach—finished going over everything from safety protocols to dress code to expectations. This would be a weight lifting class, we would have reading and tests on major muscle groups as well as understanding how to train them. We would be working out on different muscle groups daily and we had to partner or triple up

Jake and I were in lockstep almost immediately. When we were told to get to know each other and work out our goal sheets, I headed straight for him and dumped my bag to the side. "Man, it's good to see you."

"Same," Jake said, shaking my hand. "Mom told me she'd heard from your dad and that you guys were planning to move here, but I didn't know you'd already made it."

"Barely. We got in like five days ago, and it's been all running to get everything set up. Mom already has shifts at the hospital and Dad will be starting at his job this week or next."

"This is so cool that you're here," Jake said with a grin. "You gotta try out for football."

"Didn't I already miss the tryouts? And the summer practices?"

"Kinda but, I know a guy." He shoulder checked me. "C'mon."

Our weights teacher, the coach, turned out to be the coach for the junior high's football squad. He gave me a once over and then told me to show up after school to run some drills. No guarantees, but maybe I could get some time to fill in until he saw whether I was a good fit or not.

"Catch me at lunch," Jake said when we separated for classes. The gorgeous blonde was in my third period math class but she was up front and the only seat left for me was in the back. Damn, she vanished as soon as the bell rang. I swore she could move.

But this time I had a name.

I'd ask Jake about her. When the lunch bell rang, my brain already ached from the sheer number of "introduction" and "first of the year" speeches I'd received. It was nice that Jake was waiting for me right outside the lunchroom.

"Hold up," he told me when I would have gone on inside. "Waiting on some friends."

"Sure." I'd just leaned back against the wall next to him when I spotted the blonde again. She was strolling in our direction, talking animatedly to a tall, lanky guy next to her. His response made her laugh and I swore it was like being dropped inside of a bell as a gong sounded.

The vibration went straight through me. She was still smiling, laughter in her eyes, when our gazes locked. The lyrics to Savage Garden's "I Knew I Loved You," made absolute sense to me.

"Bubba, this is Frankie and Coop," Jake said and it was like all the sound rushed back in at once. "Guys, this is Bubba. Friend of mine from Germany. He's new."

"Wait," Coop said with smirk. "You have friends outside of us?" He wrapped his arm around Frankie's shoulder and I had the sudden desire to break it. "Well, what do you know?"

"Fuck you," Jake said, laughing as he dragged the door open. Frankie elbowed Coop, then stuck her hand out to me.

"Welcome," she greeted me as she shook my hand, but the eye contact didn't last anywhere near as long as I would have liked. Instead, she glanced past me to Jake. "You're really growing in your old age. Developing new people skills. Welcoming friends to our circle. I'm so proud."

She mimed wiping away a tear and I cracked up as Jake made a face at her and then shook his head. "Bubba doesn't count as new. So he's in. Deal with it."

I was? Fine by me. I hadn't realized how hard I was staring or how obvious it was as she and Jake led the way toward the line picking on each other or how Jake pretty much body blocked anyone from running into her.

"She has that effect on people," Coop said as he bumped my shoulder with his. At my glance, he touched the corner of his mouth. "You have a little drool right here.."

The flash of teasing in his eyes helped and I shook my head before giving him a little shove away. "Shut up."

He was still laughing when we caught up and she glanced back at us, a question in her eyes.

"Bubba just had something on his face," Coop said without an ounce of apology. "Don't worry, I fixed it."

At her raised brow inquiry in my direction, I found myself thanking Coop mentally. "I don't see anything," she murmured. "All good now."

Yeah. Yeah it was.

Seeing her had captured my attention. Hearing her laugh had snared my heart. But the fact she smiled at me and then talked to me.

All I could think of was soulmate. What a stupid fucking word it was, but at the same time it fit. Clearly, I kept those thoughts to myself. But I ate lunch with them every single day and it wasn't long before I had her number and we were hanging out.

Maybe all the last minute rushing and not being able to pick classes was worth it. Sure, I sat on the bench for half the year in football, but I got my times to shine. I found an old friend and new friends all on the same day.

Even better, I met Frankie.

I had no idea why all of that went through my head as we sat on the bus heading for graduation, but it did. Six, almost seven years ago, I couldn't have imagined how this worked out. Hell, at the beginning of the school year I'd thought we'd doomed it before it could really start.

Yet here we were, beyond rhyme and reason.

All because I met Frankie and she was the best damn thing to ever happen to me.

DAUGHTERS & DISCOVERY

HANK - ALTERNATE POV SCENE

"*I* was looking for Frankie Curtis," I said, eyeing the young man who opened the door. A boyfriend? Probably. Though that came with its own kind of twist to my chest. She was so damn grown already. Right, get it together Hank. "I'm Henry Jackson."

The guy answering her door went stiff, his eyes narrowed, and there was no mistaking the cool assessment in his expression. I couldn't see past him into the apartment and I didn't press except, he kept staring.

"I did get the right apartment?" Did I get the address wrong? "Sorry, if I'm coming by late. I drove here straight from the airport and I got lost once."

Coming late? Yeah, eighteen fucking years Hank. The mental scolding didn't do me any favors right now. I could nurse the guilt of missing my daughter's whole life later.

"No," he said slowly, some warmth sneaking into the chill of his voice. "You're at the right place." He glanced over his shoulder once, but didn't move. I had a feeling, that door wasn't going to budge if he didn't decide to open it.

It seemed to take an eternity before he nodded and

backed up a step. Then she was there. The slender, athletic build with a wild fall of golden blonde hair. Holy shit, she looked like Maddy. But where Maddy had a cool, almost cold edge to her there was nothing of that in this girl's cautious manner.

And her eyes…. the rich, warmth of verdant green. Goddammit. Hate for Madeline Grayson swelled in my chest to the point it threatened to suffocate me. Frankie reached for her boyfriend's hand and she lifted those eyes to meet my gaze steadily.

"I'm Frankie," she said with a half-smile, her unease at all of this communicated itself perfectly. Oh sweet girl… me too. She went to extend her hand and hesitated. "I mean, yes, I'm Frankie. Would you like to come in Mister—or is it Professor…"

I clasped the offered hand before she could withdraw it. Her palm was a little sweaty, but then again so was mine. I could handle a lecture hall full of kids and wrangle all three of mine—one would think this wouldn't be so damn hard.

"Hank," I told her. Meeting her like this was both a shock and a wonder. I'd missed so damn much, but look at her. Look at the way she faced me even when her own fear was there. "Call me Hank."

Would I prefer Dad? Fuck yes I would. That would take time though. Time and effort. I'd been absent for all of her life, but that wasn't her fault. If I needed to earn that trust with her, the I would damn well be patient and take the time.

"And I can come in or we can go somewhere. I don't want you to feel cornered or ambushed, just… You called and you mentioned graduation and I thought if you were reaching out that maybe you wanted to meet me and I've wanted to meet you."

The words spilled out in a rush, but I wasn't kidding. I

wanted to meet her. I had since the attorney contacted me. She'd called...

Focus Hank, I snapped at myself mentally. She called. Maybe I jumped the gun a little but, actions spoke louder than words.

"I did want to—Yeah, it's fine, come in." She beckoned me indoors even as she backed up. The air was warm outside and the interior much cooler.

"You have company," I said, catching sight of the others in the apartment. It wasn't just Frankie and her boyfriend. They had friends over. "I'm interrupting."

"It's fine, these are my boyfriends, you'd have to meet them anyway."

These are my...

Wait. "Boyfriends?"

She nodded, the corners of her mouth curving into a real, if shy smile. "Yeah, that's Jake and..."

"Ian Rhys, sir," the young blond offered even as he extended his hand. We shook hands briefly, then the second blond approached.

"Coop Brennen," he said, grinning. "Boy next door and resident best friend as well as boyfriend."

Frankie laughed. "Smart ass."

"Benton," Jake said as he took his turn for a handshake.

"And I'm Archie," the fourth said, moving forward to stand next to Frankie. He was a dead ringer for his father, Maddy's on-again, off-again...what was his name? "Standish."

"Eddie Standish's kid." It wasn't a judgment, but it was like falling into some kind of time warp. I'd seen Maddy and Eddie together. We weren't friends, I'd been a TA and they'd been in one of my classes.

Where Maddy had been cool and dominating, Frankie radiated warmth and affection. Standish's kid wasn't like him either. There'd always been a wariness to Eddie. A discomfort like he wasn't always sure where he stood, but his desperate love for Maddy had also been clear—even if they cheated on each other regularly.

"Unfortunately," Archie said with a half-smile. "Hopefully you won't hold that against me."

"Not at all," I assured him even as Frankie leaned into him. I didn't miss the flicker of fear over her face as he spoke. Then again, who knew what they knew after all of Maddy's lies… "Just surprised," I admitted and then glanced at Frankie again. She was… I could picture her when she was the twins' age almost too easily. She reminded me of Chloe, of who Chloe could become when she grew up and it was both heart wrenching and utterly magnificent. "I'm going to make this weird and keep staring, just ignore me for a bit. I promise I'll get over it."

"It's okay," she said with a laugh. "It is weird. I mean… Are you looking to see how I'm like you or how I'm like her?"

Five minutes with her and I didn't see Maddy anymore. Yeah, some surface similarities, genetics more than anything else. But she was not like her mother at all. "More me than her, I mean, you've got her coloring. But those are my mom's eyes and that little—crinkle right there at the corner of your right eye? That's us too. Jackson family trait. We all do it."

The most adorable of open grins spread across her face.

"Yeah, see," I said, glancing at her circle of guys who kept a watchful eye on the both of us.

They were protective, it shown in the way they all stood, one foot angled toward her. Jake and Ian were both ready to block, that was clear from their posture. Coop seemed the most relaxed, but Archie made up for that in how he kept a very focused gaze on me.

"I'm making it weird. Kelly told me I do that because I talk, talking is my thing and I get chatty and then—well, everything kind of comes out jumbled. Great when you're lecturing, can keep the room engaged, not so great when you're meeting your adult daughter for the first time and she has no idea who you are."

Right, definitely making it weird. I needed to get this under control

"He is so Frankie's dad," Coop said in a low voice, before he pressed a kiss to her temple. "If it's all right to call you, Hank, sir, why don't we all sit and I'll grab some coffee. We could order in food if you're hungry. We pretty much decimated the leftovers already."

"Hank is fine, boys," I said, taking the offer of a lifeline. I wanted time with Frankie and she had... "Boyfriends," I muttered, then shook my head. "That'll take a little getting used to. Chloe's all of seven and she's not allowed to date until she's thirty."

I let them take their seats first, then chose the love seat to be closer to her. Meeting my daughter for the first time. The world had shifted when Maddy reached out to me saying she was sick and she needed to find a paternal match.

First it was outrage, then worry, and ultimately, disappointment. If the tests excluded me, that was good, I didn't miss out on a child's life... then Frankie's attorney called.

Maddy lied to me, not once, but twice. I'd missed out on so much and my whole world flipped upside down.

"Chloe is your daughter?" Her soft question grounded me.

"See, there I go... yes." I shifted forward to pull my phone out of my pocket. Then I flipped through the photos app to pull up a picture of all of us. The twins and Alec all got their mother's coloring, but Alec looked a lot like me. "This is Kelly, she's my wife—she's also looking forward to meeting you. I thought about bringing everyone, but Kelly insisted that it should just be us at first, then when you're ready you can come meet your siblings."

The little catch in Frankie's breath, the flash of her teeth over her lower lip, and the way her knuckles went white where she gripped Archie's hand were all tells.

"If you want," I rushed to assure her. "No pressure. I mean, yes, this is pressure me showing up, but really no—I... I wanted to meet you. I'm very sorry I didn't know about you. She never told me. Not until she asked for a DNA sample because you were sick."

Worry darkened her expression.

"I know you're not," I continued keeping my focus on her. "Mr. Wittaker explained. Of course..." I cleared my throat as emotion clogged it. "I'm sorry about that either way. And I'm very glad you're not sick."

"No." Apology coated every word. "I'm not. And I'm sorry she made you think I was."

"Yeah well, that was then and this is now and when your attorney called, I was... I was surprised but I told him I'd already done a sample and I didn't mind doing it again. Apparently, once I agreed to it, the lab released the results. I told him, I wanted to speak to you and that I would welcome any contact."

"He told me," she admitted. "I wasn't... Okay confession time, I wasn't sure about meeting you. I had no idea...and Maddy and I aren't... Well we're not close. She didn't tell me anything about you either." Her nerves were right there and holy shit did I feel that. "And maybe I was a little afraid."

Right, my little girl was afraid. Get your shit together, Jackson. Didn't matter what came next. Time to make it better for her.

Missed the first eighteen years, and I didn't want to miss another moment.

DEFIANCE AND DEDICATION BONUS SCENES

FATHERS & FAMILIES

KELLY - DELETED SCENE

"Dad," Alec said, staring at Hank across the table. For his part, Hank had been doing a fantastic impression of a professor reading through papers though he hadn't turned a page in twenty minutes nor made a single mark with his pen.

"Hmm?"

"What if I don't like her?" The question was delivered in Alec's very sober and serious manner, concern radiated off of him. This wasn't a flip attempt at being funny or a taunt in order to get his father's attention. The genuine reflection in the words made my heart ache for our altogether far too grave son.

The question pulled his father away from worrying so I focused my attention on dinner and let Hank and Alec discuss this. Alec often went to one of us when he needed to figure something out, and in this case, Hank was the better one to answer. In fact, I was fairly certain the man I loved so much *needed* to answer this for himself as much as for Alec.

"Well, that's a possibility," Hank said slowly, not dismissing Alec's concerns in the slightest. I had to keep my back to them to not betray my smile. "I suppose, she may not like you either. That would be challenging."

"I hadn't thought about that," Alec admitted. "Chloe and Craig are way more annoying."

It took everything I possessed to not laugh. He didn't even mean it in a cruel way, just that they tended to be loud and playful to his far quieter demeanor.

"You know," Hank said, the chair creaked as though he stretched. He had an office that was *way* more comfortable for grading, but instead, he sat at the tall table in our kitchen that we used more for homework and food prep than eating. He did it because he wanted to keep me company in the evenings. "The only thing we can do is keep our fingers crossed. She doesn't seem the type to dislike someone just on principle."

"That seems reasonable," Alec said. "And if she's taking over as the eldest, she will have to be patient."

I waited for it, because there was no mistaking where this was going.

"That means I don't have to be..." The barest suggestion of slyness echoed in that trailing sentence.

"True," Hank agreed. "But it doesn't mean you should be impatient or try to push her to see how much you can get away with. Unlike you, she hasn't had younger siblings—or any siblings for that matter—she's been alone. Far too alone."

The last three words were a hushed exhale like he hadn't meant to say them.

"You did say that before," Alec admitted. "That's kind of sad even if the twins are a pain in the—"

"Alec," I said in the exact same breath as Hank. I turned away from the spaghetti boiling on the stove.

"I was gonna say butt," he informed us, but the gleam in his eyes betrayed his amusement.

"Uh huh," Hank clucked and then pointed his pen at him. "I'm wise to you, Mister. Is your homework done?"

"Yes, sir," Alec said. "May I go play the X-Box while you finish getting dinner ready?" That question included me.

"I don't mind, but don't taunt your brother."

"I won't," Alec said, pivoting on his heel. "I won't have to. I'm breathing. That's taunting enough."

I barely survived not laughing until the door closed behind him leaving Hank and I in the kitchen. When my gaze met his, he chuckled softly and I had to press a hand to my mouth.

"I blame you for that," Hank said with a smile. "That dry, dry sense of humor is all you."

"Bullshit," I murmured. "That's all you. You forget, I have met your mother."

He gripped his chest as if my verbal arrow had lodged a hit. "And here I was thinking you'd liked Mom."

"I adored her, but I also know where your sense of humor comes from."

"I can accept that charge," he admitted, then glanced back at the paper. For a moment, bewilderment creased his expression as if he didn't even remember reading to where he was. With an exasperated sigh, he raked a hand through his hair before he flipped back to the beginning.

"She wouldn't be coming if she didn't want to meet us," I reminded him gently.

"She's put it off all summer," he said, worry rustling with each word and his gaze fixed on the paper.

"Yes, but what did you tell me?"

"Her mother is a raging narcissist with delusional issues. She's been through an emotional ringer. She and the boys she is dating—boys—"

He groaned and I bit back another smile as I went through the motions of draining the spaghetti. The sauce and meatballs were all ready, but I still needed to get the garlic bread into the oven.

"I can't believe I wasn't there for the first date or the first dance or the first—" Anger decorated the deep sadness present in his regrets. "I should have pushed that—bitch when she called me the first time."

"You didn't know," I reminded him. "You told me then that if her child was yours..."

Hank turned in his seat and I paused mid-butter on the french loaves I'd separated.

"You didn't," I repeated. "You told me when she called. You offered her everything she needed to do the DNA test and then you sat by the phone and waited for a week."

"And she still didn't tell me the truth."

"No, but your *daughter* did. Granted, she reached out via her attorney." I offered him that opening and Hank smiled in a way that told me he knew exactly what I was doing.

"She had every reason to be cautious of a complete stranger she'd never even heard of," he said, his defense immediate and absolute. "Of course, then said stranger just showed up on her doorstep."

"And as uneasy and nervous as she was, what did you tell me?"

"She's so damn smart, Kelly. There's so much intelligence in her eyes and more, so much compassion. She's—she reminds me of my mother and my grandmother. There's a kindness in her, but also a wit. The hurt is there, you can see it, lurking below the surface. The expectation of pain and disappointment. If I'd been there..."

"If you'd known," I said, leaving the bread for the moment and wiping my hands on a towel. Crossing over to him, I tapped his nose. "You, Mr. Jackson, are one of the most dedicated and conscientious *men* I've ever known and you are an amazing father who makes me fall in love with him every single day for how much you love our children. Frankie is going to be no different. You love her, you'll be patient, and she's coming. Give her time, give yourself time…"

"What if she doesn't like all of us?" There it was, so much like Alec. That heart of his so damn ready to just embrace everyone but at the same time, worried he might smother or chase her away.

"Impossible," I reminded him. "We're amazing. We have to be, to keep up with you."

His snort made me smile for real. When he tugged me to him, I hugged him. The comfort he needed right now just made me love him more.

"Families adapt," I reminded him. "When we had Alec, we had to adapt to not just being the two of us and then the twins."

He chuckled against me. "They were a surprise."

"Yes, they were." No one had realized it was even twins— somehow—so Chloe or Craig, we'd never figured out which had covered for the other. Sneaky little darlings. "But we adapted. Even Alec, who worries so much."

Hank had worried too, his light squeeze reminded me of how he'd not slept for a week. The twins had been smaller because there had been two and had needed time in the NICU. Hank was there every single night, looking after them, spending time with them, and me. Then with Alec, he'd been a gift, involving him in everything—including the planning to prep for two when we'd only readied for one.

Pressing a kiss to the top of his head, I said, "That's why you and the kids have spent the whole summer, bit by bit, trying to put a room together for her."

"You gave up your sewing room for her," Hank said with a sigh.

"I gave up nothing. I can sew just as well downstairs in the basement as I can upstairs. This just means Frankie has her own space here and that's important. All of our kids need that."

Tilting his head back, Hank smiled. "Mrs. Jackson, I do believe I am not the only one burdened with a huge heart."

"Oh, darling, it's not a burden except that you haven't let me go down there and just hug that child and drag her back here where I can look after her properly."

He laughed. Truly laughed. "Baby steps, Kel. You're way more mom than she's used to."

I sniffed. "I'll fix it."

"I believe you."

But some of the worry had drained from his face and I dropped another kiss on his lips. "Good. Now, try to grade at least one paper, dinner will be ready in ten."

"Yes ma'am."

He sat a little straighter in the chair, focused a bit more, and the cloud of concern hovering over him had lightened. Like Hank, I wished we'd known about Frankie a lot sooner. I couldn't wait to meet that young lady. She'd utterly charmed Hank, I had zero doubts she'd charm the kids. Chloe was already her biggest fan.

The fact she was as worried as her father about how they would all do told me it would all be fine.

Families adapted.

Ours already had. Frankie would figure that out soon enough.

GOLDEN & GRATEFUL

ARCHIE - THANKSGIVING IN COLLEGE

"*M*aybe next year," Frankie said as she stretched her legs over mine. I ran my hand up and down her calf as she made a face at me. From the hurried chatter I could just make out, Chloe was not a fan of Frankie not coming up for Thanksgiving. The temptation to tickle her feet was right there, but I behaved. A cold front had moved in the day before and there was snow blowing against the windows. It was kind of nice to just be curled up with her in our living room, hot coffee in our mugs, and the cats sprawled out around us while the fire burned merrily.

Granted, it was a gas fireplace but so much better than nothing and Frankie always got tickled when we just turned it on. We'd been debating a movie when her phone rang because today was going to just be us—and Jeremy—but mostly us and we weren't going anywhere. The only place we had to be was right here.

"I get that." Frankie's soft laugh pulled another smile from me. I loved that she loved her new family. Even if she remained a shade reticent and wary. I'd rather we were all cautious until one hundred percent certain. It was so much better for her huge heart, even if she'd already fallen in love with her sister. "Chloe, emotional blackmail will only go so far."

I raised my eyebrows, should I swoop in and interrupt? But she only rolled her eyes and smiled as she shook her head.

"No, that's exactly what you were doing. Alec's right. Uh huh...no, I'm very well aware that it's sisters before bros, but... uh uh. No ma'am." Toes curling, she leaned forward to claim her cup and took a sip as Chloe offered up her defense. "Exactly. So, I'll call on Thanksgiving Day, and we can talk then, but I'm not driving up there this year."

A moment of silence.

"Because I have plans."

I grinned.

"No, that's not code for anything."

Oh, I could fix that.

As if reading my mind, she jabbed me with her toes.

Chuckling, I cupped her ankle and settled her legs back across me.

"Wonderful, yes, I love you too—go on and help your mom, I'll call on Thursday." Another couple of minutes of reminding her she already promised to call and then Frankie hung up with a groan. "Man, little sisters can be annoying."

If she didn't sound so fucking happy about it, I might have worried. "Jake and Coop have been telling you that for years."

"Their sisters are adorable though."

"According to Coop, so is yours." I grinned. "I'm actually looking forward to meeting the little spitfire."

"She's gonna wrap you around her little finger just like this," she said with a snap of her fingers.

"Impossible," I told her as she settled her coffee down and

I could shift to pin her to the sofa. "Someone else already has me completely wrapped around *her* finger."

"Oh yeah?" She shifted her legs so she could wrap them around me. It was both sensual and comforting. Getting hard around her was as easy as breathing, but having her just wrapped around me was the kind of thing I'd never known I needed.

"Yeah," I told her, cupping my hands against her head so I could just study her. "Body and soul. I'm sure your sister is cute, but I'm very firmly taken and damn happy about it."

She laughed. "You are so smooth sometimes."

"Only sometimes?" I pulled back and stared down at her. "Try all the time."

"No, because occasionally you are a great big dork who dirty talks his way out of trouble and I let you."

"You let me?" Lips pursed, I shook my head. "So that's how it is?"

"Oh yes," she informed me. "That's exactly how it is."

"Uh huh." As soon as I skated my fingers down her sides, her eyes widened.

"Archie!" Her squeal as she tried to wiggle away made me laugh, but it was too late for her. I had all her ticklish spots memorized.

Unfortunately, she knew mine and retaliated even while she was laughing. It was all fun and games until we nearly knocked her coffee cup over and I froze. Her eyes went comically wide with horror and I eased up, pulling her with me and then with great ceremony handed her the coffee mug.

We were both panting, her eyes sparkled, and her cheeks were flushed from the laughter. I probably wore the stupidest grin on my face. "So," I said. "What did you want to watch?"

She snickered. "I don't know—I think that's where we were when Chloe called."

True. I reached for the remote and started skimming through the channels until I found the one with all the holiday movies. No matter how much we complained, we never objected when Frankie wanted to watch them. Well, we didn't complain much.

Halfway through the first one, I was glaring at the screen.

"We don't have to watch this," she murmured.

"You like it."

"Yeah, but you're clearly not enjoying it."

"It's not that." We had finished our coffee already and I needed to take a break and go on the hunt for more. Only one of the cats had returned to join us after the tickle war and he was curled up in her lap.

"Then what is it?"

"That moron," I said, pointing at the screen. "He's too fucking busy for her? It's about to be Christmas and he sent his secretary to get presents and he hasn't even noticed she's not in town anymore."

Frankie grimaced.

"And that kills me, she's great and he's clearly an idiot." I wrapped an arm around her. "No way in hell would I ignore you at Christmas."

"Archie, you don't ignore me at any other time."

True. That mollified me a little and I pressed a kiss to the crown of her head. "Good. If I do, just slug me."

She elbowed me gently and I glanced down to find her grinning. "What are you going to do when she falls for her best friend now that she's back in her little town?"

I considered it for a long moment. "Be glad that your best friend loves you as much as I do."

"Smooth, Archie, very smooth."

Chuckling, I just snuggled her closer and we finished the

movie and rolled into the next one. Surprise, surprise, the city idiot didn't know what he had until he almost lost her. That was never going to be me. I knew exactly what I had and what I'd always wanted. She was right here. We were golden.

For that, I'd always be grateful.

When the phone rang closer to lunch and it was Coop, I paused the movie and answered with a, "Greetings, best friend in the small town, don't worry, corporate boyfriend is definitely taking care of our girlfriend just fine."

Frankie dissolved in laughter as Coop hummed. "Someone got sucked into the holiday movies…"

Yeah, see, he got it.

BRAVADO & BFFS

FRANKIE - DELETED SCENE

I was already on the way down the stairs when the doorbell rang. I'd kind of hoped I'd get there *before* he rang the bell, but Dominic Walsh was both swift *and* efficient.

"I got it," I called out for the guys who were upstairs playing a new game Jake had gotten for his birthday and for Jeremy who was down here somewhere. Sliding my phone into my back pocket, I opened the door to Dominic.

He looked every inch the lawyer in his dark suit, with a long, what looked like wool, overcoat and nice dress shoes. Sharp, professional, and not bad looking I supposed. It was hard to tell, though I did like his smile because it actually reached his eyes.

"Good morning," he said, his breath fogging in the cold air. I stepped aside and pulled the door wider to let him in "Merry Christmas," he continued as he undid the top buttons of his coat while I closed the door behind him.

"Merry Christmas," I greeted him with a laugh. "This could have waited until after the New Year. I hate to think I've dragged you out during the holiday."

"Yes and no," he said, his eyes twinkling as he played along. "Also, nothing to worry about. I won't even take up that much of your time."

I took his coat. "Well, come on, let's see if we can bribe Jeremy into coffee while we talk.

"Why are we bribing Jeremy and who is here, Baby Girl?" Jake made it halfway down the stairs before he paused. "This is…"

"Dominic Walsh, Jake Benton," I introduced him. They'd met him *briefly* before but they'd still been more than a little irritated with my choices and I didn't think they cared for Dominic much.

Jake descended the last few steps and took the hand Dominic extended. "I didn't realize we were having company?" The question in his pale blue eyes sought reassurance.

"It's not about Maddy," I promised him. I could do that. I'd asked Dominic to come, but I couldn't tell them yet. I would, surprise be damned, if they needed it. But Jake nodded, the relief palpable.

"Good. What are we doing then?"

"Just have some papers for Frankie to sign," Dominic said. "Won't take long at all and then I'll leave you to your holiday."

Curiosity flared in his eyes and I could have predicted it, Archie wandered down because Jake hadn't come back up.

"Right, let's go on through," I said, still holding Dominic's coat. "The boys can go back to their game and I'll be back up to root for you in a little bit."

"Who's here?" Coop called down and I didn't roll my eyes but this was a little comedic.

"Walsh," Archie answered, but unlike Jake, he didn't shake Dominic's hand.

Yep, time to move. I headed for the dining room and kitchen. It was a fairly public area of the house, but it would also work so we could sit at the table and I could sign the paperwork.

This was a huge transaction and I'd never spent this kind of money before. It had required moving into a trust account, then authorizing an agent, filing the tax paperwork, then transferring it. While that could all be handled electronically, *this* part still required my signature.

Jeremy was just putting out a pot of coffee and a pair of mugs on the table. I shot him a grateful look. He was in on my plans because he'd helped me track down the right car. We'd poured over the different models for two weeks to get the one I wanted for Archie.

"Mr. Walsh," Jeremy said as he took the coat from me. "Can I get you and Miss Frankie anything else?" The distinct emphasis on our names wasn't lost on the guys.

Archie's eyes narrowed and Jake frowned, but Coop slid over and pulled out the chair I had my hand on the back of. "Need us, Beautiful?"

I could have kissed him, and since I could, I did. He dipped his head with a grin as his lips brushed mine once. A promise for later.

"I'm good. Really, this won't take long."

"Then we can wait," Archie volunteered. Sometimes, they made surprises hard.

"I'm going for pizza," Ian called. "Anyone coming with?"

Coop chuckled. "Probably not Bubba."

While they didn't sit at the table with us, they moved out into the sitting room—where they could see us and most likely listen, but not be in the middle.

Okay. We could work with that.

"Pineapple on mine please," I called.

"I wouldn't forget, Angel. Is your guest staying for food?" Subtle.

Dominic's lips twitched as he took opened his bag and

pulled out three file folders. They were a lot thicker than I was thinking. Rather than waste time, I got coffee poured for us. Jeremy gave the boys look, then glanced at me.

I lifted my shoulders. Not much we could do with this. It would be fine. We'd made it this far.

He nodded.

"Right," I repeated from earlier as I leaned forward. "What do we have?"

I'd just pretend it was fine for the guys to listen. Dominic understood what was at stake. He also made a good confidant for top secret surprises.

"We'll start with the trust paperwork," he told me. "Thank you," he added as he picked up his coffee and took a sip. "We went over all the changes last month, but I just finished having it drafted. I read through it—" He slid the first folder over to me. "I've marked where you need to sign, but as always, read through the areas we changed and make sure the language works for you."

"Right…" I flipped it open and sure enough it was the trust paperwork. Bless him, he'd not only marked the pages for me to sign, he'd included sticky notes with the details that we'd changed.

"I made sure to include the provisions you asked for," he continued, then paused when I turned the page. "We split it across three of the accounts, while the trust as a whole is one fund, we're not investing it all in the same manner. Spreading it out may slow the income, but…"

"…it's better for the overall risk," Archie supplied and Dominic glanced at him.

"Exactly."

I bit my lip as I scanned the words, before I added my signature. "You were able to add the fund at the school for the LBGTQ+ resources…"

"I was," Dominic said. "But, I made sure to include it as

partial tax shelter for your income. The donations will always mark a ten percent slice off the overall income per quarter, with the first donation being a flat fee."

That would work. Rachel had been talking about the center and the resources it offered for college kids who were just figuring out their sexual identity or needed more support. She volunteered there when she could, but they needed a bigger space and more counselors.

"This is excellent," I said as I followed the notations down. Dominic had detailed bulleted requests for where we'd like the money to be used. "Can we do this?"

"We can. It doesn't mean they'll follow it. The donation, and the subsequent pledge gives them the money to use at their discretion. But, it doesn't hurt to make the request. As they say, money talks."

"Bullshit walks," Jake volunteered and I didn't laugh. Coop did, but I didn't.

"Thank you." Those signed, he handed me the next folder.

"These are the investments that you've already made, most of them are just for your review and to sign that you did authorize it. They'll go over to the accountants and tax attorneys for later filings."

I made a face, but the second page was where the sale paperwork for the car began. It would be in Archie's name, but I would be the signatory to the full purchase. It had been paid, along with the tax, title, and license. There were provisions for the alterations made to assure it was street legal.

"I was thinking of dropping something off for Rachel after the holidays."

"She's not a huge fan of flowers," I told him, frowning at the language on the engine changes. It had been certified by the mechanics and the experts, but maybe I should ask Jake— then again that would mean sliding this to him and trying to sneak it past Archie right in front of him.

I was good, but not that good.

Yet.

"Well," I said with a blink. "She likes flowers, but she used to work at a florist when we were in high school, so she's kind of picky."

"I like a woman who knows what she wants and isn't afraid to ask for it."

A laugh escaped me. "Then Rachel is perfect."

"Yes," he said. "She is. But I would like to do something. I didn't get to see her before the holiday. Thoughts on what she'd like? Jewelry? Chocolates? A teddy bear?"

I frowned. "Teddy bear?"

"She has one, in her room," he murmured. "Thought it might be something she collects. Or likes to do. The woman is somewhat hard to pin down."

I finished signing the last few pages and then moved to the final folder that had a Christmas card in it along with a set of keys. I made sure everything stayed in the manilla envelope and then glanced over at Dominic.

"Well, she likes photography," I offered. "But gifts are personal."

"Yes, they are," he agreed with me and took the file folders back sans the manilla envelope. "Those are your copies. Everything else will be certified, filed, and then I'll send over the duplicates after."

"Thank you."

"You're welcome," Dominic said as he tucked the folders away, then pulled out another one. "As for presents. I hope you'll enjoy this. Maybe just don't open it until Christmas."

Surprise flickered through me at the cheerful red envelope, but he was already rising and finishing his coffee, then the guys practically swarmed us to escort him out. Coop looked so damn amused it was funny. Thankfully, during the distraction, I passed the manilla envelope with the title and the keys to Jeremy and he secreted them away.

It wasn't until we were back upstairs and Ian had returned with the pizza that Archie asked about the red envelope. I'd just set it on the coffee table.

"He said not to open it until Christmas," I reminded him.

"Yeah, but we're rebels and I say we can open it early," Archie declared. "Who's with me?"

Ian and Jake voted yes, but Coop shook his head. "I abstain, it's Frankie's gift."

That earned a few crestfallen faces and I couldn't resist them so I opened the envelope and pulled out the card. It was a pair of huge googly eyes with a Santa hat on.

Inside, Dominic had written *naughty girl, you weren't supposed to look until Christmas. Enjoy the tickets.*

The tickets were for Hamilton and I laughed. We'd been wanting to see it and they were almost impossible to get. He'd also gotten us five tickets.

"Eh," Jake said, his nose wrinkled. "That's almost too good a present."

"Then you're going to have to help me come up with something for him."

There was more grumbling but when I climbed into Archie's lap and kissed him, they changed the subject.

Whew. Just two more days and I could spring my surprise.

That was a lot of kissing, but totally worth it.

On all counts.

SONGS AND SWEETHEARTS
BONUS SCENES

PAYBACK & PALS

RACHEL - UNPUBLISHED SCENE

I did a little sidestep over to Rachel, cause who doesn't love our girl? Christmas, a trip home, a blast from the past—good times, right?

Christmas in Texas was an experience. One not everyone appreciated. A part of me enjoyed getting away from the bitter cold in New York. You got on the plane wearing layers, stripped most of them away after you landed. Texas was not New York.

I had to cover up some other layers while I was here. Visits home on the holidays could mean a lot of things. Fights. Tears. Tears and fights. Drinking. Cold, unforgiving silence. Laughter, music, and boozy fun. You just never knew what it was going to be. So for a few days, I could pack away my personality and just make peace.

At least I had an exit strategy these days. A timetable. The light at the end of the tunnel wasn't four years and a graduation away. Uncle Basil greeted me in baggage claim. His bloodshot eyes were a concern, but he didn't smell like a distillery. So—improvement?

"Hey," I greeted him with a hug. "Where's Mom?" Yeah

that was a loaded grenade of a question but Basil just gave me a kind of careless shrug after he kissed my temple.

"Your cousin is pregnant," he warned me and the disdain beneath the words feathered out.

My cousin? "Basil, I have fourteen different cousins. Can you be more specific?" I shouldered my camera bag more tightly. My wallet, cash, phone, and more were also stored in my purse which was in my carry-on. Since I got two, I made sure my camera bag was with me.

He gave me one of those looks that had me grimacing.

"She's fourteen."

"Fifteen on her last birthday," he said with a sigh. "Old enough to be messing around, too young to understand the consequences. She's so damn proud of herself. Gonna marry her pimply-faced baby daddy and raise kids. That's now her goal in life."

Kill me. I could hear it coming…

"Your mother has gone to try and talk some sense into her sister—" Dorothy Ann was also *his* sister, but I didn't correct him. Dorothy Ann and Basil didn't speak. As far as I knew, they hadn't exchanged a single word in my hearing for most of my life. They didn't even mention each other by name.

"Besides being a grandmother, what sense does she need?" I spotted my bag and went for it. Basil followed along amiably, taking a hold of my carry-on bag by the handle so it bumped along with us.

"Oh the usual melodrama," he said, his tone so filled with disgust it was hard to ignore. "Her life is over, she's failed her, and she disowned the girl already."

Fuck. My. Life.

"She threw her out?"

He just gave me a tired look. "She had sex out of wedlock

and is now pregnant. She's stained the whole family with her heathen behavior."

Kill. Me.

Great.

"Where is Rain now?" Why was I even asking? His bushy eyebrows went up. She was at home. "Fuck, she's staying in my room, isn't she?"

He gave me a sorrowful sigh. "We've got some of Ohio down…"

"Thank you for the warning. They opened a new hotel, right?"

"Already booked your room. Making your mother pay for half of it, I got the other half."

"You didn't have to do that."

"No, we did. I'd have booked my own room if she'd let me get away with it. No need for both of us to drown in the madness."

The temptation to see if I could just fly back to New York was strong, but—it was the holidays. Frankie deserved some time with the guys by herself and I had to visit family to shut them up for a few months.

This was what I did. I'd just rent a car while I was here. And honestly, Christmas in a hotel sounded way preferable to all the family drama. I'd probably rescue Rain for part of it though. Make sure she actually had time to think with everyone shouting at her about what she had to do.

Fifteen.

Fuck that.

Three days later, I was sitting in a booth at Mason's, drinking a shake and reading on my digital tablet. I'd spent the morning finishing my Christmas shopping for the family in between taking Rain to a doctor's appointment. Afterward, she'd asked me to take her to her boyfriend's place.

Yep. My house had become ground zero and she just wanted to see the pimply-faced kid she was dating. I got a good look at him too. Granted, not my type, but his genuine happiness at seeing her hadn't been faked. But they looked so young it just made me want to bang my head against the table.

Her words of *this is what I want* circled endlessly in the back of my head, so I went for the dirty, dirty smut of gang bangs and enemies to lovers to just get away from it. Just because it would not be my choice, didn't mean I could disrespect hers even if I wanted to shout but *you're a baby too!*

The door jingled and I spared it a brief glance like I did whenever anyone wandered in on the quiet afternoon. Mason's wouldn't be hopping with the after school crowd when school was out. The glance up and then down again had been automatic, but I blinked as I tried to refocus on the screen in front of me before glancing up again.

"Rachel?"

Fuck. I hadn't imagined it.

"Sharon," I said in as neutral a tone as I could muster. Two plus years past all that shit in high school and I still had no fucks to spare for her. This cunt had made Frankie's life hell and she was grinning at me like we were long-lost pals?

"Oh my god, look at you!" And of course, she crossed right over to my booth then invaded my side of the booth in a cloud of eye-watering perfume and breath mints. She gave me one of those awkward size-squeezes of a hug. "You don't mind if I join you? I mean I can't stay for long. I just slipped in for a drink before I headed to the mall."

Yay me.

She didn't wait for me to answer before sliding into the seat opposite me. A waitress who looked as painfully young as my cousin wandered over and took her order for a diet coke and onion rings then wandered away. I took a drink from my shake and Sharon shook her head.

"You aren't worried about the freshman fifteen?"

I snorted. "Not a freshman." And with all the walking I did in New York? No, it wasn't a concern. Besides, I let myself have cheats when I wanted them. Starving yourself just made you hangry and bitchy.

Not that Sharon needed help.

"That's true," she said with a sigh, then the waitress was back with her soda. After she left, Sharon stripped the paper off her straw. "How is—where did you end up going?"

"Away," I said succinctly. "Where you should consider going now."

She laughed. It was uneven and a little hollow, but she laughed. "You always were a blunt thing. I promised I wouldn't stay long, but we haven't caught up in ages. We used to be friends, remember?"

Was she legit scolding me right now? For fucking real?

Thankfully, the waitress brought her the greasy onion rings. Now, if I were a real petty bitch, I'd give her shit about the deep-fried foods.

While I might be a bitch, I wasn't that petty.

"We were never real friends," I corrected her after the waitress left. Poor thing would probably curl up and die if someone looked at her cross-eyed. Better to keep her out of the line of fire.

"Now that's just bullshit." She actually looked offended. "We were all friends, you, me, Maria, Patty, Cheryl—"

She broke off on the last.

There was a name missing from her list.

Among many others, but a very specific name.

"I just want to be polite and catch up." Now the note in her voice went more than a little strained.

"Okay, let's catch up then, but let's not pretend we were friends, Sharon. You were a social climbing, backstabbing, selfish, overbearing, and mean fucktwat in school. Most of those are fine, I'm definitely a little selfish and more than a little mean. I've even been known to be overbearing, but I never tried to deliberately stab a so-called friend in the back or climb over her to get to a guy."

Nor would I ever.

"And furthermore," I continued, cutting her off when she would have interrupted and pointed a fry at her. "You tried to terrorize someone you once called a friend. Trust me when I say you don't have the first fucking clue what it is to be a friend. Fortunately, you were unsuccessful in all your little attempts to character assassinate and drive a wedge between *Frankie* and her guys."

All pretense of politeness fell away from Sharon's face and her lips compressed. "We don't need to discuss her."

"Oh, but we do, you see—*she* is my friend. *She* has been a better friend to me than I was to her at times. *She* put up with a lot shit, *a lot*. And all you did was capitalize on her misery and try to make it worse. Thankfully, you failed. But you did give them a lot of meaty material."

"What...?" Confusion clouded her gaze.

Like I said, I wasn't a petty bitch. "Bound Hearts? Surely you've heard them. Great album. The group is touring right now. All the rage on TikTok with clips from their debut."

"Yes," she said slowly, and I just grinned before I took a bite of my fry. Comprehension took a minute but watching it slowly ripple over her face was really delightful. Totally improved my day.

"Meaty material, and they're happier than ever. Maybe we should thank you for holding their feet to the fire." I made a show of thinking about it. "The guys really closed ranks around her the more you tried to tear her down, the more they lifted her up."

Her smile was sickly thin and quickly fading.

"Nah, scorpion is gonna scorpion. But she's happy and in love and they adore her and you're—well—you."

Without a word, Sharon slid out of the booth and left her onion rings untouched and her soda barely drunk.

"Aww," I said with mock-concern. "Leaving so soon? I thought you wanted to catch up."

"You're such a bitch."

I grinned. "Yes, I am." She only scowled in response and stalked toward the door. Guess I was getting stuck with the bill for her food. Excellent investment. At the jingle of the door, I called out, "Merry Christmas!"

With a glare, she all but stomped out to her car and I cackled to myself. Not petty in the slightest. That felt good. Even money said she would listen to every single one of their songs and try to dissect which part was a reference to her. That was gonna live rent-free in her head for a while.

I pulled the onion rings over and took a bite out of one before turning my tablet back on to resume reading. The holiday was already looking better.

SINS & SECRETS

FRANKIE - UNPUBLISHED SCENE

*T*he phone rang at four in the morning. Dragging myself up right, I stared at the vibrating device on the nightstand. Ian and I got to sleep not two hours earlier. Had it been two hours earlier? Wait... where were we? My brain was all cobwebs and fog. Snatching the phone before it vibrated off the nightstand, I stared at the caller ID.

The guys and Rachel—along with Jeremy and Hank—were the only people who could ring past the do not disturb. Hitting the answer, I slid out of bed and whispered, "Hang on." If she was calling me this early in the morning then she had to need something.

I still wasn't sure where we were. The tour had taken us to all kinds of clubs, bars, and other venues across California, to the Pacific Northwest, then farther west. We could wake up in one state, then be in another that night before we had to hit the road for a third. Sometimes we got hotels—like this one—and a couple of times, we'd just slept in the car or SUV or whatever was working as our transport.

I dragged on some shorts. Okay, I'd been wearing shorts the night before. We were somewhere warm. Fuck, I hoped so. I found the hotel room card and then crept over to the door. It made a little squeak as I opened it and I glanced back at the bed. Ian was still out.

Good.

With care, I stepped out into the humid air and made a face before closing the door behind me. Definitely warm. The rooms along this block were all dark, and the parking lot was full.

"Sorry," I murmured to Rachel as I made my way along the second floor balcony toward the stairs. The ground was cool under my bare feet. "I didn't want to wake Ian up."

"S'okay," Rachel said. Well, slurred really. "I probably shouldn't have called. It's four in the morning."

Four in the morning. Oh, we were in the same time zone. At the end of the block were steps leading downstairs. I perched on the top one so I could glance back in case Ian came out.

"You should...go..." There were other words in there, I swore, but they were not intelligible.

"I'm awake," I said, scrubbing a hand over my face. "I don't want to go. What's wrong?"

"Nothing." If the muffled and slurred speech weren't disturbing enough, the fact she half-sang those last two syllables would have demanded a response. "Really. Nothing. Go back to bed. Pretty boy in your bed. Have fun with the pretty—"

"Rachel." I tried not to sound impatient or irritated. I wasn't either of those things. "What's wrong?"

"I'm drunk," she admitted. "That's what's wrong. Went out with your boys tonight—they were being my wingmen."

I bit my lip.

"Jake promised he would get me laid."

Nope, I wasn't laughing.

"We had fun, cute bartender at this place. You know, she and I hooked up a few times."

No, I didn't know but I made a little sound of agreement.

"So, she wanted to hook up. Kisses like a damn demon. All tongue and teeth. Really good with the tongue." There was a sigh, like she couldn't believe she was admitting this. The slurring words weren't helping either. "But nothing happened."

"Okay. Is this a good thing or a bad thing?"

Rachel let out a little sound of absolute irritation. "I don't know."

"Been there," I admitted.

"Yeah? You tried to hook up in a bathroom bar with a girl you knew would eat you out until you screamed and not ask for a damn thing back then turned her down cause she wasn't the guy driving you nuts?"

"Well—no."

A moment of silence, then she sniffed. "Good."

"Oh, I'm going to regret this, but why good?"

"Cause if you said you had let some girl go down on you in a bathroom, I was going be really butthurt." If it wasn't for the element of misery in her sigh tangled up with all that regret and longing, I might have laughed.

"I'm sorry," I said. "What can I do?"

"Nuffink. Nuffink anyone can do. That son of a bitch with his magic dick and pierced tongue has ruined me. It's really annoying, Frankie. No guy is that good in bed."

Not going to argue that point.

"Especially not guys who have secrets." Something squeaked, just the whoosh of it and I could picture her falling back on a bed. "I think I'm gonna puke."

"Then sit up and don't bounce. If you need to vomit, go to the bathroom. Are you at the brownstone? Do I need to call Coop to come help?"

"Oh fuck you," she muttered without any heat. "I do not need someone to hold my hair and that's not why I'm gonna puke."

"Okay."

The silence dragged on, but I could hear the soft sounds of her breathing, so I waited her out. I wished I was there. Rachel sounded like she needed a hug—bad.

"I'm sorry," she said in a much softer voice. "You just want to help and I woke you up and now…"

"Hush. This is what a best friend is for. As I recall, you've listened to me whine and complain and cry and even waffle more than once."

A beat. Then. "True."

I chuckled.

"But you're worth it."

"So are you smart ass." Then because she'd brought it up. "Dominic cares, Rach."

"It doesn't matter." Not even the slurring could soften the hardness behind those words. Before I could say anything else, she said, "He's all sins and secrets, Frankie. So many secrets."

"What kinds of secrets?"

"I—it's not important," she said after a moment. "Not something you need to know." Though she sounded a little more sober. "I wish I didn't know."

That just made my heart hurt. "Want me to kick his ass?"

"No. I don't want you to bring it up with him at all." There was that sigh again. "I shouldn't have called."

"You say that again, I'm going to kick your ass." I slapped the bug away from my leg and stared down the steps.

"Wow, you even sound like you mean it."

"Impressed?" I didn't laugh but then neither did she.

"Yes. And maybe a little horny."

Now I laughed and her soft huff came over the phone. "Rach, I want to help. I hate that you're hurting."

"I'm not hurting. I'm—complicated."

"You are hurting," I argued, but that wasn't what she needed from me. She'd never drunk called me before. Hell, I didn't think I'd ever seen her drunk. "I just wish I could fix it."

"Me too," she admitted. "But I'll get over it." Then there was another sound, like a light flicking on. "I have to. It's better if I do."

"Uh huh."

"It's five in the morning," she said after another long silence. "You need to go to bed, what is it, two there?"

"No," I said. "It's five."

She groaned. "Where are you?"

"No clue."

"Then how do you know it's five?"

I laughed. "Cause it said five on the clock in the hotel room."

It took a moment, then she joined me laughing before the sound of water turned on. The shower. "Right, that means you've had what? An hour of sleep?"

"Two," I said primly. Well mostly two, but I didn't think she wanted to know about Ian and I spending thirty minutes unwinding *after* the show. Two counted. "But I can totally go back for at least one more."

"Go do that. I'm gonna shower. Then—something. They're probably gonna go running soon." The absolute disgust in her voice made me laugh.

"Well, I don't recommend it if you're still drunk."

"I don't recommend it if I'm sober," she countered. "Go back to bed you rock star bitch and forget I bothered you. Let's just pretend this whole call didn't happen."

"No," I told her softly. The running water still in the background promised me she hadn't hung up. "You're my friend, that means I hurt if you're hurting. When I get home—you and me? We're having a long, *sober* conversation about this."

"Yeah." The way she elongated the word said 'no,' loud and clear. "Might need some lubrication for that."

"Then we'll get trashed and talk about it." I could do that.

"If we're both trashed, who is gonna hold our hair?"

I chuckled. "We'll take turns."

"I can live with that. Now I'm hanging up on you, I smell and I need to brush my teeth."

"Rach?"

"Yeah?"

"You know I love you, right?"

There was a really long sigh on the other end of the phone. "I do know that and you're a sappy bitch for telling me."

I grinned. "What does that make you?"

"Lucky as fuck," she said, then made a kiss smacking noise at the phone before she hung up.

I stared at my phone for a moment and then rubbed a hand over my face. Flipping to the texts, I fired off one to Coop.

Me: *Is Rachel really okay?*

I didn't think he'd be awake, but he answered.

Coop: *Nope. But she's still lying to everyone, including herself. Jake's gonna kill Dominic at this rate.*

I frowned.

Coop: *Go back to bed, Beautiful. We'll keep an eye on her.*

Coop: *And I won't let Jake kill Dominic.*

Coop: *Yet.*

I sent him three kiss emojis then promised to call later.

Jake wasn't the only one who wanted to kill Dominic. Sins and secrets, huh?

Yeah, I wanted to know what the fuck was going on there too.

LEGACY AND LOVERS
BONUS SCENES

BROTHERS & BOYFRIENDS

COOP - DELETED SCENE

*W*e waited for the waitress to finish taking our order and moving away before we focused on each other. Jake had been the last to arrive, but he had practice and then had to grab a car to come uptown. Archie had his phone in his hand while Bubba drummed his fingers against the side of his cup, eyeing Archie's phone and whatever he was searching.

"Do I need to start?" Jake asked before draining his glass of water. I nudged mine over to him. I wasn't planning on drinking it anyway. He lifted his chin in thanks.

"I don't think you need to," I told him in between sips of coffee. The diner was one of our favorite spots. Normally, we'd have this kind of discussion at home, but Frankie was still resting and we wanted to avoid arousing any suspicions. Especially if she misinterpreted anything.

Honestly, sometimes, it was funny. The rest of the time? Not so much. And I'd personally slug the first one of us, myself included, who made her cry.

"No?" Jake asked when Bubba and Archie kept their

attention on the phone. "Then it's just you and me planning this?"

"Fuck off, Jake," Archie said without glancing up. "We're trying to find the right one. I know I saw what I think will work and we're going to need to do a custom order, but I want to show you what I was thinking."

I hid a smile at Jake's faint smirk. "Just making sure you were still paying attention."

"Stop trying to bait him," Bubba said with a brief glance at us. "That doesn't help."

"Man, you used to be fun." The mock pout did what the bitching didn't, they laughed and my grin deepened. "Fine, while you two sad sacks search, let's talk about how we want to propose."

"I had a thought on that," I said, putting the coffee cup down. "I've been thinking about this for a few years."

"Of course you have, Mr. Well-Adjusted."

"Don't hate, you'll get there when you grow up." That earned me a middle finger, of course, when I added, "if you ever do," he just snorted and shook his head.

"Got it." Archie made a little fist pump of triumph. There was more animation and engagement to him recently. The past year had been hard on him, Frankie had worried and so had I. Hell, all of us had, but he was making his way back toward us and for that, I was damn glad.

The waitress returned with plates loaded with burgers, fries, and fresh drinks all around. She even brought the Coke I'd ordered to have with my meal and I drained the coffee.

No sooner did she leave than my phone pinged with a message. So did Jake's. I pulled it out of my pocket and thumbed the screen open so I could look at it.

"This one is in three parts, but we can customize one to be in four," Archie said. "I say we work it so each one has two diamonds and then whatever other stone we want to add to it, that way it's balanced, then we have them work the loop in."

The infinity loop, like our tattoos. Not a bad plan. Jake munched on a fry as he studied it.

"We have a lot of options with metal, but how big do we want it—I mean she can't have more than a half-inch at best between her knuckles and the first joint."

"We can talk to the jeweler," Archie said, waving off the concern. "I'm thinking titanium or something as strong. Just because that's what the commitment is. But also, we can have matching rings crafted when we're looking at the bands part."

"Are we going to discuss how we handle the legalities now?" Bubba had taken a bite of his burger to punctuate the question and I glanced back at the ring.

The idea of interlocking rings where we each gave her one that would then form a whole held a lot of appeal. This conversation was almost as funny as it had been inevitable, really.

"No," Archie said after a moment, his tone more thoughtful than confrontational. "That's a conversation we have to have with her."

"Agreed," I injected. "This is about asking her, planning how we ask her and making it clear that we're all committed to this."

"You think she doubts that?" Jake considered, his eyes narrowed.

"No," Bubba answered with a sharp shake of his head. "She doesn't doubt us. I'll be honest, even when she thought we were being dicks, she didn't doubt that we cared. We've made this work for the past four years and we're going strong."

I agreed with all of that.

"No, Frankie doesn't doubt us. The tour put a lot of

things into perspective."

"Fuck," Archie said with an exhale. "Did it ever." He finally set aside the phone. "I'm all for you guys going platinum, but next time, I'm just coming along."

"Same," Jake muttered. "I fucking hated being five thousand miles away when she needed us."

Agreed, but I didn't have to throw that in. "We handled it." I pointed to Bubba with a french fry. "More, Bubba handled it. He kept us looped in, we were there on the phone and on video calls. Granted, while not *ideal*, we were there. We've made this work and we're even balancing the more hard-headed personalities among us."

I didn't even glance at Jake or Archie and they still flipped me off, but Bubba laughed. "Good point."

"Fine, we're saints." We were so not, but Archie's exasperation was funny. "Who asks first?"

"Not you," I said with Bubba and Jake's echoed comments piling on top. "No offense," I said, continuing as Archie seemed torn between insult and amusement.

"I'll let you know if I need to take it."

I grinned. "The point," I pressed on before Jake or Bubba could jump in. "Not you because I think we all should have a carte blanche on our own proposals. We have our own relationships with her, then we have the one we built as a family. You," —I pointed a fry at Archie— "will absolutely go over the top with whatever you do and that means it's a good capper. Mine is likely to be a lot more personal."

"Are you saying mine won't be personal?" Sometimes, I enjoyed Archie's needling and other times, I just wanted to throw food at him.

"No, dickhead," Jake answered. "I'm saying your idea of personal is a whole orchestra and sky writing. It's definitely got style, don't get me wrong. You're also exceptional at planning the big things that knock her right off her feet. But

Coop is right, I want my own proposal. I want to plan it, propose, and make it personal. Then maybe cap off all our proposals with a big group one."

"Or..." Bubba said slowly, before taking a drink of his soda. "We propose, but we ask her not to answer. Not immediately. I like the idea of keeping it personal, one thousand percent. But I also want her to *know* for damn certain we're coordinating this. That we are asking her as individuals, but we're all in this together. We all want to marry her."

"Brother Boyfriends unite," Archie said with a grin and Bubba just chuckled.

"So we propose, in our own ways, on our own schedules. But we also set a timetable so that we can go in order."

"You already know the order, don't you?" Archie asked even if it sounded mostly rhetorical.

"Sure, but I'm open to discussion. After all, I proposed to her already."

"You were five." Jake flicked a french fry at me.

"Still counts and she said yes long before she met you bozos. So, I think we go in the order we fell for her."

"Which means in the order we met her," Bubba said and nodded.

"That means I'm definitely last." Instead of being remotely irritated, Archie seemed pleased. "Since every proposal is personal, I get to do whatever I want—right?"

"Why do I think this is going to be both hilarious and cringe-inducing?" Jake threw in, but then he bumped Archie's shoulder with his fist. "Short answer, yes, you do whatever you want."

"Are you going to incorporate the group ask?" I was curious because that could go either way.

"I think so," Archie said. "Let me do a little more mental planning. Jake, do you have graph paper?"

"Yep." He pulled it out of his backpack and set it on the

table, then passed over a pencil. Archie pushed his plate out the way and started sketching.

"Do you think we should ask her dad?" Bubba mused.

"Nope," Jake said even as Archie shook his head.

"No, I think we tell him. Like if we want him involved at any point in the proposal, but as much as I like the guy and Frankie adores him—he doesn't get to make this decision for her. No one makes this decision for her."

We all agreed.

"Fair deal," I said, tackling the next uncomfortable part of this whole thing. "Custom designed and built ring is going to be expensive and before you say you can cover it, I want to pay for my own ring for her."

"Same," Bubba said.

"Yep." Jake gave a thumbs up as he leaned toward what Archie was drawing. "We need to budget for it."

For once, Archie didn't mumble a complaint. He just nodded. "Equitable, well-balanced, and committed."

"How very mature of you," I teased and he snorted, before he snagged a fry of Jake's plate and flung it at me. I caught this one and just ate it.

"So that just leaves *when* do we ask?"

"When the rings are ready," I suggested. "That gives us all the time to plan out what we want to do."

Agreement reached, we ate and watched Archie draw with Jake adding some suggestions. Bubba and I also offered up some ideas, but by the time we finished lunch and ordered cheesecake to take home to her, we had a basic ring design and a budget.

And I already knew exactly how I was going to propose.

I couldn't wait.

DREAMY & DEVOTED

FRANKIE - DELETED SCENE

*L*aughing, I made my way off the dance floor while fanning a hand toward my face. The club was amazing, the music was fantastic—but even better, everyone was here. My friends. My family. I glanced down at the rings on my finger—my fiancés.

That sent a little thrill through me. At the bar, I found a spot where air conditioning was actually blowing downward. Stopping there, I tilted my head back to let the coolness wash over me.

"What can I get for you?"

When I opened my eyes, the bartender was standing there. "Water, please. Ice cold."

He chuckled. "Coming right up."

If I had alcohol right now, I might throw up. I'd danced with the guys, multiple times. Danced with KC. Danced with Chloe. Danced with Dad. Even Alec and Craig had gotten pulled into the action. It was all so overwhelming and at the same time—amazing.

"Hey," Rachel said as she slid up to the bar next to me. "You good?"

Sweat gleamed on her brow and her lips were a little swollen. I didn't make any comments on that because she was still working on *her* and that was the important part. The bartender brought over the ice water and I grasped it gratefully as Rachel ordered one for her and a soda. Holding up a finger, I downed about half the glass.

Between the chill of the water and sitting under the fan, I didn't feel like I as overheating as much. "Oh, I'm fine—just hot."

Rachel laughed. "You've been hot forever, why is that an issue now?"

I rolled my eyes even as I laughed. She grinned and when her water got there, she clinked her glass with mine.

"Cheers, gorgeous," she told me. "I still think you're nuts for taking on four of them, but they might almost be worthy of you if they keep spoiling you the way they are."

"I adore them," I reminded her. "They're perfect just like they are."

She made a gagging sound, then grinned. "I'll give them credit, they make you smile and that's the important part."

"I miss you," I confessed and she sniffed.

"Of course you do, because I'm awesome." She managed to hold the arrogance for all of five seconds before we were both cracking up. Another couple of drinks and I was almost not boiling alive when she added, "Are you happy? I mean for real? This is—" She motioned to the club, the Greek themes with its columns and nooks, the dance floor and the stage.

"It's Archie," I reminded her. "And yes, I am happy. Like—no caveats happy."

"No caveats?" Rachel raised both eyebrows. "That's something."

"Right?" When Dad and Eddie asked me out to dinner tonight, I'd had an idea that something might happen.

Archie's was the only proposal left, but… "It's everything," I admitted. "Rach, I have a family. A huge family. Not just Dad and Kelly and the kids, though that's so cool. I have Jeremy and Eddie—I couldn't imagine Eddie being 'family' but he is. Then the guys…they're everything. We've had some ups and downs, but they're still my best friends and they love me and I love them—"

"You know there might be something wrong with you," she teased.

"Maybe, if there is, I don't want to fix it. Because there's also you."

"Saving the best for last," she said, grinning.

"Absolutely, Mr. Thorns."

That cracked her up all over again. "I still think I could give these guys some tips but after today, I might have to admit Archie's got the romance and showmanship down."

Laughter bubbled up through me as effervescent as the champagne that had been flowing since Archie "popped" the question. "He does," I said.

"Okay, all dreamy swooning aside—this what you want? Marriage to all four of them? You guys are ready for it?"

"Can anyone be really ready?" I asked before I drained the water and the bartender slid another over to me. I mouthed thank you and he winked at me before Rachel groaned. "What?" I said swinging a look at her.

"He's flirting with you."

I held up my hand. "Sorry, I'm taken." We stared at each other for a beat and Rachel's lips trembled.

"But you noticed he was flirting."

"I didn't care," I said, rather than admit that I wasn't really paying attention to the bartender. Nice guy brought me water. So what if he winked? He wasn't one of my guys.

"That was the right answer," Jake said as he slid up behind

me and wrapped his arms around my middle. Thankfully, I wasn't dying from heat stroke but even if I was, I'd still have leaned back into him.

Eyes closed, I just drank in his nearness as he pressed a kiss just behind my ear. "Rachel."

"Jake."

I cracked my eyelids open to find Rachel giving us an indulgent smile.

"Looking after our girl?" Jake asked.

"Always," she said. "Also, you look ridiculously happy."

I grinned.

"Don't hate," Jake teased and I elbowed him. He gave a gentle oomph then squeezed me lightly. "Fine, we love Rachel, we just don't tell her that. We're much better at the snarking and the threats."

"This is true," Rachel agreed. "Now, go away, I want time with my BFF before you guys drag her back out to the dance floor."

"I was thinking of stealing away to a private room," Jake mused. "Maybe celebrate a little more personally."

Rachel made a gagging sound.

"Don't worry," Jake said, still grinning. "You're not invited."

"Oh my god," I laughed and tilted my head back to look up at him.

"Too much?" His eyes were practically dancing and I smiled as he brushed his lips to mine.

"Nope," I promised. "You're perfect."

"No ma'am, that's you. But I will let you girls have a drink. I'm gonna threaten the bartender so he doesn't flirt with you again."

"Jake—"

"Hey? It's me." Then he winked and gave me another kiss

before he slipped away and when I glanced back at Rachel, she was laughing.

"Ridiculously happy," she commented. "And I am glad. I still don't think anyone is ever going to be good enough for you, but those four come the closest."

"They're perfect for me," I said. "They've always been perfect for me, even when I didn't see what they felt or were asking me for."

Her expression softened. "Want to go find a table with our waters and gossip for a bit?"

"You have anything good to tell me?" I raised my brows. Her smirk was adorable.

"Maybe, you'll just have to work at getting it out of me."

The bartender had brought over two fresh glasses with ice water and no winks. Scooping them up, Rachel and I weaved through the crowd. There were well-wishers and more than one quick side hug as we climbed the stairs to the second level. It was definitely cooler up here.

"Rache?"

"Hmm?"

"Spill."

"Damn," Rachel said, lips quirking. "Foreplay, Frankie. Foreplay. You want me to come clean with the details, you need to work me up to it."

I rolled my eyes and laughed. "You're terrible."

"And you love me, so don't bitch."

It was true, I did love her. "Fine...have I mentioned how beautiful you are to me?"

"That's better," Rachel said and when she winked, I held up my left hand.

"Still taken."

"Don't I know it."

There was a beat and then we were cracking up all over again. I caught Archie's eye from across the room and he raised his glass to me where he was talking to Eddie and I grinned, before I blew him a kiss. Coop had Trina on the dance floor and Ian was—there he was, he was dancing with Chloe and she was laughing.

I couldn't adore them more if I tried.

"So damn gone on them," Rachel commented.

"Yep," I admitted. "One thousand percent."

FAREWELLS AND FOREVER
BONUS SCENES

AMBITIONS & ANTICIPATION

FRANKIE - POST FAREWELLS AND FOREVER SCENE

I rocked Charlie gently. His sniffles had gotten worse, but it was just teething. Sweet baby boy was just precocious trying to cut them all at the same time. Izzy had been like that. Thankfully, Joshua had spared us, cutting his teeth with barely a whimper or a roar. He just got it done.

Not that I minded, Charlie just needed extra cuddles when his temperature was up and I felt the same way. It was nice to be cuddled when you weren't feeling well. Cuddling them was one of my favorite things to do, especially when they were soft and warm from their bath, smelling sweet. I rubbed my cheek against his hair as we just rocked together.

Jake had looked after him while I showered, then I took Charlie in the shower to wash him up too. The falling water always made him laugh. Now that we were dressed again, Jake left me to settle him while he grabbed a shower. The guys would be home soon.

"Hey," Archie said softly, and I blinked slowly to find him kneeling in front of the rocking chair. "Little guy is sacked out. Let's put him in bed, then we're putting Mama to bed too."

A yawn escaped me even as Archie eased Charlie from me with the kind of expertise he and the guys had developed over the last few years.

"Shh," Archie hushed him as Charlie stretched and let out a little complaint. I rose slowly to follow them, even as I did my own stretch. Charlie's cheeks weren't flushed anymore and his lashes barely trembled as Archie made the smooth transition from holding him to settling him into the bed.

It wouldn't be long before Charlie, like Josh and Izzy before him outgrew the toddler bed. It made me a little sad. But only a little. I loved every new stage, even when they wore me out.

Sliding an arm around me, Archie nuzzled a kiss to the top of my head. "Mrs. Standish," he murmured. "You need me to settle you in bed too?"

There was more than a little heat kissing the end of that offer and I smiled.

"Yes," I told him and his eyes darkened. "But after lunch, please. I'm starving."

My stomach let out a gurgle right on cue.

"And I really do want some us time, just the five of us— and after, I promise you can put me to bed and do whatever you want with me."

Head tilted, he appeared to consider my offer. "Can we keep the us time to thirty minutes or less?" He waggled his eyebrows. "You're looking especially luscious and I missed you."

"Maybe not that fast, but we'll see what we can do." I smothered another yawn before it could escape. Tangling my fingers with his, I drew him out of Charlie's room and we checked that the monitor was on.

The smell of lunch reached me before I even hit the top of

the stairs. Someone had gone to Sleepy Pete's. They'd brought home meatball sandwiches.

I was about to die and go to heaven. The mouthwatering red sauce, rich meat, and layers of parmesan on toasted bread. "Oh, I'm in love," I said as we hit the last step on the stairs.

Archie chuckled. "Never let it be said I don't spoil you with everything."

"I wouldn't dare let *anyone* say that," I promised him as I half-danced toward the deck where Jake and Ian were waiting. Coop was just coming in the door and I grinned as I beckoned to him with a curve of my hand.

Yes, I wanted all of us in one spot. I wanted to savor their company. I just wanted to *be*—but meatball sandwiches had been procured and I was *starving*.

"I see you followed your nose, Angel," Ian teased as I reached him. I steadied myself with a hand against his chest as I rose up on my tiptoes to kiss him. "Jake called and said you needed the protein."

I didn't kick Jake, because he wasn't wrong. "Honestly, this just smells delicious, but it's even better because you guys are here."

Coop freed his tie as I reached him and I welcomed him home with a kiss. Then we were settling around the table as the sandwiches were divided out along with drinks. Jeremy arrived with drinks for everyone. Mostly water, but there was also iced tea.

"I'm going to take care of some errands and I'll pick up the children after school. Do you need anything else?" He gave me an appraising look. Since Jeremy had already learned my news, I just gave him a smile.

"Everything is perfect, thank you Jeremy."

He nodded and I swore he could look serene and smug at the same time. It was nice. The guys played catch up, Jake and Archie discussed a little business while Ian filled me in on the proposed tour and Coop drifted back and forth between the conversations as we ate.

But when we were done, Archie said, "Okay, it's been an hour, Mrs. Standish. I think I've earned my time to put you to bed."

"Well, that's one way to be blunt about it." Coop chuckled, but Archie just shrugged.

"Subtlety went out the window when we had to start running interference with the kids to make sure we got time with our girl."

"True," Jake said. "That's just gotten tougher with each addition."

"But worth it," Ian mused aloud. "I like our family."

"It's just about perfect," Archie said. "In fact, if we stop now, Charlie will be going to school in three years or less, then we get all day with Mama again." He gave me a playful leer and I let out a deep sigh.

"Well, I hope you aren't too attached to that idea. I know it's good to have ambition, but I've waited all week for you to get home—"

I didn't even have to say it, Archie straightened in his seat and his gaze zeroed in on mine. "Yeah?"

"Might need a raincheck on those all day play dates for roughly five years and seven months…"

His expression shifted. They all did. Coop and Jake high-fived. Ian leaned back in his chair and looked so damn pleased, but it was Archie I focused on. Archie who'd never once worried about the fact that despite our lack of protection, it was the other guys who got their shots at fatherhood before him.

We'd only been trying for a few months again…and we'd been so busy. A glimmer of tears reflected in his eyes as

Archie began to smile. "When do we get to find out boy or girl?"

"Probably another eight to ten weeks, Arch," Coop said. "Why? We taking bets?"

"Hell yes," Archie said, his grin growing. He paused a beat and studied me. "Do we get to find out ahead of time or do you want to wait?"

"We can do whatever you want, Papa," I promised. "Though it looks like I'll be touring pregnant again."

"A short one," Ian said firmly. "With healthy breaks in it. I don't want you exhausted."

"Agreed," Archie said, tapping his chin. "We need to modify schedules. Josh took a lot out of Frankie while she was carrying Charlie and Izzy is just going to want to take over everything."

"We got this," Jake said. "We know all the tips and the tricks… also, we should hit the gym to keep up our stamina for when her sex drive goes overtime."

"Oh hush," I said shaking my head, then focusing on Archie. "That's the best part."

Archie laughed. "No, babe. The best part is you. Every-thing else is just…" He blew out a breath. "You're pregnant?"

"Yep."

"And everything is good? All healthy? No concerns?"

"Nope. Though I think my stretch marks are gonna have stretch marks." I'd given up worrying about a flat tummy ever again.

"Tiger stripes for the win." Archie blinked. "Wait a minute —excuse me gentlemen. Our wife said I could put her to bed and do whatever I wanted with her. I want to celebrate. So y'all are on the Toddler Patrol."

He didn't wait for permission before tugging me to my feet. All the way up the stairs, I swore I could *hear* his brain going a mile a minute and when we made it to our suite, he pressed me up against the closed door and studied me.

"Is it okay if I'm a little terrified this time?" he asked, his voice solemn as hell.

"You've been terrified every time," I reminded him, but I cupped his face. "Your secret is safe with me."

All of their secrets would be safe with me. Always.

"This is true. So, just to confirm—health checks are good and sex is still on the table?"

"Oh, Mr. Standish," I informed him. "I may not be able to have coffee, but I would still like to get a little cream."

I couldn't resist. His eyes lit up at the comment. "Oh, Mrs. Standish, please put in your order. I will make sure to fill you up…but first, get naked please. I haven't seen those breasts or that gorgeous pussy in far too long and it's time to get reacquainted."

Wrapping my arms around his neck, I lifted my face toward his and he rewarded me with a deep, lingering kiss.

"We're gonna have a baby," he whispered. "Fuck, I love you so much."

We were gonna have a baby.

"Oh shit." He paused as I lifted off my shirt.

"What?"

"We need A names," he told me.

"Archie?"

"Yes, Babe?"

"I'm going to get naked. So are you. We can work on names later."

"Yes, ma'am," Archie said. "Getting naked now."

SECRETS & SOULS

FRANKIE - DELETED SCENE

*T*he following is a new scene that would take place in Chapter Twenty of *Farewells and Forever*.

LIFE WAS WEIRD. IT COULD GO FROM BEING RIDICULOUSLY BUSY to almost too routine. Other times, it could be so full it was overwhelming and still leave you aching as you missed the people who weren't there. Then there were days like this—when your best friend helped you with a secret plan with no questions asked.

"How are you doing?" Rachel asked. "We can take a break."

"Oh don't you start," I scolded, despite my amusement at the question and dropping a hand to rest on my hip. "We've been doing this for twenty minutes. I'm hardly going to wilt like some delicate fucking flower." As it was, we'd barely even started taking pictures.

"I will if I want to," Rachel countered, mutiny filtering into her expression. "You were tired when you got here."

That was an accusation.

"Yes, because it was a long drive and I still have to pee every thirty seconds." I wouldn't deny it. "That does not make me hapless or on the verge of collapse." Archie had wanted to drive me in and he'd only stopped fussing when Jeremy took over the driving duties.

"No, but you are *very* pregnant. I mean—" She straightened and swept a hand in my direction. "Girl, there is robust and full of life and then there's you."

"Thanks." I wasn't sure if it was my baleful expression or my tone, but Rachel cracked up. Warmth flooded her eyes and her smile expanded. Both managed to puncture my irritation with her. "Seriously, thanks."

"You are welcome. It doesn't hurt that you're fucking beautiful," Rachel said with a wink. "It also lets me indulge you when you decide to get cranky."

"You're lucky I love you," I teased her and she grinned without even an element of irony.

"Oh, I'm very well aware of how lucky I am—I almost wish I could work so that I could be a fly on the wall when you show them these pictures." She hid her face on the last, snapping another picture as I tilted my head. Almost eight months pregnant. If you'd told me I would go out of my way to document this moment, I'd have laughed.

Everything was swollen, from my feet to my hands. It was hard to sit to lay down to stand—pretty much anything. And I constantly had to pee. At the same time, there was a thrill involved in every step of the way. The guys were...

"Perfect," Rachel murmured as the snap of her camera brought me back. We were in the city. It was a surprise gift for the guys—all these photos—and Rachel had helped me with the secret keeping, going so far as to arrange a private shoot at the studio. She'd also done my hair and make-up with the help of her girlfriend. It had been my first chance to really sit and talk to her. I liked her.

A lot.

Still, the fewer who had to keep our secret, the less chance it had of getting out. Her girlfriend slipped off and left the two of us to do this and Rachel had a dozen different ideas from the sweet to the sexy. Since I trusted her, I let her set the tone.

"What's perfect?" I asked, turning to face her. The baby shifted and I dropped my hand onto my stomach to soothe him or her. We'd voted three to two to wait and see. The guys argued constantly about the idea of a boy or a girl. They were in love with the idea of a girl. Right up until they remembered that boys like girls and then they'd all get growly and scowly.

It was adorable.

A laugh escaped me and Rachel grinned as she snapped another photo. "Your expression was perfect and now it is again—want to share what dirty thoughts are going through your head?"

"They are not *dirty* thoughts," I said with a sniff but it did little to diminish her smile. "I'm just happy." I really was. As uncomfortable as being pregnant was, I liked looking forward. I liked anticipating... I liked how the guys were alternating between excitement and irritation with each other and the process.

The prospective grandparents weren't much better and Rachel—for all she gave me hell—she'd been thrilled for me from the moment I told her I was excited. Thrilled and supportive.

I wouldn't trade a single moment of it. Not even...

All at once the whole bubble seemed to tremble and Rachel lowered the camera. "Frankie?" Concern reflected in her eyes and her tone.

"Do you think, if Maddy had this kind of support I do now when she was having me..."

"No," Rachel said abruptly and I blinked. "Your mother could have had all the support in the world, she chose to walk away from all of it. She made it about her, not about you, not about the future. She made selfish choices."

I swallowed, rubbing my hand against my abdomen. "I wish…" I did and I didn't. I had Kelly. She wasn't my mother, but she was a mom and she showered me with affection whenever I let her. I had Sara, Ian's mom. I had Carly and Alicia—and even Klara. I had a lot of maternal figures who wanted to be there, but none of them tried to be Maddy.

None tried to take her "place."

"I wish…" Closing my eyes, I had to fight back the sudden surge of tears. Most of the out of control emotions had eased in the last couple of months. But there were still momentary crying jags and wild laughter. "I shouldn't—" I couldn't complete the thoughts.

They were selfish.

One more snap of a camera and then Rachel caught my hand and tugged me over to the windows. The city sprawled out beyond. I swallowed around the lump in my throat.

"There is no should and, of course, you wish," Rachel said in a tone that brooked no arguments. In fact, it was so absolutely reasonable and no nonsense, it demanded I focus on her. "You miss your mom. You wish you could connect with her right now. That's okay and you have every right to feel that way—"

Tears burned in my eyes. "Sometimes it feels so stupid and others…"

"I know," Rachel said with a sigh then she wrapped an arm around me and leaned her head against mine. Closing my eyes, I rested on the strength she offered. "I wish she'd been a way better mom to you so she could be here right now. I wish you could have every goddamn thing you've ever wanted."

I sniffled, then summoned a smile. "My life's not so shabby…"

"No," Rachel said, agreeing with me. "It's not." She didn't have to say anything else. As much as it irked me to miss Maddy, I did—but it wasn't *Maddy* I missed so much as who Maddy *could* or maybe *should* have been.

"Love you, Rach."

"Love you too," she whispered.

We stood there for a few more minutes while I got my wild emotions back under control. The tears evaporated, slowly, and the ache in my soul eased.

Finally, Rachel blew out a breath as she moved away and I didn't miss how she dabbed at her own eyes. Right, time to get a grip for both of us.

"What's next?"

"Topless photos. I want to enjoy what pregnancy has done to your breasts and we can take pictures that will make those idiots you married drool."

I laughed. This was what inspired the photo shoot in the first place. I'd seen photos of Demi Moore years earlier and the imagery had always stuck with me.

"Fair warning," I said as I dried my own tears. "Big boobs *hurt.*"

"Beauty is pain," she deadpanned.

We locked eyes for a long moment before we both cracked up. Yep, life could be painful too but it was also full of moments like this.

Moments I wouldn't trade for anything.

AFTERWORD

Thank you again for being on this journey with me. Thank you for always asking about characters we met along the way. We've seen KC's series and Emersyn's. I haven't forgotten our queen of the cacti, Rachel. She will absolutely be getting her series and it is coming.

I can't wait to see what's next.

xoxo

Heather

ABOUT HEATHER LONG

I *love* books. Not just a little bit, but a lot. Books were my best friends when I was growing up. Books didn't care if I was new to a town or to a class. They were always there, my trustiest of companions. Until they turned on me and said I had to write them.

I can tell you that my own personal happily ever after included writing books. I've always said that an HEA is a work in progress. It's true in my marriage, my friendships, and in my career. I am constantly nurturing my muse as we dive into new tales, new tropes, new characters and more.

After seventeen years in Texas, we relocated to the Pacific Northwest in search of seasons, new experiences, and new geography. I can't wait to discover what life (and my muse) have in store for me.

Maybe writing was always my destiny and romance my fate. After all, my grandmother wasn't a fan of picture books and used to read me her Harlequin Romance novels.

Follow Heather & Sign up for her newsletter:
www.heatherlong.net
TikTok

ALSO BY HEATHER LONG

82nd Street Vandals

Savage Vandal

Vicious Rebel

Ruthless Traitor

Dirty Devil

Shamelessly Loyal (Novella)

Brutal Fighter

Dangerous Renegade

Merciless Spy

Reckless Thief

Fierce Dancer

Bay Ridge Royals

Shamelessly Loyal (Novella)

Battle Lines

Deceptive Truce

Wicked Surrender

Violent Chaos

Desperate Victory

Blue Ivy Prep

Problem Child

Mad Boys

Party Crashers

Money Shot

Throne Taker

Lone Star Leathernecks

Semper Fi Cowboy

As You Were, Cowboy

Shackled Souls

Succubus Chained

Succubus Unchained

Succubus Blessed

Shackled Souls (Omnibus)

STANDALONES

Kiss of Fate (w/Blake Blessing)

Taste of Karma (w/Blake Blessing)

I'll Be Home... (w/Tate James)

Untouchable

Rules and Roses

Changes and Chocolates

Keys and Kisses

Whispers and Wishes

Hangovers and Holidays

Brazen and Breathless

Trials and Tiaras

Graduation and Gifts

Defiance and Dedication

Songs and Sweethearts

Legacy and Lovers

Farewells and Forever

Wolves of Willow Bend

Wolf at Law

Wolf Bite

Caged Wolf

Wolf Claim

Wolf Next Door

Rogue Wolf

Bayou Wolf

Untamed Wolf

Wolf with Benefits

River Wolf

Single Wicked Wolf

Desert Wolf

Snow Wolf

Wolf on Board

Holly Jolly Wolf

Shadow Wolf

His Moonstruck Wolf

Thunder Wolf

Ghost Wolf

Outlaw Wolves

Wolf Unleashed